THE MAKING OF HER

Susie Nott-Bower

© 2012 Susie Nott-Bower

Published by Linen Press, Edinburgh 2012
1 Newton Farm Cottages
Miller Hill
Dalkeith
Midlothian
EH22 1SA

Email: lynnmichell0@googlemail.com
Website: www.linenpressbooks.co.uk
Blog: linenpressbooks.wordpress.com

ISBN: 978-0-957005006
Cover photograph: Ray Spence, Arcangel Images Ltd
Author photograph: Roger Nott-Bower
Cover design: Submarine, Edinburgh

THE MAKING OF HER

Susie Nott-Bower

ACKNOWLEDGEMENTS

With many thanks to Mr. James McDiarmid MSc FRCS (Plast) Consultant Plastic and Reconstructive Surgeon of McDiarmid-Hall Clinic for his help with checking the accuracy of medical details and data. Any errors are mine. He bears no resemblance at all to the terrible Mr Marcus Templeton!

Thanks to Kate Harrison for her generosity in reading the manuscript and writing a lovely review; to Hubert Fiebig for translating the extract from Ahead of All Parting by Rainer Maria Rilke from the original German; and to all my fabulous friends who have read and critiqued and kept my spirits up and listened to me droning on about it all (you know who you are).

Excerpt from *The Voyage of the Dawn Treader*, Copyright © 1952 by C.S. Lewis. Reprinted by kind permission of HarperCollins Publishers Limited.

Excerpts from *Burnt Norton*, from *Four Quartets*, Copyright © 1944 by T.S.Eliot. Reprinted by kind permission of Faber and Faber Limited.

And finally, thanks to Lynn Michell, Director of Linen Press, for picking me out of the slush pile, and for her endless belief and encouragement, not to mention her meticulous editing.

For my parents, who made me.

JO

I'll tell you a story.

It's what I do. Though the words would once have stuck in my disbelieving throat.

Long ago, you and I might have sat before a fire, haunch to haunch, the flames licking red and gold as my words meandered into your ears. Today, now, I tap each word on a plastic keyboard and watch the sentences flicker on the screen:

Long ago, I'd tell you a fairy tale – about an Ice Queen who melted, a Princess who kissed her Prince awake, a Magician who changed gold into lead. Today, now, I'll tell you a story about the so-called real world: about middle age and makeovers, counselling and cutting rooms; about my valiant friend Clara and how she found her heart; about me and how I lost mine.

There is a fire. He lit it for me earlier. It shifts and sighs and crackles, restless in its city grate, and my fingers tap-tap-tap and the clock wheezes and chimes and I hear his soft footsteps on the stairs.

And I'll tell you how I came to find my beloved. In time.

'Jo?' he says, from behind the study door. His voice is gravel and honey. Like his kisses, it rasps and soothes. He told his own stories, once. Long ago and in a different language. It grieves me that he is silent now. Seven months, three weeks and a day I've lived in this house. Ten long years ago, he locked the door to the basement room and left his soul inside.

'Yes, my love?'

We hold our breaths. Oh, I could open the door and pull him in. Pull him down on to the faded Chinese rug before the fire or on to the old daybed with the grumbling springs and we could lose ourselves in one another, as we do. Only a recollection stops me, from our beginning: about passages not taken, doors left unopened and rose gardens never explored.

There's a clumsy, discordant sound, of wood cannoning against wall, and then his footsteps on the basement stairs, the rattle and click of an unaccustomed key as a door opens, creaking, and closes.

I breathe, and bend again to the keyboard.

I'll tell you a story of weakness (mine), and pride (Clara's), and stubbornness (his). I'll write of a time when Clara and I were half the women we are now, and of our search for what was missing. Of how we came into our own.

And when the story's finished, I'll be able to say: I made this.

But the story will say: Ah, but I was the making of you all.

Far away, almost inaudible, the first, hesitant string of chords, and his hoarse voice, singing…

PART ONE

you take me to the water
you tell me
you're gonna bathe my wounds away
and your midnight hair winds about my throat
and your river fills my mouth
and I'm drowning in your tears
strip me down, love
tear my will away like petals
love me, love me not, love
strip me down

Extract from WATER INTO FIRE
Music and lyrics by Pete Street
© Flame Records

JO

'Off out again?'

'I'm going swimming,' I say.

'Swimming?' Iain's eyes travel slowly down my body, from my limp hair to my thick ankles. *What's the point?* remains unsaid, but I hear it all the same. There is nothing for me to react to. Only shadows.

*

The changing room at Hammersmith Baths smells blue and puce, of chlorine and hot feet. The floor is caked with talcum powder, and a pair of broken goggles lies tossed and forgotten beside the overflowing bin. There is a free locker by the toilets, its door hanging open. I spread my towel over the slatted wooden seat.

A gaggle of girls – they could be any age between fourteen and seventeen – cluster round the mirrors, teasing and tarting the strands of their mermaid hair, their lips barely parting for text-talk tattle. Stripping off my clothes and exposing my disreputable old body to their cool eyes feels almost impossible. I'm tempted to take off my glasses first. It's what I always do when I'm stressed. Without them, the hard world becomes soft and malleable, less threatening. But I won't give the mermaids the satisfaction. Bending, I ease off my shoes and place them side by side at the bottom of the locker. Deep in my bag, my mobile rings. It stops before I find it.

The girls at the mirror are silent now, alerted by the mobile's siren call. They are done, temporarily, with their tight little concerns, and are searching the room for sport. I turn my back on them, unzip my trousers and pull them down. They graze the floor, picking up talc and stray hairs. I brush ineffectually at them, and pull off my jumper.

A snort, completely unmuffled. The mermaids' faces are expressionless, but one – with black-painted talons and a studded nose – holds my eyes, boldly and coldly, for a full ten seconds. I can feel my skin reddening, only too aware of what she sees: my giant, faded bra, the elastic long exhausted, my breasts slipping down towards my stomach like melting wax.

I haul the rubbery costume up over my belly and dare a utilitarian glance in the mirror. A middle-aged woman, her hair, once the red of hot embers, fading to ash. Dimpled flesh spilling out of a sagging costume that has lost its stretch. Like its owner. The locker is full to bursting with my oversized clothes. What if I could tear off my skin, layer by unwieldy layer, shove it in the locker, turn the key and walk away? What if I could step down into a transformed pool – magically dark and moonlit, with no bored lifeguard, no chlorinated sting – and slip, with barely a ripple, under the surface? What then? What then?

I pick up my towel and wrap it tightly round my body. Last of all, I pull off my glasses, drop them into my bag, squeeze the bag on top of the pile of clothes, and lock the door. As I pass the mirror, and the blurred, smirking girls, the mobile reprises its sing-song refrain, muffled and mocking. I let it ring.

CLARA

'Cut!'

Clara's shoulders drop with relief. 'Great stuff, people – that's a wrap.'

It's done. It's going to be all right.

Better. It's going to be extraordinary.

Happy birthday, Clara. A good day's filming; the best of presents. Which is fortunate, since it's the only present she's likely to get.

Down on the studio floor, the interviewee, chin-up and defiant, is gone before Clara can thank her. The crew is suddenly galvanised into action, unplugging and stowing equipment, eager for the curling hospitality sandwiches, the vinegar wine, and home. House lights are switched on and working lights are dismantled. *The Body Politic* set stands abandoned, no longer glowing like a jewel in the darkness of the studio, but a tawdry collection of painted flats fed by cables.

Clara forces herself to take a deep breath of dry, stripped air. Like tap water, it's already passed through too many bodies. Her temple throbs and the all-too-familiar tide of red heat floods her. In a moment, her face will be shiny and her neck turkey-cock red. She gropes in her bag for a tissue.

'Clara?'

Her assistant producer, Alix, stands a pace away, willowy and white-blonde, half a head taller than Clara. Half her age. Twenty-five, and thinks she knows it all.

'What?'

'Are you all right?' Alix's tone suggests she's addressing an elderly, and slightly batty, relative.

'Perfectly. Why?'

'You look a little… flushed.'

So would she if she'd barely slept the previous night. So would she if her brain was in a fog, her bladder in overdrive, her concentration shot, with nothing she had tried – from green tea to red clover – helping at all.

'I got the cut-aways you asked for.' Alix's tone is ice-cream, sweet and cold. 'And a couple of other shots you might find useful.'

The implication is that, without Alix's contribution, *The Body Politic* would go under. Clara clamps her lips shut. No doubt Alix will construe her silence as another symptom of impending senility.

Thank God for Gary. The cameraman, shrugging into his jacket, approaches and holds out his hand. 'Good luck with the edit, Clara. Should be a good series.'

'Thanks, Gary. A pleasure, as always. Till next time?'

He looks at her. 'You've heard the rumours.'

ProDoCo's up against it. They all know it. Something – or someone's – going to have to give. Please God, don't let her lose Gary as well. Don't let them decide she should be camera operator as well as director and editor.

'Oh –' Alix says, as if she's just remembered. 'Richard wants to see you.' She turns on her heel and melts into the mêlée.

'She's on the ball, that one,' Gary remarks, his eyes following Alix's progress to the green room. Is this is an indirect dig at Clara's own performance? Stress has been playing a jangling tune on her nerves, ricocheting round her system like a pinball. Did Gary notice the script shaking in her hands when the interviewee, a government minister in a Jaeger suit and pearls, suddenly broke down on camera, her careful make-up mask sliding down her cheeks as Gary zoomed in on her face?

I'm no bloody Iron Lady. I lost a child. But I had to keep on going. I had to, don't you see? The woman's voice had been wet and muffled. *And now it's all too late…*

Great television. Why did it feel like someone had kicked her in the stomach?

Gary's staring at her. 'Coming for a swift one?' It's a long-standing ritual, nothing to do with her birthday. She's been careful not to mention birthdays for years.

'Sorry,' she says. 'Got a date with the cutting room.'

*

'All done?'

It's Richard, her executive producer and old friend. He too looks worn and distracted.

'At long last, yes. You wanted to see me?'

'Yeah, later. You'll be editing?'

'No.' She gives a weak grin. 'I'll be out on the town, celebrating.'

'Celebrating?'

'Joke. Of course I'll be editing.' Her mind's already in the cutting room, selecting shots, scraps of dialogue, music. Why is her body so reluctant to follow? Editing has always given her a buzz – the thrill of making a show with a message, a show with balls. She presses her palm to her aching forehead. *What's happening to me?*

He looks at her. 'Clara, take a break. You're done in. Go home and get a few hours' sleep.'

'Impossible with this schedule. I'll be burning the midnight oil for weeks yet.'

'No let-up, is there? Why do we do it?'

Clara smiles faintly. 'Roll on the next one.'

Richard's face flickers. 'Clara, I need to…' He glances at her. 'I'll drop by the edit suite later, OK?' And he's gone, shambling down the corridor. Suddenly, from the back, he looks like an old man.

*

'Yes?'

Damn. It's Iain. Clara's fingers tighten around the phone. Iain's voice is a high, mosquito whine which exacerbates the ache above her temples. What must it be like for Jo, her best friend, living with it every day?

'Is Jo there?' She reaches across a pile of scripts for her bag and the paracetamol. The cutting room – or Edit Three as the likes of Alix insist on calling it – deep in the bowels of ProDoCo is airless and claustrophobic.

The weight of the world is in Iain's sigh. No doubt he resents her dragging him away from the Great Work.

'No, Clara. She's out. *Swimming.*'

'Oh.' She rummages in the bag with her spare hand.

'Why don't you ring her mobile?'

'I have.'

She can hear him creaking around, pacing, doubtless running a habitual hand through what's left of his ginger hair. Her skin prickles with distaste.

'I wish,' he says, 'you'd have a word with her. You are, after all, her best…' the implication is *only*… 'friend.'

'About?'

'She's never in, lately. I'm having to manage *everything.*'

She'd roll her eyes if they didn't hurt so much. Jo has told her that Iain is always out. At conferences, he says, and seminars and interviews. Where the hell is that paracetamol? Her fingers encounter a scrap of paper and her heart gives an unaccustomed lurch. Iain's fractious voice drones on.

'She doesn't seem to appreciate that, without me, the bills wouldn't be paid. We are, after all, in a recession…'

The skinflint. The only recession that really bothers Iain is the one taking place in his hairline.

'Great plays don't get written by magic. *You* should understand, Clara. The hard work and application that creativity entails…'

Iain S. Coe, celebrated playwright and pompous prick. Leecher of Jo's creative energy and eater-away of her self-esteem. Living with Iain must be like driving with the handbrake on.

'Clara? Are you there?' Iain's irritation rasps down the line.

'You're breaking up...'

If only. And she cuts him off.

She places the crumpled scrap of paper, with its hastily scrawled number, on the desk in front of her, her fingers smoothing it out. Reflected in the blank screen of the monitor, her eyebrows are pushed together in a frown as if objecting to her plan. *Tough,* she tells them. *I'm going to do it.* She picks up her mobile again.

'Clara?'

It's Richard. She presses the cancel button on the mobile, feeling ridiculously guilty. As if she's been caught doing something selfish. As if she's been caught wasting time.

'How's it going?'

She rotates her aching shoulders. 'Good. Some exciting stuff.'

Richard nods. His attention is elsewhere. Probably on his impending liberation. Early retirement. Beyond giving and receiving congratulations, they haven't discussed it. Did he jump, or was he pushed?

'Not long now, eh?' She attempts joviality.

'Sorry, what?'

'Freedom. R & R.'

'Oh. Yes.' He hesitates. 'Clara, we need to talk.'

'About what?'

'What's next. For you, I mean. Me, I'll be sitting by the fire with my feet up.'

'With Linnie and a glass of beer?' Linnie worked at ProDoCo for years as Richard's hyper-efficient PA before he had the sense to marry her. 'So what do you have in mind?'

Richard pulls up a chair. 'I've been talking with Stanley.' Stanley Barforth, Richard's replacement, fresh from the BBC. Cherubic face. Designer glasses and designer stubble. Never looks directly at her. 'You're not going to like this.'

'Oh?' She pulls out a tissue and dabs at her upper lip.

Richard clears his throat. 'You must have heard. ProDoCo's struggling. Output has to be trimmed. Staff too, in some cases.

Otherwise we're going down the pan.'

Something icy slithers down her back. This is it, then. How dare he? How dare they?

'He's sacking me?'

Richard shifts in his chair. 'No. No, not at all. You're highly valued. You know that. But priorities change. Ratings are dropping. There's a lot of pressure on us to make more… viewer-friendly programmes.'

'Dumb down, you mean?'

'I wouldn't put it exactly in those terms. Clara, there's no easy way of saying this…'

'Spit it out, Richard. I can take it.'

He's speaking slowly now, as if reluctant to voice the words. 'We want you to make a different kind of show.'

'How, different?'

'You've heard of extreme makeovers?'

'Plastic surgery? Boob jobs and facelifts?'

'That's right. How would you feel about making a show about that?'

'Sure.' The fear's draining away now, leaving her mind clear. 'I can do it from a feminist viewpoint. Bring in some experts. Look at the history of women mutilating their bodies, female circumcision, foot-binding…'

'No, Clara. Not that kind of show.'

'What, then?'

Richard sighs. 'A standard makeover. Ugly duckling transformed into swan scenario.' He's avoiding her eye again. 'We thought we might call it *The Making of Her*.'

Her heart thumps in time with the throbbing in her head. So this is what ProDoCo has come to. She rallies.

'The words "old" and "hat" spring to mind. Nobody's making that crap any more. I thought Barforth was brought in to liven things up…' She catches Richard's expression, and changes tack. 'Isn't it in ProDoCo's interests to invest in something original? Something groundbreaking? Not, in effect, to go backwards?'

Richard grimaces. There's something he's not telling her. 'Sorry,' he says. 'I shouldn't have asked…'

He's going to offer her something else.

'…because there isn't, actually, any choice in the matter. It's this or nothing.' Richard pulls ineffectually at his straining waistband. 'There's neither the budget nor the market right now for high-end documentaries. I wish it were otherwise.'

Clara rubs her knuckles over her aching eyes. Thoughts collide and hiss. Stuff bloody ProDoCo. She'll go. There are other stations, other jobs…

Richard reads her mind. 'Leaving's an option, of course. But the whole industry's in the doldrums, thanks to this bloody recession. And, er…'

'And?'

His expression struggles between sympathy and seriousness. 'Why d'you think I'm on my way out? Television's a youth industry…' His voice tails away but the implication of the words seems to grow, taking up all the air. She swallows and finds her throat dry and tight.

'Hold on to what you've got, Clara. That's my advice, for what it's worth. If you jump ship, there'll be no coming back. There's a host of ambitious young producers like Alix, all hungry, all with years ahead of them, ready to beat down the door for your job.'

She finds herself shredding the damp tissue. The white nubs stick to her fingers.

Richard looks at his own hands. 'One other thing…'

'There's more?'

'Alix is going to be kicking her heels now you've finished filming.'

'As opposed to snapping at mine?' The tissue is falling apart in her hands and dropping to the floor.

'We can't afford to keep her at a loose end. I've asked her to start researching suitable candidates for *The Making of Her*. She can put out some ads and set up interviews. Narrow the field down while you finish editing this series.'

Enough. She swings her chair to face him. 'Let me get this clear. You want me to make a tacky, formulaic programme with the assistance of a manipulative, self-serving little madam, about a person I haven't even chosen?'

'Well, obviously the final decision will be yours.'

'Thanks! That makes all the difference.'

Richard places his hands on each arm of her chair. 'Clara, we've known each other a long time…'

'All the more reason why you should understand how I feel about this.'

'…and I'm not going to be around to back you for much longer.'

'Back me?' The words burst from her lips before she can stop them. 'That's a laugh.'

He pulls away, his face closed. 'All right. The bottom line is this. If you don't take it, the programme will go to Alix. Which would put you in a very vulnerable position.'

She clenches her suddenly-cold fingers under the desk. Stinging, rebellious tears threaten. She blinks, hard.

Richard, relenting, leans towards her. 'Look, calm down. Think about it. Sleep on it. Let me know after the weekend.'

She can smell the relief on him as he half-heartedly pats her on the shoulder and beats a retreat. The cutting room door swings firmly and silently shut.

The scrap of paper flutters on the desk as if reminding her of its presence. Such a fragile thing. She could drop it in the bin and forget the whole ridiculous idea. Instead, she finds her fingers on the mobile again, picking out the number and shaking as if they no longer belong to her. When a distant voice at the other end of the line – might as well be the other end of the world – replies, she looks quickly behind her, almost hoping for Richard – anyone – to be there. But she's on her own. Massaging her temples, she begins.

JO

The ProDoCo doors slide open. I run my fingers through my wet hair, hoping I'm reasonably presentable. Foolish of me not to have made use of the hairdryers, but I couldn't bear to spend a moment longer in the changing rooms. Besides, I had to pick up Clara's fiftieth birthday present. Knowing Clara, she won't be celebrating, but I feel it's incumbent on me to provide at least a portion of birthday cheer.

Darren, at reception, grins at me. 'Evenin', love. Come to see 'Er Majesty?'

'I have.' I feel an absurd gratitude that he recognises me, since I only come occasionally, when Clara's on her own. My evening visits to ProDoCo give me an excuse to get out of the house. Out of myself. Iain will no doubt have plenty to say on my return. Iain can bloody well wait.

'Edit Three tonight.' Darren turns back to The Sun. 'You know where to go?'

I nod.

Descending to the basement in a clunky lift which smells of electricity and burning rubber, I think, fleetingly, of Persephone, voluntarily going down to Hades. There's a certain grim relief in leaving the light behind and burying oneself in isolation and darkness. The doors shudder open, revealing a dimly-lit corridor. I knock quietly at the door of Edit Three. Each time I come here, the whole place seems more shabby and neglected.

Clara is frowning at the monitor screen, attempting to balance her mobile between her shoulder and her ear while prising the lid off a plastic cup of black coffee. Her eyes are underscored by bruised half-circles. An open bottle of paracetamol lies on the desk, along with several dog-eared pages of script. Her stress is palpable.

'Jo. Thank God.' Clara's thin, intense face breaks into one of her rare smiles. She puts the cup down and drops the mobile into her bag. 'I've been trying to get you…'

I lean down and hug her. 'Happy birthday.' I delve into my shopping bag and pull out a bulky, tissue-wrapped box and a card.

Clara grimaces. 'Thanks. I'll open them later.' *You know I don't do this* hangs in the air between us. Too bad, Clara. There are no cards on the desk, nor even a celebratory drink. And I bet it's the same at home. The day of Clara's birth goes resolutely ignored every year. Except by me.

'Sit…' She pulls over a chair, after removing several files from its seat.

'You look exhausted.' I pull my coat off and feel my hair, damp and dripping, on the back of my neck.

'I'm always exhausted. *You* look like a drowned rat. Here…' Clara pushes the coffee towards me.

I subside into the chair, grateful for the semi-darkness. Drowned rat? Beside Clara, I feel more like a bag-lady. My body always seems to be attempting to escape from its clothes, while Clara somehow manages to look chic and self-contained in her uniform black suit, even at the end of what, judging by her expression, has been a horrendous day. Which she is clearly needing to share.

'So what's happened?'

'Bloody Barforth…'

And Clara is off, her frown deepening, her back ramrod straight, hands gesturing regally. I suppress a grin. Her Majesty, indeed.

'They want me to make a crappy makeover show… dumbing down… behind my back…'

I settle back and try to take in the mixture of fact and invective, listening, as I always do, to the many levels of what is being said. Anger, yes. Natural, under the circumstances. But something else, something quivering and uncertain which I've never heard before in Clara's voice.

'And then he as good as said I'm too old to get another job!'

On her birthday. Suddenly I know that the gift is a terrible mistake. 'What about all your experience? The awards you've won?'

'What about them?' Clara hurls a ball of tissue in the general direction of the bin. 'What does experience count for where the Barforths of this world are concerned?'

'Fifty is the new thirty,' I say. I read these wise words in a magazine full of images of underage, underweight models.

'Fifty,' Clara replies, 'is the new geriatric, at least in my game. I'm well past my sell-by date. Not only on the shelf, but shoved to the very back of it.'

For a moment, the girls in the changing room loom again. I push them firmly down and concentrate on Clara.

'And I thought I'd finally got shot of Alix. What the hell is Richard thinking of?'

'Can't you just grit your teeth and do it? This makeover thing? You're always telling me how volatile the television business is. If you wait it out…'

'What, and lose the last shred of integrity I have left?' Clara stands and begins to pace the room. 'These programmes are dross. Worse. They're insidious. They sell lies…'

'Do they?'

Clara gives me a *what's-the-matter-with-you* look. 'Come on, Jo. They peddle the line that a perfect body means a perfect life. They're using fear. Women's fear of ageing, of being alone and invisible. Fear of losing their identity…'

'Why do you talk about women as *them*? As if you belong to a different race?' I stare down at my thighs, splayed over the seat. 'Don't you ever feel insecure? Afraid?'

Clara hesitates. 'About the way I look? Never.'

The edit suite is stuffy. My head feels tight. I see my face, pale and plump and all too substantial, reflected in a blank monitor screen. Lucky, lucky Clara to have been born with confidence. Or to have acquired it along the way.

Clara subsides into her seat, fanning her face with a page of script. 'Anyway, who's going to watch this bloody programme? It's been done before, a thousand times. Come to that, who watched it all first time round?'

A rhetorical question, but… oh, what the hell.

'Me.'

I drop my head to hide my burning cheeks. I don't need to look to know that Clara is staring. Indeed, I can read her thoughts. Can this be Jo, whose inner life has always been far more significant to her than anything on the outside? Jo, who has slipped seamlessly into middle-age as if she were made for it?

Well, I'm human too. I pull off my glasses.

'I did. I watched them. Sometimes. When Iain was holed up in his study. They soothed me. Like bedtime stories.' I hear my voice rising, like a child's. 'They're contemporary fairy-tales. Stories about transformation. Caterpillars turning into butterflies. Frogs into princes. Look at Cinderella, the Little Mermaid…' The mermaids in the changing room appear. To mock me.

'The Little Mermaid?' Clara's lip is curling. 'Patriarchal nonsense. The woman having to adapt to fit into the man's world. And every step she took sliced her like a blade, remember? Is it worth being cut to ribbons just to fit in?'

'Maybe. For some women. Yes.' Why am I arguing about this when I am here to bring birthday cheer to Clara?

'What's going on?' Clara is staring at me. 'This is about Iain, isn't it?'

'No more than usual.'

'Why the hell do you stay with him, Jo?' Clara seems glad to pour her scorn in a familiar direction. The almost-argument has unnerved us both.

I rub at my glasses with a corner of my jumper. 'Because. Because… I'm used to him. Because of our work. The plays.' Not that my name ever appears on them. Not a single credit. Not even as the copy-editor. 'Anyhow, under the circumstances, I could ask you the same question. Why stay?' Below the belt, yes. But maybe it will distract her. The ruse works.

'Why should I be forced out?' Clara's face is flushed and self-righteous. 'I'll go when – and *if* – I feel ready to. I've worked here for twenty years. I'm good. And I'm not about to let Alix grab my job.'

So it's a matter of pride, as it so often is with Clara. I decide to change the subject. 'How's *The Body Politic* going?' Clara has been immersed in an investigative series about the private lives of female politicians.

'Great,' Clara says. 'She finally broke. Today. On camera.' I feel a stab of pity for the unknown woman. Clara's eyes flick towards the empty screen of the monitor. 'Just the editing now, and it'll be done.'

I glance at my watch. I ought to be going, but I string out the conversation just a little longer.

'You love it, don't you? The editing?'

'Yeah. Never thought I would, when Richard first made me learn.'

'So what changed?'

'I discovered what editing can do.' A ghost of the old, effervescent Clara. 'When I edit, I cut away the dross. Get to the heart of it. Tell the story *my* way.'

'I wonder,' I say, 'what it would be like if we could edit our own lives.'

'How d'you mean?' Clara is restless now, only half-listening. Her fingers are creeping towards the keyboard.

'Which bits would we cut away? Who – what – would we keep? Which story would we choose to tell about ourselves?'

Clara presses a key. The monitor glows and glares. Her unspoken mantra hovers in the air between us: *Wake up, Jo. Step into the real world.*

Dismissed, and faintly irritated, I put on my glasses and haul myself to my feet. 'I thought I'd tell Iain tonight. About sending out my stories. I've almost finished them.'

My babies. Conceived on my own. Without Iain. Am I brave enough to let them go – out into the real world? Are they good enough? Am I?

There's no answer. Clara is tapping at the keyboard, my birthday present forgotten on the desk beside her. On the screen, a woman in a smart suit is crying: 'I can't go on like this. I've had enough...'

You and me both. I pick up my bag and coat and make for the lift.

CLARA

Ten o'clock. Clara opens her empty fridge-freezer and drops three cubes of ice into her vodka. Ice for the Ice Queen. That's what they call her at ProDoCo, behind her back. Who cares? So long as they leave her in peace to get on with what she does best.

The editing is going well, which is all that matters. Sod Barforth, Alix and the whole pathetic makeover nonsense. It will pass. It usually does. Jo was right. She usually is.

She carries her drink over to the window. A new, young moon curves like a promise over the Notting Hill rooftops. A couple of hours and her birthday will be over for another year. A milestone, this one. Millstone, more like. She yawns. Her body aches with exhaustion but her brain is in overdrive, as usual. No point in going to bed yet, though she has to be up at six tomorrow. The black rectangle of the TV crouches in the corner, waiting. Most people relax in front of it. No point, for her, in trying. It's work. Stimulation, comparison, analysis.

She asked Jo, once, how she wound down.

'I potter around the house,' Jo said. 'I tidy things. I wash up.'

'Wash up?' Clara's only concession to housework is stacking the dishwasher, and she doesn't do that very often. The ProDoCo canteen is grim, but it stays open till late. Her colleagues divide into two camps: those, like Richard, who survive on chips and beer, and the low-carbers, like Alix, whose major consumption, between endless Diet Cokes, appears to be the odd blood orange.

She looks around for something to tidy, but the house is immaculate. Her cleaner came today. The aluminium-and-glass tables gleam, the leather sofa is burnished and the sweet smell of beeswax emanates from the floorboards. Anyone would know, as soon as they walked in, that this was the house of a single professional woman. No toys overflow from the cupboards; there are no tacked-up garish drawings on the fridge; no family photographs. A limited-edition Hockney is reflected in a series of floor-to-ceiling mirrors, while the laptop glows, waiting, on the coffee table. Awards fill the spaces on the walls, and on the mantelpiece her BAFTA winks a blind, bronze eye.

Maybe she can fool her mind into relaxing by changing out of her work clothes and getting into her pyjamas. She sets down the glass and moves to her dressing room. When she pulls off her jacket, it remains rigid, its shoulders stiff. She locates the hanger and sets the jacket and her skirt to join their companions, hanging in efficient ranks in shades of black, white and grey. She tosses her shirt, still clammy, into the laundry bin, and returns to the bedroom. Her pyjamas lie folded on the pillow. Their soft warmth comforts her skin. The bed is made and the duvet plumped and turned back. Sleeping pills on the bedside table, to deal with the nightmares. A box of tissues, to deal with the hot flushes. No man, cluttering things up.

Time to face it. Him. It's only once a year, after all. Why can't he take the hint and leave her alone? The envelope lies on the coffee table, waiting for her, full of Dan; one each year, for seven years. Why can't he just let go? Move on? Like she has.

See you at home, he used to say. Or: *I'll be home about seven.* She had always been irritated by his choice of the word. Why did he have to domesticate things? The concept of *home* felt claustrophobic and hemmed her in. *It's a house,* she had told him. *Just a place to sleep in.* He had laughed – in the early days when he had first moved in. Somewhere along the line, it had stopped being funny.

Sharing her house with a carpenter was the most ill-advised decision of her life. Although he kept his tools in the cellar and showered as soon as he came in, there would always be a breadcrumb trail of sawdust or pencil-shavings of wood which fluttered from his clothes to the carpet. At first it was exciting, part of the territory of Dan. The scent of him, the tang of sweat above the wild notes of oak or ash; the taste of woodsmoke. He brought a new flavour into her house, and her life. Something fierce, almost. Alien.

She drains the vodka. Her head swims, just a little. She rarely drinks. But if not tonight, when? She sets the glass down on one of the aluminium tables, the last of the ice cubes clinking and melting, and picks up the envelope. Better get it over with. If she could toss it in the bin, unopened, it would be simpler. One year – *soon* – she will.

Her name and address sprawl across the surface of the envelope. Art-college writing. The stamp is stuck on at an angle, as if thrown. Only the postmark – from Cornwall, as always – sanctions and officialises it. She tears the seal slowly, carefully, and draws out the card.

A seascape. Painted in watercolour in Dan's inimitable style, the waves are real enough to wet her fingers. She swallows and opens the card.

Happy returns, Clara. The words tumble and roll over the page. *Perhaps one day you will?* And his trademark signature of a swan, stamped from a wooden block on to the paper.

Return? If he only knew. If she'd told him the truth back then, her carefully constructed world would have disintegrated. Just like that. Her life would have been sucked away, just like it is sucked away, nightly, in the dream.

*

Jo's gift is a cake. An iced birthday cake. A completely useless cake, since Clara avoids carbohydrate and never celebrates birthdays. Neither tasty, nor tasteful. Fifty pink candles have been painstakingly pushed into the blue-white icing to form the words *Happy Birthday Clara!* and a box of matches has been thoughtfully provided. *Dearest Clara,* says the card. *Please celebrate this, your half-century. And make a wish!*

Her half-century. God, that sounds ancient. What would Dan think of her now? What would her life be, if they'd stayed together? What would... Quickly, she stifles the thought. Her heart is beginning to pound again, as it so often does. Stress, her doctor says, but she's not so sure.

Right.

She lifts the cake out of its tissue-swathed box and carries it into the kitchen. It just fits into the sink. Then she returns to the living room for the cards and the matches. The first match blazes and dies. She drops it on the draining board. She has a sudden recollection of herself as a child, in bed, reading the story of The Little Match Girl. Jo's fault. All that stuff about modern fairy tales and transformation. She strikes and lowers a match to the tip of a candle, again and again, until the cake blazes, just as all the cakes of her childhood did, inviting her near to warm and to wish. What happened to all those wishes whispered into thin air? Who, if anyone, heard them?

She picks up Dan's card. Holding it in the tips of her fingers, face-down over the flames, she watches as it catches, then goes up in smoke as the fire takes hold, eating up Dan's waves. Suddenly, it blazes up as if in anger and burns her finger. She lets go. The card drops into the candles and is consumed until there's nothing left but blackened shavings, which dirty the icing. The candles flicker on, triumphant.

And make a wish!

Clara draws in a deep breath, conjures up a face, a person. *I wish... I wish you were here. I wish I hadn't...*

But it isn't Dan's face.

She blows, again and again and again, until every candle is extinguished. Her breath sends the ashy shreds of paper floating and flying around the kitchen, settling on the polished steel surfaces and the newly-cleaned tiles.

Now, at least, she's got something to tidy.

She unlocks her hands, which seem to have twisted themselves into some kind of prayer, picks up a dishcloth, and begins.

JO

The grandfather clock on the landing wheezes and strikes eleven. I'm standing at the door of Iain's study, listening. To gauge his mood.

Silence. A burst of irritable tapping. A longer silence, punctuated by a heavy sigh. It's always like this when he's working up to something. Or just working himself up. My intuition – I call her The Voice – is speaking clearly: *Not tonight, Josephine.*

The Voice is my barometer. I check in with her regularly, as other people tune in to the weather forecast or the news. She gathers up sensations: she whispers, hints, suggests at things felt but not named. Unease has slipped like smog into my awareness for some weeks now, but hasn't yet crystallised into a definable shape. I am uncomfortable. I want to focus on the germ of an idea for a story which has been tugging at my attention for days. A story about an invisible woman and how she comes to be seen.

Down in the kitchen, I'm faced with the left-over clutter of our supper. Convenience food, chosen in haste at the supermarket on my way back from ProDoCo, and ill-received by Iain. Knives lie abandoned on the table, their blades crossed in unlucky, jagged angles, and tomato ketchup smears the plates. The scene resembles the aftermath of a particularly bloody battle. Which it was, in a horribly silent way. Our wars are fought with the weapons of domesticity: the gunshot slam of the door, the missile of a sprouting potato aimed to miss the bin, the slingshot bickering over chores and utensils and vegetables. The fact that we butcher our relationship in the arena of the kitchen seems apt. After all, we began it, back in 1979, over a meal.

*

He asked me to pass the gravy. Not exactly memorable as first words go. Surprising – no astounding – that he slid into the seat directly opposite me when he could have chosen any of the prettier, thinner women from the creative writing workshop we were both attending. I hated eating in public. Still do, particularly when I'm required to talk at the same time. Things get mixed up. And a plump woman eating is an open invitation to derision. I wasn't only plump then, but fey and bookish. I knew my deficiencies as far as men were concerned.

Iain S. Coe. Attractive, in a precise, wintry, writerly way. Before I heard him speak, I thought he was an American. I was taken aback by his drawling English accent.

'Everyone assumes that,' he said later, smiling. 'Actually, I changed my name by deed poll.'

'Why?'

'Because I'm going to be a great playwright.' He winked. 'Get it?'

It took me a moment to catch on. Eugène Ionesco would – perhaps – have been flattered.

I passed him the gravy. Our eyes met briefly. During the course of the meal I passed him the sugar, the coffee and the cream. And he asked me questions.

Where did I live?

Ah, The Smoke. Did I know the Henley-Bartons in Hammersmith?

Was I enjoying the workshop?

He'd been on it before. He called the tutor 'love'.

Had I been writing long?

He'd published five short stories. And was writing his first play.

He spoke at length, hardly pausing to swallow his food – roast beef with all the trimmings. This disappointed me. Dreaming over him in the workshop, I had imagined him a vegetarian. I heard him mention 'my ex-girlfriend' three times when he was talking with the other students, but with me, he extolled the virtues of celibacy and solitude. I found myself nodding agreement, longing to extricate him from both states. After dessert, he turned to me in front of the others and said, 'That was quite a good piece you wrote.'

I reddened with pleasure and embarrassment.

'I've a few thoughts about improving it. Want to come back to my place for a coffee after class?'

*

I carry the used plates to the sink and turn on the hot tap. Outside, there's nothing to see except a black expanse of shrubs, haloed by the jaundiced light of a Chiswick street lamp. Condensation courses down the pane. I glance down at the radiator to check on the spider. He's large, with long thin legs, and from time to time he lowers himself from his lair to scoop up the flies trapped in his languid web. Sometimes I find the remains of smaller spiders squeezed dry, their dark blood spotting the skirting board.

Upstairs, a door squeaks open. The floorboards groan as Iain crosses the landing. Then comes the syncopated beat of his footsteps on the stairs.

Round Two.

Iain marches into the kitchen and begins clattering spoon, cup and kettle. Every sound transmits irritation. The fridge door opens, and slams.

'There's no milk.' He sounds almost pleased.

I don't turn from the sink. 'True.'

'Why didn't you pick some up? Along with that putrid cod supper?' Iain's mouth will be pinched into its customary pained expression. He'll be running his hand through the roots of his ever-ebbing hair in a gesture both self-important and foppish. He saw Hugh Grant do it once and now he can't stop himself. I imagine each pass denuding a little more of the carefully-tended orchard of his coiffure. He gets the make-up girls to backcomb it when he's on TV.

'You were out long enough to buy a bloody banquet.'

I pull the plug. The stained water circles and drains. Funny how we managed to eat a whole meal in virtual silence, only for open verbal hostilities to break out at this late hour. *Tears before bedtime*, as my mother Julia used to say. Only they won't be Iain's.

'I dropped in on Clara,' I say. Lately, I've taken a masochistic pleasure in goading him. And any mention of Clara makes him boil and spit. 'It was her birthday.'

His weighted silence is full of the implication that my time is all leisure, all luxury, while he is bound, like a contemporary Prometheus, on the rock of Art. He conveniently forgets that I was up six nights in a row last week on *Parity*, the current play – proof-reading, suggesting solutions and even rewriting.

I dry my hands on the tea towel. I can feel him watching me, sizing his words.

'Clearly, Clara's birthday is paramount. As is *swimming*. You don't really give a shit, do you?'

He's baiting me, wanting me to snipe back, as I so often do, thus giving him the opportunity to tell me I'm impossible to live with. Accommodate him, and he treats me like a doormat. Stand up to him, and he tells me I'm cold, unloving and unlovable. He pounces on irrelevancies and magnifies them, obscuring and muddying my thoughts. Arguing with Iain is like standing in quicksand.

Now he's pouring hot water into his cup, purposely allowing it to slop over the sides on to the work surface and to run down to the floor.

'For God's sake, Iain!' I can't help myself.

Triumph flares in his face before he steps on to the safe ground of his martyrdom. 'That's right. Just when I'm really struggling with a scene, you start needling and nagging. How often do I have to say it? I need *peace* when I'm writing. Peace of mind. And you stir things up, every time. Why do you do it? To get some kind of reaction? To remind me you're here?'

Fat chance. I make for the door. There's little point in biting back, and besides, tonight I haven't the energy. I'd rather be out in the hall, sandwiched between the boots and the bookcase, pounding away on the old manual typewriter, getting my idea down on paper.

'Can't even stay in the same room with me?' Beneath the provocation, Iain's voice is a child's, fear and fury mixed. 'Fuck it. Don't bother. *I'm* going.'

He shoulders past me, jogging my arm with his cup. Boiling liquid spatters my trousers. The kitchen door slams. I crouch in the stinging silence, pressing my leg with my fingers until the smarting eases. Then I tear sheets of kitchen roll and wipe up the mess on the floor. Like Alice, except I'm in a pool of tea, not tears. Beneath the radiator the gossamer web sways slightly. The spider has withdrawn into his lair.

Slowly I stand, switch off the light and make for the typewriter. From Iain's study, I hear the rapid tap-tapping that signals his muse has returned, at least for now. The argument has refuelled his energy and restored his confidence.

The more he swells, the more I shrink. He squeezes me dry.

*

I should have paid heed to The Voice on that early summer day in 1979 when Iain ground the gears of his battered Morris Minor along the highways and byways of Somerset. But I was young then, and hopeful, and thought I was in love. I didn't want to pause, to discover, to be disillusioned.

My visions of an ascetic retreat, a half-timbered barn or a tumbledown woodland cottage were shattered when we pulled up outside a new-build house on an estate on the outskirts of Bristol.

'Are we here?' I asked, hoping otherwise.

'This is it,' Iain replied, with some pride. He led the way up the drive, fishing in his pocket for a key. I gazed at the rows of little boxes, as far as the eye could see.

There was nothing actually unpleasant about Iain's home. It was clean. Everything was arranged with soldierly precision. It was also completely devoid of atmosphere. As I looked round his cold, orderly rooms my heart shivered and sank.

'Nice,' I said. It wasn't a lie. The adjective described Iain's home perfectly. Everything was *nice*: mannered, polite, in-its-place. Not a crumb or a newspaper or an un-plumped cushion. No open books, no half-eaten snacks, no dirty socks. No paintings. Just a large glossy photograph of Iain with his arms around a woman, presumably the ex-girlfriend.

'Want to see my writing room?' Iain offered. Clearly this was an honour.

He led me upstairs to a single bedroom where a grey melamine table with tubular legs and a leather-effect swivel chair nudged a bookshelf of *How To* editions, together with a book of quotations, Collins English Dictionary and a well-thumbed thesaurus. On the table, beside a pile of papers, stood a black typewriter.

'Is this what you write on?' I reached to stroke its keys. 'I wish I had one.'

'Do you type?'

'I did a year at secretarial school.'

'Ah,' said Iain. 'I'm strictly a two-fingered operator. It takes an age.'

'If you ever want anything typed up…'

'Thanks,' he said. 'I'll bear that in mind.'

Somehow, we never got around to discussing my work. After two cups of instant coffee, I retired to the toilet, squatting among the arctic tiles, averting my eyes from the athlete's foot powder, the Easygrow hair oil and the cut-price toothpaste. When I returned to the living room, Iain was lying on the sofa, naked from the waist down. His trousers had been folded, together with his Y-fronts. With his long, bony shanks and small head, he resembled a daddy-long-legs. His erection was impressive.

He wanted me. Or so I told myself, as he plunged into me under the stony gaze of the ex-girlfriend. Afterwards, he had me sit on the sofa while he heated Fray Bentos steak pie and tinned potatoes, setting the tray on my knees with a flourish which I found strangely moving.

Later, when he revealed that by day he taught English in the local grammar school, I shut my eyes to that part of his life. Instead, I encouraged him to pour out his writerly dreams, his plans and ambitions. When, in the following months, he mentioned the ex-girlfriend – which he often did – or when he wrinkled his nose at me and suggested that I lose some weight, I dragged the five published stories and the play-in-waiting to the forefront of my mind.

He wants me soon became *he needs me*. At first I was merely the typist, on the black-gilled, recalcitrant typewriter whose keys stuck together and trapped my fingers if my attention lapsed. I couldn't help noticing that much of his play was pedestrian. I told myself this was because it was his first draft. But there were promising passages which I seized on like a terrier, and Iain followed any revisions I suggested with a touching eagerness. I became used to being woken at two or three in the morning – Iain's best writing hours – to find him tearful, fearful, needing my input and my support. Nine months later our partnership brought forth not a child but a finished manuscript. By the time the play found an agent, and that agent a producer, Iain and I were married. And I became Jo Coe, which amused Iain no end.

*

Funny, isn't it, how your adversary can become, over the years, your friend? Or vice versa, in the case of Iain and myself. The black typewriter and I are wary allies. We rub along together like an old married couple. I've learned to avoid its snares and pitfalls, and it tolerates my predilection for Tipp-Ex. In rare interludes between complaining about the noise, Iain has taken to calling it *the old dinosaur.* I refrain from pointing out the tautology.

Clara, of course, can't understand it. 'That thing's out of the dark ages. Get a laptop, for God's sake.'

But there are many reasons why we stick together, me and the typewriter. At the keyboard, I'm a boxer at the gym, punching letters with bravado, taking pleasure in each indentation. Making my mark.

No room for prevarication. It's do or die. I love the physicality of our relationship. Let those who wish idle over the laptop, with its virtual, cerebral blandness. For first drafts at least, I'll use a carriage and a ribbon. When I roll in a fresh sheet of paper, I'm transported back to before I became the joke, Jo Coe, back to a time when my abilities were recognised and encouraged. The Davina Lucas Secretarial School, in one of the grimier corners of Hammersmith. The place where Clara and I first met.

But I digress. My fingers are poised over the keys, ready to begin. Never mind Iain, who will stamp downstairs after the first few sentences, yelling about peace and inconsideration and earplugs. The keys hit the paper forcefully and satisfactorily, one hard-gained letter at a time, until I have a title. *Now You See Me.*

And they will. They will.

*

'You didn't marry Iain.' Clara, on the phone, soon after the wedding.
'What?'
'You married the writer in him. The writer in yourself that you won't acknowledge.'

Far easier to see it in him. Far easier to bask in his reflected glory than to step into the spotlight and expose myself to potential ridicule.

'Without you,' Clara said, 'Iain would be dead in the water.'

I didn't believe her. Not then.

Babies were out of the question. Iain's peace, he reminded me, was of the essence, and besides, the second bedroom (the nursery-sized single) had been commandeered for his study. Our physical relationship drooped and died soon after we married, when Iain resigned from his teaching job to channel his energies into writing. As royalties increased, he invested in a shiny new computer, mainly, he said, to make my job easier. Because from time to time, he'd recline on the daybed like Barbara Cartland and dictate his thoughts to my quick fingers.

'You don't need one of these,' he said, 'for your little fairy stories.'

My 'little fairy stories' were never real work. Real work earned its way in the world. Real work stood in the spotlight of public scrutiny and took its bow. Real work was visible. No wonder my stories languished, unseen, for all the years of our marriage. As I did.

*

My fingers ache from the typing and the cold. Upstairs, I can hear Iain's voice, but not his words. From the querulous tone I suspect he is complaining to someone. I prefer not to speculate on who this might be. Often these late-night calls precipitate a departure: an urgent meeting with a director, a radio show to record.

I pray to Saraswati, the goddess of writing: *Tomorrow. Please.*

The worm, you see, is turning. Of necessity, to the computer. I know that no-one in the publishing world would look at a manuscript where the 'i's were too faint to read and the pages were dotted with Tipp-Ex. Only a fair copy, fresh from the hard-drive, will do. Iain's increasing absences find me in his study, feverishly typing and cutting and pasting.

Iain shows little curiosity as to how I spend my time. It is as if I only exist in his presence. I carry my stories secretly in my heart, in my belly, and, more recently on a memory stick which I secrete in a box of tampons in my dressing-table drawer. I hear them crying for me in the night. I have to resist them, for Iain snores next to me and – so far – he is unaware of my plans.

CLARA

The man sitting opposite Clara smiles – a lop-sided grin which starts in his eyes and works its way down to his mouth. She can't remember the last time she met a stranger – a man – outside work. Sitting in this yellow-painted room in a pool of weak autumnal sunlight, she surreptitiously places a hand over her heart, which is beating quickly. Loudly.

David Wood. She had liked his surname. Straightforward and practical. No messing about. But now that it comes to it, why the hell is she here?

He doesn't seem in any hurry to start. He's still smiling, searching her face. He is not what she expected. She had imagined him older: pedantic, a pullover-wearer, maybe sandals. In fact, he is balding but youthful-looking. His face, while lined, has the high-planed bones of a dancer. There is no pullover. She checked for sandals when she came in and found his feet incongruously bare. He sits with them splayed on the rug between their chairs. She averts her eyes.

The silence between them lengthens. Her anxiety turns to irritation. She pushes words wilfully into the space between them.

'Like a blind date, isn't it?'

He raises an eyebrow. 'How so?'

'I don't know you. You don't know me. Here we are. Stuck with each other for an hour.'

The grin again. 'Is that how it feels?'

'Worse. I'm a therapy virgin. And you know what they say about first times…'

'What do they say?'

Does he have to be so literal? 'Never mind. I'd like to start now, actually.'

'Haven't we already started?'

'Properly, I mean. I'd rather not waste any more time.'

This is a mistake. What can he know, sitting up here in his ivory tower, about real life? He is cushioned from it in his sunny-side-up room lined with books, far above the madding Camden crowd. Even the traffic roar below is muted. What could he ever understand about ProDoCo, or about Alix and Stanley Barforth? About extreme makeovers?

His gaze has a particular intensity, as if he is listening to her whole body, top to toe.

'What has brought you here?'

She pulls at her hair in a vain attempt to cover her face. It had begun – what was it, just a week ago? – in the ProDoCo toilets.

*

She had been taking sanctuary from another tough day in the studio, running cold water over her wrists and grimacing at her reflection, at the line between her eyebrows – the result of years of focusing and frowning. Perspiration had leeched away patches of foundation. Hardly a convincing Ice Queen. Still, she had a reputation to keep up. A reputation which would carry her through this period of no more periods. If it wasn't for the small detail of the hot flushes.

Voices in the corridor, approaching.

Unable to face chit-chat, she had dodged into a cubicle, where a tampon lay curled at the bottom of the toilet bowl. And no loo paper – just an empty cardboard roll. Couldn't ProDoCo manage to pay a cleaner anymore? She squatted above the seat, irrationally irritated by the presence of the tampon. She should be grateful to be rid of all that. No more monthly cramps interrupting her schedule, holding her hostage to her gender. Except her body had her prisoner, more than ever before. Dan would call it karma, if Dan was still around.

'He's *amazing*…'

It was Lisa, her PA, talking about her latest man, no doubt. Lisa was older than herself and twice-divorced but remained full of an unshakeable optimism as far as her marital prospects were concerned. Internet dating had a lot to answer for.

'Reaaally?' Clara stiffened at the cut-glass drawl. The hint of cynicism. Alix.

Now Lisa was in the cubicle next door, pulling at loo paper. 'Whatever, Alix. When you get to my age, you may understand.'

'I doubt it.' Alix's voice floated in from the sinks, distorted as she applied lipstick. 'Why would any sane person pay – what is it? – fifty quid for an hour of navel-gazing with some shrink when they could buy a copy of *Psychologies* and do it for themselves?'

The toilet flushed. The door opened.

'Because,' Lisa's voice was cool, 'there comes a time when life gets too much. More than you can manage. I'm not talking about how-can-I-be-more-positive questionnaires and articles on life-coaching. This man is magic. He's helping me turn my life around.'

'How did you find him?'

'Richard. Some connection of his.'

'Dangerous.' Clara could imagine Alix's smirk. 'I can just see the two of them having a heart-to-heart about you over a beer. Not good for the CV.'

'Alix, give over.' Lisa's laugh was forced. 'He'd never tell Richard anything. Professional ethics. It's all totally confidential.'

'Only kidding.' Alix yawned. 'Oh well. Back to the slog. The Ice Queen's struggling this morning. I'd better go and keep an eye.'

'Leave her alone, Alix. And come down off that high horse. One day it'll buck you off.'

Alix's laughter echoed out of the door.

Clara looked down at her left hand, which was hurting. Her nails had gouged into her palm. And both hands appeared to be shaking. Lisa was still out there. Clara stood, pushed open the door, and watched Lisa's face redden.

'Youth,' Lisa said. 'They think they're invincible. She'll learn.'

'Yeah.' Clara fiddled with her hair. There were white-blonde hairs in the sink. *Just ask.* 'That man you were talking about…'

'David?'

'I've a friend. Who needs…'

Lisa was scrabbling in her bag for her address book and scribbling a number down. 'He's worth every penny. And more. Tell your friend…' Lisa flicked a quick, questioning glance at Clara in the mirror, 'that he's a life-saver. Nothing less.'

*

'Clara?' He's waiting for an answer.

She feels the flush coming, hitting her like a wave and sucking her into its blind, red undertow. Sweat starts out under her eyes. A droplet slides down her cheek, betraying her.

He's still looking at her. Her thighs are sticking to the leather seat.

'What's happening?' he asks.

She bends to her bag and pulls out a tissue. 'Hot flush. The change!' She laughs, without humour.

'Why are you laughing?'

'For God's sake!' Her embarrassment sparks into irritation. 'This is like some crappy sit-com.'

'Sorry?'

'Where the therapist does nothing but ask questions.'

'Ah.' He pauses. There's a glint in his eye. 'So, why were you laughing?'

The sun has gone in. She feels chilled and wraps her arms around her body. 'I was being cynical.'

'About?'

'That phrase. 'The change of life'. Nothing's changing in my life, except for the worse.'

'And you want your life to change for the better?'

Is he for real? Clara counts to five, slowly, before replying. 'Obviously. Doesn't everyone?'

He remains silent, refusing to take up her gauntlet. This is the game that therapists play: answering a question either with a question or with silence. Well, two can play at that. She deliberately shifts her eyes to the window. There's a pigeon on the sill, roosting, a wretched-looking ball of feathers. A clock somewhere behind her head is ticking steadily, measuring out her time at a pound a minute. Why the hell is she here when she could be putting that time to better use in the cutting room?

Because of the memories. Because of the fear. Because if she spends much more time around Alix she will either kill her or go mad. Neither of which – as Alix herself would no doubt point out – would be good for the CV.

All right.

'I don't know where to begin.'

He nods. 'It doesn't matter where. Start anywhere.'

She tells him about her job. About her exhaustion. He listens intently.

'Have you seen a doctor?'

'Of course. He says there's nothing physically wrong with me.'

'So your work has become stressful and frustrating. What about the rest of your life?'

'What rest of my life? I have a house in Notting Hill. My cleaner spends more time in it than I do. No pets. No plants. No social life to speak of. No relationship.'

A sudden, lurching memory of Dan's body. The smell of him, the rough skin on his hands from hours of working with wood. Sweat and sawdust. And the seven long absent years between them.

Out on the windowsill the pigeon has been joined by another. They flap, jerking their necks at one another in a mating dance. Relationships are for the birds. She sits up straighter.

'What about friends?' His voice is gentle.

'I've a good friend. Yes. Jo.'

'Have you talked to her about this?'

'No.'

'Because?'

Clara hesitates. 'I've known her for thirty years.'

'Long enough then,' he says, with a hint of that smile, 'to trust her?'

'Of course I trust her. It's just… I've always been the strong one. I can't let her see me… like this.'

'Like what?'

She picks up the glass of water that he's placed beside her chair. The water slops about and she realises her hand is shaking. She puts it down again. 'I used to love my life. My work. Every morning I'd be up and raring to go. Now I wake full of dread. What's happening?'

'What do you think is happening?'

She stares at him. Why is she paying fifty pounds to have her questions bounced back at her?

'I'd hoped you might give me some answers.'

He smiles rather sadly. 'I'm here to provide a space where you can find your own answers.'

Unexpected, angry tears fill her eyes. She feels like a child; a child who wants the adult to make it all right for her, to hold her, to tell her what to do. The words leap from her mouth, bypassing her brain.

'I have dreams…'

He nods, waits.

'I'm standing at the edge of the sea. Just me and the grey water. And the tide's going out, pulling at the pebbles under my toes. But then it gets stronger. Crueller. The sea sucks away the sand, everything, from under my feet. The whole world's being sucked away. And I know that it's going to suck me away. And then I'll be gone. Extinguished. Like…'

'Like?'

She stops. 'I don't know why I'm talking about that. I came to talk about work.'

'Perhaps,' David says, 'you are talking about work.'

She stares at her hands. 'Look. I need to sort things out. As quickly as possible. I don't want to spend years in analysis. I want you to show me what's wrong so I can fix it and get on with my life.'

Silence. She looks up and meets David's mild eyes.

'Clara, this isn't a garage.'

'What?'

'You're talking as if you're a dodgy car. And I'm certainly no mechanic.'

'You think this is funny? It's my life we're talking about. I may be just an unimportant hour in your working day, but...'

'You're not unimportant.'

'Look. I don't know why I'm here. I'm not someone who spends overmuch time navel-gazing.' *Shades of Alix.* 'I have better things to do with my life. I just...'

'Yes?'

'I just... need help.'

It hurts to say it. She feels angry with him for making her do it.

'Yes,' he says again. 'So how do you think I can help you, Clara?'

She grits her teeth. 'If I knew that, *David*, I'd be sitting where you are. Or I wouldn't be sitting here at all.'

'You seem angry.'

'Brilliant. Send that man to the top of the class.' Her voice is strident. He doesn't seem offended, but neither does he respond. She picks up her bag. 'This is a waste of time.'

He raises an eyebrow.

'It's like shouting into an empty cave. All I get back is an echo.'

He sits back in his chair. The silence feels loaded and locked. The clock, ticking above her head, signals the passing of empty, unsolved minutes, the precious segments of this fifty-minute hour she's paying for, in which she hoped to find salvation. She looks at her hands and sees her knuckles pale with clenching, the bone showing white. When she looks up, he is still watching her.

'I'm not used to this. It doesn't feel normal. It feels false and... and dangerous.'

'Dangerous?'

'I'm not used to these silences. This space.'

'Do you have no space in your life?'

'None. There's too much to fit in. Deadlines...'

'So how does it feel to have this space, now?'

'Threatening. Like it's stopping me from getting on with things.'

'What things?'

'My life.'

He leans towards her. She catches the scent of lemons, tart and sharp. 'But this is your life, Clara. Right here, right now. This.'

'But it's empty. There's nothing here.'

'Is that how your life feels? Empty?'

How can it? Her life is chock-full. Isn't it? She stares into the silence.

'It's almost time,' he says. The clock's hands click towards closure. 'I'd like to suggest something.'

Maybe he's going to give her a solution.

'If you decide to come back, I'd invite you to use this space to explore the parts of yourself you're unfamiliar with. Your mystery. Perhaps the answer – if there is an answer – lies there.'

New age mumbo-jumbo. She stands up.

'I'm not the soul-searching type. Not even sure I've got one.'

He moves to the door and quietly opens it.

'Goodbye, Clara,' he says. 'Go well.'

She stalks through the waiting room, clatters down the stairs and jerks open the front door to a wall of traffic noise. Back to ProDoCo. Nowhere else to go.

JO

In Iain's study, last night's drawn curtains reveal just a chink of cold morning light. He left yesterday afternoon, citing a crisis meeting with a producer, to be followed by an early-morning radio interview for the *Today* programme. Naturally this necessitated an overnight stay in his usual Portland Place hotel. Before leaving, he took pains to train his hair over the bald patch, and to douse himself with copious amounts of aftershave. I hope John Humphrys is appreciating his efforts. Meanwhile, the study – and the computer – is mine.

As dawn broke, I made the final revisions to the last story, then, crossing my fingers, I clicked Print. Now the printer is chugging out crisp, precious pages. A sudden wave of joy breaks and floods through me, followed immediately by something resembling grief. The process of writing my stories is the closest I'll ever get to the miracle of motherhood. Is this how it would feel to watch a child grow and then fly the nest? I don't know. I will never know.

The street outside is waking – a dog barks, a milk float clanks past, dustbins are being emptied and letters flap on to the morning mat. The printer's repetitive cycle has become a lullaby. My eyelids droop.

'What are you doing?'

Iain is standing in the doorway. I had not expected him until lunchtime. My tired brain registers something different about his appearance but I am too busy watching his eyes. They scan the desk, move across the neat piles of paper, then drop to the printer just as its telltale grinding betrays me and ejects the final page. The silence is raw.

'I'm printing my stories,' I say. 'To send out.'

'Send out?' Iain bends down and stares at the pages on the printer tray. His face is unreadable. 'How long's this been going on?'

I almost laugh. It's as if he's discovered me in bed with another man. Have I committed literary adultery?

Iain strides to the window, wrenches the curtains apart and throws up the sash.

It's his hair. He has done something to his hair. The floppy gingery fringe is gone, replaced with a kind of blond stubble. With green highlights.

'It stinks in here…'

I know he's blustering. He's delaying the confrontation until he has mapped out the area of combat. Harsh morning light dazzles me. I grip the edge of the desk and pull myself upright, wincing at the stiffness in my knees.

'I'm sending my stories out to some agents,' I say again. To make sure he hears or to convince myself? And then, because I can't help it: 'What have you done to your hair?'

Iain flings his jacket on to the filing-cabinet. I register the smell of sweat and, under the tired aftershave, another, unfamiliar scent. One of his shirt buttons is missing. His face works its way into habitual self-pity.

'You've always been secretive. Always shut me out.' This opening salvo seems to energise him. His tone rises, like a mosquito on overdrive. 'No wonder I feel so excluded in our relationship.'

Excluded? Him? Iain has a way of turning things round so that floor becomes ceiling. Inside down, upside out.

Now he's in full flood. I've always suspected that his real, secret ambition is to be an actor rather than a playwright. Declaiming is his verbal element.

'…shared everything I've ever written with you… been completely open…'

I watch his mouth opening and closing. I smell stale garlic and red wine on his breath. I stare at the green highlights, then at the gap in his shirt where an overabundance of white, hairless belly is revealed. The Voice whispers urgently but Iain is making too much noise for me to hear her.

'...tampering with my computer... private space... do you have any idea how... how *invaded* I feel?'

Suddenly I am full of righteous fury.

'Fuck you, Iain!' The word jolts me awake. 'You don't feel *invaded* when I'm in here proofing and editing, do you? This has nothing to do with your so-called privacy. This is about the fact that what I do matters too.'

Now I've started on this track, I can't stop. I've opened a Pandora's box. All the resentments I've tamped down over the years. All the pain. 'You want to keep me small. Insignificant. Manageable. Everything is just fine as long as I don't rock the boat. As long as I stay in my place. Down in the hall, that is. On the typewriter. With my *little fairy stories*. As long as I never grow...'

Just for a moment, I look into Iain's eyes, and I see that he's afraid. Maybe he feels small, too. Maybe I've been carrying both our portions of insignificance. Tom Thumb and Thumbelina. And just for a moment, I feel sorry for him. It doesn't last longer than the time it takes for him to bend and pick up the last sheet of my manuscript, holding it between finger and thumb as if it is poisonous, his body rigid with antipathy.

'Fairy tales.' He manages to convey a world of triviality in the two words. 'Do you honestly imagine there's a market for this stuff?'

'There might be.' My voice is high and quivering, like wind through telegraph wires. Already the anger is draining away. Why can't I hold on to it?

'You're a dreamer. You live entirely in your own head.' Iain grabs my arm and pulls me over to the mirror. 'If you paid more attention to what's blatantly obvious, you might do better.'

I see the reflection of my face, pallid in the harsh morning light. I see my beaky nose, my glasses at half-mast; the estuaries that run down from the corners of my mouth; the flotsam of grey in my hair.

I turn to the open window and suck in breaths of stark morning air. Iain leans on the desk, watching me. The tempo slows. I feel like a character in one of his plays.

'It's time you saw someone.' Now he's wearing his *I-know-what's-best-for-you* face.

'What?'

'A doctor.'

'I'm not ill.'

'Since your... menopause,' he struggles with the term, 'you've been even vaguer than usual. You forget things. You drift around like a ghost. Or else you're aggressive and overreact to everything. And you've put on even more weight. I understand it's to do with your time of life, but frankly, it's worrying.'

I open my mouth to speak but nothing emerges.

'Rosalie agrees that your issues are probably hormone-related.' Rosalie Rogers. His publicist. A pillowy, curvaceous blonde with a mind like a razor. 'But she thinks you should get some psychological help as well.'

'What the hell are you doing, discussing me with Rosalie?'

Iain ignores the question. He waves my final page at me. Already it looks sparse, flat. 'And now this. Dabbling in writing is one thing. Deluding yourself that you can be published is something very different.' The Voice is screaming, but her screams are silent and I can't lip read. Iain gives a tiny belch and changes tack.

'Remember when Clara came to dinner?'

How could I forget? Clara and Iain are always an explosive combination. I had attempted to forestall any arguments with vast amounts of food and wine but after an hour of listening to Iain's views on contemporary play writing, the decline of modern morality and the importance of his *art*, Clara had changed the topic abruptly and asked me if she could read one of my stories. My fingers had trembled when I handed it over. Iain stood up abruptly, setting the glasses on the table rattling. Clara merely glanced at him.

'In fact, why don't *you* show one of Jo's stories to someone, Iain? You must have lots of contacts in the publishing world.'

Iain blustered but eventually agreed. Had he read it? He certainly said nothing. More likely, he had dumped it in the nearest bin.

Now it would seem that he hadn't.

'I showed your story to my publisher. Against my better judgement. But of course, Clara knows best.' Iain runs his fingers through what's left of his hair. 'I wasn't going to tell you. But now you've forced my hand.'

I want to shield my head, my body, from what is about to rain down upon me. Not blows – Iain has never been physically violent – but hurtful, unbearable words. Iain knows how to destroy. He knows exactly where my softest, most vulnerable places lie. He knows how to squeeze the life out of me succinctly and efficiently.

'They said your writing was immature,' he says, stressing each syllable. 'Unpolished. Derivative. Unmarketable.'

My legs are shaking. There is no pain. Just a gaping wound that will weep blood forever. Or so it feels. My project, destroyed by his words, lies between us like a corpse. I stare at my manuscript as if it still might give me the strength and energy to fight back but it is just a pile of paper. A thing.

Iain is still talking. 'You're a good copy-editor. And a fast typist. Stick to what you know and what you *can* do. Rejections are painful. Even I know that. Your state of mind is fragile enough without subjecting yourself to all that negativity. If you *must* write, keep it where it belongs. As a hobby.'

I focus on the gap in Iain's shirt and the faint smell of her, of Rosalie, on his body. On his breath. 'Get out.' Is this my voice? 'Just go.'

'Oh, I will…' He has me by the arm and is dragging me out of the room. He holds me tight, his fingers digging into my flesh, as he turns the key, removes it from the lock and shoves it in his pocket. 'So now let's see how *you* like being shut out.'

'Iain, you're being ridiculous. Open the door.'

'Fuck *you*, Jo,' he says, and crashes his way down the stairs. The front door slams.

I sit down abruptly on the landing carpet. It is only after several, silent minutes that I begin to cry.

Iain is gone for five days. I go through my routines in the empty house but my life has slipped into a minor key: a mournful rhythm underpins my living. And as the days shunt by, the rhythm slows and stops. Sometimes the phone rings. I don't answer it.

When Iain returns, it is in a four-by-four driven by Rosalie. From an upstairs window I see him, pale as the wind, advancing up the path. I hear him let himself in, pause in the hall, then climb the stairs. The top of his newly-shorn head, touched with green, rises towards me.

'I'm not staying,' he informs me. 'I've come to get my things.'

Brushing past me, he unlocks the study door. I watch as he packs his computer, his printer, his notes and his books and carries everything out to the waiting vehicle.

'Where are you going?' I ask as he pushes past me on his way to the bedroom. He ignores me. There's the clatter of hangers, the wooden scrape of drawers opening and closing, the zip of his suitcase-on-wheels.

He hefts the case downstairs. The front door slams.

Much, much later, I go to the study. My manuscript lies where I left it, minus its final page. I pick up a sheet and read. The words are meaningless. I can find no connection with them. *Put it away, Jo. Out of sight.*

I slide my fingers around its bulk and lift it to my breast. Then I carry it out of the study and across the landing. My mother's voice follows me down the stairs. *Stupid, stupid child. Get out of my sight.*

CLARA

A half-moon gleams over the Chiswick rooftops. Clara presses the doorbell. Again, nothing. She's been trying Jo's mobile all day and has left countless messages. The landline rings forever.

She bends to the letterbox, forces it open and squints through the aperture. The hallway is dark and littered with mail but the door to the living room is partly open, momentarily illuminated by a flash of blue-white, then another.

'Jo?' Her voice is swallowed by the darkness. She stands and moves to the side gate, fingering her way along the wall of the house towards the back garden. It, too, is cast with a white-blue, wavering light. The living room curtains have not been drawn. She moves to the French windows. For a moment, her own reflection stares back at her, backlit by the moon. Then she sees Jo.

Jo is swaying, alone and barefoot, in the flickering glare of the television. She is wearing a white nightdress that flares around her as she twirls and turns. Her hair, twisted into a plait, whips her wet face. She moves like a child, unselfconsciously, as her pale woman's body bounces and sways. Her hands are clenched incongruously at her sides, as if defying the rest of her. A bottle of wine, a half-empty glass, an open book and a pair of scissors lie on the coffee table.

Clara moves closer to the French windows so that her breath mists the glass. Jo looks like a goddess, a wraith from one of her own stories. Unrecognisable and somehow unreachable. The wall of glass between them could be a wall of stone.

Jo suddenly lifts her arms above her head, her mouth grimacing in a letterbox of pain, and opens her hands. A cascade of white falls around her like swansdown or confetti, like the flakes in those childhood snow-globes, and she suddenly stops moving – a puppet whose strings have been cut – and collapses on the sofa.

Clara is tempted to back away into the darkness. Only the combination of the bottle – Jo rarely drinks – and the scissors forces her to tap, then bang, on the cold pane.

Jo's expression, on registering her presence, is strangely blank, as if she wishes Clara weren't there. Her cheeks stain with a flush. After a moment, she picks up a woollen throw, draws it around her body and moves, somewhat unsteadily, to unlock the French window.

'Jo. What's going on? I've been calling you…'

Jo stands back to let her in. The room smells stale, of wine, sweat and tears. The sofa cushions are pressed into thick creases and the grate is full of ash. On the television screen, a rock concert gives way to an advert for the latest anti-wrinkle cream. Clara picks up the remote. The screen convulses into darkness.

Jo sinks back on to the sofa, pulling the throw around her body. She doesn't invite Clara to sit. Some fragments of cut-up paper lie where they have fallen on the coffee table. On one, the words *my betrothal*. On another, *betrayal of.*

'Where's Iain?' The question seems apt, though there are many others Clara might ask under the circumstances.

'Gone.'

'Gone where? What do you mean?'

Jo doesn't answer. Clara crosses the room and clicks on the overhead light. In an instant, the pale goddess is reduced to a washed-out woman wearing a grubby gown.

'Welcome,' Jo says, with the slightest of slurs, 'to the real world.' She picks up the glass and drains it.

'I'm going to make you a coffee.' Clara eyes the bottle. 'A strong one.'

Jo shrugs and picks up the open book lying on the table.

In the kitchen sink, plates are stacked high. Clara moves those that are obstructing the tap and fills the kettle. She finds one mug at the very back of a cupboard and sets to work washing another. An open packet of sugar, a coffee-stained spoon impaled in it, trails white crystals over the work surface.

Jo is still reading when Clara sets down the mugs on the sticky surface of the coffee table.

'Jo?' Clara hears the edginess in her own voice. She reaches over, takes the book from Jo's hands and lays it down. Hans Christian Andersen. *The Ugly Duckling.* The paper fragments whisper and shift.

'What's all this? What have you done?' Clara gestures at the scissors and the paper.

Jo smiles. 'Cutting room,' she says. She picks up a mug, lifts it to her mouth, then, wincing at the heat, replaces it. Her glasses have steamed up. She takes them off and rubs them with a corner of the throw. Without them, her face looks shorn and innocent. Like a little girl's.

'What about Iain?' Clara attempts to impose some order on a confused tangle.

'Gone,' Jo says again.

'Another woman?' The words come out too quickly, but Jo appears unmoved.

'Rosalie.'

'His publicist?' Clara feels only a grim sense of relief. Trust bloody Iain to have a replacement lined up before he leaves.

Jo puts her glasses back on. 'I imagine,' she says, enunciating carefully, 'that you think it's a good thing. Probably you're right. He's been impossible for months.'

For ever, more like. Clara reaches for Jo's hand. Jo shrugs her fingers away and begins to trace and retrace an invisible pattern on the fabric of the throw.

'Good riddance,' Clara tries. 'Rosalie doesn't know what she's letting herself in for.'

Jo's mouth twists into a facsimile of a smile.

'And now,' Clara adds, 'you can get on with your writing.'

Jo stands abruptly, rattling the mugs on the coffee table. 'Better clear up,' she says, casting her eyes around the room as if trying to decide where to begin. For a moment, she stares at her reflection in the ornate mirror over the dead fireplace. She picks up the wine bottle.

'She was right, of course.'

'Who?'

'Julia.'

Jo's mother. Clara had only met her once, shortly before she died, but she had witnessed the way Jo shrank in her mother's presence, while the emaciated Julia took centre-stage, dragged on her ridiculous pastel cigarettes and drank gin. 'About what?'

'She said that I would waste my life and that I'd never amount to anything. She said that I would never hold on to Iain.'

'For God's sake, Jo! Your mother was a lush. She ran away. From life and from you. Hardly an authority on success.'

'But she was right, wasn't she?' Jo pushes her glasses up the bridge of her nose. 'I have wasted my life. Haven't I?'

Clara fights the temptation to lie, but what good would it do? Jo always knows when she is avoiding the truth.

'Anyway,' says Jo. 'It's gone now. All of it. Iain, our work together, my writing –'

'What? What's Iain done with your stories?'

'Nothing. It was a… fantasy. Thinking I could write…'

'You can write. You write like an angel.'

Jo is kicking at the scraps of white paper all over the carpet. Word dust.

Clara hauls herself to her feet. Every bone in her body aches with tiredness. She should be in the cutting room. She should be in bed. 'Right. First, we're going to clean up. And you're going to sober up. And then we're going to talk.'

Jo mutters something and ducks her head. It sounds suspiciously like, *Yes, Your Majesty.*

JO

My house glows, even if I can't say the same for myself. Clara has even routed the spider by gathering him up in a duster and flinging him into the garden. Maybe he will be happier there among the weeds and the worms. Upstairs, water fills the claw-foot tub, into which Clara has sprinkled a sachet of bubble-bath, circa 1980. A Christmas present from Iain. Does he give Rosalie sachets of bubble-bath? Rosalie would expect Jo Malone at the very least.

Clara is sitting on the edge of the bath. Her back, usually ramrod-straight, is hunched. In her dark shirt, the sleeves rolled up for business, she resembles a small black fly. Not much buzz left. I feel a stab of guilt. That's the trouble with sobriety; no wonder my mother fended it off at all costs. Sober, you feel everything denied by the drink. Including headaches. I rub my forehead.

Sensing my presence in the doorway, Clara turns and stands up. 'Get in.'

A blush crawls up my neck to my face. I can no more undress in front of Clara than fly to the moon. I glimpse our indistinct figures in the misted mirror: Clara in her sharp office suit, her hair still a perfect, shiny bob in spite of the housework. Me a plump, lumbering giant wrapped in a stained flannelette dressing-gown. On Clara's face, incomprehension shifts into understanding.

'I'll be back.' She disappears towards the stairs.

The water is violet-foamed. It smells of Turkish Delight and icing sugar. It swirls, hot to my touch, in the white font of the bath. I drag off my glasses and place them carefully on the side of the wash basin. I pull off the dressing-gown, drop it on the bath mat, drag off my knickers – avoiding the mirror – and step into the bath.

My skin turns ruby red. I reach for the soap and rub it slowly under my arms and over my breasts.

Dirty little girl. My mother Julia's voice, hysterical and high, on the day she dragged me inside from the garden where I had been making joyous mud-pies in the rain. She smacked me – stinging blows across the back of my legs. *Trust you to ruin my bloody day.* She pushed me into the bathroom. She stood over me while I climbed into water that was too hot. She wrenched the old flannel from my small fist and replaced it with a scourer. *Get rid of that dirt. Now.* Then she lit a cigarette and watched while I raked the scourer over my fat little stomach again and again until she was satisfied and my skin was red-raw.

Did my mother imagine that under all the mud and grime, beneath the skin and puppy-fat, she might find a real little girl? One she could be proud of?

Hearing Clara's footsteps on the stairs, I slide under the water, the foam tickling my face and hiding my breasts.

Clara is looking down at me, her brows pushed together as if the sight of me wallowing in the water is anathema to her. 'So, what next? Are you going to give up on yourself?' Her voice echoes around the tiles and prods my throbbing head. 'You want to prove Julia right?'

'Pass me a towel, please.'

Clara grudgingly hands one to me.

'And please don't look?'

I haul myself out of the water, glimpsing the reflection of my body, pink and glistening as a suckling pig, in the mirror. The towel is warm and dry.

'Well?' Clara's back is still turned.

'I'll look for a job.' It's the first thing that comes to mind.

'What sort of job?'

'Secretarial, I suppose. Though I doubt I have the qualifications.'

'You can learn. But you're not giving up on your stories.'

'Clara,' I say, 'let them go. I have.' I shrug myself into my dressing-gown.

'You're going to send them out. Remember?'

What I remember is cutting the stories into shreds. 'They're in bits.'

'Then print them out again.'

'Iain's taken the computer. And the printer.'

'But you've saved them somewhere?'

I nod reluctantly, thinking of the tampon box. 'On a memory stick.'

'Then I'll print them out from my laptop at work.'

I don't know whether to hit her or hug her. 'You're already run off your feet.'

'So?' Clara, in this mood, is not to be argued with.

Today, her brusque determination has triggered a turning-point of sorts. A punctuation in the endless sentence of my existence. I think of Iain and Rosalie bedded down in Rosalie's chic Hampstead apartment, making the beast with two backs.

Suddenly my shoulders are shaking. My cheeks are wet.

'Clara,' I whisper. 'Iain. He's…'

Clara turns, her face softening at the sight of mine. Tears are pouring down my cheeks. She holds out her arms to me. I shake my head.

'What is it?' she says. 'Bloody Iain…'

'He's dyed his hair,' I reply, wiping my eyes with the back of my hand. *'Green.'*

CLARA

'The fillet steak. *Very* rare. And a glass of the Beaune.'

Marcus Templeton returns the menu to the waitress, running his eyes efficiently over the girl's body. Clara hates him already.

A lunch meeting is standard: a means of establishing a working relationship. Marcus will perform the surgery in *The Making of Her*. Therefore Marcus must be courted, having — as Richard's informed her — generously agreed to waive his fees. Generosity? More like bloody free publicity. From the instant she stepped over the threshold and was asked by a liveried attendant if *Madam would like to leave her coat?* Clara's inner anarchist has been rapping at the glass of her professional facade.

Marcus rose from the table, breathing urbanity, as she approached.

'Ms Williams. May I call you Clara?' Without waiting for her assent — which wasn't coming — he took her hand in his soft, dry grasp, holding on to it just a little too long, and suggested that they order first and then discuss the show. Clara nodded perfunctorily. She was on his territory and must conform to his rules. It was his idea that they lunch here at his club in Wigmore Street. Convenient for his consulting rooms in Harley Street, of course.

The restaurant is panelled, a cushioned sanctuary in the heart of London's frenetic buzz. Baroque lamps create intimate pools of light; waiters and waitresses glide dimly from table to table like solicitous moths. Music murmurs in a soothing undertone. The clatter of cutlery is restrained. Conversation is polite, punctuated by the high notes of women's laughter and the low rumble of male bonding.

The business of ordering done, Clara places her laptop on the table and prepares to begin. Marcus raises a discreet eyebrow.

'Laptops aren't encouraged in the restaurant.'

'Oh. I'd hoped to take notes.'

'Perhaps you could do so later. After all, this is an informal meeting. Just a getting-to-know-each-other session, yes?'

My way or the highway. She closes the laptop and returns it to its case. Marcus is tasting his wine, approving it. His pale, hairless hand is devoid of rings except for a gold signet on his little finger. His head seems large compared to the rest of his body, as if a camera is zooming in on it. She has to check the impulse to lean back in her chair, away from him. He must be in his early sixties, yet his face is barely lined and there is no trace of a belly beneath his pink-striped shirt. Has he had surgery himself?

'So, Clara. Tell me about *The Making of Her.*' He's taking on the guise of interviewer.

'We'll follow a woman through the various stages of her... transformation. Interview her beforehand, find out about her life and her history, how she feels about the way she looks. See how she's perceived by a random sample of the public.' Clara takes a sip of water and swallows a sigh. 'We'll film you preparing her, film the operating and the recovery period. Then we'll reveal her to the public again and show the difference surgery's made to her life.'

'And do you have a candidate yet?'

'No. I'm still editing my present series. Alix, my assistant...' she grimaces, 'will be placing advertisements shortly.'

'What kind of woman will you be looking for?'

'Someone with an interesting story, hopefully. But I need to know from you what sort of woman would be most suitable for plastic surgery?'

Marcus coughs. 'Personally, I'd prefer to use the term *cosmetic* rather than plastic – at least as far as facial surgery and breast augmentation is concerned. Plastic surgery is a general term covering both reconstructive and cosmetic surgery. A point which I'd like to get across in the filming.'

'I see.' Pompous ass. 'So reconstructive surgery is for people who've lost parts of their body, or been burnt?'

'Indeed. And, of course, for women who've had mastectomies.'

'And cosmetic surgery is purely for...' she wants to say *vanity* but curbs herself '...aesthetic improvement?'

'Broadly speaking, yes. Although the emotional impact cannot be underestimated. When a woman feels unhappy about the way she looks, her whole life suffers. An improvement in self-esteem is often the most important result of the procedures.'

The inner anarchist digs her sharply in the ribs. 'Wouldn't self-esteem be better achieved through something less invasive, like...' she remembers David Wood's room, '...therapy?'

'Certainly, a woman could spend five years on a psychiatrist's couch and perhaps eventually come to terms with her body. I can give her the same result in a single session.'

He talks as if he is a magician, bestowing confidence in the wave of a scalpel. Her head feels heavy. She would lay it on the tablecloth if she could. What a shame he can't cut away exhaustion and despair along with the fat. She takes another sip of water.

'So what kind of woman shall I look for?'

'In physical terms, a woman aged between, say, forty and fifty-five. Healthy. A non-smoker. She'll have to pass certain medical tests. The best results occur when the patient is mentally and emotionally stable and realistic about what can and can't be achieved. Again, we'll carry out psychometric tests to ascertain this.'

Two plates descend on their table, bringing an aroma of undercooked meat. Marcus's steak basks juicily among potatoes dauphinoise and lurid green asparagus. Lacking any appetite, she has opted for an omelette with salad.

'Have you ever filmed an operation?' Marcus helps himself to mustard.

'No. This is not the sort of programme I usually make.'

'So I understand.' He cuts into his steak.

'Oh?' She looks up.

He smiles. 'I've been doing my research. You make investigative documentaries. And you hold, so I'm told, pronounced feminist views. How do you square those views with working on a programme like *The Making of Her*?'

What's Richard been saying? Or if not Richard, who? Clara watches the blood ooze out of Marcus's steak, the sharp knife slicing through the crimson flesh and his mouth moving as he chews. Her stomach turns.

'I do have personal reservations. Yes. I make no secret of it.'

'And they are?'

'Changing a woman's appearance isn't, in my opinion, the most effective way of solving her problems. It just reinforces the idea that exteriors matter most. It encourages women to measure their worth through other people's eyes.'

Marcus impales another bloody piece of meat. 'Go on.'

'If women change their bodies to suit an elitist, collective idea of ideal femininity then they'll...' she remembers Jo's unexpected attack. 'Then we'll never feel at ease in them.' Marcus smirks, as if he can read her mind, but she ploughs on. 'Our bodies become man-made, manufactured. Products. Made for consumption.'

Like that meat and drink he's guzzling. Every mouthful paid for by a woman's self-loathing. Every sip of wine a measure of a woman's fear.

Marcus seems unmoved by her rhetoric. 'Mightn't a woman feel more powerful, more confident, if her body expresses her inner beauty? Mightn't she feel more authentically herself?'

He's playing with words. Playing devil's advocate. For him, this is an amusing way of passing the time. He has made short work of his steak. Pink juice coagulates in pools. She pushes the remains of her omelette to the side of her plate. Marcus takes a piece of bread and mops up the remaining juice. 'Isn't it every woman's right to choose what she does with her own body?'

'Of course. But such choices should be made from a position of integrity, not fear.'

A drop of pink splashes Marcus's tie. She watches him dabbing at it with his linen napkin. He looks up and catches her expression. Then he places his knife and fork together. They face her in a sharp, clinical line.

'It would seem,' he says, 'that your heart isn't in this programme.'

'My personal views and my professional ethics are separate things.'

'Perhaps then,' says Marcus, 'you should examine your own sense of integrity. Is it right for you to make a programme you don't believe in?'

She straightens her back and meets his cold eyes. 'I'll do the job to the best of my ability. As I always do. The programme will be good.'

He is staring at her. His eyes are ice-blue. Is he wearing contact lenses?

'If I didn't believe in your professional ability, I would not have agreed to the project,' he says. 'You do realise that, don't you?'

A gauntlet has been thrown down. She nods. Marcus proffers his wine glass to her tumbler of mineral water.

'To a stimulating working relationship.'

Can he be flirting? Her stomach squirms in disgust. Reluctantly, she clinks her glass against his.

*

Citing urgent work commitments, she left as soon as she could. There was a brief tussle over the bill, which Marcus appropriated despite her reminder that ProDoCo was paying; in claiming victory, she felt he had shifted the basis of their lunch from the professional to the personal.

Now, outside, she takes great gulps of grimy London air, thankful for its polluted familiarity. She needs to walk, fast, away from Marcus Templeton and his hothouse carvery of a world.

She turns into Harley Street. All along its length, limousines are parked bumper to bumper, ignoring the imminent threat of traffic wardens. Others draw up, disgorging clients. Most are mature woman, their unnaturally smooth facial skin surgically stretched over their bones, but there are younger women too, carrying chic carrier-bags labelled Jaeger, Chanel and Joseph. They walk confidently to their appointments with their private surgeons, dentists and complementary therapists, whose practices line the street. One pair are wearing the hijab, only their eyes visible as they flap up the steps to a brass-plated entrance. Only now does Clara remember that this is where Marcus has his consulting rooms. Hastily, she turns and walks back in the direction of Oxford Street.

Too late. A greatcoat topped by a large, unmistakeable head is moving rapidly towards her. Damn. She had hoped that he would settle to a leisurely brandy in his club. She crosses the road and ducks into the miniature oasis of Cavendish Square. Shielded by a scrubby privet hedge, she sinks down on a stained bench, keeping her back turned. What on earth is she doing, hiding from the man who will soon be part of her team?

The exposed little square is a welcome relief after the claustrophobic cosseting of the private club. She is surrounded on all sides by moving columns of traffic that halt with a growl at the lights before accelerating away. On this closing autumn afternoon, the brown-hued garden is deserted, dotted with empty benches and waste bins overflowing with the remains of lunchtime sandwiches and discarded newspapers. The only diners here are the downtrodden pigeons that peck desultorily around the bins and, on the far side, a bag-lady who rummages in them. Under Clara's buttocks, the wooden seat is hard and cold.

Maybe she should flag down a taxi and make a quick getaway. She steals a glance towards the other side of the road. Marcus has stopped and is shaking hands with a shorter, younger man who looks, from behind, vaguely familiar. No choice but to stay put.

The rush-hour heaves into gear. Cars, taxis, bikes, all carrying people to appointments, meetings and destinations. Busy people with a purpose. Like herself. Every train, tube or taxi journey provides an opportunity to open her laptop or switch on her mobile. Dan used to laugh about it, calling her a *human doing*. He used to sing *do-be-do-*

be-do as an irritating reminder even while his warm fingers massaged the knots in her neck. In return, she had berated him for his lack of ambition, his laid-back attitude to life and his wholehearted enjoyment of the present. Had she been envious of his ability to slow down and be still? When did she last stop and do absolutely nothing?

'Mind if I sit beside you, dearr?'

The bag-lady is standing over her, one hand holding a long-expired sandwich, the other gripping a pull-along trolley overflowing with detritus. The West Country accent, with its burr and slow cadence, is incongruous here. The woman has her pick of any of the dozen or so empty benches in the square. Why choose this one? She clearly wants company. Someone to talk at. Or else she is going to beg for money. And she's probably been drinking. But then again, she has more right to sit where she chooses because her choices are so few. Clara darts another glance towards Marcus, who is still in conversation, and shuffles along the bench.

The woman nods, exhales and lowers her bulk on to the seat. Lines are etched deep into a face dominated by a huge, bulbous nose. Her feet are encased in a ragbag of materials – newspaper, fabric and string.

The woman seems disinclined to talk. She crumbles the hard, discoloured crusts and tosses them for the pigeons that flap and shudder around their ankles. Clara half-heartedly kicks her foot, scattering them. The woman looks at her.

'What's the matter, dearr? Don't like birds?'

'Not these. They carry disease.'

'Ahh.' The woman grins. 'Dirty little buggers, eh?'

'Yeah.'

The woman breaks off another crust and tosses it among the pigeons. Clara shoos those nearest to her away.

'Like reading, do you?'

'Sorry?'

The woman is wiping her hands on her trouser leg. 'Like books?'

'I don't get much time.'

'I like to read. I gets books from the skip over Camden way. They throws them out of the college.' She chuckles. 'Too many books for them students with their computers and all that.'

She rummages in her trolley. 'What about this? Handsome, in't it?' She holds out a book. 'Want to see?'

Clara takes it. A thin volume of poetry by someone called Rainer Maria Rilke. It's far from handsome. It is stained and spotted with what might be bird-droppings. The woman is breathing heavily, leaning close. Clara tries not to inhale.

The woman's finger jabs at the name on the cover. 'He's a bloke, even though he's got a woman's name. *Maria*, see?'

'Right.' She makes to hand it back.

'You take it, dearr. You have a read. Do you good.'

'No, no. I couldn't. It's yours.'

'Dear of yer! I got plenty more in 'ere.' She gestures to her trolley. 'You have it. Go on.'

'Oh, well… thanks.' Clara pushes the book into her bag. She can throw it out later. She glances behind. Marcus is striding away up Harley Street. His companion is walking in the opposite direction.

'I'd better be going.' She rises but the woman grasps Clara's wrist in her horny, rough hand.

'Don't you go believin' any rubbish about them birds. They got names. Every one. You remember that.'

Safely ensconced in a taxi, Clara looks back at the square. The woman is ambling off towards Portland Street, her trolley bumping behind her. Nothing to hurry for. Nowhere to go. *Do-be-do-be-do.*

The taxi noses down Wigmore Street, but gets stuck behind a sleek black limousine that is illegally parked outside Boots. A large, dishevelled man, his grey hair tied in a ponytail, flings open the near-side door and hurries into the store. Behind, traffic is backing up. Clara's driver leans on his horn, creating a dissonant symphony with others down the line. A window in the rear of the shrouded limousine rolls down a few inches. Further along the street, a traffic warden is strolling towards the fracas, pen at the ready.

'Urry up, mate! Do 'im!' Clara's driver is rubbing his hands gleefully.

A short man hurries past the crowd that is gathering on the pavement. He tip-tups in polished leather shoes, his man-bag swinging from his shoulder, designer glasses dwarfing his little-boy face. It's the man she saw talking to Marcus. It's Stanley Barforth.

The shop doors slide open and the pony-tailed man returns in the nick of time, carrying a plastic bag. He yells something in a Glaswegian accent and hops into the limousine. The traffic warden is busy fixing a fine to the windscreen of a nearby Fiat. The limousine pulls out and proceeds in a leisurely fashion down Wigmore Street, its stark number plate – PS OFF – offering its own succinct commentary on the situation.

'Bastard,' mutters Clara's driver. 'Thinks 'e owns the bloody road.'

'Probably does,' says Clara, watching Stanley Barforth disappear into Marcus's club. 'Money talks.'

So that's how it is. The old boy network still performing the mutual scratching of backs. Marcus is a rich man with an ego that needs feeding. ProDoCo needs investment.

The Making of Her suddenly makes perfect sense.

PETE

'Boots! Pull over!' Jongo yells, unnecessarily loudly in Pete Street's opinion, blasting him with a wave of cigar smoke and whisky.

Ed, the driver, swings the limo in the general direction of the kerb, provoking a cacophony of screeching brakes from the cars behind.

'What kind d'ye want?' Jongo is already half out of the limo.

'Paracetamol. Strongest they've got.'

'Eh, laddie! Anybody'd think you'd got hammered last night, if they didnae know better.'

Jongo MacBride is, in his own words, *nivver one to hold back*. Over the decades, Pete has learned to live with his manager's idiosyncrasies: his habit of emphasising the most unlikely phrases in his sentences like a ham actor and his fondness for foul-smelling cigars and malt whisky. Jongo, for his part, has learned to curb his smokes in Pete's presence, if only for the sake of his master's voice. But he boldly goes where no man has gone before in terms of stomping over Pete's sensitivities.

As Jongo slams the car door behind him, Pete presses a button and the window slides down an inch or two. It's a toss-up which is the lesser evil – Jongo's distinctive aroma or the danger of being recognised by anyone old enough to remember him. As the *eau de Jongo* dissipates, it's replaced by the hot fumes of exhaust and the not-so-silent fury of the vehicles behind. This is madness. Why the hell didn't he stay at home? Jongo's fault. As so much is.

Just because he'd made the mistake of rubbing his temples earlier this morning. Jongo, of course, had leapt on it.

'Headache, laddie?'

'Yeah.' Easier to agree. Heartache, after all, was harder to treat.

'Eh.' A pause, as Jongo scrutinised him. 'You need a dose of *fresh air*, if you ask me.' Pete hadn't. 'Nothing better to clear a sore head. An' it's time you got out in the world. Ever since…' Jongo hesitated in an uncharacteristic attempt at diplomacy… 'ye've become *hermetical*.'

Pete longed to hermetically seal Jongo's lips by telling him to shut the fuck up. Instead, he'd somehow been bullied into accompanying Jongo on this totally pointless jaunt.

Now the noise level around the limo is overwhelming. People are yelling obscenities from car windows. Furious fists hit horns. Pete presses the button that winds the window back. *Come on.* Come on, Jongo. Move your ass and let's get home.

The limo door is yanked open and Jongo deposits a plastic bag on Pete's knees. 'Got a bottle o' water while I was at it,' he says, 'so you can tek a couple now.'

Pete delves into the bag. The pack of pills is large. The plastic water bottle is cold and clammy in his palm.

'How's your head, laddie?' Jongo asks earnestly.

'Going off.'

'Ye should *see a doc.* You're gettin' through too many of they pills. That's the third lot in *as many weeks*.'

'Leave it.' Pete shoves the pills in his pocket and takes a swig of water. The hooting behind them ratchets up. Lucky he doesn't really have a headache, otherwise what with the noise and Jongo he'd be bloody dying by now. Ed, who is of a philosophical bent, turns in his seat.

'Taxi drivers, eh, Mr Street? All them years of doin' The Knowledge. You'd think they'd learn a bit of sense along the way.'

He takes his time letting off the brake and flicks a practised V-sign out of the window as the limo slides out into the traffic.

JO

Horses sweat. Men perspire. Women merely glow.

My mother Julia's adage. She had one for every occasion.

A whistling woman, like a crowing hen, is neither use to God nor men.

And her favourite:

Hell hath no fury like a woman scorned. I gaze at myself in the bedroom mirror. Here, undoubtedly, stands a scorned woman. Where, then, is *my* fury?

My glasses slide down my nose and I push them back up. Must keep the real world in focus. Especially today. It seems that I have somehow changed into a horse, since sweat is running coldly down the small of my back and *glowing* is the last word I would use to describe the woman in the mirror. This sweating has nothing to do with the menopause or with the season, which is decidedly autumnal. No. This is fear.

I toss my greying mane, which flies out in split ends. A real woman would have gone to the hairdressers before an interview: would have planned her outfit down to the last detail days before.

I glance at my watch. One-fifteen. The interview – for a receptionist and general office administrator in a local public relations agency – is at two-thirty. And I have nothing to wear. Clothes cover the bed. Shoes lie on the carpet. Somehow, like the woman in the mirror, my wardrobe has aged and altered behind closed doors. Like me, it is wrinkled and worn. How am I supposed to cobble together a wearable ensemble from these jumble-sale rejects? It will have to be the trouser suit since all the skirts make me look six months pregnant. Never mind that the waistband cuts into my midriff and there are shiny areas on the knees and cuffs. As to a bag, Old Faithful will have to do, even if it doesn't match. My shoes, at least, are new. Plastic and stiff, they are already squeezing my feet unmercifully, pinching at every step. Like the Little Mermaid. Is this the price I must pay for entering the real world?

And talking of the real world, the doorbell rings. Right on cue. Just as I'm tugging at the jacket of the trouser suit in a vain attempt to persuade it to cover my bottom. It's Clara, carrying a parcel.

'Your stories. Send them off. Now.'

'I can't. Not now. I've got an interview at…'

'Do it.'

She stands over me while I stuff the stories in a padded envelope and address it to the first agent on my list. I glance at my watch. Two-fifteen. Panicking, I throw on my old black coat and rush into the street. But Clara has no mercy. She grabs my arm and marches me to the postbox on the corner. There she stands and watches while I drop the envelope in.

'Don't forget,' she calls after me as I turn and totter down the High Road in the general direction of the interview, 'fortune favours the bloody-minded.'

If only Julia's sayings had been more along those lines.

And now here I sit in the waiting room, an ugly duckling among a flock of sleek swans, none of whom is a day over thirty. Surely we should each have been given a separate time slot? Maybe there has been some kind of hold up.. The receptionist, whose job we are all after, hardly seems to care. She chews gum and plays solitaire on her computer, sighing audibly every time the phone rings and counting down the minutes to her departure.

My heart is fluttering feebly at my ribs like a moth trying to escape. To distract myself, I thumb through a magazine. The models look affronted as I turn the pages with fingers that are strangers to a manicure. What am I doing here among these media savvy beauties with their sparkling acrylic nails?

The clock over the reception desk ticks through two-forty-five. Through three. Three-thirty. There are just two of us left now, me and a young woman in a pink suit who was greeted effusively by name when she arrived a short while ago. She is now gazing down at my swelling ankles.

The receptionist's phone buzzes. 'You can go in now,' she says, vaguely. I stand up, feeling my trouser legs peel away from the plastic seat.

The receptionist frowns. 'Not you. Her.' The pink woman grins and sashays off towards the door marked *Interviewing*.

'But I've been waiting since two-thirty.'

'You'll be going in shortly.'

'But that woman came in after me...'

'You'll be going in shortly.' The tone is dismissive. I return to my seat.

Hell hath no fury like a woman scorned. Why, why then do I feel like a limp rag?

At five to four, the phone buzzes.

'There's still one more,' the receptionist states, bored. 'I know. I *know*. All right –' she raises her eyes to me '– you can go in now.'

*

'Please take a seat, Mrs Cow.'

'Coe.' I can't risk further misunderstandings. 'Josephine.'

The seat is warm from the previous candidate. The interviewing panel do not introduce themselves. A boy of about twenty-three with hair gelled into aggressive spikes is picking his teeth with a pink paperclip. A woman in her thirties is yawning, her eyelids bowed under the weight of a mass of sooty black eye shadow. The desk is littered with plastic cups and empty water bottles. The air smells tired. A fly bumbles morosely at the window pane.

'Sorry for the wait.' This is the boy. He doesn't sound particularly sorry.

'Why don't you tell us about yourself?' sighs the woman. They both gaze at me without interest. I push my glasses up my nose.

They promptly slide down again.

'I'm fifty.' *Too much information, Jo.* 'I have a typing speed of eighty words a minute…'

A look of pained wonder passes between the pair.

'What applications have you used?'

'I'm sorry?'

'Excel? PowerPoint?'

This is an unknown language. 'I'm sure I can learn.'

A silence – as if each is hoping the other will speak. Eventually the woman recites: 'And-what-do-you-think-you-can-bring-to-this-job?'

'Enthusiasm. Responsibility. Maturity.'

The boy gives a tiny smirk.

'I have good written skills. I'm numerate.'

'What?'

'Good at numbers.'

'Oh. Right.' The boy eyes his watch.

The woman shuffles papers in a concluding sort of way. 'Do you have any questions at all?'

The air feels so weighted down with lethargy that I can barely form the words. 'What would my duties be?'

'Duties? Didn't you read the ad?'

'Yes, but…'

'Receptionist. Telling people where to go.'

The boy smirks again, shifts in his seat and takes up the refrain. 'And some typing, emailing. You know. Press releases. Whatever.'

'And the hours?'

The woman sighs again. 'Variable. Ten till six usually. Four weeks' holiday. All right?'

'Yes.'

'Right. Well, thanks. You'll be hearing from us by the end of the week.'

I have waited two hours for an interview which has lasted approximately six minutes.

*

'The very first tear he made was so deep that I thought it had gone right into my heart. And when he began pulling the skin off, it hurt worse than anything I've ever felt.'

The doorbell is ringing. I place my book face down on the table. The postman hands me a thick wad of mail, held together with an elastic band. He doesn't look at me.

I watch him walk away down the path, hunched over his burden of letters. Brown, sodden leaves lie downtrodden on the path. Autumn is drifting inexorably into winter. I should go out and walk myself out of this mood. Treat myself to a coffee and a cake. See a film. The very thought of such activities exhausts me. In the six days since the abortive interview, I have hardly stirred from the sofa, finding solace in my childhood books. Hans Christian Andersen. The Brothers Grimm. And now, best of all, C.S. Lewis and his story about the boy who was turned into a dragon. I am hungry for other people's words, for other people's worlds. I know I am regressing. Back to the years before Iain, back to a time when books were my sanctuary from Julia's carping criticism, my companions during her echoing absences. I drop the mail on to the coffee table and pull the old throw over my knees, psyching myself up to the task of separating Iain's mail from my own. Very little for him comes to this address – presumably because he has informed the Post Office that he is no longer resident in Chiswick. His mail will be redirected to Rosalie's.

I slip the rubber band off the pile of envelopes and begin trawling through them. There are three for me: two business envelopes with typed addresses and a large manila envelope, addressed in a script which seems familiar.

I begin with the business letters. The first is from the PR company:

Dear Mrs Cow,

Thank you for attending an interview with us recently. Unfortunitly – hah! *– we are unable to offer you the position, but wish you all success for the future.*

Yours, etc.

I tear the paper in half and drop it into the bin. The second letter is from Woodhall Platt, Solicitors:

Dear Mrs Coe,

We have been instructed by our client, Iain S. Coe, to initiate divorce proceedings. Please be kind enough to advise us whether you will be seeking representation in this matter and if so, apprise us of your solicitor's details.

Regarding the shared residence, our client requests that suitable arrangements be agreed between you.

Yours faithfully etc.

I stare at the words. Can he do this? When he is the one who has left? When he is bedding down with Rosalie? Is he counting on the fact that I won't argue my case?

Hell hath no fury…

Perhaps I have bitten my tongue so often that I have severed it. I set the letter aside.

I stare at the manila envelope. Given the contents of the solicitor's letter, both my name and my address already seem obsolete. Then I realise why the writing looks familiar. It's my own.

The moths in my chest are not just fluttering, but swerving dangerously. The Voice is yelling *Don't!* But I tear open the envelope. Inside are my stories, just as I sent them. No note, not even a standard rejection slip. Across my covering letter someone has scrawled a single word in black ink. *No.*

I carry my stories to the kitchen and drop them in the waste bin. I wipe at my cheeks, which are wet, and return to the sofa, and my book.

Eustace, the boy who has been turned into a dragon, is standing beside a pool, where a great lion, Aslan, has ordered him to 'undress'. The boy tries unsuccessfully to scratch away the thick dragon-skin. Then Aslan uses his claws to rip it off, deeper and deeper, layer by excruciating layer. Finally, stripped naked, Eustace is thrown into the water. And he realises that he has been turned into a boy again.

I sit. I wonder. What would it feel like to be stripped of everything that has accumulated over the years? To start afresh, clean and new?

To become a woman again?

CLARA

'Got a minute, Clara?'

It's Alix. Ice-blonde hair pulled back. Nails French-manicured. Long legs lean and unblemished. Accent cut-glass.

'Can it wait?' Clara is struggling to edit a tricky sequence of shots for *The Body Politic*. Alix has an in-built radar for breaking Clara's focus.

'Sure.' But Alix doesn't go. She places her notebook on the desk and swivels in an empty chair, her eyes on the screen.

Clara presses Play. The sequence unfolds. The first four shots are good. Very good. But not the fifth. Alix's expressive silence says it all. Clara deletes the shot and replaces it with another. Better. But now there are sequencing problems…

'Clara, I don't want to butt in, only…' Alix's sublimely confident upper-class tones shatter her already fractured thoughts. Clara sighs. 'Yes?'

'What about a shot of the ex-husband there? One of the ones I got? It would give him a presence early on.'

Shit. She'd forgotten all about those shots. She retrieves one and includes it. The scene unfolds seamlessly. She senses Alex nodding. And she experiences an almost overwhelming urge to place her hands about the girl's slender white neck and squeeze.

'Thanks.' Her throat closes around her reluctance to say the word. 'So. What do you want to talk about?'

Alix smiles. 'Just to update you on *The Making of Her*.'

As if she is the senior producer. As if this is her project. Clara reaches for her coffee, but the cup is empty.

'I've been talking to Marcus,' Alix says.

'Marcus?' When did Alix meet him?

'Marcus Templeton,' Alix enunciates, as if Clara is very old or very deaf. 'And he agrees that we really must choose someone soon. After all, his people need to organise medical and psychometric testing...'

'I'm aware of that.' Clara's heartbeat quickens, thuds and echoes in her ears. How dare Alix imply that she's dragging her feet?

'...so, anyway, we've established a profile of the kind of woman we're looking for. I've put advertisements in The Mail, The Standard and the usual women's mags. We should get the first responses next week. Then I'll arrange interviews. I'll have our woman within the month.'

Clara is aware of a quivering sensation in her legs. As if the ground is being sucked from under her.

'Alix.' Steady. She must keep her voice steady.

'Yes?'

'I see no reason for you to stay on after the next couple of weeks. I'm sure Richard will be needing your... skills... elsewhere.'

Alix lowers her lashes. 'Really? That's not the impression I got from Stan Barforth. He seemed to think I should stick around. Just in case.'

So she's in cahoots with Stanley Barforth too. Nausea rises to accompany the ringing in Clara's ears. She swallows, hard.

'In case of what, exactly?'

'Well, you might need help. After all, this *is* new territory.'

'Alix, I've no idea what you mean by that remark.' Clara forces herself to speak evenly. 'And I certainly won't need you after I take over.' Her head is swimming. Is she going down with something? 'I'll tell Richard. Let him know he can allocate you elsewhere.'

'Won't it be Stan Barforth's decision? After all, Richard'll be out soon.' Alix's face is expressionless but her tone subtly conveys derision for Richard, for Clara, for the whole outmoded status quo.

'It will be my decision. As producer.' Clara turns back to the frozen screen. If Alex doesn't get out quickly, she'll say something she may regret.

'As you wish.' Alix picks up her notebook and stands. Her vacated chair swivels on its pedestal.

As the cutting room door swings shut, Clara grabs the empty coffee cup and screws it up with a crackle which should be satisfying, but isn't. Bloody Barforth. Bloody Marcus. Bloody, bloody Alix. Her knees are shaking. There is a strange ache in her chest. What's going on? She drags in a breath. Another. She hears herself muttering words and questions like a mad woman. *You think I can't do it? A formulaic, done-to-death disaster of a show? You think it's beyond me?* The sound-proofed walls close in on her. Papered on them are Alix's smile, Marcus's overbearing head, Stanley Barforth's empty eyes. She propels herself from her seat.

Sweat is snaking down her sides. Her world is wobbling like a spinning top just before it skids sideways and crashes. She wants to scream, but there's no room in her throat, no way out.

Is she dying? Going crazy? She half lowers herself, half falls into her chair, fumbling for her mobile. Jo? Her fingers itch to dial the number. But no. Not fair. Jo is fragile. Who, then? Who?

David Wood's phone rings. And rings. It is lunchtime but surely his receptionist should be there?

Please let him answer. Please. This neediness is as terrifying as her physical symptoms.

'Hello. This is David Wood. I can't get to the phone right now, but please leave your message, together with the time you called and your number, and I'll get back to you as soon as I can. In case of emergencies, I can be contacted on…' She dives for a pen and scribbles the number on her script. His phone rings for a long time before it is picked up.

'David?' The word comes out shrilly.

'Who is this?' A woman's voice. David's wife?

Clara takes a deep, struggling breath. 'Is David there? I need to speak with him.'

There is a moment's pause. Then: 'Can't it wait till he gets back to the office?'

'It's urgent.' Sweat is trickling down her face like tears.

'They all say that.'

How incredibly fucking rude. Forcing herself to ignore the barb, she repeats her request.

'He's working. Probably.' The woman's tone is vague. 'Leave your number at his office.'

The receiver is replaced.

She rings the office number again. This time his receptionist picks up.

'Clara Williams. I came once before. Can I see David? As soon as possible?'

'I'm sorry. David's fully booked today.'

'Please.' Every other word seems to have deserted her. 'Please?'

There is a pause. 'Just a moment. I'll put you on hold.'

Clara slumps in her chair. What if he says no? What will she do?

The receptionist is back. 'You could come at the end of his appointments. At nine o'clock?'

'Yes. Thank you.'

Can she hold on? Maybe she has overdone the caffeine. Maybe she should eat. She makes herself walk to the canteen, where she forces down a salad and substitutes a bottle of mineral water for her customary coffee. Then, blocking her ears to the cries of her body, she returns to Edit Three and focuses on the screen.

*

She is an hour early. Maybe his eight o'clock appointment won't turn up. No such luck. David's door remains resolutely shut. She bites the skin around her thumbnail. Her only distractions are the other clients arriving for their appointments with the therapists who share the practice. She stares at them as they come and go, trying to read their expressions. Do they feel better after their fifty minutes? Beside her, a beautiful elderly woman sits, her age-spotted hands clasped loosely in her lap, radiating calm. Was she a mess too before coming here?

David's door opens and a nervous-looking young man in corduroy trousers sidles out, head down. David appears behind him. He is wearing a blue denim shirt hanging over jeans, and his feet are again bare. He sees Clara, gives her a brief smile, then widens the door to allow the elderly woman to enter. She greets him with familiar pleasure. David touches the woman's shoulder lightly as she moves into the room past him, and Clara is surprised by an unexpected flash of... what? Resentment? Why should she feel proprietorial about him? She cannot answer this question. All she knows is that she is needy. Nakedly needy. She wants to be in that woman's place, already unburdening herself under David's steady gaze. She strains to hear what may be passing in the room and catches an occasional burst of laughter. What is there to laugh about? The clock ticks on towards nine.

At ten to nine, the door opens. Clara stands up. The elderly woman, still serene and smiling, hovers in the doorway. She leans towards David and they briefly embrace. David then retreats into the room and shuts the door. Clara sinks back in her chair.

Nine o'clock. The receptionist is gathering her things and putting on her coat. At last. At long last. The door opens and David waves her in as he bids goodnight to the receptionist.

There are candles on the mantelpiece and the two chairs are bathed in pools of warm light from simple wooden-based lamps. She catches the same scent of lemon, mingled with a whisper of the last client's perfume. And another scent: something male and unknown.

'Clara.' David folds himself into his chair. His eyes are tired, but the smile is just as welcoming. She glances at the clock. Only fifty minutes.

'I had... an experience today. That's why I've come back. I wasn't going to...'

He nods. 'What happened?'

She tells him about her encounter with Alix. About her physical symptoms. 'It was terrifying. I thought I was having a heart attack.'

'Sounds more like a panic attack.' He is gazing quietly at her. Scanning her from head to toe.

'A panic attack?' Is he implying she is neurotic?

'You've been under a lot of pressure for a long time. Your body has to express what it's feeling. A panic attack is one way of letting off steam.'

'But I wasn't panicking. I was furious.'

He studies her, saying nothing.

'I was! Alix was completely fucking underhand, going to Marcus behind my back. She was undermining my position, suggesting I can't do my job...'

In the silence that follows she hears the strident echo of her words. They sound alien here, too loud.

'Clara,' David says. 'Do you think that anger is your default position?'

'What?'

'Remember last session we spoke about you exploring the unfamiliar parts of yourself?'

She nods.

'Anger seems very familiar to you. Is it, perhaps, the emotion by which you recognise yourself?'

She takes a rapid breath to argue the point, then closes her mouth.

'Might your anger be your champion? The part of you that comes to your defence when you feel under attack?'

What the hell is he saying? Doesn't everyone get angry when they are attacked? She thinks of Jo. OK, not everyone. But Jo's mildness has hardly been a benefit to her.

David's voice is gentle. 'It's fine to have the capacity for anger. But I sense you may be feeling it *instead* of a range of other emotions. What do you think?'

'What emotions?'

'That's for you to identify. What might be lurking under this anger?' He sits back.

More bloody questions. She swallows her irritation. 'How should I know?'

'Let's go back to your encounter with Alix. What were you feeling?'

'I felt undermined. Betrayed. And when she'd gone, I felt I was in a straitjacket. Like I couldn't move. I couldn't break out. Claustrophobic. Imprisoned. I was scared...'

'You were scared.'

'You're suggesting I was frightened rather than angry?'

'Maybe.' He draws a leg up, so that his bare foot rests against his thigh. The bones of it are long and expressive, like the planes of his face. 'Forgive me,' he says, 'if you've heard this metaphor before, but it's easiest to liken the psyche to an onion.'

'Now we're talking vegetables?'

He doesn't rise to this. 'The outside skin is tough. It's the part the world sees and recognises. But if you strip it away, underneath you'll find green skin, then white. Layer upon layer. Until you come to the softest part of all, the heart.'

She wants to ridicule him and his theory. 'I'm allergic to onions. They make me cry.'

He looks at her. 'The layers represent feelings. We all wrap emotions around our hearts so that no one will know us at our most vulnerable.'

'What, even you?'

He says: 'Most definitely even me.'

She tries to imagine him angry, furious or frightened, and fails.

'What are you feeling right now?' he asks.

Feeling? She casts her mind around. 'Hungry.'

He seems to be trying, unsuccessfully, to hide a smile. She glances at her watch. Forty minutes. The question jumps from her before she has time to consider it.

'Do you believe people can change? Really change?'

'If I didn't, I wouldn't be sitting here. What about you?'

'On the outside, yes. You can move house, get a new job, a new partner. Even...' she remembers Marcus's white hands '...a new face and a new body. But that's not real change, is it?'

'It's an interesting question. There's an old alchemical saying: *As above, so below.* In other words, what happens on one level affects and perhaps transforms what happens on another. So you could argue that changing the outside will have an effect on what's happening inside. We're all just bundles of moving energy, after all. I think everything we do has an effect on everything else, whether we know it or not.'

'So, me coming into this room has changed you?'

That lop-sided grin. 'It's certainly had an effect on me. Yes.'

They sit in silence for a moment or two. The silence doesn't feel threatening. Which is progress.

'In my world,' she says eventually, 'there's no time to do this. Every minute has to be used effectively. Every decision must be faultless. There's no opportunity to be less than perfect.'

'That doesn't sound very forgiving.'

'It isn't. Mistakes are seen as failure. Ageing is seen as failure.'

'And yet you're human. And humans, by their nature, are fallible. And they age.'

'Tell that to Alix.'

David raises an eyebrow. 'What is it exactly about Alix that challenges you?'

'She represents everything that's... that's wrong about television today. Oh, she's efficient. But she's a ratings-chaser. Quantity over quality, every time.'

'Do you feel threatened by her?'

'You must be joking!' A flush looms. She scrabbles in her bag for a tissue. 'Women like Alix are two-a-penny. They come swanning in with their posh accents and their ready-made connections.' She dabs at her forehead. 'Did *she* start at the bottom and work her way up?'

'Like you did?'

'Of course. I learned to type. That's how it was, then.'

She and Jo, at the Davina Lucas Secretarial School, full of hope and the promise of a better future. And her hard work had paid off. Eventually.

David shifts in his chair. 'Is there anything about Alix that you recognise in yourself?'

'Nothing.' Clara drops the tissue into the bin. 'She's ambitious for all the wrong reasons. She's cold. And she's after my job.'

A sudden memory of herself at thirty, talking to Richard about a senior producer.

Isn't it time she retired? She really is getting past it. Why doesn't she step aside and give one of us a chance?

'Clara?'

The enormity of the idea lodges in her throat. She could never have been like Alix, could she? Her nails are biting into her palms. 'I'm good.' The words burst from her. 'I'm very good at my job. There's so much more for me to do. They're wrong…' Hot tears prick at her eyes and she blinks furiously. She knows perfectly well that the quality she finds absolutely unnerving in Alix is her certainty. Because her own confidence, the mainstay of her self-image, is crumbling.

David is leaning forward. 'Clara. I'm sure there's more for you to do. And I'm sure there's more to you than they – or you – are aware of.'

She looks at him. He means it. She glances at her watch. Nine-twenty. Only half an hour left. The now-familiar anxiety makes her restless. 'Can I get up? Move around?'

'Feel free.'

He sits and waits as she stands, feeling exposed and self-conscious. She walks over to the bookcase. She recognises none of the books. *Everyday Zen. The Road Less Travelled. Care of the Soul.* Protruding from beneath the bookcase is a box, its interior painted blue, half full of sand.

'What's that?'

He follows her gaze. 'The box?'

'Is it a litter tray?' He might just be weird enough to keep a cat in the therapy room. She imagines him stroking soft fur with the soles of his long feet. The ghost of a shiver runs through her.

'It's a sand tray.'

He must be a paediatric therapist too. 'For kids?'

'It can be. But adults can use it too.'

'How does it work?'

'Want to try?'

Here we go again. A question answered with a question. Yet rather than irritating her, it feels soothing.

'If it won't take long.' She returns to her seat.

'It takes as long as it takes.' He hefts the box into the space between the chairs, which he pushes back, out of the way. He lowers himself to the floor, motioning her to do the same. It's strange and unsettling to be so close to him. Down on the floor, all the formality has gone. She can smell him. Warm skin and crumpled cotton. There's a ring on his wedding finger. She remembers the cool tones of the woman on the phone. What would it feel like to be married to a therapist? Does his wife resent his clients' need for his attention and his care?

'So, what do I do?'

'Whatever you want. You can play with the sand. You can pour water into it.'

Her jaw tightens. 'Is that it? How's that supposed to solve my problems?'

'Clara. You can try it, if you want to. It's up to you. But if you choose to do it, you need to do it wholeheartedly.'

The clock is ticking. Candlelight flickers over the surface of the sand, illuminating the fine grains. Oh, what the hell. She plunges her hands in, conscious that he is watching her. The sand feels cold and fluid. She pushes her hands deeper until they disappear. She pokes one finger above the surface. She is a child, dress tucked into her knickers, squatting in the soft sand at the playground. She looks up at David, then returns her attention to the sand. Over and over she scoops up a handful and lets the grains sift through her fingers.

'How does it feel?'

She doesn't want to stop. She circles her palm over the surface of the sand and feels its soft surrender.

'Real,' she says. 'It feels real.'

'Would you like some water?'

'No!' The question is an intrusion.

'Clara?'

'I prefer it dry.'

She pushes her forefinger into the sand and draws a spiral. Pressing deeper, her finger comes into gritty contact with the bottom of the box and reveals a tiny ovoid of blue. Now she is burrowing with both hands, pushing sand out from the centre of the box to the edges. The blue circle grows. A lake, a lagoon. No. An oasis, a space. She finds herself taking a deep breath. If only she could find a way to that blue circle and stay there forever.

The clock ticks on. David unfolds his long legs, stands up and moves across the room to a cupboard.

'You can use these too, if you want.'

'What are they?'

It's difficult to tear herself away from the sand with its blue island. She resents having to leave. Reluctantly, she brushes her hands together, shaking off this new world, and gets to her feet. She stands next to David at the cupboard. He opens the doors.

Row upon row of tiny objects. There are figurines – a sword-swinging Samurai warrior, a fairy princess, a hundred others. And tiny animals. There are wooden houses and trees. A skeleton. A spider. A bell. A tea-set. Flowers, feathers and stones.

Her fingers reach without conscious control and grasp a tiny baby. She knows that the baby is a girl. She returns to the sand tray and places the baby in the centre of the blue circle she has exposed. Her eyes fill.

'Clara?' David's voice is gentle.

She shakes her head. A tear drips into the sand. She covers up the dark pockmark. More tears. More dark spots in the sand.

He reaches for a box of tissues and passes it to her. She pulls out a handful and presses them to her face, hiding. Then she sits back on her heels, balling the wad of tissue between her palms. She stares at the baby in the blue circle.

'I can't remember when I last did that.'

'Which?' he asks. 'Cry or play?'

'Both.' Oddly, she doesn't feel embarrassed. She feels soft and full and clean.

'Tell me about the baby.' David says. 'Imagine you're her. What does she feel?'

Clara swallows. 'Safe. Peaceful. She feels…' Tears well up again. 'She feels… happy.'

'And what does she want, this baby?'

'She… she wants to be perfectly still. She wants to be…'

Do-be-do-be-do.

'To be… wanted.' A flush of self-consciousness spreads from the top of her head downwards. For a long time, she stares at her hands. Then she looks up, straight into his eyes, daring him to laugh at her. What greets her is compassion.

'To be wanted,' he repeats.

'For herself. For just who she is. Without having to do anything or prove anything.'

'To be wanted. Just for being who she is,' he says softly.

'Yes.'

Silence. She is aware that he is glancing at the clock.

'It's almost time, Clara,' he says. 'Would you like to come again?'

'Yes,' she answers. Without sharpness. Without hesitation. 'Yes, I would.'

JO

I am sitting among the other dinosaurs in the Natural History Museum with a letter from Iain in the bag on my lap. Above me, the giant articulated bones of a Tyrannosaurus Rex soar towards the canopied ceiling. Beside me, a little girl bites into a chocolate bar as her mother reads from the guide.

'– and this one's sixty-five million years old!'

'Mummy, how old are you?'

The woman catches my eye and grins. 'Almost as old as that dinosaur.'

The child's expression is serious above her chocolate-smeared mouth. 'No, you're not! If you was old as that, you'd be dead. Or else you'd be growed up to the ceiling.'

The woman takes the child's hand and hoists her off the seat and their laughter echoes away.

I feel a reluctant affinity with the giant creature suspended above me. Dinosaurs and middle-aged women. Past our sell-by dates. Obsolete. Although, judging by the crowd flowing around it and pointing at it, the dinosaur has the advantage of visibility. We dinosaur women live unnoticed and disregarded.

Lately, I feel like a ghost in my own life. As if I have no substance, no flesh or blood. As if I have been reduced to dust. Apart from my brief forays into the world, where people only notice me if I'm holding up a queue or if I blunder into someone's path, I barely exist.

When the letter clattered through the box this morning, joining the newspaper and sundry junk mail, I found myself unable to open it. I had almost managed to expunge thoughts of Iain from my mind. The pinched, upright writing was a shock: so familiar, yet so far removed. I had expected another solicitor's letter, having ignored the last. I felt a sudden pressing need to leave the house.

I hurried out into the damp mist of a winter morning, the unopened letter fulminating at the bottom of my bag. Reaching Chiswick High Road, I jumped on the first bus that pulled up – a bus which carried me to Kensington. I sat for some time beneath the golden memorial to Albert, gazing at the skaters, the lovers and the tourists. It was too cold to sit for long. My feet took me past the V & A and onwards until the need for a hot drink and a free seat propelled me into the Natural History Museum.

I can put it off no longer. I draw out the envelope and tear it open. I imagine Iain's tongue licking the flap. The paper is blurred. My eyes seem unwilling to focus. I push my glasses up my nose.

Iain has used our headed paper – the stationery he spent a week or more fussing over, deliberating about the design. His name is at the top in an overblown curlicued font. Our shared address is beneath, in plainer characters. At the time I had accepted the omission of my name. A portent?

Why has Iain chosen to write to me on this paper? Probably because he is too stingy to let it go to waste and because I am the only person he can use it for now that he no longer lives at this address. Or is it a jibe at me, a reminder that the home we once shared will soon be sold? Not for the first time, I wonder where I'll go. There will be money, of course. Unlike the stationery, the house is in both our names. At the time it had seemed unnecessary but Clara had urged me to make sure that I was included in the formal paperwork. I can almost hear her voice now, here, at my shoulder, telling me to read the bloody letter and get it over with.

Dear Jo,

I am not dear to him. So far, this letter is a travesty of attribution. I'd rather dwell on this fact than on its contents. My chest is beating and booming like those pulsating cartoon hearts. I glance around. Unsurprisingly, no one is looking at me.

I think we both know that our parting was unsatisfactory. I feel the need to sit with you and talk face to face. Let's meet for supper – on Thursday at eight – at Estrella's, as we used to. I look forward to seeing you there.

Yours,

Iain

I stare at the words, hardly able to assimilate them. Estrella's. Our old rendezvous. Our treat to ourselves at the end of a busy week. Iain's frugality didn't extend to eating out, although he always made a point of reminding me I was meant to be on a diet. We haven't been to Estrella's for perhaps two years.

Unsatisfactory. The ambiguity and understatement of the word disturbs me. It seems an odd way to describe our last encounter: his refusal to speak with me or to look at me. What has changed his mind – if, indeed, his mind is changed? What can he want to discuss with me *face to face*? Perhaps he wants to push me into hurrying the divorce. To sort out financial arrangements and the sale of the house. But surely that will be taken care of through the solicitors? I bend to read the words again, trying to wrench meaning from them.

Deliberately, I focus on his assumption that I will be free on Thursday night. How typical of Iain. No *if it's convenient*. A simple supposition that I will be available, that I will come. And he is right. That's the hard bit. I am all too free to run to his side.

An insidious thought creeps in. Perhaps he is regretting his hasty decision to divorce.

Perhaps he and Rosalie have split up and he has nowhere else to go. Perhaps he wants to come back.

Yours, Iain.

Is he telling me obliquely that he is mine? And if so, do I want him, along with his new green highlights? Would Iain's sniping remarks be more bearable than my mother's carping refrain, which has taken up residence in my head? My heart yearns towards the familiarity of being needed, of being used. In the best sense. It is my redundancy that hurts more than anything else.

I know, of course, what Clara would say. *Don't you even think of meeting him, Jo! Iain's a pain in the ass. You're well rid of him.*

But Clara, with her busy, purposeful career, does not have to deal with these empty hours. She does not have to grapple with this growing sense of uselessness.

Don't judge me weak, Clara, for going along to see what he has to say.

After all, there has been no real communication between us since he left.

After all, there are practical things to sort out.

Let your lawyers do the sorting out, Jo. You know how tricky Iain is. Keep your distance.

Clara's voice? Or The Voice? I fold the letter and return it to my bag. I'll think about it. Decide nearer the time. But in my heart, I know the decision is already made.

*

Iain is late, of course.

Arriving punctually at Estrella's, I explain to the maitre d' – who shows no sign of remembering me – that I am meeting Mr Coe and that he has booked a table. I hope this is the case. The maitre d' leafs through the diary. For a terrible moment I am certain this is a cruel joke: that Iain never intended to meet me; that he simply wanted to put me through the agony of waiting, just to underline the drab loneliness of my situation. But *This way, madam.* I am led to a table by the window, where a candle flickers, a tardy symbol of my lack of faith. Self-conscious in my new black dress and shorter-than-usual haircut, I settle into the proffered seat. *A drink, madam?* I shake my head. I'll wait.

Estrella's has moved on. The wrought-iron, bistro-style circular tables, which always rocked when you cut into your food, have been replaced with square oak. An extravagant flower arrangement almost obscures the kitchen. The waiters, who used to resemble musicians in a shabby orchestra, now wear striped butcher's aprons around their skinny hips.

My new shoes are cutting into my feet just as they did at the impossible interview. I had hesitated over wearing them – perhaps they were jinxed – but then deliberately squeezed my feet into them. Where had superstition got me so far in life? I would not have my future determined by a pair of shoes. I surreptitiously ease my feet out of the hard plastic and cross my fingers beneath the tablecloth.

And here is Iain, striding ahead of the waiter to join me, leaning down to kiss my cheek, almost suffocating me with the heavy scent of his aftershave. The green highlights are still intact. He is wearing grey chinos rather than his ratty old cords and, somewhat incongruously, a pair of orange suede moccasins. Did Rosalie choose them? He looks sharper, younger. As if the time he has spent away from me has refreshed him.

'Jo. Good to see you.' This has to be for the benefit of the waiter. He bares his teeth at me, and I am dazzled by a white wall of enamel. I wonder, fleetingly, how much it cost.

'Hello, Iain.'

'New hair?'

I nod. He doesn't pass comment on it. The maitre d' arrives, shooing away the hovering waiter and shaking Iain's hand.

'Mr Coe!' He flicks a glance at me. 'You see, we have your usual table…'

His usual table? It has been two years at least since we were here. Is it pain or humiliation lodging in my chest, almost taking away my breath?

Iain, oblivious, spreads his linen napkin, peruses the menu. 'What would you like? Don't stint yourself. This is a celebration.'

'A celebration?' Right on cue, the wine waiter arrives. Iain takes his time swilling the wine around his mouth and rolling his eyes. Thankfully, he doesn't spit it out afterwards. Having poured us both a glass, he says:

'*Down in the Dark* has been optioned for a film,' and settles back for the inevitable congratulations. A small but precise hole is being drilled through my heart. *Down in the Dark* was our last baby. I wasn't there to see it take its first faltering steps into the commercial world.

He is raising his glass to mine. 'To success.'

I swallow. 'How's *Parity* going?'

Iain hesitates. 'Pretty well. Of course, I've not had much time for writing recently, what with radio and conferences. You know.' He takes another sip of wine. 'What have you been up to?'

'I've been busy,' I say, knowing that he won't ask for details. He doesn't. 'In fact, I've been looking for a job.'

He raises his eyes from his glass. 'Oh? Doing what?'

'PR.'

'With whom?'.

'I don't actually have it yet but I've been asked for an interview.' Not a lie, exactly.

Iain's mobile rings. He stands and walks off towards the toilet, his shoulders hunched protectively around the phone. After some minutes, he returns, smiling, the new white teeth gleaming in the restaurant gloom.

'Sorry about that. Business.' Rosalie business?

Our food arrives. I find that for once I am entirely without appetite. Part of me longs for Iain to come to the point. Part of me dreads it. I feel like a fat fly suspended in amber. Iain is ascertaining that all is in order, that our glasses are refilled, the condiments supplied. Finally, he turns to me.

'Jo.'

'Yes?'

'There's something I'd like to discuss with you.'

Get on with it. Please.

'I've been thinking...' He forks in a mouthful of risotto, chews and swallows. Making me wait. 'I feel I may have acted rashly. Said some things that... while true... perhaps shouldn't have been said.' He suddenly reaches for my hand and imprisons it in his own. His palm is warm and damp.

'Jo. There's a lot of history between us, and I don't want to lose that. Do you?'

I find myself speechless, which Iain takes for assent.

'We've achieved a lot together, haven't we?'

I nod. This, at least, seems true.

'So why don't we carry on?'

'You mean, you want to move back in?'

Iain hesitates, releases my hand. 'Not precisely that. After all, there's Rosalie to consider.'

'What?'

'I have to… consider her feelings.'

He has to think of Rosalie's feelings. After a moment, I gather myself. 'So what, exactly, is it that you want?'

Iain smiles, taking another opportunity to show off the teeth. 'We're a good team, you and I. And as you said, you need something to keep you busy.' He appears not to notice my intake of breath. 'Why should our… change of circumstances… affect our working together?'

I swallow. 'You mean, you want to carry on living with her – with Rosalie – and have me work with you on *Parity*?'

He nods. 'There's no room at Rosalie's place for a proper office so I could come over to the house and use my old one. It would be convenient for you, too.'

I open my mouth, willing something to come out. Nothing does. I'm painfully aware that in a terrible sense Iain is offering me a lifeline: a chance of restoring my sense of purpose, of usefulness. I hate him for the power he holds over me, for dangling this tempting morsel under my nose. The pathetic part of me wants to grab at it. But The Voice is speaking now, loudly and unambiguously. She is telling me that if I take the bait, the last vestiges of my pride will be gone and I will be tethered irrevocably to Iain by the cord of my own need.

He is waiting for my reply, the familiar pursing of his lips indicating growing impatience. A cacophony of responses lurches around my brain. He glances at his watch, sighs. 'If it's a matter of payment, I'm sure I could come up with something.'

I grip the table, struggling to find my voice.

'I thought... do you know, I actually thought that perhaps you regretted leaving. That you might have realised you still cared for me.'

'Well...' he blusters. 'Naturally, I still... *care* for you.'

'Like you might care for an old dog? A favourite armchair?' I am half standing, my voice rising. People are looking.

Iain's features have assumed their customary self-righteous expression. 'You must be aware that you've rather let yourself go.'

Dinosaur woman. I want to push his smug face down into the remains of his risotto. To douse the green highlights in red wine. I want to kill him slowly, tortuously, as he is killing me. Above all, I want to be safe at home, my head in a book. Under the table, as if they have a life and a will of their own, my feet are slowly re-encasing themselves in the hard plastic shoes.

'Sit down, Jo, for God's sake. People are staring.'

'Who cares?' I'm beyond worrying now about making a fool of myself. The maitre d' hovers at the periphery of my vision. Iain takes out his wallet and counts out notes.

'I thought we could work something out. Rosalie was right.'

'What?'

'She said this was a bad idea. That you and I are so opposite in character and understanding we should never have got together in the first place. But I hoped we might salvage something from this mess we've made.'

What you hoped, Iain, was to gain my services as editor and chief hand-holder for as little remuneration as possible.

Iain's voice is cold. 'I was offering this as a favour to you. As a kindness. What are you going to do with your life? You've no qualifications. No training. Who else is going to take you on?'

I gaze down at the top of his balding, stubbled head. My mind is suddenly clear.

'As it happens, Iain, I know precisely what I'm going to do. Something I'm perfectly qualified for. Which doesn't involve you at all.'

I drop my napkin into my congealing meal and walk out, leaving Iain alone with the bill. The shoes cut into my feet at every step.

*

The pleasure of writing the letter is so great that I almost forget that I actually intend to send it. I have denied myself the relief of writing for so long it is like turning a tap on full. Words stream from my fingertips and hit the paper running. My tears blur the text as I lean in to read it. Quickly, I bundle the sheets into an envelope, lick it shut and hurry out into the November mist to post it before I can change my mind.

CLARA

'I've found her!' Alix's eyes shine with self-righteous fervour. 'This is definitely the one. She's perfect.' Clara can't bear to look at her.

She, Alix and Richard are holding a meeting in Richard's office on a muggy December afternoon. A few early Christmas cards, pinned to the pockmarked notice board, flap in the warm air from the radiators. *Peace on Earth. Good will to all men.* Clara swivels her chair away from Alix and her laptop so that she faces the window. Far below her, pinprick headlights move through the darkness like an animated string of beads. She sees her own reflection: drawn and drained of colour by the fluorescent strip-lights. It is too hot and dry in the office. The air feels starved and stale. Alix sips from a bottle of water. In spite of her mounting anxiety, Clara sticks to black coffee.

Alix opens the laptop and turns it so that Richard has a good view. Clara coughs. Alix reluctantly angles the screen slightly towards her.

The woman is perhaps fifty. She's smiling self-consciously at the camera, her hands held palm out at her sides like a little girl. Her hair is bleached blonde. Her skin is freckled and sun-damaged. Her cleavage, inappropriately flaunted, is wrinkled. She's wearing a short, shiny skirt, revealing lumpy thighs.

Alix says: 'Patricia Wells. Forty-five, married to Terry, four children. Works as a waitress. She wants to be made over because she's always been unhappy with the way she looks and has never been able to afford surgery.'

Clara sighs. Richard turns to her. 'Clara?'

'Boring.' She drains her coffee.

'What?' There is a tiny crease in Alix's perfect white brow.

'Do you think that viewers will want to watch a very ordinary woman being cut up to look twenty years younger?' Richard glances sharply at her. Too harsh. The Alix effect.

'I thought,' says Alix, 'that the point was to find someone whose appearance could be changed dramatically? I mean, I hadn't realised that we were searching for Germaine Greer.'

'More's the pity.' Clara keeps it *sotto voce* but Richard throws her another warning glance.

Alix continues: 'Patricia's just the kind of woman we want. Ordinary women will relate to her. She'd be amenable to whatever Marcus decides. She's desperate to have this chance. Of all the women who applied, I know she'll show the greatest improvement.'

'I think we're missing a trick, here.' Clara swivels her chair towards Richard, deliberately excluding Alix. 'Hardly rocket science, is it, to find a woman like Patricia and produce a pedestrian programme – just like all the others?' She glances at Alix, whose face is even paler than usual. 'What we need is an angle.'

'What are you thinking?' Richard asks.

'We need a woman who is intelligent. A woman with character. Someone you wouldn't expect to apply for a makeover like this.'

Alix says, 'That wasn't the brief I was given.'

Clara smiles. 'It's a matter of thinking outside the box, Alix.' Alix's foot is swinging, as if she'd like to kick Clara. *Good.* 'How many women applied?'

'Two hundred and twenty.'

'Of whom how many were no-goes?'

'About half.'

'Will you get the applications, please? I'd like to take a look.'

Alix darts an entreating glance at Richard. He sighs. 'Alix, if you'd get the forms, we'll have one last trawl through.'

Alix stands, closes the laptop with a click, and leaves the office.

'Clara.' Richard's tone is admonitory. 'There was really nothing wrong with that woman.'

'Is that what we want? A clone of all the women on all the other shows?'

'*The Making of Her* is a makeover show. Please don't lose sight of that. It's a very simple concept. We don't have to make it complicated.' He looks at her. 'This fuss isn't about Patricia what's-her-name, is it?'

'Whatever can you mean?' Clara feigns innocence.

He doesn't smile. 'It's about proving a point. This is getting personal, isn't it?'

Of course it's bloody personal.

'You know my feelings about Alix. But putting that aside, I've no desire to make a predictable show. And Patricia is predictable.'

Alix returns, carrying a pile of applications, which she dumps with a thud on the desk in front of them.

'Thank you, Alix. Perhaps you'd get us some coffee?'

Alix flushes. Richard says, 'I'll get it.' He looks at Clara, puzzled and – what? Disappointed?

She bends to the applications, skimming each form, casting them aside to join a growing pile. Most are Patricia lookalikes, with their greying roots and embarrassed smiles. Any one of them would do. She is aware of Alix sitting, arms folded, her foot swinging back and forth. Has Alix already found the best of the bunch?

Richard returns with coffee. 'Perhaps,' he says, 'we should reconvene later.'

Alix stands.

'Wait. What's this?' A bulky letter, awkward among the other applications. Alix leans in to look.

'Some nutter. She goes on and on. Using a manual typewriter, no less.'

Clara scans the pages. Each word looks as if it has been branded on to the paper with the force of desperate fingers. 'Have you read this?'

Alix flushes again. 'I read the first page. But she doesn't qualify. She didn't fill out the form, or give an address. Just a mobile number. And she hasn't even bothered to include a photograph.'

Hell. Nor has she. The power of the writing is such that she feels she knows this woman. Can see her, feel her. She bends to re-read the letter.

'I am plain. Not ugly, as such…'

'You'd pass me by in the street. As the world does. Unremarkable…'

'Age is leaving its indentations all over my body… screwing me up like an unwanted letter…'

This woman knows how it feels to be obsolete and passed over. She hands the letter to Richard and turns to Alix.

'Sarah Miller. Fifty. Lonely, unloved. A thinking woman. Please arrange for her to come in, Alix. I want to meet her.'

JO

Get a move on, Jo.

Another of my mother's refrains. How it would annoy her to see me like this. Sitting alone and bare-faced at my kitchen table in my dressing-gown. Far better for me to be perched opposite Iain at Estrella's, the pretty, painful shoes cutting into my feet, my lipsticked mouth set in a compliant smile. My head nodding at Iain's opinions like those nodding dogs in cars. The ones that always face backwards, towards the past.

Well, mother, I am moving on. Even though every step feels like I am carrying a millstone and walking in treacle. Or, to mix yet more metaphors, like I am all at sea and my frantic waving attracts not a life belt but a straitjacket. Iain has managed to move on with the aid of a lover, some green highlights and a new set of teeth. Can it be so simple?

This morning, I took myself to Chiswick Library, where I copied out uplifting quotes about dealing with hardship. *Reculer pour mieux sauter*, the French advise. My schoolgirl French translates this as 'recoil in order to better leap ahead'. The Americans are more motivational: *When the going gets tough, the tough get going.* Clara would vote for that one. I prefer the Eastern view: Sun Tzu said that when the battle gets hard, it is best to disappear, and to reappear later when strengthened. Excellent advice, given that I am an expert in invisibility. It is the art of reappearing which has so far eluded me.

But now I am back at my old oak table in the kitchen, making a list of my assets. Philosophy has been abandoned for now in favour of facts and practical action.

1. This house

Half of it belongs to Iain. But half a couple needs less space than a whole one. And half a Chiswick house is worth a lot more than a whole one in, say, Brixton. I could buy myself a flat somewhere near Clara. Notting Hill is too expensive, but Hammersmith is possible. Or Barnes. Perhaps, on long walks along the towpath, Clara and I can rebuild our friendship. Clara has been distant and distracted, and I sense that it's not all down to stress. Is there something she's not telling me?

I pull off my glasses to rub my eyes. What wouldn't I give for clarity? A sense of purpose? In this real world, I am as out of place and unwanted as the Ugly Duckling, flapping from farm to cottage to barn, longing for an open door and a welcoming smile. Will I ever find a place which feels like home?

Concentrate, Jo. I push the glasses back up my nose.

2. *Furniture*

Which pieces will Iain want? Few, I suspect. He has taken all the portable, expensive items like the computer and the music centre. There will not be room in Rosalie's bijou apartment for our heavy Victorian wardrobes, nor this solid table. Unless, of course, he and Rosalie pool their resources and move to a bigger place. Iain might prefer life without me, but life without a study will be intolerable. And he'll have to hire a secretary, since his efforts to recruit me have fallen on stony ground. Which leads me to another asset:

3. *My skills*

I suck my pencil. Iain's words echo in my head. *Who else is going to take you on?* No one, obviously, in the corporate world. The abortive interview made that perfectly clear. Perhaps I could go freelance. Advertise myself as a copy-typist. Type up other people's manuscripts.

I place my pencil down on the list and get up. A person can only do so much recoiling. Classic FM is playing something appropriately mournful on the old analogue radio. Iain has taken the digital. I need diversion and comfort. I twiddle the dial to Radio Four.

Libby Purves is talking about creativity and solitude. Her guest, a well-known painter, is being amusing about the diversions she seeks

during the long hours alone in her studio. A lively discussion ensues.
Then:

'I'm sorry, but I really must come in here —'

The familiar, mosquito tone cuts through the airwaves. Iain.

'Yes, Iain?' There is a note of weariness in Libby's voice.

Iain clears his throat, rather noisily. *'Don't you think that rather too much is made of this concept of artist-as-recluse?'* He doesn't give Libby, or her guest, time to reply. *'I, personally, feel that the true nature of the artist is relational… that only in a loving, reciprocal relationship can an artist, or a playwright of course in my own case, function at his best…'*

I jerk the dial clockwise through the fuzz and hiss of white noise, through foreign stations, through scraps of talk-radio. I am out of my comfort zone, radiophonically. Then, cutting into the cacophony, comes a delicious silence: the blessed clarity that comes when you are tuned in. And into this silence comes the voice.

Not The Voice. She has been lying low since the blood-letting in Estrella's. Another voice. A beautiful male voice that simultaneously soothes and scratches and seduces. I stand stock-still in a rare shaft of winter sunlight and listen. Dust motes glitter before my eyes like airborne diamonds, turning and basking in the sound.

The notes, played on a guitar, steal into the air like strangers. They seem tentative, but I hear the confidence underpinning each one. Their hesitancy beckons me close. Their certainty holds me fast. A restless tug of war between rock and classical, the music winds around my body like a scarf, wanders into the corners of the kitchen and caresses my cheek. And underneath the warming notes, I hear something harsher: an intimation of fire, of heat and desire. I find myself moving to it. Caught in its embrace, I glide around the oak table like Ginger Rogers.

All too soon, it is over. The announcer says:

'And that was "Changing the Story" from a musician we hear too little of today, Mister Pete —'

The phone is jangling above the radio.

'Yes?'

An unknown voice. Female. For a crazy moment I imagine it is Libby Purves asking for my views on solitude and art. But it is not Libby.

At first, I forget who I am. Or rather, who I am supposed to be. Then I paste a smile on to my lips and say, *Yes. Yes, I can do that.*

As I replace the receiver, the radio is playing The Doors' 'Light My Fire'. I feel anything but fiery. More like knocked sideways by a great wave. My head is swimming. Even my eyes appear to be leaking. Tears of joy or sorrow? I have no idea. All I know is that it is time to rewrite my story. To begin a new chapter. Under a new name.

CLARA

It is five a.m. and Clara is awake. The dream is still with her.

David Wood is wearing a green surgical gown. On his head he wears a matted crown of twigs and grasses. He is operating on her with a fine golden knife. She is awake. She looks up at the masked faces peering down at her: Alix wearing an icing-sugar gown, Jo in a wedding dress with a fiery red veil, and another shadowy female figure whom she cannot identify. She watches David make the first cut; her blood flows over his hands like water. Now they are moving towards her left breast. Her breath catches. He slips his hands inside and draws out her heart, holding it up like a trophy. Out fly a pair of birds, their great wings beating white as they gain the sky. David is smiling. That lop-sided grin. *Clara*, he says quietly. *Clara, are you a pigeon or a swan?*

I want to be a swan.

Clara pushes back the heavy duvet, reaches for the box of tissues and dabs at her hot face and chest. She half expects the tissue to be stained red with blood. Her heart is beating fast behind her ribs. Where it should be.

She forces herself away from the dream. Focuses on the day ahead and her meeting with Sarah Miller – the woman who will really go under the knife. A shiver of reluctant excitement runs through her.

Sarah Miller's letter had been so open, so frank; her pain tangible in every line. The lack of a photo, though, is worrying. Why apply for a makeover programme and not include an image of yourself? Clara's cheeks are suddenly burning. What if Alix's reasons for dismissing Sarah Miller as a possible candidate are correct? Under normal circumstances, Clara herself would have discounted the woman. Alix knew that. Richard knew it too. No wonder he had looked so puzzled. So disappointed. And sending Alix to fetch coffee had been out of line.

What made you do that?

David's voice. Not judgmental, but sad, as if she has not lived up to his belief in her.

It was pride, David. I'm not proud of my pride.

The alarm is bleeping. She turns it off and heads for the bathroom. A hot shower will wash it all away. Richard and the guilt. David Wood and the disturbing dream. As the water courses down her body, she finds herself muttering a dogged mantra:

She will be right. She will be right.

Is she talking about Sarah Miller or herself?

*

'Clara, I only hope that this woman will be suitable.' Richard's voice on the phone is cautious. He's probably watching his own back, knowing that Stanley Barforth's designer glasses are firmly focused on it. 'Because if she isn't, we have to go with Alix's candidate. You know that, don't you?'

'She'll be suitable. I feel it in my bones.'

The truth is that her bones are aching with anxiety. She is staking her reputation – and her future – on a woman who could be a disaster. Clara crosses her fingers and glances at the clock. Three minutes late. What if Sarah Miller doesn't even show up? Has Alix deliberately… *Stop being paranoid.* Clara swivels in her chair to face the window, where the grey world of a London morning goes about its business. She takes a gulp of bitter black coffee and jumps at the sharp tap on the door.

It's Alix; her face an alabaster mask. 'She's here.'

'Send her in.'

Voices murmur outside, then there is a second, hesitant, tap.

'Come in.'

The door opens slowly and a familiar figure slips inside. It's not the woman she is expecting.

What is Jo doing here? She never visits Clara in her office, only in the cutting room at night when she is sure to find Clara alone. Has there been another crisis with Iain?

'Jo. Are you OK?'

Jo nods.

Clara frowns. 'Look, I can't talk right now. I'm interviewing someone…'

Jo's face is white. She does not retreat. Instead, she moves towards Clara's desk.

'I know,' she says, her voice unsteady. 'I'm her.'

'What?'

'Sarah Miller. I'm Sarah Miller.' Jo gropes for a chair and collapses into it as if her legs are unable to hold her. 'Sorry, Clara. I used my second name and my maiden name.'

Josephine Sarah Coe, née Miller.

Clara sinks into her own chair. She must still be dreaming. She can hardly look at Jo, who is suddenly a stranger: a plump, middle-aged woman with red-grey hair in shapeless clothes, her eyes bleak and her pale mouth opening and closing.

'I want to be made over,' Jo is saying. 'I need to be.'

Clara is dimly aware of the working world ringing and chattering beyond the door while here, in her office, Jo is having some kind of a breakdown.

'Sorry.' Jo pushes her glasses up her nose. 'Really. I know this puts you in a difficult position…'

Difficult? She doesn't know the half of it.

Clara struggles for rational thought but her mind will only focus on irrelevant detail. She gestures at the letter that lies between them.

'Whose phone number did you use?'

'Iain's old mobile. It's been in the kitchen drawer for months.'

'And why the typewriter?'

'Iain took the computer. And if I wrote it by hand you would have recognised my writing. Of course, I couldn't send a photograph or an address. I wanted it to be a fair decision. Fair on the other women, I mean.' Jo smiles, shakily. 'I thought that, given the odds, if you did choose me it would be a miracle. It would be meant.'

What a mess. What a fucking mess.

'Why? Jo, for God's sake, why? What made you do this?'

'Metamorphosis,' Jo says, as if this is explanation enough. 'It's what I want. I've been thinking about it… reading about it. Clara, I've tried. I've really tried. But whatever I do, I come up against *No*. So… maybe I need to do something more drastic. Maybe I need to… to tear away the old me and start again.'

'What are you talking about?' *I don't need this.* Not now. Especially not now. But Jo's still talking, soft and low, as if she's telling herself a story.

'At first, I dismissed it. I told myself it was one of those crazy ideas you have when life's pulling you way down. But it didn't go away. And then Iain…' She stops and grimaces. 'Anyway, now I'm sure.'

Iain. That explains it. Jo is reacting to something Iain has said or done. She isn't thinking straight. Clara reaches out a hand.

'Look, I know you've been through hell with Iain but he's out of your life now. You can do anything you want…'

'Exactly. And I want to do this.'

'No, Jo.' The words sound weak, even to herself. Does Jo know how much she wants – needs – to be persuaded?

'Let me do it.' Jo is staring at her. 'I don't want to be Jo Coe anymore. I don't want to be a pathetic woman who's wasted her life.'

'Then go home and write.'

Jo stiffens. 'I can't write. Not after…' Her face closes down. 'I just can't.'

'Can't?' This is ridiculous. 'Are you telling me that you're prepared to go through an extreme makeover, that you're willing to subject your body to a surgeon's knife, but you haven't the courage to pick up a pen and do what you love most? For God's sake, Jo. You're a writer, through and through. Isn't it time you accepted yourself for who you are?'

A long, futile pause.

'Remember what you told me about editing? About cutting a programme?' Jo is twisting her hands in her lap, but there's a different note in her voice.

'So?'

'How you start out with perhaps ten times more material than you need? Then you cut it down, layer by layer, until you get to the heart of it?'

Until you come to the softest part of all, the heart…

David Wood's words. For a moment Clara is back in his yellow room. Safe.

'That's what I want.' Jo is gazing at Clara as if she is trying to force her to understand. 'To cut through the dross. To find out who I might be, under all this.' She pulls at her fraying jumper. 'Like in the story.'

'What story?'

'There was a dragon. Well, a boy. And a lion tore off his dragon skin, layer by layer…' Jo's face lights up.

Clara wants to shake her. 'For crying out loud, Jo.'

'What?'

'We're not talking about some idealistic… fairy story. This is the real world.'

'Oh?' A flush of red crawls up Jo's neck to her face. 'You mean the world you inhabit?'

'It's a hell of a lot more real than the one in your head.'

Jo is on her feet. 'What makes you an expert about reality? Or for that matter, an expert about me? *Your* world is make-believe.' She waves her arm to encompass the office, the whole of ProDoCo. 'Look at you – you shut yourself away in the studio, in the cutting room, playing god!' Clara has never seen Jo so angry. 'When do *you* plan to step out from behind your precious camera and actually notice how the rest of us live?'

'It's my job.' Which is now even more on the line.

Jo rubs her eyes. 'Sorry. That was uncalled for.'

Through the glass panel in the door, Clara sees Alix staring at them, very still, tapping her teeth with a biro. Surely she hasn't heard the exchange? On Alix's laptop screen is the other woman, Patricia Wells, frozen in time. Alix is smiling. A secret, self-satisfied smile. Clara longs to wipe it off her face.

'Sit down. Jo. Try and see this from my perspective, please. I've gone out on a limb for this. Alix had already found someone for the programme. I insisted on having you instead. That puts me in an untenable position. Talk about a conflict of interests…'

'No one knows. No one needs to know.'

A traffic jam has formed on the West Way. Distant horns blast, lights flash. Clara thinks of Richard's words. *If she isn't suitable, we'll have to go with Alix's choice.* She imagines Alix smirking as she spreads the word around ProDoCo. *The Ice Queen screwed up again. Definitely past her sell-by date.*

Hell. But once more, she tries to marshal arguments against Jo's plan.

'Think of the women watching this show. Watching you. What kind of an example will you be setting? Think of your feminism.'

Jo's head snaps up. 'Think of yours, making the bloody programme.'

'Cheap shot.'

Jo nods. 'All right. But I don't feel… feminine any more. That's the point. I feel indeterminate. Neuter.'

'And you think a new pair of boobs and a facelift will change that? You'll still be the same person inside.'

'It's complicated…'

'It's all too bloody simple from where I'm standing.' She's up to her neck in shit, either way.

She stares down at the West Way, wishing she was in one of those tiny cars, speeding away from this charade. Is Jo in any fit state to do it? Can she really pull this off?

Can I?

Slowly, slowly, her mind is returning to its familiar professional tracks. 'You do know you'll have to see a psychiatrist? Go through a whole battery of tests?'

'Yes,' says Jo. 'I know that. What are you implying? That I'll fail?'

'What do you think?'

'Please, don't patronise me. I'm neither stupid nor mentally unstable.'

'No, you're neither of those things. But you are… delicate.'

'Sensitive, Clara. Not fragile. Anyway, I promise you that I'm ready for this. Really. In body and in spirit.' She presses her lips closed.

'Right.' Clara stares Jo down. 'You want to know the full lurid details? Let's start with this body of yours. The body you insist on hiding even from me. You'll have to expose it. Not just to the crew, but to the public. They'll tear you apart, Jo. Viciously and without pity. You'll be stripped naked for the world to see and judge.'

'They can't say anything that I haven't already heard. From Julia. From Iain.' Jo dips her head. 'From myself.'

'OK. That's just the beginning. You'll be heavily anaesthetised. Under for hours. Nine hours, to be precise. Usually, procedures on this scale would be done in two sessions, but not this time, because ProDoCo wants to save money on filming time. Of course, this suits our surgeon, Marcus, perfectly because he can flaunt his magic powers. Your body will be broken, suctioned, reconstructed. You'll spend days, maybe weeks, in hospital. You'll look, and feel, like a car-wreck. The wounds could become infected. It could all go wrong. You could die.'

Jo blinks. She swallows. 'I know the risks.'

'Well, I wouldn't do it.'

'No.' Jo swivels her chair back and forth. Back and forth. 'No, you wouldn't. But you don't have this,' she prods at her nose with a finger. 'Or these.' She gestures at her breasts. 'I have only this one chance. If I change the outside, then maybe the inside will follow. Can you please try and imagine that, Clara?'

You could argue that changing the outside will have an effect on what's happening inside. David again.

'Clara, you chose me,' Jo is saying. 'Of all the women who applied, you thought I was the most suitable.'

'I bloody well wouldn't have if you'd sent a photo.'

'Look at me. If you didn't know me, would you choose me now?'

Clara looks. The clear morning light illuminates every line, every grey hair, every excess pound. Jo is, indeed, perfect for *The Making of Her*. Inside and out.

'Are you sure, Jo? There'll be no going back after this.'

Is that an infinitesimal shadow passing across Jo's face? If so, it's gone in an instant. 'Yes. I'm sure.'

'You'd better not live to regret it.'

And I'd better not, either.

A sharp knock. Richard pokes his head in.

'Clara? Just wanted to…' He sees Jo. 'Sorry. I didn't realise you were still interviewing…'

Clara could put an end to this ghastly charade right now. She could tell Richard the truth and live with Alix's self-righteousness. She looks at Jo. Jo's eyes are fixed on Clara, mutely entreating her. Clara watches Richard narrow his eyes as he sizes Jo up. Then his face relaxes into a broad smile. When he turns to Clara, he gives one emphatic nod. He's stepping forward, holding out his hand to Jo. Clara takes a deep breath.

'J… Sarah, this is Richard, my executive producer. Richard, this is Sarah Miller. The star of *The Making of Her*.'

PART TWO

you fooled me with your secrets
you were dry
you're gonna leave me cold as ash
and I locked my doors, shuttered up my soul
and you trampled on my hope
laughed and took my life away
strip me down, love
tear my dreams away like petals
love me, love me not, love
strip me down

Extract from WATER INTO FIRE
Music and lyrics by Pete Street
© Flame Records

PETE

On the first floor of his tall, thin Islington house, Pete Street sits by an open window, trying not to think of loss and love, while across the room his manager, Jongo MacBride, sings:

Should auld acquaintance be forgot
And nivver brought to mind?

If you can call it singing. A hoarse conglomeration of bass, whisky and phlegm.

'C'mon, lad, gie us some backing…'

Pete sighs and pulls the guitar to his knee. Why does Jongo insist on spending New Year's Eve with him? Probably – he picks out the lumpen chords of 'Auld Lang Syne' – because nobody else will have him.

'Put your heart intae it, laddie! Gie it a wee bit of welly…' Jongo's breath is redolent with alcohol and bonhomie. He is wafting a fart-smelling cigar about – the only day in the year that Pete allows it – and stamping in time with the words. The floorboards shudder.

We twa hae run about the braes and pou'd the gowans fine
But we've wander'd monie a weary fit sin auld lang syne.

As Jongo pauses for breath, Pete hears the sweet, simple sound of bells. St Mary Magdalene Church, just around the block. E-major scale. Then fireworks pop and crackle to the baying accompaniment of revellers. What the fuck does it all mean? Why should a random date on a calendar signify anything so momentous and so inconceivable as a new beginning?

Jongo leans out of the window into the night air, whistles at the unseen party-goers, belches and bellows: 'Eh, *another new year…*'

Tomorrow, and tomorrow, and tomorrow. The Bard knew about the monotony and fruitlessness of life, Pete would bet on it. The bells have stopped. He picks out a few chords. They sound infinitely better without Jongo's accompaniment.

'It's bloody Bawtic in here.' Jongo is slurring. He always lapses into deep Glaswegian under the influence. There's the clink of bottle on glass and the sharp smell of whisky. 'C'mon, bawbag, gie yoursel' a wee drap.'

'I don't drink. Remember?' The temptation to break the guitar over Jongo's thick head is strong. Only it would be a waste of a good instrument. He strums, hard, on the strings. Clean chords can cut through fumes and memories. Usually. Only tonight the guitar, too, is slurring, blurring. *Jesus.*

'Bugger off home,' he mutters. 'Or go and sleep it off in the spare room.'

Jongo, however, is not so easily dispatched. He's collapsing into his usual chair, still swallowing whisky. Out in the hall, the landline is ringing.

'Will I get it?' Jongo's glass hits the surface of the table.

'No.'

The phone rings on, pealing in the new year in its own monotone way. After it stops, Jongo says, 'Why don't you gie him a ring?'

'Who?' *Don't go there, Jongo. Not now. Not ever.*

'The wean. Wish him a' the best…'

Pete clenches his fists. Jongo's tactlessness can be epic when he's pissed. 'Leave it.'

'But he'll be −'

'Leave it, Jongo.'

Silence. Jongo blows his nose loudly and copiously. Then, in an entirely different tone, he says, 'Now, laddie.'

What? Is Jongo revving up for his annual pep-talk?

'A date *for your diary.*'

'Haven't got one.' Don't need one.

'March 1st. 8 p.m. The YUKs.'

The UK Music Awards. Poor relations to the BRITs. Pissed-up

youth, leather-clad wrinklies – like himself – and the obligatory bust-up offstage. Or on it, to the delight of the viewing public. 'No way.'

Jongo stands, wheezing, and moves towards the fire. 'Eh, but this one's a must. They're *honouring you.*'

'What for?'

'Lifetime achievement award. The dog's bollocks, eh?'

Bloody hell. Pete's skin prickles with horror and humiliation. 'Forget it.'

He's got a studio full of awards. Down in the basement. A room with bars on the windows and sound-proofed walls. A room he hasn't entered for a decade. Ten years ago he locked the door, and locked it has stayed. He is not about to open up old wounds. Auld acquaintance *should* be forgot.

'C'mon, laddie, it's a *grea' opportunity.*' Jongo's Glaswegian realism thunders at his unwilling ears. 'You've got tae come out *and accept the thing.*'

'Why?'

'Sales, my lad. Sales.'

'Don't need money.'

'Well, *I* do, laddie. How else will I keep m'self in malt?'

Having Jongo around is like having another ex-wife. He thinks of Katia. Hears her flat, cold voice. Even the memory of her sucks the air from his lungs. Deliberately, he slams a mental shutter down on her. On all of it.

A lifetime achievement award. This is it, then. The sum of his ambition. The sum of his discomfort. He doesn't qualify, of course, for Best Single, or Best Solo Artist. They are reserved for today's kids, squeezing out their songs between snorting lines of coke. The platinums on his basement walls testify to his own success. And to the desert years ever since. Deserted years. Meanwhile, the music business nags him for interviews and appearances. They tell Jongo he provides nostalgia. Well, they can whistle for it. He'd sooner jump into a snake pit.

Bloody Jongo. Brokering the deal for the album. *Pete Street: Greatest*

Hits. Regurgitating his past. Another tired old collection from a tired old man.

'It's time for a change, lad. You know it is.'

Pete keeps his face low over the strings.

'Ye've got to get out intae the world. Wake up, lad. Stop being a bloody *recluse*.'

He will not be drawn. It's his life. He'll live it as he chooses.

'I've accepted, anyways.' The clink of bottle on glass. 'On *your behalf*. Happy New Year, laddie.'

Still two months away. He doesn't have to go.

Doesn't have to hang around, either. He's got the pills. He's got the choice.

The guitar screams a cacophony of protest, splintering the air.

CLARA

The end of a year. The end of an era.

A fitting time to chuck in the towel and start afresh. Clara peels off another layer of clothing, fans her hot face with a paper serviette and forces her expression into one of stoic indifference. Pleasure is too much to ask. Retirement parties are dire at the best of times.

Typical of Richard and Linnie to choose New Year's Eve to throw open the doors of their genteel Ealing townhouse to a mass of jostling bodies aping bonhomie, gyrating to the sounds of the sixties and exhaling the mingled aromas of hot mince pies, alcohol, sweat and perfume. Tomorrow morning, next year, Linnie will hoover up trodden-in crumbs and de-stain carpets and upholstery. Richard will pile broken glasses into the bin – well-wrapped in newspaper – and clank countless bottles into the recycling boxes. And his long career at ProDoCo will be over.

The Christmas tree spews piles of needles on to the oriental rug each time a reveller brushes past. Linnie, her greying bun coming down, squeezes from group to group offering more canapés, more sausage rolls and more hospitality to people she hardly knows. The party is an uneasy mixture of old friends and working acquaintances. Richard appears to have invited everyone he can think of in a final frenzied burst of generosity. Clara watches him touring the room, tie loosened, receiving congratulations – wholehearted from his contemporaries and specious from the younger members of staff, who cannot imagine anyone actually deciding to stop working. Seeing pity in their eyes, Clara turns away.

Where does she fit in? Among the oldies? The worn-down, burnt-out, done-their-timers? Or with the driven and ambitious? The likes of Alix? She has no wish to talk to anyone here except Richard and Linnie, and they are fully occupied. There are others she intends to actively avoid. Alix, blonde hair loose down her back, chalky breasts translucent under a moss-green silk tunic, her long white neck exposed, is swaying provocatively to the Beatles. Her body appears to be off-duty, but Clara knows better. Alix is assiduously working the room. Her half-closed eyes are scanning her fellow guests, appraising them: her pale fingers are ready to grasp the ankles of the person on the rung above. Since Clara took over *The Making of Her* and relieved Alix of her duties, Alix has been icily polite. Yet Clara senses that she is waiting, poised to strike.

This whole charade is sickening. The undertones, the cold realities lurking beneath the facade of a fond farewell to Richard. The forced you-will-enjoy-yourself New Year veneer. Jo will be sitting at home, on her own for the first time on New Year's Eve. Clara should be keeping her company. But Jo had been quick to brush away her apologies.

'Of course you must go. How could you miss Richard's leaving party? I'll be fine.'

The guilt, however, persists. Not only because she has abandoned Jo, but because a part of her is relieved to have done so. What was it Diana, Princess of Wales, said in that famous interview? *There were three of us in this marriage, so it was a bit crowded.* Since that day in the office, there has been an extra, unwanted person in her friendship with Jo: Sarah Miller.

So far, Sarah has presented a calm and inscrutable mask to Marcus, to the psychometric testers and to the crew. She has sailed through the medical, the tests and the initial filming. And Jo? Jo has retreated into that unreachable place in herself; the place she goes to hide. Now that their friendship has become a working partnership, Jo seems determined to preserve her independence. Sarah Miller, her on-screen persona, continues to exist after the cameras stop rolling. Is she protecting Clara or herself?

'Clara –'

A hand brushes her bare arm. Marcus's great head looms down at her. She nods.

'Marcus. Hello.'

Marcus's eyes dip, momentarily, to her exposed cleavage – a look which makes her want to cover her body, scrub off her make-up, screw her hair into a bun and zip herself into an impenetrable layer of formality. He epitomises everything she detests in a man. Patriarchy, vanity and egotism. As he leans in towards her, she steps backwards. A distasteful little dance.

'Quite a party,' he says.

Clara attempts to ignore the tiny rat-bite shivers of irritation that his presence provokes and forces a smile. 'Richard deserves a good send off. He's been an excellent mentor – and a friend.' Saying the words makes Richard's leaving real. Until this moment, it has been theoretical. Now, as she watches him pumping the hand of a colleague, his tired face lit up in gratitude, she feels she is losing a father, a brother. Richard has always been there, a kindly male presence. And who will she be left with now? Bloody Barforth, with his stupid glasses and his man-bag. And Marcus Templeton with his poncy practice in Harley Street and his friends in high places.

'May I get you another drink?' Marcus bends his head towards her. A tang of cologne and something else that is clinical and sour. She shakes her head.

'So,' he says. 'We have an excellent candidate for *The Making of Her*.'

'Yes. She's very suitable.'

'Provided that she can lose some weight, of course.'

'She's motivated.' Already Jo seems less substantial. *Her* Jo is literally disappearing, pound by comfortable pound.

Marcus moves closer. 'And what are your plans for the holiday?'

Clara wishes she had bad breath. 'What holiday? I've forgotten what holidays are. I'll be cutting the material we've shot so far and making preparations for the filming.'

Marcus's eyes are appraising. 'Give yourself a break. I'd like to take you out for another meal. Get to know you a little.'

Trust him to come on to her now. Their working relationship is fragile enough as it is. He probably seduces by the book. She steps back again.

'Thanks, but I think we should keep our relationship… strictly professional. Don't you?'

She has got through to him. Marcus's face stiffens as if she has slapped it. But before he can reply, Alix, her eyes dark in her pale, perfect face, brushes past him, then stops in apparent surprise.

'Marcus! I didn't know you were coming.'

Marcus's features assume an animated smile. He takes Alix's hand and bends to kiss it. 'Alix. How delightful to see you. I was wondering what had happened to you.'

Alix flicks a glance in Clara's direction. 'I'm not working on *The Making of Her* anymore.'

'Oh?' Marcus, one eyebrow raised, turns briefly to Clara, then back to Alix. 'Why not?'

Alix's silent gaze hands the responsibility to Clara. There's a challenge in her eyes. Clara returns the stare. 'Alix was researching for the programme while I finished my previous series. *The Making of Her* only requires one producer.'

'A pity.' Marcus turns to Alix. 'Perhaps you'd like to dance?'

Alix smiles. 'Love to.'

Marcus places a hand on her silk-clad hip and escorts her into the heaving crowd without so much as a backward glance at Clara.

In the kitchen, Linnie is removing another tray of sausage rolls from the oven, her forehead beaded with sweat, coral lipstick bleeding into the tiny lines around her mouth.

'What can I do?' Clara sets down her glass and prepares to be commandeered.

Linnie smiles, baring large, uneven teeth. 'Nothing at all, Clara dear. Everything's under control.'

Clara believes it. Organisation is Linnie's middle name. She is the mainstay of a dozen committees, the kind of woman people turn to when they need someone to take charge. How will the dynamic between Linnie and Richard change now that Richard is retiring? Linnie reads her mind.

'Eat, drink and be merry, for tomorrow...' She laughs. 'We won't know ourselves, rattling around this house together. Dickie seems to think he's going to play more golf, but I can't see it.'

'Nor can I. Richard doesn't know the meaning of the word "leisure", for all his complaints. He's a complete workaholic.'

Linnie looks at her. 'You two are as bad as one another. When did you last take a holiday? You look worn out.'

'Thanks.'

They smile at each other. This is an old, well-trodden path. Linnie turns her attention to the sausage rolls, ranking them in neat battalions on a plain china plate, and delivers her thought directly, as she always does.

'It's time you got out and met some folk. Look at you now, skulking in the kitchen when there are lots of nice men out there. Don't you think?'

'Linnie, every man here tonight is either a work colleague or a happily-partnered friend of yours and Richard's.'

Linnie frowns. 'Not *every* one. I grant you, most are.'

'It's an incestuous world, television. As you and I both know.'

'Well, it didn't do me any harm.'

'True. You got a diamond. You both did.'

Linnie wipes the worktop and fiddles with the dishcloth. Clara knows what's coming.

'I don't suppose you've seen anything of Dan?'

'No. I haven't.'

'He's still in Cornwall?'

'I believe so.' A sudden memory of Dan's birthday card swallowed by the candle flames.

'What a shame. He was a good man.'

Clara picks up a wooden spoon and attempts to balance it on her finger. 'We were chalk and cheese.'

Linnie, rinsing glasses, muses. 'Funny expression that. Certainly, on the surface, chalk and cheese are two very different entities. But then, as words, they're similar in form. Both one syllable. Both beginning with "ch". Not that opposed.'

Dear Linnie. So easily distracted by words. Throw a tempting phrase in her direction and she'll pounce, worrying at it until she can extract its exact meaning.

The door opens and Richard blunders in. His hair is ruffled, his jacket undone, his trousers at half-mast below his stomach. He gives Linnie a smacking kiss on the lips. 'All right, my treasure?'

Linnie removes a tiny piece of fluff from his jacket. 'Dickie, I want you to talk to Clara.'

He looks at her. 'I talk to Clara all day. What do you want me to talk to her about?'

Clara retreats towards the door. 'Your wife's back on her hobby-horse. Ignore her. Anyway, I need to pee.'

*

The toilet seat is wet. Some lazy man who can't be bothered to raise the seat. Clara perches above it and allows her bladder to empty at length. The door handle turns and she freezes, hoping the bolt works. There's a sharp knock.

'It's engaged!'

Silence. Then, in the bathroom next door, the sound of retching. *Oh, God.* Clara wants to go home.

She pulls up her knickers, opens the door and glances into the bathroom. A woman is leaning over the basin, breathing heavily. Clara taps half-heartedly at the open door. 'Are you all right?'

The woman turns, her eyes not quite focusing. She is forty-ish, auburn-haired and, even with green-tinged skin, beautiful. Without moving her head, she slips backwards to lean on the edge of the bath, wiping her mouth with a hand that almost loses its way. She is wearing a wedding ring.

'Shall I get your husband?'

The woman raises her chin and gives a dank, humourless smile.

'Oh, my husband…' she slurs. 'Good idea. Send for the cavalry!'

'What's his name?'

The woman casts her eyes up. 'His name? Oh, he doesn't have a *name*. Just a title. *Saint*. Look for the one with the halo.'

The last thing Clara needs is to get involved in some marital dispute. 'Look,' she says, 'I can do one of three things.' The woman squints up at her. 'I can fetch your husband. I can get you some coffee. Or I can leave you here. Which is it to be?'

The woman considers this. 'No husband. No coffee. Glass of water.'

Clara goes downstairs and returns to the kitchen where Linnie, looking tired, is half-heartedly stacking the dishwasher. Clara retrieves a dirty wine glass from the sink, rinses it and fills it with tap water.

Linnie raises an eyebrow. 'Going teetotal?'

'Not for me. There's a woman throwing up in your bathroom. Won't let me get her husband.'

'Oh?' Linnie doesn't seem unduly concerned. 'What does she look like?'

Clara describes her. Linnie sighs. 'That'll be Jessica. She does this with disturbing regularity. We wouldn't invite them, only her husband's one of Dickie's oldest friends.'

'Which one is he?'

'He isn't. Or rather, he isn't here. They arrived together – a bit of a miracle in itself – and then she started a row, as she usually does, and he went home. Can't say I blame him.'

'She called him a saint. With heavy sarcasm.'

'Always does. He *is* actually rather a saint. But she hates it. I think she feels his goodness is a rebuke to her. Go on, take the water and I'll ring him. Ask him to come and fetch her.'

The woman – Jessica – has revived a little when Clara returns. She is sitting on a wicker clothes basket, smoking a cigarette. Clara ostentatiously waves away the fumes and offers the water. Jessica blows smoke over her shoulder in a practised way and takes the glass with a shaking hand.

'Close the door, will you?' Clara ignores her and opens the window instead. Icy air streams in. Jessica's eyes widen slightly and she shivers. 'Do you have to do that?'

'If you have to do *that*.' Clara gestures at the cigarette. 'You certainly seem intent on an early grave.'

Jessica smiles. 'What's to live for? Love?'

There is something likeable about this woman, even if she is a lush. Also something... familiar.

She gazes at Jessica. They certainly haven't met. She wouldn't forget that hair or that face. And yet...

Linnie's head appears around the door. 'Jessica, dear. I think it's home time.'

'Where is he?' Jessica stubs out her cigarette in the basin and takes another slug of water.

'On his way. He says he'll wait in the car.'

'Well, he can wait a bit longer.' Jessica pulls a pack of cigarettes from her pocket, extracts one and struggles to light it. 'I'm busy talking to...?' She looks at Clara.

'Clara.'

'Her. I'll be down in a while.'

Linnie raises an enquiring eyebrow in Clara's direction. Clara nods.

'I'm not stupid,' complains Jessica. 'Or insensible. Yet.'

Linnie retreats. Clara sits on the edge of the bath.

'So, Clara. Are *you* married?'

'No. Thank God.'

'You are right,' says Jessica, 'to thank him. Marriage isn't all it's cracked up to be, I can tell you.'

'Linnie says your husband *is* a saint.'

'Oh, he is. Which makes it hard for a sinner like myself. Or maybe he's a saint because I'm a sinner. Or I'm a sinner because he's a saint. Who knows?

'I don't believe in saints. Or sinners.'

'Well, it hardly matters, anyway.' Jessica seems bored. 'It won't last.'

'What won't?'

'My marriage. Like me, it's on its last legs.'

'Are you sorry?'

'Hardly.'

'Is he?'

'Don't think so. What do they call it? Irreconcilable differences? Anyway,' she flicks the ash in the direction of the window, 'I want a child.'

'Oh?' Jessica is hardly an advertisement for marriage. What kind of a mother would she make?

'And he doesn't. So I intend to find a man who does. Leave my husband to his sainthood and strike out on my own.'

She's talking as if her husband is disposable. As if she can just chuck him away. Consumerist mentality. If this one doesn't work, get another one. Another man, another life.

Jessica takes a last, sucking drag at the cigarette and drops it into the toilet. 'So that's my plan. What d'you think?'

'I wish you luck.' Clara thinks of Dan. Perfect father material. She ought to introduce him to Jessica. If they were still on speaking terms. Her throat constricts.

Jessica sighs. 'I'll need it. Meanwhile, there's the rest of this bloody night to get through.' She hauls herself up and stands, wobbling. 'Oh fuck,' she says. 'I'd better get downstairs before I throw up again.'

Clara holds out a hand. 'Come on. Take my arm. I'll see you out to the car. Where's your coat?'

Jessica shakes her head. 'In a pile, somewhere.'

'The bedroom?'

'Maybe.'

'What's it like?'

'Original.'

*

128

The bedroom is in darkness but a streak of light from the en suite illuminates Richard and Linnie's enormous bed, its satin cover wrinkled and slipping under a toppling pile of coats. Jessica's coat is easy to spot. It is indeed original: ankle length, bright orange fake fur. It must clash horribly with that red hair. Clara retrieves it, folding it over her arm.

The en suite door opens. Alix exits, closely followed by Marcus.

'Oh…' Alix says. Her tone holds more satisfaction than surprise. Framed in the light from the doorway, she and Marcus are an imposing pair; although the effect is diminished by the fact that Alix's tunic is pulled down to her waist, exposing her breasts. Most women would turn away. Cover themselves. Alix merely stands, while Marcus, behind her, fiddles with his cuff.

'Clara.' Alix's tone is cool.

So this is the way of it. Well, they thoroughly deserve one another.

Alix smiles. She turns her face up to Marcus and slowly, deliberately, kisses him on the mouth. Clara turns to go, grateful for Jessica's coat, which offers her some cover. Reaching the landing, she glances back. Marcus is staring at her over Alix's shoulder. Alix may be the cat that got the cream, but Marcus looks like a dog torn between two bones.

*

Like an elderly couple, she and Jessica link arms and make their way downstairs. The party slurs and stumbles around them, anticipating the countdown to Big Ben. In the hall, Linnie appears at Jessica's other side and together they escort her out of the front door.

The air outside cuts like a knife. A few flakes of snow flutter down and melt into the white frost on Richard's front lawn. Further down the road, a car is flashing its lights. Once, twice.

'There he is,' says Linnie.

'Good-oh,' mutters Jessica, whose eyes are closing.

A man emerges from the car and walks rapidly towards them.

As he approaches, his balding head is caught in the light of a street lamp. Clara drops Jessica's arm. It can't be, surely…

'David!'

'Clara.'

His face is white. She remembers the question she asked him. Whether he – even he – ever felt vulnerable or fearful. And she remembers his reply: *Most definitely even me.*

Jessica turns slowly towards her. 'You know each other?'

Clara hesitates, then nods. Jessica smiles in a knowing kind of way. 'Oh. Confidential, is it? Doctor and patient?'

David takes his wife's arm. 'Get into the car, Jessica. Thank you,' he adds to Clara and Linnie.

'My hero,' says Jessica, with venom. They turn towards the waiting car as the midnight sky explodes with a thousand fireworks.

'Clara, dear,' Linnie says, 'it's none of my business, but...'

'Don't ask. And please, don't tell Richard?' Linnie nods reluctantly, hugs her and wishes her a happy new year.

*

In the taxi, images loom and retreat: Alix kissing Marcus, her bare breasts pushing into his shirt. Linnie picking fluff from Richard's jacket. Jessica dragging hungrily on her cigarette and talking of babies. David's white face.

The taxi driver jams on the brakes to avoid a pair of drunken revellers who are staggering in the middle of the road. Clara's bag spills its contents over the floor.

'Sorry, love,' the driver says, over his shoulder. 'Lunatics.'

Clara switches on the overhead light and bends to pick up her things. Phone, purse, make-up bag. The Rilke book is lying face-down, one of its pages bent under it, like a broken limb. She has been carrying it around with the vague notion of giving it to Jo. She retrieves it and smooths the twisted page.

The overhead light yellows the paper.

You, the first
lost loved one, who never arrived...

Funny how love always seems to be linked with loss. Certainly always has been for her. Better, then, to keep a cool head and a frozen heart. Stick to sex like Alix and Marcus. A simple transaction.

Who knows whether the same
bird did not sing through each of us
Yesterday, separate, in the evening?

She sees David's face, white in the darkness. In that moment, something passed between them. But what? Is it a leavening? A kind of equality? Because she knows now that David is neither a hero nor a saint but someone like herself. He hurts just as she hurts. Clara longs, suddenly, to tell him what she knows. She wants to talk with him, one to one.

Only it will never be one to one again. Jessica, of the brusque, cool anonymous voice on the phone, will always be there between them. David's wife. The third person in the relationship.

JO

'Happy New Year, everybody!'

The presenter, trailing streamers, links arms with his female co-host as the band plays the first strains of 'Auld Lang Syne'.

I press the remote and the gaudy picture abruptly disappears. Next door, raised voices sing the same refrain. Outside, people are spilling on to the street. A glass breaks. Cheers. All this frenzied celebrating – and for what? All those resolutions to be made later today among the debris, the hangovers and the blurred memories of the previous night: the only sanctioned opportunity to begin again. To get it right this time.

Happy New Year, me. I take another sip of wine, another handful of peanuts. Breaking my diet. Breaking my own resolution to do better. Today, later, I will go back on the wagon: I am too far down the road to turn back now. At least this really will be a new year. There's no avoiding that. I feel the familiar moth-like tremor in my chest. A new me.

For the first time in my life, I am in the spotlight. The camera lingers like a lover over my face and my body. When I speak, people listen. I am indispensable: the star of the circus that is *The Making of Her.* I am the chosen one, singled out not for my beauty but for the absence of it. *Fancy that,* I think periodically. I am wanted for everything I am not. The aching emptiness I struggled to fill with food and words, the invisibility that dogged my days, have become my Unique Selling Points.

Just so long as I keep up the deception. Sarah Miller – my second self, my shield – will carry me through *The Making of Her* and into the new. It was Sarah who stood statue-still on a pavement on Chiswick

High Road wearing – as instructed by Clara – an old pair of Iain's tracksuit trousers with a tawdry zipped-up fleece. It was Sarah, grim and unsmiling, with her face bare and her hair unwashed, who gazed into the middle distance while Gary and the crew circled her. It was Sarah who was offered up as carrion to the critical crows: an endless moving jury of Christmas shoppers who grinned, gawped, assessed and condemned. Half-cut, most of them, with seasonal celebration, and all the more cruel for it, pronouncing on Sarah's age and on her disintegration:

'Sixty to sixty-five, I'd say…'

'Looks older than my nan.'

'Them lines round her neck…'

And the clincher. A child, fresh from the local pantomime, clutching her mother's hand, staring up at me.

'Is she an Ugly Sister, Mummy? Is she real?'

I asked Gary to stop recording. He didn't. The camera zoomed in, its piercing eye recording my every reaction, invading my space, probing at my flushed, distorted – ugly – face, at the tears spilling out of my eyes. It wasn't Sarah Miller who broke down. It was me. Jo Coe.

My mobile bleeps. A text, from Clara. *Happy New Year!* Sent well before midnight, caught up no doubt in the frenzy of messaging through the ether. I can't blame Clara for preferring the facility of a text to the potential awkwardness of a call. After all, I have distanced myself from our friendship. I can no longer be emotionally open with Clara; it is too risky while my emotions swing wildly between certainty and draining doubt. I need to hold on to the certainty and maintain the mask. As *The Making of Her* grinds into gear, I am all too aware of Clara's tension. I sense the shifting loyalties in ProDoCo. I pick up the cold undercurrents between Clara and Marcus.

Marcus Templeton. I had imagined a green-gowned magician who would wave his wand and puff! transform the old Jo from awkward duckling to sleek swan. But this is the real world, and Marcus is not a sorcerer but a surgeon. He wields a scalpel, not a wand. So I laid aside my childhood books and substituted them for *Cosmetic Surgery for Dummies*. Now I read about blepharoplasty, rhinoplasty, belt lipectomy, abdominoplasty, submuscular augmentation and liposuction.

I wipe my salty hand on my dressing-gown and carry my drink to the hall, where the typewriter crouches, spider-like, on its spindly table. Friend or foe? The fury that propelled me out of Estrella's and to the typewriter was short-lived but filled with pure, sizzling energy. Firing off the letter, my fingers pumping the keys, I was filled to the rim with righteous anger, determination and strength. I was sure that it was The Voice telling me it to apply for *The Making of Her*. But intuition is sometimes indistinguishable from fear. Or longing.

My heart is dropping out of the safe confines of my chest like a plunging lift. What if I've got it all wrong? What if The Voice wasn't telling me to write a letter to ProDoCo? What if she was telling me to write?

I remember Iain's description of my stories. Immature. Derivative. I remember the agent's rejection letter with its single damning *No*.

I put down my glass. A whistling *crack!* from the back garden next door signals another pyrotechnic onslaught. I bend to the typewriter, run a reluctant finger over its cold metal keys. This machine has translated my fragile thoughts into bold, irreversible print so that they can be read – and torn apart – by the real world. But it is an obsolete thing. A dinosaur, like myself. I'm seized by the desire to make a gesture – a New Year ritual that will signal my separation from the past: from Iain, from Julia, from my painful, childish dreams. The corners of the typewriter bite into my palms as I carry it to the front door, where I wrestle with the lock.

The night air is redolent with the fumes of spent fireworks. Snowflakes fall hesitantly like confetti or ash. I set off down the path to the gate and across the empty road to the Gardams' house. Jon and Louise Gardam are away for New Year. The house stands dark and shuttered. I hesitate for a moment at the gate to the back garden, then shoulder it open.

My slippers are wet with slush from the street. A rocket streaks into the sky; it screams and explodes in an anticlimax of tawdry sparks. The grass is stiff with frost. The pond lies at the bottom of the garden like a black mirror, secret and deep.

A sodium fountain shoots white light from next door, garishly exposing my silhouette and that of my burden in the water's surface. I consider removing my dressing-gown and my night-dress and wading in naked. But reality, like the cold, bites. And anyway, the pond is only two feet deep. I remember Louise telling me so. Instead, I climb on to the stone surround, crouch beside the water and, stretching my arms as far as they can bear to be stretched, let the typewriter go.

It's gone, easily and quickly absorbed by the dark water. My dressing-gown gapes open at the chest from my exertions. I pull it around myself, shivering. Down in the primordial swamp at the bottom of the pond, the typewriter is safe from me. And me from it. I am almost free.

*

I pull open my underwear drawer. There, nestling under the baggy old knickers, lies my abandoned journal and, beside it, the tampon box. I shake out the box. The memory stick falls into a bra cup. I gaze at the tiny device. This small piece of plastic holds eighty thousand of my words, two years of my life and yearnings too numerous to count.

Just for a moment, I hold it in the palm of my hand. Then I drop it and raise my foot to stamp. A sharp pain shoots through my heart. I bend down and rescue the stick. I replace it in the tampon box. Not yet.

Instead, I lift out the journal. I feel a tiny sliver of excitement in my belly – a stirring like the first kick of an unborn child. I pull open the cover. Pages of words, not printed and proper, but sprawling and crawling. Black and blue patterns on white ground. Hurts, hopes and dreams.

Down in the living room, I pull the old throw around my shoulders, take the journal into my lap and draw a thick line under the last entry. I turn the page to a virgin sheet.

I am allowed to write a journal. Anyone can write a journal. No one but me will ever read it or judge it. I pause, savouring this moment of pure permission. Then I lower the pen to the paper and begin.

CLARA

Secrets.

It's Clara's first session with David since the New Year's Eve party when his world and hers collided. Will he be angry that his private life with Jessica has been so mercilessly exposed? Will he suggest she sees another therapist? He won't. He *won't*. Clara bites down hard on her lip. The clock above the receptionist's desk ticks towards eight a.m.

She is early, as usual. It's still dark outside, though a streak of pearl is opening in the east, making the yellow street lights look tired and wan. Clara hugs the radiator. The receptionist, taking pity on her, hands her a mug of black coffee.

'Would you like a magazine?'

'Thanks. I've got a book.'

She pulls the Rilke out of her bag. She carries it with her, for company. Rilke seems to think that solitude is salutary. Necessary, even, for personal growth. But where do you draw the line between solitude and loneliness? Did loneliness begin seven years ago when Dan left her? She had coped with it then by accelerating the pace of her life and cramming in ever more work, like a bulimic crams in food. Now, thanks to Jo's presence, she can no longer take refuge in her job. Why the hell hadn't she swallowed her pride, gone with Patricia Wells and allowed Alix her moment of triumph? Jo would have put her life back together without resorting to surgery. Maybe she would even have thanked Clara for her narrow escape.

Clara sighs. Why hasn't she told Jo about therapy? About David? Is she perhaps punishing Jo for involving her in the Sarah Miller deception? Or is she playing a childish game of tit-for-tat: *you withdraw from me, I'll withhold from you?* Whatever the reason, the result is more bloody solitude.

Marcus remains a splinter under her skin, questioning her decisions in front of the crew and undermining her authority. At least she is spared his heavy-handed flirtation since the night she interrupted him kissing Alix. Whether that relationship was a one-night stand or something more lasting, she has no idea. Nor does she have any desire to know. She rarely sees Alix these days, thank God. Stanley Barforth has temporarily demoted her to work as a researcher on a series about strippers.

Eight-twenty-five. Clara shifts in her seat and takes a gulp of coffee. David's door opens and she hastily swallows. A suited city bloke with briefcase and braces walks out. Off to the Tube and the office. She strains to catch a glimpse of David, but he is already closing the door.

Last night the loneliness got to her. Sleepless, she experienced a visceral need for someone to be there beside her. Holding her. Touching her. A memory of Dan's hot, urgent physicality aroused her, but it was David's face which sent her over the edge into blessed oblivion. The cold light of morning brought only shame and guilt. She certainly won't be relating that episode in today's session.

*

'Clara. Come in…'

David offers her a quick, wary smile. She sits, allowing the familiar citrus smell of the room to wrap itself around her while he settles opposite her.

'How are you today?' His tone is formal.

'I'm not sure.' She finds it difficult to look at him. His expression now, serious and self-contained, is so different from the face she conjured up last night.

He waits while she struggles for words, all of which feel clumsy and wrong. She glances down at his hands. His wedding ring is still in place.

'Do you want to talk about New Year's Eve?' he asks.

So he is acknowledging it. She nods, clears her throat and wills herself to ask the question. 'Have things changed? I mean, between us… because I met your wife?'

'Has something changed for you?'

Back to the question-with-a-question ploy.

'No. Yes. I didn't realise you were Richard's friend. Or that you and… and Jessica…'

'Of course. I'm sorry that you became involved.' He leans forward. 'Clara, you know that I can't discuss my personal life here. It wouldn't be appropriate.'

'Appropriate for whom?'

He ignores the question. 'I just want you to know that as far as I'm concerned, nothing has changed. In terms of your therapy.'

'It has, though,' she bursts out, 'hasn't it? Everything has changed. I need to talk about what's happening. For me.'

He looks concerned. 'Go on.'

'It's forced me think about how dependent I am. On these sessions with you. And to think about relationships.'

He pulls one leg up on to his knee, holding his bare foot. His eyes do not leave her face.

'I don't know how to do relationships,' she continues. 'There's a relationship language that I don't speak. And I'd imagined that you had a perfect marriage.'

David's face contracts slightly, but he nods again.

'Only now that I've met Jessica…'

'Yes?'

'I realise your life isn't perfect either.'

A flapping at the window. The pigeons are back, jostling for space on the narrow sill.

'Life is never perfect,' David says. His tone is calm but the expression in his eyes belies it.

'You can have a perfect moment.' Like last night. She flushes and stands abruptly. 'Can I do a sand tray?'

He nods. Is he relieved? Has she let him – and herself – off the hook? He carries the sand tray over and lowers it into the space between their chairs. She goes to the cupboard, opens the doors and ponders the rows and rows of figurines. How to choose?

'Just let them talk to you.' He reads her mind.

Cowboys and Indians, stars and spiders, teacups and swords and… a little plastic television. She continues searching. Still the television beckons. Reluctantly, she picks it up.

'What have you got?'

'A television. I don't want it. Not in here. But it's drawing me to it.'

'Good. Anything else speaking to you?'

At the back of the cupboard, almost hidden, is a gleam of white. She reaches in and draws out a miniature bride and groom. They are moulded out of plaster, conjoined. Black-and-white. Man-and-woman. She brings them to the sand tray, kneels, and places them on the rug.

'I don't know what to do with them.'

David's voice is gentle. 'Play. There's no right way to do it. Just see what happens.'

She bends to the sand, her fingers automatically beginning to shape and mould it. Now she is pushing the sand into the middle of the tray, humping it into a ridge that divides the tray in two. On one side of the ridge, she places the television. On the other, the bride and groom.

'This is what it feels like. My life.'

'And where are you?'

'Here.' She points at the side with the television.

'And the bride and groom?'

'I'm separated from them. They belong to someone else's life. Not mine.'

She gazes at the black-and-white figurine. She imagines white plaster being poured into hundreds of identical moulds in a foreign factory. She imagines someone painstakingly painting each figurine. Probably a woman. A woman with a face like Jo's. Visionary and intent, creating the fairy-tale ending. The perfect pairing.

'What do they have to say?' David's voice shatters her thoughts.

'What?'

'The bride and groom.'

Feeling foolish, she picks up the couple. They are just toys. She can hear nothing but the throaty moan of the pigeons on the sill and the distant swish of traffic. Then, the faintest whisper. The bride. She stares at the cherry-painted bow of the lips.

'Clara?'

'She… she's saying she wants to be free. She doesn't want to be joined to him.' The voice is Jessica's. *Leave my husband to his sainthood and strike out on my own.* Clara's face is burning.

'And what does he have to say about that?' David remains impassive. Doesn't he know Jessica is planning to leave him?

Clara looks at the groom, his face plaster-white under his top hat. 'He says he loves her. He asks her to stay with him. But she's telling him that it won't work, that he must go, that…' She stops.

'Yes?'

'It's not…' Not David and Jessica. 'It's Dan. Dan and me.'

'Who's Dan?'

'He's – he was – my partner. I… I made him leave.'

'You made him leave?'

'Yes.' She swallows.

'Why did you do that?'

'We – he – it wasn't working. We were too different. We wanted different things.'

'What sort of things?'

'He wanted me to leave London and move to the sea. He wanted to start a family.' Her heart is beginning the familiar, stressful pounding. 'I needed to stay here. I had my career. So much I wanted to achieve.'

'Tell me about Dan.'

Clara traces a finger over the pale mask of the groom. 'He was a carpenter. A Buddhist.'

She remembers him sitting cross-legged, back straight, for long, still minutes. There was never any hurry. He would be holding a piece of wood and just staring at the grain. He said that he was allowing it to talk to him and show him what it wanted to be.

Like she is doing now with these toys.

'Dan would've been good at this. He loved to play.' *Do-be-do-be-do.*

'And what about you?'

'Life's not a playground. There's so much that needs to be changed.'

'Such as?'

'Injustice. Prejudice. Violence. Ageism…'

'That's a lot to take on.'

'Oh, that's the tip of the iceberg. I'm not going to sit still and do nothing…'

'And Dan could?'

'Dan was happy to live in his Zen world. Playing with his wood, laughing, making love… I told him to go. Told him to follow his *bliss*. That's what he used to call it. His bliss.'

She had been so cold. She had told him to leave, over and over again, like a harsh mantra that splintered their last days together. In his face she saw hurt, bewilderment, and then a final hardening into resolve.

When he spoke to her on that last morning, his Irish accent had been pronounced and alien: 'Even my leaving has to be dictated by you. You're emasculating me, Clara. Sucking the heart out of us. Wilfully. As you do with everything.'

And she had cried out, furious and fearful: 'I have to, because you're so passive! So bloody fluid. The way you just accept everything…'

Rare anger had flamed in his face. 'I accept *you*, Clara. But you can't cope with that, can you? You think people should love and acknowledge you for your success and your achievements, not for yourself.'

At the door, he had turned, held her shoulders and kissed her, simply, on the mouth. 'I'll say it one last time. I accept you. And that doesn't make me weak, however much you want to believe that. I hope one day that you'll understand.'

Then he had left, his head bowed, his face closed to her. She had never seen him again.

She sits motionless, gripping the figurine.

'What happened after he left?'

Oh, plenty. She blinks hard and lays the figurine down in the sand. The couple lie side by side like effigies on a medieval tomb. Quickly, she scoops sand and covers them.

'You buried him?'

'Yes. He called a few times. It was too hard.'

'And now?'

'I'm not in contact with him. What's the point?'

David is looking at her steadily, saying nothing. The silence lengthens.

'It's over. Finished. Nothing would have changed between us. Even if…' she stops.

'Even if what?'

'Nothing.' Her hands are gritty with sand. 'Better, surely, to use my energy on the things I can change.'

David is silent. She rubs her hands together and watches the tiny grains falling on to the rug.

'Sometimes,' he says, 'people try to change the world as a substitute for changing things closer to home.'

A familiar anger rises, burning, in her throat. She wants to pierce his smugness. She wants to provoke him. To push him away.

'Is that why *you* do what you do? It's easier, isn't it, to sit here and focus on my problems than to sort out your own? To analyse Dan and me, rather than you and Jessica?'

'Touché.' David's face flickers into a slight smile but there is no other reaction. She sees him standing in the falling snow, alone. She sees Jessica stumbling into the passenger seat. She sees their two silhouettes conjoined as the car drives away.

'I'm sorry.' But it's too late. Her words cannot be retrieved. Like fencers, they face one another. Has her rapier hit its mark and wounded him? She desperately needs him to be intact. She doesn't want to have power – her familiar, lonely power – over him. She holds her breath.

'Sticks and stones, Clara.' Now he's grinning properly, the old lopsided grin. 'And you are right. People in glass houses shouldn't throw them.'

Clara lowers her eyes and pokes an embarrassed finger into the sand. The ridge crumbles under her touch. Her heart is thumping, not with fear, or stress, but with something else, something way outside her comfort zone.

Gratitude?

Not exactly. What she feels is closer, perhaps, to love.

JO

I am more than my body. I am more than my body…

I am writing, curled around my journal, in a corner of the sofa. Rain taps at the French windows and swirls in the gutters. I glance at my wrist, but my watch is not there. It is still lying on the bedside table where I left it last night. The living room clock shows seven-twenty-five. My eyes ache. All night I was tossed by dreams and tormented by scraps of sensations which were impossible to pin down.

So I gave up on sleep and carried my journal, heavy now and almost full, down to the living room. Today, Monday, is a precious day off. Marcus is busy with his regular clinic. Clara is preparing for tomorrow's filming. The day is my own, which is a blessing and a curse. The blessing is my release from the exposure of *The Making of Her.* Under the glare of the lights, the scrutiny of the camera, I am an insect on a pin: all skin, all surface. The curse is that I have to deal with my feelings. And the only way to do this is to write them down.

I crouch over the paper and strain to deliver words which refuse to surface. I can only write this monotonous litany: *I am more than my body.* I stare at the words, willing them to reveal their meaning. But they are only marks. They mean nothing.

I head for the kitchen. I am not hungry. But something dangerous and momentous is rising in my gut, and I need to stuff it back down. I need the familiarity of food.

I reach for the bread and a knife. The loaf is blurred and shaking in my hand. I drop the knife, pull off my spectacles and rub my eyes. Tears are falling down my cheeks without apparent cause. For what? For whom?

Blinded by my weeping, I lean on the worktop for support. The palm of my hand closes, in slow motion, over the knife blade. I watch as the flesh gapes red and raw.

Only then does the hidden dream of my tossing night reveal itself. I am naked. Stepping down into a pool – a pool of cleansing and transformation. I wade in deeper until my belly is covered, then my breasts. Until the surface of the pool closes over my head. And then I taste the water. Except that it isn't water.

It is blood.

My chest is heaving with keening sobs. My whole body is crying – my ears, my shoulders, my stomach, my thighs. Blood flows down my wrist and drips on to the tiles. I reach for a paper towel and press it to my palm. A salty sting.

Back in the living room, words appear of their own volition, ink and blood mixing on the page. They say it all. Everything I have avoided. Not just this morning, but for weeks.

I can't do it. I can't do it. I can't.

I wipe my wet face with a sleeve. The words are true. The game is over. I stand up as slivers of thoughts chase through my mind.

I must tell Clara, as quickly as possible.

And I must bind up my hand.

The filming. Marcus's time. All wasted.

And I must dress.

They will have to find someone else.

And if I get to ProDoCo by nine, I can get it over with.

I close the journal and hurry to the bathroom. To the bedroom. Then I throw on a jacket and step out into the rain-dark morning.

*

ProDoCo is brightly lit, a star ship among the tower blocks and the council estates of Shepherds Bush. The doors hiss open at my approach. Last time, I came to beg Clara to choose me for *The Making of Her.* Dear God, what was I thinking of?

'Nice weather for ducks.' It is Darren, on reception. He waves me through. In the lift, I practise what I am going to say.

Clara, I'm so, so sorry. I've made a terrible mistake. I've realised I can't do this after all. I must face Clara's wrath and withdraw. I want to retreat to my old life: to my journal, my books, to the safety and familiarity of my own skin.

The lift doors open. I hurry through the outer offices. Clara's door is shut. I am just raising my hand to knock when it opens and Alix emerges, a form in her hand, almost cannoning into me. For a moment she looks at me without recognition. Then her lips part in a smile.

'It's… Sarah, isn't it?' I nod as she drops the sheet of paper into her bag and offers a manicured hand. Her eyes flicker over my own bandaged one. 'Alix St Clair. We met when you came to be interviewed. How's it going?'

'Actually,' I say, 'I need to see Clara. It's rather urgent.'

'Oh?' There's a wealth of expression in the syllable. Alix throws open the door and steps aside so that I can see the empty office. 'Clara's out.'

'Out?' It never occurred to me that Clara might not be here. She is always here, except when she is filming or in the edit suite. So why is Alix in her office? 'When will she be back?'

'Who knows?' Alix gives a tiny toss of the head. 'She wouldn't tell *me*. Lately, she just disappears. Once or twice a week. Could be for a couple of hours, could be less.'

'I'll wait, then.'

Alix says, 'I was on my way down to the canteen. I need a break. Sodding boring research job. Want to come for a coffee?'

I am about to refuse, but something in Alix's eyes challenges me.

'All right.'

*

Stirring grey-brown liquid in an institutional cup, Alix appraises me.

'Hurt your hand?'

'Just a cut.' I pull my sleeve down over the bandage.

'So how are you coping with the filming?'

I sip my coffee. She will not have the satisfaction of knowing, before Clara, what I am about to do. 'All right, I think. It took a while to get used to it. All those people…'

Alix nods. 'Yes. It can be pretty overwhelming. How are you getting along with Clara?'

'Very well.'

'Really?' The tone is light, but I sense poison. Diluted, but definitely there.

'You sound surprised.'

'Not exactly *surprised* but… Clara's not been particularly easy lately. Or so I hear.'

'Oh?'

'But then the menopause can't be much fun. The mood swings, the hot flushes. A difficult time, I imagine.'

Easy to imagine in the safe knowledge that she has another twenty-five years to go.

'Clara works harder than anyone I know.' I instantly regret the words.

'Yes?' Alix's tone is lazy now. The silent implication is that I am not likely to know the meaning of hard work. 'Of course,' she adds, 'Clara's been here an age. Longer than anyone else.'

'She must be very experienced.'

Alix smiles, stretching her legs out and examining their line. There is a pause. She doesn't seem to find it awkward. Eventually she says, with the hint of a yawn, 'It's inevitable, I suppose, to begin to lose the plot at her age. After all, she's heading for retirement…'

'She's only fifty!' Too quick. Would Sarah know that?

'Reeaaally?' This time, the word stretches to infinity.

'Yes. The same age as myself, actually.'

Alix pauses. 'Ah. Yes. In her prime, then.'

Patronising, snide little madam. I feel myself flushing.

'Are you trying to tell me something, Alix? If you are, please do so, and do it straight.' Did I really say that?

Alix's eyes flicker over me, assessing me. Then she pushes her cup aside, glances around and lowers her voice. 'Between you and me,' she says, 'Clara's on pretty dodgy ground. It wouldn't take much for her to be given the push.'

I swallow. 'What do you mean?'

'Old dogs. New tricks. Clara is old-school. She lets her principles get in the way of the job. And right now of course, she's rather out of her depth. I dread to think,' Alix adds, clearly not dreading it at all, 'what would happen if anything went wrong. With *The Making of Her*, I mean. Clara would be out on her ear.'

Oh, God. I had imagined a fracas, Clara being rightly furious. But not this. Not this.

Alix stands. 'Well, back to the grind. Want to see if Clara's back?'

I shake my head. 'I think I'll have another coffee.'

'I'll tell her you're waiting, shall I?'

'No,' I say. 'It's all right.'

Alix gives me a speculative glance. 'I thought it was urgent?'

'No,' I repeat. 'I forgot. I'll be seeing her tomorrow. For the filming. It can wait till then.'

Alix holds out her hand. 'Well, best of luck… Sarah.' The pause speaks volumes. 'I guess you'll be unrecognisable next time we meet.'

She turns neatly, and catwalks to the lift.

I drain my cup. The dregs are bitter, and cold.

*

I walk. Through rain-soaked Shepherds Bush Market with its stalls of gaudy cloth, plastic homeware and exotic fruits. My hair is plastered to my skull. The traffic, jerking and stuttering, echoes my jagged thoughts. And Alix's words.

Dodgy ground… out of her depth… the push… out on her ear…

I am in Hammersmith. Cars, cycles, taxis and buses pour around the island of the Broadway Centre and the underground. Should

I catch a bus or get the tube? At the crossing I hesitate, slapped by wet plastic bags and bumped by umbrellas. A black limousine with a personal number plate – PS OFF – hisses through the lake at my feet and baptises me with a wave of dirty water.

'Get a move on, love…' The lights have changed and someone is nudging me. The people behind are elbowing past. I don't want to go home. I turn in to King Street, past the Council Offices with their anonymous escalators and concrete walkways. My legs carry me down a long-forgotten but familiar alleyway reeking of urine and beer, to a damp, deserted courtyard.

The Davina Lucas Secretarial School

The plaque is still on the wall but the windows are boarded, the panes broken and blackened. Someone has been sleeping in the doorway; a grubby blanket and a couple of empty lager cans stake claim to the steps. The letters 'S' and 'h' have been scratched out to leave *cool* and the door has been sprayed with garish graffiti. I peer through the letterbox. The hall is clogged with junk mail, but otherwise it is just as it used to be.

Thirty years ago.

Clara and me, grinning at one another behind Davina Lucas's back as she stoops to inspect our typing. Davina's bluestocking stockings are just visible under her pleated skirt. Her pursed lips tut at Clara's haphazard work. *Too rushed, Clara, as per usual.* Then an abrupt nod over my conscientious, careful typing. *Take pride in the process, ladies, like Josephine.* Later, Clara pulls me, laughing and complaining – *Davina will see us!* – out of the school and into the Cardamom Café for elevenses. A quick, rebellious fag for Clara and a Kit-Kat for me, plus two cups of brown builders' tea and Neil Diamond on the radio.

When did life get serious? When did we stop laughing? So long ago, it seems, that I cannot remember. Back then, our hopes and dreams seemed attainable. The Davina Lucas School was a portal to freedom. Now, like me, it is worn down. Shuttered and shattered. I sink down and sit on the wet step. What to do?

I must back out of *The Making of Her*, of course, just as I intended.

No nonsense about offering up my body for the sake of Clara's career. I am no sacrificial lamb. So why the hesitation? Surely I am not still chasing the magic of metamorphosis?

No. The magic was, is, an illusion. I wanted to believe that Marcus could carve away the failure, the rejection, suck out the old Jo along with her fat. Sluice away Julia's ugly-duckling daughter and Iain's invisible wife. I bought into a story – not a children's tale, but an adult fantasy about bodies and beauty, visibility and value. So there is no earthly reason why, knowing this, I should continue. And yet… something unwanted niggles and whispers. *You started this,* it says. *You chose this path, wittingly or unwittingly.*

My head jerks up. The Voice is back.

I shiver. Have I embarked on a process that once begun – like giving birth – cannot be refused? I remember my dream. The pool of blood closing over my head, filling my eyes, my mouth. Drowning me. The damp is seeping into my haunches, yet I sit on. The Voice has been AWOL for weeks. Why does she have to return now? And why does she always have to be so bloody *right?*

Because I know. I wish I didn't, but I do. This knowing is lodged deep inside my flesh. In my very bones. I must go on with *The Making of Her* but with my eyes, at last, wide open. I must find out what it intends for me. I must see this process through. Slowly, consciously and meticulously, just as Davina taught me.

I touch the plaque with a shaking hand. As I do so, The Voice is back again, whispering.

It will be the making of you.

The little courtyard is dark now. I brush down my trousers and run my fingers through my dripping hair. Then I set off down the alley and walk into the real world.

PETE

Pete Street wakes to the laughter of his ex-wife, an erection straining up his belly and the familiar seeping sensation of dread.

In his dream, Katia was waist-deep and naked in the river, her heavy black curls oiling the water. She was dropping pills, one by one, into the river, counting them out in her flat, metronome voice. *He loves me... loves me not.*

'Give me them...' he shouted. But he couldn't wade in after her. He couldn't leave the boy.

Katia smiled. Then, as if bored by him, it, she tossed the remaining pills into the water, creating a furious fizzing all the way to his toes.

Now, she said, her small, cruel face glinting white, *if you want to swallow your pills you'll have to drink the river.*

He rubs at his eyes. Sleeping's torture. So is waking. Better get up now or he'll be pinioned to the bed by thoughts and memories. Getting up – in the non-erection sense of the word – is hardest of all. His hand strays towards his cock.

Fuck. She'd love that.

A cold shower will wash away Katia and shock the erection into submission.

Beside his head, the mobile shrills. He picks up his shades and shoves them on. Stupid, but necessary. With them on, the world can't see him.

'Mornin', Mr Street.' Ed, his driver. 'Hope I didn't wake you?'

Pete runs a hand through his tangled hair and clears his throat. 'Had a nightmare.'

Ed chuckles. '*To die, to sleep,* as The Man said. *To sleep, perchance to dream. Aye, there's the rub.*' When Pete doesn't comment, he asks: 'Will you be needin' me today, Mr Street?'

Pete stands. Moves to the bathroom. 'Not today, Ed.'

There's a silence, then Ed says casually, 'Will Mr MacBride be over?'

'Probably.' Pete sets the shower hissing, turns the temperature to ice.

'Be sure to call me,' says Ed, with a wink in his voice, 'if anything comes up.'

*

Rain drums against the living room window as if trying to force its way in. But the guitar's where he left it, in the corner against the wall. And the fire is there, ready for lighting; Jongo laid it last night. Everything present and correct. He likes that.

An insidious thought sends him to the kitchen. He gropes in the cupboard behind boxes and tins until his fingers find the three identical packets. He touches them. His talismans.

She can fuck around with his dreams. But she can't mess with reality.

CLARA

'Running…' Gary nods from behind the camera.

'And…' Clara checks the shot in the monitor at her feet '…action!'

Marcus smiles at the camera. 'Plastic surgery, which includes both cosmetic and reconstructive procedures, doesn't, of course, involve the use of plastic. The word comes from the Greek *plastiko*, meaning "to mould". Plastic surgery moulds the contours and infrastructures of the body to create a normal, or in the case of cosmetic surgery, a more aesthetically pleasing, appearance…'

The camera widens to include Jo, standing naked save for her knickers, her face closed and her body all too visible under the harsh, probing lights. That long-ago evening after Iain's departure, Jo had taken care to hide her body beneath the bath water and behind a towel. She had exposed her feelings, but concealed her flesh.

And before that? Clara hasn't seen Jo's naked body since they were in their twenties, on holiday, in the days before Jo's marriage to Iain and his wounding remarks about her weight. Back then, Jo's body had been plump and full. Full of itself. Now it looks exhausted, as if it's given up a fight. As if it can no longer hold itself together, but is collapsing, falling into the shape of the old woman Jo will become.

Clara has filmed women's bodies many times in her career: women who have been raped, women who have self-harmed, women who have starved their flesh into submission. But ageing is a subtler process. It wreaks its havoc and its destruction almost gently, year by inevitable year, slowly squeezing the juice from the body. From Jo's body, and also from her own.

Quickly, she lowers her eyes to the image on the monitor. Sarah Miller. She must concentrate. Make sure Gary's getting all the shots she'll need. She must listen to Marcus's words. She must deliver this programme efficiently, just as she has always done.

'Thank you, Marcus.' He nods, coolly. Their relationship is now, literally, clinical. 'Would you move into describing the ageing process and how it relates to Sarah's body?' She turns to Gary. 'Start on a close-up of Marcus and follow him.'

Marcus takes up his position. 'Let's begin by looking at what happens when skin ages. Over time, the connective tissue which supports the face loses its elasticity, partly due to the natural effects of gravity. Sun damage will, of course, speed up the process.' Gary is gradually panning to Jo's face. 'This is the case with Sarah.' Marcus places his fingers on Jo's skin, pulling it up and back. For an instant, the young, hopeful Jo is there, until Marcus releases the skin. 'What I propose for Sarah is a full facelift, including rhinoplasty – restructuring her nose.' The camera's eye follows his hands down Jo's body. 'I will lift and augment her breasts...' he traces patterns over Jo's breasts, which, without support, have fallen almost to her navel '...and remove the excess fat from her stomach and thighs.'

Clara looks at Marcus, fully and expensively clothed in his Savile Row suit, Paul Smith shirt and leather brogues as he fingers Jo's exposed flesh, pronouncing on her deficiencies. The old fury rears up but just as suddenly loses its potency. Why blame Marcus for doing his job? She might more reasonably blame herself for doing her own. Witnessing – no, worse: recording and broadcasting this shaming experience. And in so doing, heaping more fear and repugnance on the uneasy relationship women have with their own bodies.

'And... cut.' Her call is late. Marcus came to the end of his speech some time ago and Gary is raising a quizzical eyebrow. Jo remains still.

'That's it for today. Thanks, everyone. Thank you, Sarah. That was... great.' Jo gives a small half-smile, takes her robe from Lisa and quickly shrugs it on.

'Are you OK?' Clara lowers her voice. Before Jo can answer, Marcus intrudes between them.

'Sarah, is there anything else you'd like to talk about before surgery?'

Jo flushes and shakes her head. 'I know what to expect. I just want to get it over with.'

'Absolutely. Don't worry. And do call me if anything occurs to you. Otherwise, I'll see you tomorrow.' He shakes her hand formally, as if they'd just met at a party, and without looking at Clara, moves off.

Tomorrow. Surgery day. The day of Jo's rebirth as a new and improved model. *Wednesday's child is full of woe.* Clara shakes the thought away. When she turns to Jo, she is gone.

*

Eleven p.m. Clara is propped up in bed, checking emails. She should be winding down after the day's filming. Taking a hot shower, getting some much-needed sleep. Except that there's tomorrow's filming schedule to check and recheck. Besides, sleep is accompanied by dreams. David-and-Dan conjoined, arousing and tormenting. Even in her waking hours, Dan's face, Dan's voice intrude, distracting her with his bloody *do-be-do-be-do.*

She and Dan are over. Done with. Finished. So why does he keep resurfacing, like some drowned ghoul in a horror movie?

Because of therapy, forcing her to dig up her past. Because of David.

When she's not dreaming about David-and-Dan, or being sucked away by the sea, she dreams she is in court, petitioning for custody of her own job. The judge is Marcus, his great head ponderous in a white wig. Counsel for the Prosecution is Alix. Beneath the folds of her black gown, Alix carries a fine-bladed knife, which she uses to carefully cut away Clara's precarious hold on her career.

Daytimes are little better. She often sees Alix sitting with the other assistant producers in the canteen, coldly assessing Clara and her menopausal madness: waiting, sharp-eyed, for her to lumber into a quagmire of her own making and quietly expire.

Her eyes ache as her fingers punch the keys. The night is heavy with an approaching storm, the air hollow like held breath. Her laptop sits between her legs, its electromagnetic warmth penetrating the duvet. Strange bedfellow. And with this thought comes another memory of Dan.

He is spread out, dozing, beside her, the duvet pushed back because of the heat. Through the open window, she hears the sound of an urban dog-fox barking. She is propped against the pillows, straining over the laptop. He reaches a warm hand to her thigh, caressing her, murmuring, 'Clara, switch off. Enough, now.'

She ignores him, focusing on the tiny virtual egg-timer, the endless swathe of information flowing and unfolding under her fingertips.

Much later, as the laptop plays its valedictory song, she turns to him, wanting release. He is sleeping silently beside her, his chest rising and falling. She bends to his slumbering cock, her hands working at him until he is hard, a tiny tear of semen shivering on the tip. His eyes are half open now, watching her as she straddles his body, already wet for him, guiding him inside. He doesn't touch her. They don't speak or kiss. Anger fuels her movements as she pushes at his passivity, goading him towards climax. When it comes, it's dry, empty. Only then does he speak.

'Clara, you bring a whole new dimension to it.'

She is half asleep, half aware of his semen slimy on her thighs. 'To what?'

Dan's words are so quiet she barely hears them. 'The making of love.'

And in the morning he is curiously removed, waking early, shrugging into his work-clothes, setting about his day.

The memory brings a sweat. She can feel it stealing up on her, tightening the space between her eyes, making her wait for it, like an orgasm, then releasing through her in its customary wet, burning heat: not a relief but an invasion, a red rape. She reaches for tissues, mops her face and her chest. The wind gusts in the branches of the tree outside her window, its leaves scraping at the glass. A dry, electric flash is quickly followed by a growl of thunder.

She hates lightning and remembers Jo, who delights in it, telling her how her father used to carry her, as a child, out into the garden during storms, trailed by Julia's irritable complaints... *For God's sake, Tony, don't take her out there... stupidity... danger... wet carpets.* Jo told her how the rain ran down the back of her neck, tickling, how the lightning flashed the garden into lurid daytime and how the thunder growled like a great dog in the sky as Jo and her dad counted, together, the spaces in between.

Clara forces her focus back to the screen. Arrangements for Jo's surgery roll down the page. Not Jo, Sarah. Not that fresh, excited child in the thunderstorm, but a sad, middle-aged woman about to go under the knife.

Another lightning flash. She hunches her shoulders, anticipating the dry heave of thunder, which follows immediately, right above the house. The room is plunged into darkness as the bedside light is extinguished, though the laptop merely flickers before moving automatically to battery mode. A power cut. All she needs. Outside the window, the leaf-scraping ceases, surrendering to the wet rustle of heavy rain in foliage. She pushes the laptop away, feels for her slippers and pads to the window. Water streams down the pane. Beyond, the street lights glimmer and an occasional window is still lit. Not a power cut, then. The storm must have tripped the fuse.

The fuse box is in the cellar, two flights down. When did she last go down there? Not for years. When she bought the house, she'd planned to tank the cellar, lower the floor and convert it into extra living space, yet somehow a combination of her heavy workload and the cellar's silent inertia meant it remained just as it was when she moved in: dark, slightly damp and low-ceilinged. Dan had sworn when he struck his head on the joists, and moved around crab-like to retrieve his tools. He'd offered to do the work: to clear the cellar and make it habitable. She had prevaricated. Let his suggestions slide away. *Why bother? What would we use it for? It's better left as a store.*

Dan was sensitive to the fact that she owned the house. He moved around her belongings with grace, staking few claims. Except for his altar in the corner of the spare bedroom; his sitting-place. On this subject alone had Dan the Flexible proved implacable. Twice a day he would sit, his back to the room, facing the altar. Meditating. When she asked him what he meditated *on* he told her that his teacher gave him riddles: *What is the sound of one hand clapping?* What, she thought privately, was the point of that? But something deeper in her knew that the cellar would have been the perfect workshop for him: something he would never admit. Both of them, stubborn. Subterranean arguments, never voiced. *Your territory. Ours. Commitment. Obligation. Love?*

She feels her way down the stairs and into the kitchen. There's a torch in the drawer. Its steady light gives her comfort and control. She pulls open the cellar door and descends. It's icy down here. Her slippers crunch slightly on who knows what. The torch beam swings around, sliding over cardboard boxes, rusted paint tins, a discarded chair. She ducks her head to avoid the cobwebs hammocking from the joists.

The fuse box is under the stairs. Stupid place to put it. And, equally stupidly, she's piled up boxes around it like a barricade. Stooping, fearful of spiders, she pulls the nearest box out, its base scraping across the cold cement floor. Heavy. What does she have in that? Probably old paperwork: tax paraphernalia, scripts from long-ago programmes. No love letters or photographs, obviously.

She shoves the box away behind her and it crunches into something solid. There's an empty, teasing silence: her shoulders tense as she senses an object toppling, falling through air. Something shatters on the concrete floor. And something else, lighter, drops and rolls.

She can just reach the fuse box. Leaning across the remaining boxes, she flips open its cover, illuminating the row of switches in the torch beam. The trip switch is up. She clicks it down, hears the familiar hum of the fridge-freezer in the kitchen above her head, feels rather than sees her relieved breath clouding, cold, around her. Carefully she backs out, the heel of her slipper crunching down on a shard of whatever it was that broke.

She switches on the light. The cellar is revealed, grey, bare and sorry for itself. The floor is scattered with glass fragments. An old green vase, unused for years, has been knocked off a mildewed bookcase. And lying in the pool of shattered pieces, a small wooden box. She bends and picks it up. It sits comfortably in the hollow of her hand like a pigeon's egg. Her name – Clara – has been carved into the lid. The wood has been so finely worked she can barely see the join between the upper and lower parts. But there is an exquisite gold hinge and, on the other side, a tiny lock. Encumbered by the torch, she tries to pull it open but it is tightly shut. She turns it upside down. Carved into the base is Dan's trademark swan. Something solid inside rattles.

There must be a key. She drops cautiously to her knees among the shards of vase, using the torch to illuminate dusty crevices and corners. Nothing but a few dead, spider-wrapped flies. She extinguishes the torch and carries the box up to the kitchen, where she washes her grubby hands. The box sits mute on the worktop.

In her bedroom, she switches off the laptop and climbs under the duvet, holding the box close to her body as if her warmth might melt it open. Waking with the light, five hours later, she finds it pressed into the soft flesh of her breast. It leaves a reddened glyph, like a scar.

JO

Marcus is marking my body with a pen. I glance down at myself and see broken lines, crosses, sections – so innocent, innocuous, like a child's scribbles. Or like a map – the broken lines for footpaths, crosses for churches: a map to guide Marcus over the contours of my body. Stop dreaming, Jo. More like a slab of meat hanging on a hook of my own making, while the butcher marks the joints and cuts.

I blink. My head is swimming. The hospital room is too hot and I've eaten and drunk nothing for eight hours. I seem to be having an out-of-body experience. I am hovering somewhere above my own flesh, which I have committed to Marcus's busy hands. I catch a tang of aftershave. A man, not a magician. No man's fingers – apart from these – have touched me with intent for a long time. Certainly not Iain's. I remember lying awake a few months ago, reaching tentatively towards him as he snored. Even unconscious, Iain had shrugged away from me. Marcus's hands are pale and professional. They stroke my body – not in love, or even lust, but in simple clinical demonstration. Somehow, this is soothing. I can relax and receive his hands upon me, knowing that no response is expected or desired. The first time, when his fingers had circled my nipples as he described how he would lift my breasts, I wondered what it would be like if those hands were touching me in a less professional capacity. Such thoughts hadn't lasted long. Residing in my body has, after all, brought me far more pain than pleasure. Much safer to pretend I'm out there, part of the crew, gazing in upon Sarah Miller's body, objectively recording the process.

Clara is as usual hunched over the monitor, while Bill, the gnomic sound-recordist, hangs a microphone over our heads like a fishing rod. A gentle soul, Bill, in his old-man's cardigan and cords, who – as Clara has warned me – is apt to pin you to the wall and talk endlessly at you between takes, perhaps to make up for spending so much time in enforced silence, listening to other people's voices. Gary is cool, professional: rumoured to have a wife and a couple of girlfriends on the go. He looks at me with practised, remote eyes: to him, I am merely a form to be framed. And Lisa, the PA, a kind and efficient woman in her fifties, remains surgically attached to her clipboard and pen. Over the past weeks, these people have become my surrogate family. They have listened to me, followed my every move, seen me naked as a baby. Soon, they will watch me anaesthetised and laid out on a trolley and will witness, like some sacrificial cult, the cutting and culling of my flesh, the letting of my blood. They will record my reformation.

I want my journal because I long to add these thoughts to all the others I've written, from my heightened awareness of Marcus Templeton's fingers to Clara's bruised, heavy eyes and white face. A different kind of recording, but, for me at least, more important. Each night, I sit over my pages, catching the delicate sensations and ephemera of the day like a cat raising its nose to the wind to catch a scent. I do not read over what I write. It's enough to let it stream out of me on to the receiving paper, a kind of alchemy in which the base metal of *The Making of Her* is transmuted into gold. Where once I would confide my feelings, haltingly and inadequately, to Clara, I now empty myself into the safe confines of the journal. It is my confidante, accepting it all without protest or denial.

'Sarah?' Marcus's voice, shortly followed by Clara's.

'Are you OK?'

I shake my head, then nod. 'I'm fine. Just rather hot and drowsy.'

'Time to get you into theatre.' Marcus turns to Gary, deliberately cutting across Clara. 'Got all you need?'

Clara's face stiffens. Gary raises an eyebrow, glances at Clara. 'Clara?'

Clara's face is flushed. 'We've more than enough. Tea break, everyone. We'll meet in theatre in half an hour to set up.'

As the crew disperses, Clara takes my arm, leads me down the corridor to my room and sits beside me on the bed.

'Jo, talk to me. How are you doing?' Clara looks haggard and thinner than ever. I realise I've no idea what's going on with her any more. Nor she me. We have lost our connection.

'I'm fine.' This response is now my mantra. 'What about you?'

'Me? Getting by. You know.'

I don't, but this doesn't seem the moment to ask. Any minute now, the anaesthetist will be here. Clara suddenly turns, searching my face.

'I need to know, Jo. And it's OK, either way. Just tell me… are you certain you want to go through with this? It's not too late. Really.'

It will be the making of you. The Voice is still with me. I try a grin. 'And just what would you do if I backed out now? Pop out into the street and grab a stranger?'

Clara's face is set, stern. 'Your well-being is more important to me than any fucking job.' But her face flickers as she says it. Is she telling the truth? Are either of us? I reach for Clara's hand.

'Listen. I'm going through with it. It's my choice. It's all right.'

Clara ducks her head and makes a muffled sound. When she raises her face, I see a single tear in the corner of her eye. It dribbles down her cheek. What's going on? Clara doesn't cry.

'Sorry.' Clara wipes at her face with the back of her hand, like a child. 'It's just… we haven't talked for so long. About this. About anything. There are things…' She shakes her head slightly. 'When you're all done and mended, we'll catch up.' She glances at the door. 'Marcus may be a snake, but he knows what he's doing. It'll soon be over and you can start again.'

We can start again remains unspoken. We turn away from each other and when our eyes meet again the masks are back in place.

Ready for the theatre, I think. *How appropriate.*

CLARA

Clara glances at her schedule one last time. The cutting room awaits.

The operating theatre is a hot, sealed box. Slick surfaces gleam; the sharp smell of disinfectant mingles with the whisper of gas and the trickle of water running into a sluice. Bodies are swathed in masks and gowns, their genders indeterminate. Everything here is homogenised.

Except, of course, for the hierarchy. She and the crew are here on Marcus's terms, on Marcus's territory, and bound by the rules of the theatre. The scene is set, the cast assembled, and only he, the main character, is missing. Theatre staff and television crew go about their duties, distinguishable only by the tools of their trades. A nurse glides in carrying a tray of instruments while Lisa scribbles on her clipboard. Another adjusts a drip while Bill sets up his microphone and frowns, muttering, at his meter. A third studies jagged lines on a bleeping screen while she, Clara, stares at the monitor at her feet. Gary, camera on his shoulder, is filming the anaesthetist bending over the form that is Jo. Was Jo. For Jo is unrecognisable, her hair tucked away, her spectacles removed, her mouth slackening around the anaesthetist's mask, her body hidden under a flat, green gown. Only the machines acknowledge her life, bleeping out her heartbeat, hissing her breath.

Clara remembers a rare visit to another kind of theatre, for *Romeo and Juliet*. Juliet lay like this, drugged and illuminated, waiting for Romeo. Jo lies waiting, too. Not for her match, her mate, but for Marcus. No anxious husband paces outside the doors, praying for her. No one knows, or cares, that Jo is here. *No one except me.*

Sweat dampens Clara's face, accompanied by the familiar

accelerating thud of her heart and the shaking of her knees. She tries to remember David's advice: *Breathe through it, Clara. Panic attacks can't last. Breathe, and you'll come through.* Thank God for the mask. At least no one can tell. Surreptitiously, she takes a deep breath, then exhales. Again.

She glances over at Gary, waiting now, camera at the ready. He sees her looking and winks. A wave of gratitude: Gary's still on side, in spite of Marcus's attempts to ingratiate himself with the crew by buying Gary drinks, sharing jokes with Bill and flirting with Lisa. His intent, as far as she can see, is to create a bond with them while firmly excluding her. His behaviour towards her this morning was outrageous. She is used to crew politics, to office politics; but a contributor who refuses to respect her authority and who seems bent on blatantly undermining her – never. The crew are clearly confused. They must wonder what the hell is going on. Marcus is making her seem extraneous. Redundant.

Gary, professional to the core, seems impervious to Marcus's machinations. Whenever Marcus turns to him, rather than to Clara, for direction, Gary points him firmly back to her. Yesterday, after more of the same, she took Marcus aside.

'What's going on?' Her voice sounded querulous.

He smiled. 'Nothing at all, to my knowledge.'

She held his eyes. 'Look, Marcus. You're a professional in your field and I respect that. I'm a professional in mine.' Marcus had raised one eyebrow very slightly. The familiar fury crept up her throat. 'I wouldn't dream of undermining you in your work. Why are you undermining me?'

He bent his great head towards her. She could smell his breath. 'Clara, aren't you being a little... paranoid?' There's always a specious slant to his replies. Like a slimy politician.

'I'm the director, Marcus.'

'Of course you are.' He had looked amused, as if a child had just informed him that she was a grown-up.

'Then please respect that.'

'*My* respect,' Marcus intoned, his eyes pointedly moving to the crew, 'is not in question.' And he had patted her on the shoulder, which had the same effect as patting her on the ass.

There's a stir among the nurses as Marcus sweeps in. His eyes scan the room, blank and cold as he registers Clara's presence. Immediately he moves towards Gary, draping an arm over his shoulder, murmuring and gesturing. Clara quickly joins them.

'When we begin,' Marcus is saying, 'it will be necessary for the camera to stay in one place – perhaps here.' He indicates a position near Jo's knees. He allows Bill to attach a radio microphone to the front of his gown. 'Everyone else,' he glances in Clara's direction, 'must remain in the background.'

She's being dismissed, cast out from the action, thank God. She can crouch in her corner, focusing on the monitor, rather than witnessing the reality of the operation. Squeamish, Dan used to call her, when she turned her eyes from his cuts and scrapes. Well, it's true. She would probably faint if she were at Gary's side, though she would never admit it to him, or Bill, or Lisa. Jo knows it, but Jo isn't conscious.

I'm on my own.

Marcus is conferring with the anaesthetist. The room is unbearably hot. A nurse swabs Jo's exposed belly with some kind of orange-brown liquid. The flesh wobbles from side to side. On the monitor, Gary moves in for a close-up as Marcus's gloved hands pick up a blade. Clara's head buzzes as the knife slides – so easily, soundlessly – through the tender skin under Jo's left breast.

It's only skin. Just skin and fat and bone and blood, she chants to herself, a mantra to keep herself from shutting her eyes, from throwing up.

*

Halfway through.

Jo's breasts have been lifted and augmented with implants. They stand unnaturally upright. Marcus's large hands, deft with a needle, have sewn up the gaping wounds. The flap of Jo's belly has been opened like a red, glistening cave, as Marcus wielded an instrument back and forth among the blood and tissue, vacuuming up clots of yellow fat and spewing them into a basin.

Distract, Clara. She thinks of her dream: the dream of David operating on her and lifting her heart out of her body. The birds flying free into the sky. Is Jo being freed? From her ties with Iain, from her self-criticism, her invisibility? Or is she being severed from herself, changed into a person she won't recognise?

She chose this. She said she was sure. Why, then, beneath her queasiness, does Clara feel like a betrayer?

A nurse covers Jo's mutilated body with a sheet as the focus moves to her face.

'Clara.' Marcus's voice, repeating her name with an edge of irritation. For once, he's looking directly at her with those cool, blank eyes.

'Yes?' She is disoriented. Dizzy.

'Come over here, please.' It's not a request, but an order. He makes it sound as if she has been deliberately shirking her responsibility.

Her knees creak as she stands. Her head's swimming. Somehow, her legs carry her over to the operating table. Jo's words. *When do you plan to step out from behind your precious camera and see how the rest of us live?* Gary's eyes question her above his mask. He knows. He knows she's terrified.

'Ready?' A grim smile in Marcus's voice as he turns, inevitably, to Gary. Gary shrugs, nods. 'Then we'll continue.'

Marcus leans down into Jo's face, holding out his palm for a blade. Jo lies silent and receptive. Clara wants to pummel her into consciousness, to scream at her – at herself – to get out. To run. The urge is so strong that she squeezes her fists together and clenches her jaw tight. Then there's only the heavy beat of her own heart, the snaking hiss of gas, the relentless bleeping monitor, the rustle of gowns and the very faint sound of the camera turning over. And the sharp, hot smell of cutting, of blood, as Marcus runs his blade across Jo's eyelids.

*

'Somebody take her out.' Marcus's tone is dismissive. Lisa's arm is around her. Clara stumbles, knowing all eyes are upon her. She cannot control her legs. Her head is icy cold. Her ears are buzzing. She needs to throw up, but a last remaining strand of self-preservation prevents it as Lisa half-carries her towards the heavy doors and – at last, at last – they swing shut behind her.

Later, sitting in the toilet, her head thumping, she presses a ball of wet paper towel to her face. Lisa has returned to the theatre, her mind on all the shots she hasn't listed and all the time codes she's missed.

The end. Ejected by her own body, her control lost, her authority gone. The fact that Marcus and the crew have witnessed it is the ultimate humiliation. She casts around for any residue of confidence or strength. Gone. All, all sucked away. Marcus has exposed her for what she is: a director without direction. A feeble failure. Her head sinks into her hands. Richard was right. She is utterly expendable.

*

'Feeling better?'

It's Lisa, tactfully ignoring the streaks of tears on her cheeks and the fact that she's still sitting on the toilet.

'Clara?' Lisa's eyes are kind.

'Yes. Yes, I'm OK. Thanks for getting me out.' She cannot meet Lisa's eyes.

'It could happen to anyone. It was hot, the stress…'

'Not to you, though. Or Bill. Or Gary.'

Lisa touches her hand. 'Nobody's perfect. Not you, not any of us.' She stands. 'Come on. Come out and face them. They're worried about you.'

'Is Marcus still there?'

'Marcus,' says Lisa, 'is a prize shit. Everyone knows that. Anyway, the filming's pretty much over, as far as he's concerned. Don't let him get to you, Clara.'

'How's Jo? Is she OK?'

'Jo?'

Bugger. 'Sarah, I mean.'

'She's fine. It all went really well. She's still under, of course. Want to go and see her?'

'Yes. Yes, I will. I'll just…' she casts around for her bag.

'Right.' Lisa gives her a penetrating look. 'Don't worry. It's not the end of the world.'

Only the end of her career.

Not now. Not tomorrow. But soon. It's just a matter of time.

JO

'She's coming round.' A faraway voice.

Who? I can feel the pressure of warm flesh around my hand.

'Jo? Thank God…'

Everything hurts. I dare not, cannot open my eyes.

It's Clara's voice, next to my ear. 'It's all right. It went well. You're fine. Aren't you?' Clara sounds odd, as if someone's pulled the plug out of her.

I try to lick my lips, but my mouth is too dry. I can't breathe through my nose. A dampness is pushed against my face.

A flurry of movement somewhere in front of me. A door opening? Yet something in the ether alters, more as if a door has closed. Another, deeper voice. My shoulder is touched.

'Sarah.' *The Magician.* 'Sarah, this is Marcus. Can you hear me?'

I move my head, sparking a burning sensation somewhere I can't identify.

'Good. Very good.'

My eyelids feel stuck down. I force all my concentration into opening them. Sudden smarting. A sound jolts from me.

'Nothing to worry about. They're bandaged.'

I open my swollen lips and breathe. Again the damp thing, wetting my skin. Then Clara's voice, high and staccato: 'Is she all right?'

Marcus's tone is dismissive. 'She'll feel like she's been hit by a bus. Give her water, if she wants it.' Then, closer to my face. 'You've done well. The procedures went without a hitch. Now all you have to do is rest and recover. I'll come back to see you later.'

*

Clara's still here, holding my hand, anchoring me to consciousness. She gently moves a straw between my lips. Grateful water escapes the corners of my mouth and runs down my neck.

'You were talking about dragons,' she says.

'Ag-ons?'

'When you were asleep.' There's a pause. 'You look like a mummy.' Another pause. 'Does it hurt very much?'

Does it? I cast around my body. I thought it hurt, earlier. Where? I just feel floating. Amorphous.

'S'awright,' I manage.

*

'Snow!'

A nurse briskly pulls back the curtains on the still-dark January morning. Yes, I can sense its presence. The air feels a little lighter. I crane my neck, grateful, now that the bandages are gone from my eyes, for the gift of sight. Propped up as I've been since the operation, I can just see the car park stretching away below; rows and rows of silent cars, their roofs sugared with snow. Moving headlights on the road. And figures, hunched and wary on the slippery pavement.

The nurse brings me tea, with a straw.

*

Marcus examines my breasts and my belly. I catch a brief glimpse of a pair of taut, swollen protuberances, like something in a men's magazine; of a sutured belly lanced across by a great scar. A drain. Not so seductive. Clara and the crew are back, recording it all.

'Excellent, Sarah. All coming along very well.'

Marcus turns his attention to my face.

'So,' he says to camera. 'The moment of truth.'

Deft hands remove the last layer of bandaging that's been holding my face together.

Do I have a face, anymore? And if I do, whose will it be? I wince as the bandage pulls at my skin. Then cool air and Marcus's fingers, feeling.

'Very good indeed.' Is he congratulating himself, or me? He places a mirror in my hands. He seems to be waiting for me to do something.

'Don't you want to have a look?'

Do I? Slowly, I lift the mirror.

My first reaction is *What's that?* Of course, I knew what to expect. They had told me. I had seen pictures. But this isn't some prosaic piece of information, some stranger's wounds. This is my face. A swollen, caked mass of a face. Packing and padding where the nose should be. Heavy bruising under the eyes. The lids criss-crossed with stitches.

There's a long, expectant silence. Then Clara's voice, apologetic. 'Sarah, can you tell us what you see?'

What do I see? A mess. The mess I've been carrying around, inside. On the outside now, for all to see. No need to hide it anymore. I smile for the camera, feeling the stitches pull.

'Interesting,' I say. 'Ten rounds with Mike Tyson at least.'

Afterwards, the crew clap. I receive congratulations. Marcus, gracious, turns to go. Suddenly, it's urgent to know.

'When can I go home?'

'Soon. When we've taken out the drains. It should be plain sailing from now on.' He smiles.

*

If this is what plain sailing is, what kind of a sailor am I? I feel sick, disoriented, sinking. Capsized. One moment I'm marvelling as my hands trace the slopes and valleys of this new shape of myself. The next I'm drowning in discomfort, clawing at the pain which buzzes like an angry insect at my wounds: stinging my eyelids, my breasts, my belly. And wrapped around me, heavy as lead, is an exhaustion from which I fear I will never emerge.

'Quite normal, Sarah.' Marcus Templeton smiles and pulls at his immaculate cuff. 'It'll take a while for the anaesthetic to leave your system.'

But it's not the anaesthetic or even the physical pain that disturbs me. It's the sea change inside me. I am a broken wave. I am flotsam. I am fire. The magician has wielded his sharp wand, but what has he created? A miracle or a monster? Gold or lead?

Beyond that first glance in the mirror, that performance for the cameras, I haven't dared to look. The storm inside me is tricky enough to weather. I cannot face myself – or whoever it is I'll face – in any mirror. Not yet. Let the nurses take care of the wounds out there. I have my own preoccupations to attend to.

Each wave of pain is a wave of blood. A red sea, tumultuous and salty, sweeping relentlessly through my body. This body. But each time the wave recedes, I am an empty shore, a stretch of silent sand. Where is my mother's abrasive voice? Where are Iain's querulous tones? Where is the old Jo with her ugly-duckling mentality and her self-recrimination? I am all absence.

Except for one thing. A seed, planted on that pivotal day outside the Davina Lucas Secretarial School. The day when I made my choice to go through with this. A foetus, deep inside me, making its presence felt in brief, surprising moments, which jerks my lips into an involuntary smile. A will-o'-the-wisp, all air and fire. An embryo. A stranger.

*

Back in the real world.

I lie propped up under the throw in my living room among the blessed familiarity of my books, my television and my sofa while Clara clatters about in the kitchen. This is what I've yearned towards, for weeks: the comfort of home. Of friendship. Preparing for the operation, I had soothed myself by imagining this: everything returning to the way it used to be. Me and Clara, sitting as we've sat so many times in Iain's absence. Watching videos, drinking wine, exchanging ideas and experiences. Why, then, am I feeling more discomfort than relief? In conversation, Clara and I creep around one another. We are over-careful. Clara asks, warily, after my health. I ask Clara, politely, about the progress of *The Making of Her*. These superficial exchanges sting more than my wounds, which are mending and closing, day by slow day.

Could it be that Clara senses the change in me? Obviously not the outer transformation, which, with its bruising and swelling, must be all too visible. No. Is she aware, unconsciously, of the new self growing inside me? Whatever – the balance between us is subtly shifting, and I sense that it will be I, not Clara, who will break the spell between us. I who will force things into the open.

'Jo?' Clara's tone is irritated. She is at the kitchen door, a teaspoon in one hand and a jar in the other. 'I've been asking you. D'you want tea, or coffee?' Clara is grey-faced, a punctured balloon seeping air. Is she weary, as I am, of the charade between us? I stare at her, willing her to meet my eyes. Clara's gaze remains determinedly on the carpet.

'Actually,' I say, 'I'd like my journal.'

'What?'

'My journal. It's upstairs, beside the bed.'

Clara frowns and returns to the kitchen. The teaspoon clatters in the sink. Then she crosses the hall and, still without looking at me, makes for the stairs. When she returns, carrying the journal, her face is sullen, like a hurt child.

'So,' she says, not giving it to me. 'You're writing again?'

'Yes.'

Clara weighs the journal in her hands. 'All this.'

'Yes.'

Silence. She thinks I've shut her out because once I would have told her everything. And it's true.

'What have you been writing?'

'My feelings. My experiences, my thoughts…'

'From *The Making of Her*?'

'Yes.'

'You mean you've been keeping all this to yourself?'

I nod. Who else could I tell?

'Why didn't you talk to me? Tell me? You always did before.'

'It was different. We were different.' Clara looks at me. 'You would have felt obliged to talk me out of *The Making of Her*, and then you would have lost your job.' Clara stiffens but I push on regardless. 'I nearly didn't go through with it, in fact. Even when I saw Alix…'

'Alix?'

'She told me you'd be out on your ear if anything went wrong. But,' I say, seeing horror freeze on Clara's face, 'I didn't carry on because of her. Anyhow, nothing *has* gone wrong, has it? You've proved you can do it. Proved her wrong.'

Clara's expression changes.

'Tell me, Clara,' I say. 'Truth time.'

Clara sits abruptly on the arm of the sofa, still holding the journal. Words begin to tumble from her.

'I collapsed. During the surgery. Had to be carried out. They did it without me…' Her face is scrunched up, like a child about to cry. 'I lost it. My control, my authority, my credibility. And there's nothing…' Her head is bowed over the journal. 'I've been trying to hold it together for ages. But Alix, and Marcus… and just being so stressed…'

'And me,' I say. 'The fact that I pushed you into using me.'

Clara takes a deep breath. Then: 'I wanted to be persuaded. I was too afraid of losing face with Alix. With Richard. I put my job and my pride before your well-being. And before my own ethics.'

'What a pair we are.'

Clara doesn't smile.

I swing my legs to the floor, feeling the tug of my wounds, the now-familiar pains and protests from the new body. 'Anyway,' I say. 'I want you to have it. The journal. Read it, if you want to.

Or throw it out. Whatever.'

Clara looks at it.

'I would have told you,' I say. 'Of course I would. If things had been different.'

Clara mutters something.

'What?'

She pushes the journal away from her, on to the table. 'What a bloody hypocrite I am.' She wipes at her cheeks. 'There's lots I haven't told you.'

'D'you want to tell me now?'

And it all pours out. Panic attacks. Therapy. David. Jessica. Dan's box in the cellar.

'And I think I have... feelings... for David. But then, I keep thinking about Dan.'

'I liked Dan.'

'Everyone liked Dan. Was I such a bitch to him, Jo?'

Kicking her when she's down? Then a different kind of kick, from deep inside me. 'Yes. You were. Sometimes.'

Clara nods. 'I don't know what to do. What shall I do?' A first. Clara never asks for advice.

'Maybe,' I say, 'it's less about doing than allowing. Letting things unfold. Letting life provide the answers.'

'You sound like David.'

'Do I? Well, it's worked for me.'

'Has it?' Her tone is ironic.

'Yes.' I shift up the sofa towards Clara. 'I was afraid. So afraid to let this happen to me. But now I'm glad. All this...' I touch my bruised face, glance down at my body, '...is the stuff I've carried round inside. All the pain of all the years with Iain. All the wounds from Julia's criticisms. The bruises from beating myself up. This is what I've been doing to myself my whole life. And now it's on the outside, where it all belongs.'

'Better out than in, you mean?'

Dear Clara. She's doing her best to understand. 'Much better.

I couldn't heal myself on the inside. I had to see it, to know it. I feel...'

Dare I say it? I will.

'I feel reborn. And it's nothing to do with the way I look. Rather, the reverse.' I still haven't seen myself, apart from fleeting, sideways glimpses. I haven't stood before a mirror, full-frontal, naked, and faced Sarah Miller. Not yet.

'Anyhow.' I pick up the journal, offer it to Clara. 'Read it. If you want.'

Clara takes it. 'I will. When I have time.'

'It won't make easy reading, I warn you.'

Clara rummages in her bag, hands me a thin, scruffy volume. Poetry by Rilke. 'I meant to give you this. A writer for a writer.'

Why do I cringe still at the word *writer*?

'Read it,' says Clara. 'I did.'

'All right.' The book burns my palm. 'It's a deal.'

And we hug, to seal it.

CLARA

His place. Hers. Theirs.

Intimacy-in-a-box in David's little yellow room. Intimacy, but without the hazards of a real relationship. Is this why she feels closer to him, able to reveal herself more deeply than she ever did with Dan?

Twice a week. Monday mornings, when the pigeons coo and murmur, fluffing their feathers in the cold gutters above the window. Thursday evenings, curtains drawn against the night, candles flickering, close. Easier to talk then. To relax, without the imminence of work. The Thursday-evening sessions carry her seamlessly home and into bed, where her dreams still find her and David in congress, or almost so: they tremble on an edge.

Today, though, is a Monday. Pumped up for work, she brings adrenaline into David's room with her. While Jo convalesces, Clara and Lisa are making arrangements for her final 'reveal' in March: sorting out appointments with the dentist, the optician and the hairdresser; booking the studio and the crew; briefing wardrobe and make-up; inviting a carefully selected audience. She had to fight for a studio – the UK Music Awards wanted to book the whole place. Tough. Now she and Jo are OK again, she's got her mojo back: has almost managed to put the debacle of the filming behind her. Almost. Stanley Barforth is still watching her. He drops into the cutting room when she's busy with the rough cut and asks her, with monotonous regularity, how it's all going? Has someone whispered to him that she fell apart? Or is she being paranoid?

*

David is quiet today, very slightly withdrawn. During the last session, glancing up from the sand tray, she had met his eyes, unguarded, and had caught something different in his face, an expression beyond professional regard. What was it? An intensity? A shift in his perspective towards her? Part of her wants to sit with this, to embrace it and allow it to evolve. To unfold, as Jo had put it. Another part – the old, provocative Clara – wants to push him. To force it into the open. She checks his hands, as she always does, for the ring. Still there. Perhaps Jessica's threat was just a drunken boast, rather than a real intention. *Do I want her to leave him?* Once, she would have regarded Jessica simply as an obstacle between herself and what she desired. But now…

I don't want him to suffer. The thought sets off a chain of repetitious arguments in her head. Isn't he suffering anyway, with Jessica? And who's to say he wouldn't suffer if he was with someone else. Someone like herself? Dan could testify to that.

She has brought Dan's wooden box, having prevaricated over doing so for several weeks. It feels almost promiscuous, to bring it here. Like three in a bed.

'I found this.' She holds the box between finger and thumb, so that he can see it. He leans forward.

'May I?'

She hesitates. In her possession, the box feels sanctioned. Handing it over feels exposing, unfair, like an infidelity. But that's ridiculous. Dan and she are finished. She passes it across to David, watches his face as he turns it, finding the swan carved into the base.

'Dan?'

She nods.

'Where did you find it?'

'In the cellar. It must have been down there for years.'

He shakes it, gently. 'There's something inside.'

'Yes. But I can't open it. There's no key.'

He returns it to her. Their palms brush as he tips it into her hand.

Something feathery shivers inside her.

He asks, 'What do you imagine is inside?'

She turns from him and stares down at the tiny box, tracing her name on the lid. 'It's obvious, isn't it?'

He looks at her, simply. 'Not to me.'

'It's got to be a ring, hasn't it?'

'Has it?'

'Come on, David, don't be obtuse.' He raises an eyebrow. 'What else could it be?'

She wants him to understand. To agree. To be on her side.

'Did Dan talk to you about marriage?' he asks.

'No. But then, I never gave him the chance. I know he wanted commitment from me…'

'Commitment?'

'I told you. He wanted me to move away with him. To have… Anyway, he must have been meaning to ask me to marry him. And then, when things went wrong…' She shakes the box. 'It's so – *irritating* of him to have left it.'

David smiles his lop-sided smile. This is also irritating. She wants him to be discomfited by the ring. To be jealous?

'If you're so sure it's a ring, and you're so certain you'd never marry Dan,' he says, 'why do you need to know?'

'Because… because…' *Yes, why?* 'Because I don't want any more secrets. Look at me and Jo. How much better it is, now that the secrets are out.' She doesn't tell him that Jo's journal lies unopened in her bedroom drawer.

'So what do you plan to do?'

'About this?'

He nods.

'Don't know. I could try to lever it open…'

David shifts in his chair. She has come to know that this signals mild disapproval.

'Or I could go down to Cornwall and confront him with it.' Why is she being so provocative? Of course she isn't going to do that.

'You sound as if you feel he's betrayed you.'

'I thought he was gone, out of my life. And this… this *part* of him has been sitting in my cellar all the time, judging me.'

'Judging you?'

'Well, reminding me. Waiting for me. I don't know…'

'Do you need to know?'

'Yes.' She stuffs the box back into her bag and crosses her arms.

'That's that, then?' His tone is quiet, but there's a provocative edge.

'That's that.' The air between them feels heavy. The clock above her head ticks. The brooding pigeons moan, outside.

'What's going on, Clara?'

Always questions. Drawing feelings from her, leaving her vulnerable and exposed. Maybe it's time the tables were turned.

'Do you like me?' The words leap out of her, almost, but not quite, against her will.

David's face remains impassive. 'Why do you ask?'

'Because I want you to tell me.' The window is suddenly buffeted by a gust of wind and she hears the sharp cry of a seagull. Inland, out of its element.

'What do you think?'

'I don't know. Come on.' She forces a grin. 'Just for once, give me a straight answer. Do you?'

He studies her. There's no answering smile. She finds herself holding her breath. After a long pause, he says:

'Yes, Clara. I like you.'

'Good.' She breathes out, although his answer gives her less relief than she'd anticipated. 'I'd like to do a sand tray now.'

'Right.' He stands. The atmosphere is still heavy and unclear. She watches his long back, the slanting angle of his shoulders. It's hard to look at him for too long when they sit face to face. Easier to gaze out of the window or to study corners of the room. Now, as he moves towards her carrying the sand tray, the harsh morning light catches at his head, flaring around it like a halo. She drops her gaze. He places the tray between them and she sinks down on to her knees, gratefully submerging her fingers in the cool sand, spreading them as far as she can and feeling the delicious softness enfolding them. So simple. So different, in every possible way, to her life.

After a while, he says, 'I have some clay, if you want it.'

'Clay?'

He reaches behind his chair and pulls out a polythene-wrapped cube. He's never offered it before.

'All right.' She leans to it as he unwraps it. 'I haven't played with clay since I was in the infants.'

It's wet. Shiny. He cuts a wedge of it. The inside of the clay is different: paler, secret. Her hands long towards its perfection.

'Enough?' he asks. She nods.

'Take it,' he says. She leans towards him and reaches for the slice. It's heavy. Heavier than she expected. And cool. She lifts it to her nose.

'Smells of old ditches. But in a good way.'

He smiles. Something lightens between them.

She stares down at the clay. 'I don't want to spoil it.'

'How d'you mean?'

'I know I'm supposed to make it into something, but I don't want to. I just want to hold it.'

'Then just hold it.'

She does. 'It feels like –'

'Yes?'

Like a baby. So delicate to look at. Yet surprisingly heavy in her hands. The air is full of memories. Voices. Jessica, drawing on her cigarette: *'I want a child. And he doesn't.'* Selfish of her. *Selfish.*

'What's happening?' He always picks up on the unspoken.

'Nothing.' She sinks her fingers into the clay-flesh, harshly. The clay pushes up under her nails. She withdraws her fingers, obscurely glad at the clean dark holes. No longer virgin, the clay gapes at her, sullen. Gripped with a need to somehow punish it, she begins to squeeze it together.

'Clara?'

'Don't know. I want to… mangle it.' She begins to rip pieces off it, hating it now for its subservience to her probing fingers. Scraps of clay fall on to the rug. She wants to grind them in. She wants him to stop her. He doesn't.

She bunches her hand into a fist and drives it into the severed clay. Sees the shape of her knuckles embedded in it. Still, he says nothing. She lifts it, then drops it, hard, into the sand tray and watches the heavy grey ball sink into the sand. Silence.

'I've spoilt it. Shit. Why did I spoil it?'

She pulls the clay out of the sand. It's gritty. She squashes it further, knowing that she has crossed a line, that she has sullied something sacred. The sand-clay is all mixed up in her hands. She cannot separate it. It's ruined.

'I always destroy things. Always. *Fuck*. Why do I do it?' She drops the clay back into the tray. Sand shoots out over David's bare feet and over the contaminated rug.

'Clara.' He's speaking quietly. She sits, defeated, her gritty grey hands clasping and unclasping in her lap. 'Clara, what do you think you destroy?'

'Everything. Everything I touch. Look at Dan. I destroyed everything between us. And now this.'

'This?'

'You and me. Here.'

'How do you think you're destroying it?'

'Because I'm so pushy and hard. And you're so…'

'What?'

'So… beautiful.' She cannot look at him. Shame envelops her. She wants to crawl out of the room, yet she is paralysed, pinned to the floor. The silence stretches to infinity. Eventually, he speaks.

'Clara?' His hand moves to hers, folding her roughened fist in his own. The touch of him is like a door being wrenched open. Lurching, she leans up to him and kisses him awkwardly on the mouth. For a split-second, he responds. Then he pulls away.

'See?' She is beyond herself. Savage.

'Clara, sit down.' She slumps back into her chair. David's face is tense. He looks rather as he did when they collided on New Year's Eve. His uncertainty feels frightening.

'I'm sorry,' he says at last. 'I shouldn't have taken your hand. I wanted to give you… comfort. It was wrong of me.'

The lap of her skirt is stained, clay-grey. She brushes at it. Worse.

'Therapy can stir up some very strong feelings.' His tone is professional now, remote from her.

'Are you trying to tell me that this is just transference?'

'Transference happens. For you, and for me.'

'You can call it that, if it makes it easier for you.'

He looks at her. 'Whatever it is, we have to deal with it.'

'How?'

'There are two options.' The sun has gone in, leaving his face grey and closed. 'We can continue to work through it here, without acting anything out.'

Impossible. How can they sit here as therapist and client, after what's happened?

'Or?'

'Or we can terminate the therapy.'

It's as if he's cut the air between them. Cut her. She cannot speak.

'I can refer you on to someone really good.'

'And then what?'

'What do you mean?'

'What about us?'

Silence. His face is closed. 'There can't be an *us*. You know that.'

She looks down at the decimated clay and the ruined rug.

'Clara, I've… very much enjoyed working with you. Take as long as you like to decide.'

She glances at the clock. Their time is up.

JO

Who is this woman with the straight nose and the wide-open eyes?

I stare at my reflection as I do now some fifty times a day. If I keep doing it, I will surely find the old Jo peering back at me, beaky-nosed and baggy-eyed. Each day the bruising and swelling diminishes, revealing someone both unnervingly familiar and utterly different, like a very flattering portrait of myself, painted some fifteen years ago. I flick an embarrassed glance down towards the breasts and reach to touch them again. They feel globular and satisfyingly high. Confident. My hand travels to my midriff, surprised again by the dip, the gentle curve of it. Not mine. Sarah Miller's. Quickly I pull my dressing-gown together – my familiar, reassuring old towelling robe, which covers me like a dust-sheet, betraying none of the new curves and angles.

I have been unwilling to leave the house since coming home from hospital, surviving on basic rations brought by Clara. I seem to be continuing to lose weight. I no longer feel the need to binge.

Yesterday Iain called, after weeks of silence.

'Jo?' His voice was crackly and distant.

'Who is it?' I had not recognised my own husband.

'It's me, Iain.' The familiar irritated tone. 'Who did you think it was?'

'Iain. How are you?' I gazed at myself in the mirror and watched the new lips opening, stretching and closing.

'I've been better.' He didn't ask after my well-being. There was a pause. He seemed to be waiting for a response. Unable to think of one, I let it be. Eventually, he said, 'I'm coming round.'

'You can't!' There was no space between the thought and the

words. I heard Iain breathing heavily on the other end of the line.

'What d'you mean, I can't?' Then, more aggressively, 'I've as much right as you to be in that house.'

I watched myself twine my hair around my face, concealing it. Then I drew a voice from behind its curtain. A cool, impersonal voice.

'It's not convenient, Iain.'

'Convenient?' Iain spluttered. 'But I need to see you!'

'What for?'

'Parity.' For a moment I thought he was being obscure. Then I remembered the latest play. Forgetting its title felt somehow reassuring.

'What about it?'

'I've hit a problem. It's all right,' he added, 'Rosalie knows. In fact, she agrees we should talk it over.'

Well, bully for Rosalie. A sudden, unfamiliar sensation. What was it? Gasping and bending over, I recognised it as mirth. I pressed my free hand against my mouth and watched my new eyes goggling in the mirror with the effort of holding back the laughter.

'Jo?' Iain's voice was querulous. 'Are you there?'

With a supreme effort, I pulled myself together. 'Yes. I'm here.'

'So when shall I come round?'

'You can't.'

'What?'

'I said, you can't.'

'But I need to talk!'

I shook my hair back from my face. 'The thing is, Iain,' I said, speaking slowly and clearly, 'it would be a waste of time. Because I have nothing – not a single word – to say to you. Goodbye.' And I replaced the receiver.

The phone rang again, a moment later. And again. Messages were left, which I deleted without listening. I knew he wouldn't come round. He'd recognised the determination in my voice and would not try.

I move to our bedroom – *my* bedroom – and throw on a baggy sweatshirt and Iain's ancient jogging pants, which threaten to fall down. I anchor them in place with one of his old ties. I cannot, however, disguise the face. It emerges from the swathes of old clothing like a phoenix from the ashes.

All right. You win. I burrow in a drawer, pull out a dusty lipstick and draw a slash of red across my lips. *Satisfied?* There is no reply. I suspect that the new me is biding her time. She will not be fooled by this attempt to mollify her.

The doorbell rings. Peering from the window, just in case Iain has been foolhardy enough to attempt a forced entrance, I see the top of Clara's head. I run downstairs, feeling a new lightness that is more emotional than physical.

'Look at you!' Clara is trying to smile, but her face is stark and white and her eyes red-rimmed.

'What's happened?' I give Clara's stiff body a hug and pull her in. She shrugs and moves into the relative darkness of the hall, where she stands as if at a loss.

'Come through. Sit down...' I lead her to the living room. 'I'll make coffee.'

'Got anything stronger?'

At the back of a cupboard I find a bottle, which I decant into a tumbler. Clara sniffs it dubiously.

'Cooking sherry,' I say. 'It's all I've got.'

Clara closes her eyes, downs it in one and places the tumbler on the table. 'I've just come from therapy.'

'Yes?'

'I can't go to work.'

I wait.

'Jo, I've done...' Clara seems to be forcing the words out. 'I've done a terrible thing.'

'What have you done?'

'I kissed him.'

'Who?'

'David.'

For a moment, I can think of nothing to say. 'What happened?'

Clara reaches for the glass, then, realising that it's empty, drops her hand.

'He said I'd have to choose. Between carrying on and…' her tone dips '…*working it through* or… or… ending therapy with him.' She gives a weak smile but her eyes are bereft.

'Which did you decide?'

'I didn't. Couldn't. He said I should think about it. Oh, Jo…' Clara digs her fingers into her palm. 'What shall I do?'

My attention is suddenly caught by our reflection in the large, ornate mirror that was formerly Julia's, over-grand in my comfortable, lived-in room: a bequest I'd unwillingly accepted. I felt the pressure of my mother's expectations each time I looked in it. Clara is a small, hunched figure, her face tight and tense. And beside her is my own unfamiliar face with its lurid yet strangely pleasing lips. I take a deep breath and attempt pragmatism.

'Why don't you look at the pros and cons?'

This seems to calm Clara. She stands and walks to the mantelpiece. 'Yes. Yes. I'll try that.' My heart contracts at her desperation.

'Right. Reasons for staying…' Clara counts on her fingers. 'One, it's the only restful place I know, apart from here. Two. I'm learning about myself. Learning to play. And three…' She raises her head, almost shyly. 'I love being with him. He's… special.' Her face is transfigured. She looks like a child.

'Good reasons.' I wonder about transference. But then, isn't every relationship a kind of transference? 'And the cons?'

Clara drops her head again. 'It can never be the same again. I've ruined it. The… innocence of it.'

'Why did you kiss him?'

'Don't know. I was upset. He took my hand…'

'Is that allowed?'

'Probably not. I don't know.' Clara rubs her fingers along the mantel. 'Dan was right.'

'Dan? How does he come into it?'

'He said I had to control everything.' Clara wipes her fingers on her skirt. 'I didn't realise it, back then. But maybe it's true.'

Dan, with his ease of being. It had always appealed to me. Somehow, though, that very ease had brought out the worst in Clara.

Clara is still speaking. 'Why do I always have to push? To force things? Why can't I just let things be?'

'Maybe,' I say, 'you're afraid you'll never get what you want unless you push for it. Maybe,' I watch Clara's face, 'you're afraid of letting go.'

Clara stiffens. 'Letting go? Can you imagine what would happen at ProDoCo if I let go? Alix would be on my job in an instant.' The old, militant Clara is back. 'I have to be strong. It goes with the territory...'

'It sounds as if you brought the territory into your relationship with Dan. And into therapy too.'

Conflicting expressions chase across Clara's face like cloud shadows passing over land. Eventually, she says, 'I can't be seen to be weak. Letting go is weak.'

'Sometimes...' I am back, for a moment, outside the Davina Lucas School, with The Voice whispering in my ear '...it takes more courage to surrender.' I stand. 'I'm going to make coffee. Want some?'

Clara nods and follows me to the kitchen. As if she can't bear to be left alone. I fill the kettle and spoon instant coffee into mugs. Clara fiddles with the dishcloth.

'Anyway,' she says, 'I can't change the way I am, can I?'

I pour milk into the mugs, add sugar.

'I mean,' Clara drops the dishcloth and picks up a scourer, 'I'm a fighter. Aren't I?'

'Fighting's what you do. Not who you are.'

'That's what *he* says.' Clara is rubbing the scourer over her palm, back and forth. 'Who am I then?'

'You're a woman, for a start.' Everywhere I turn, I see the lips. Now they're reflecting back at me from the surface of the kettle, scarlet on steel. Clara mutters something. The kettle, boiling, obscures her words.

'What did you say?'

'Never felt like one.' Clara's eyes are fixed on the scourer.

Now we're getting somewhere. It feels easier, somehow, to talk here in the kitchen. Women's territory. 'Never? Not even with Dan?'

Clara shakes her head. 'I was beginning to feel… something. With David.' The kettle clicks off, steam billowing. I unplug it slowly, drawing out the process. 'What did you feel?'

'Soft. Full…' Clara's face is pink. 'Frightening.'

She moves abruptly away from the sink, tossing the scourer into the washing-up bowl.

'Get a move on,' she says as she grabs the kettle from me and pours water sloppily into the mugs, shoving one towards me. By the time I've picked it up, Clara is out of the kitchen. I follow her into the living room. She is standing gazing out of the French windows at the grey garden.

The soft sound of rain on the glass is like an invitation. I move to join her. A light mist is falling, whispering of still-distant spring.

'So, what now?'

'I don't know. I really don't know.' Clara's face is stricken. 'Maybe,' she says, as if trying to convince herself, 'I don't need to know. Like you said, there's no need to push things. Maybe it's best not to make a decision right now.'

Maybe she's just putting off the inevitable.

I move to the fireplace, automatically looking in the mirror for the old Jo. The new one flashes a challenging, lipsticked grin.

Maybe we both are.

PART THREE

you kissed me with your body
your red mouth
you set a fire inside my soul
crazy ruby flames fanning my desire
then you turned and put it out
left me talking to the smoke
strip me down, love
tear my hope away like petals
love me, love me not, love
strip me down

Extract from WATER INTO FIRE
Music and lyrics by Pete Street
© Flame Records

JO

I pull back the curtains, yawning. The sun, albeit a weak, winter sun, makes me squint. Down in my garden, sadly neglected, the ground is dark and ridged and encrusted with frost. But the ice on the window is melting, dribbling down the pane. I glance at my watch. Eight o'clock. A long day ahead, beginning with a cut. This time – thank God – the painless kind. The hairdresser is booked for ten.

Lisa and the crew call it, in reverential tones, The Reveal. Not a particularly apt title, in my opinion. More of a cover-up, surely, than a revelation? I am to be coloured and conditioned, sprayed with fake tan, slathered in make-up, dressed and displayed. I will be pampered and prinked and polished, pushed on to a makeshift catwalk in a ProDoCo studio and opened to the public. The Public: that same anonymous body who – was it just ten weeks ago? – pronounced me to be elderly and ugly. Young people mostly, chosen for their likelihood to over-age me. To judge me from their own comfortable vantage point of *it'll never happen to us.*

And now? In the bathroom, as I insert the new, cerulean-blue contact lenses, I wonder what they will see. Who they will see. Each time I look, the mirror seems to offer a different reflection. I've become a chimera. A wild and fanciful thing, assembled from many different parts.

Take these eyes. For decades they've been kept behind glass. Now, exposed, they start out of my face, wide-open as a child's. In contrast, my greying hair, uncut since that disastrous dinner with Iain, provides a limp and straggling backdrop for the pulled-up, stretched face. This witch's hair will be condemned, shorn and dunked in chemicals later this morning. I have no idea what they plan to do.

Goodbye hair, I whisper to it.

I load paste on to my toothbrush and clean my teeth. White and even, they belong to some American chat-show host. They make me look too healthy. They emphasise the plump redness of my lips, which have been injected with filler. Even though the swelling has subsided, the lips jump into stark relief against the pallor of my skin. They are as incongruous as the protruding breasts, which draw attention to themselves, unlike my familiar slouching pair.

The new me. I still cannot link this face and this body with any sense of self. They intrigue me and fascinate me, but they are not me. After today I plan to ignore them. After today, no one will care about them. They will be an irrelevance compared with the new self growing inside.

By this evening, it will all be over. No more crew recording my every move and my every word. No more Magician with his dry, professional hands and cool eyes. And no more holding my breath as I think about Alix poised to steal Clara's career. By this evening, my part in *The Making of Her* will be over. They will have what they wanted of me: a body that has been transformed for the entertainment of their audience. A body of information to be fed into machines, edited and transmitted. The end of the story.

And yet… I frown. The moths are back in my chest, fluttering and skittering.

What are you telling me? I ask The Voice. *I'm listening. Speak to me.*

There is, for the present, no reply. Just that familiar, shimmering, queasy beating. But I will keep listening. Such signs are to be ignored at my peril.

PETE

He fingers his jacket.

Smooth and black, early 90s. Perfect cut. Perfect fit, still, which is some comfort in view of the charade ahead.

His hand strays to his jaw. Also smooth. He's shaved with care, as he always does.

Jongo got him an electric shaver for Christmas. It's still in its box in the bathroom cabinet. Poncy convenience machine for a poncy commercial existence. He prefers the razor. The slow, regular rhythms of the foamy brush. The uncertainty of never quite knowing if he'll keep his skin.

He pulls the watch from his pocket and flips open the glass. Seven-twenty-five. Jongo and the limo'll be here any minute. Sooner it's over, sooner he'll be back here. How the fuck did he get talked into this?

He wanders to the window. The guitar, propped against his chair, calls to him. Time for a quick play? His fingers itch for the safety of the strings. He reaches for it, but his mobile is ringing. That'll be Jongo already outside.

'Yeah?'

There's some kind of interference on the line. *'Gwaaaaa-ffshhtaaaw!'*

He holds the mobile away from his ear, then listens again. 'Who's there?'

A cacophony of coughing.

'It's me.' Jongo. 'I'm took ill. Wi' the *influenza*.' Another gargantuan sneeze. 'Sorry, lad.'

A slow, pleasurable realisation. He doesn't have to go. He pulls off his shades. 'OK. Look after it. The cold.'

'Influenza. I'm *dying*, man. The car'll be there in five. Are ye ready?'

'Not going without you.'

A symphony of throat-clearing, followed by a trumpeting snort. 'You're going, laddie. Ed'll tek care of you. No arguments.'

'I'm not.'

There's a long pause. Deadlock. Jongo's left it up to the wire on purpose so he'll have to go through with it. *Tough*. He's about to cut the connection when Jongo says, 'I told him.'

'Who?' But his heart is jumping in his chest.

'Jasper. He'll be watching it on the satellite.'

Shit.

'Are ye going to let him down? Are ye going to *let yoursel' down?*'

The entryphone buzzes: Ed and the limo.

'Go on, laddie. You deserve it.'

I'm getting my just deserts, that's for sure.

Jongo's voice is fading. 'Talk to you later, lad. Enjoy it.'

'I won't.'

He thrusts the shades back over his eyes and prepares for purgatory.

JO

The dress is dazzling. Accustomed to wearing washed-out woollens, bulky sweatshirts or safe, slimming black, I almost refuse it. I cannot imagine, in my former life, even contemplating such a dress. Plunging at the front, exposing the new breasts almost to the nipple, the dress is crimson, shiny and silky. The material whispers down my body, clinging to its curves. The colour is picked up in the new, spiky red hair, in the glossy scarlet lips and in the highest heels I've ever worn. Shoes for posing. Again, red. Like those shoes in the fairy-tale which danced the wearer to death. Just looking at them makes my calves ache.

Gary zooms in for a close-up of the shoes. Of my legs. He looks at me directly now and with some degree of interest. This is unnerving. But then, it's all unnerving and, I suppose, comes with the territory. I ponder these things as an anthropologist might survey some fascinating but far-removed tribal behaviour. Other people's reactions have nothing to do with me. They are simply an instinctive response to the smokescreen Sarah Miller, testimony to Marcus's magic, a woman who bears no more relation to who I am than a cardboard cut-out resembles a living, breathing person. Sarah can pout and preen. She can spill her new, ripe breasts into the world but she is only a product: a perfect product which ticks all the boxes.

'Thank you, Sarah. Fabulous. Have a break.' Clara looks exhausted. She has been pouring black coffee down her throat all day and is tense and irritable. I asked her earlier if she'd done anything about therapy.

'No. I haven't,' she said, her eyebrows pushing together. 'I've too much else on my plate.' Clara, I suspect, is feeling the effects of life without David, but is too proud, or too shamed, to make an appointment to see him.

As the ProDoCo coffee machine defecates a grey, oily liquid into a plastic cup, I sense myself being scrutinised. None of the crew appears to be looking my way. Clara and Gary are in a huddle at the other end of the studio, muttering about shots. Lisa is scribbling intently, tucking an escaping curl behind her ear. Bill is talking at one of the young sparks, who turns his head aside to yawn. Only Marcus, immaculate in a grey tailored suit and blue-striped shirt, is looking in my direction, though his eyes appear to be on something – or someone – behind me.

'Wow.' I turn to find Alix standing inside the doorway under the exit sign. '*Don't* you look incredible.'

Alix is dressed entirely in white, like a marble statue. Her eyes scan my body, then return to my face. The moths in my chest are skittering furiously. What's she doing here?

Before I can frame a reply, Marcus joins us. He takes Alix's hand and kisses it exaggeratedly. There's something intimate under the flamboyant gesture. Is the affair still going on? He looks from Alix to me, his smile self-satisfied, as if we are both his creations.

'Snow White,' he says, smiling at Alix. Then he nods more distantly at me, 'and Rose Red.' Alix's cat-got-the-cream smile curls across her face.

'I suppose,' she says, her eyes running once more down my body, 'that you hardly recognise yourself?' Her own body leans provocatively towards Marcus.

I don't reply. It's still extraordinary to me that I no longer feel the need to respond in the old, insecure ways. Sarah Miller's face and body serve as a magical foil, providing cover, allowing me to rest safely and silently within.

Alix slants her eyes up at Marcus. 'A tribute to your skills, Marcus. They'll be queuing at your door.'

Marcus's smirk implies that this is already the case. 'Sarah's procedures have been most successful.'

I pick up my cup, about to walk away. After all, they're discussing Sarah, not me.

'I hear,' Alix is saying to Marcus, 'you've been a great success yourself. On camera.'

Marcus flicks a glance at Clara. 'Under the... somewhat trying circumstances.'

I pause.

'Ah,' says Alix, nodding. 'Yes.'

'It would have been different,' says Marcus, 'if *you* were directing.'

There's a distant burst of clapping from the studio next door. Some music awards show, Clara says.

I turn to Marcus. 'On the contrary,' I say, wondering where I've found the nerve, '*The Making of Her* has gone really well. Particularly,' I look at Alix, 'since you left.'

Alix raises a cool eyebrow. Turning from me, she shimmers up at Marcus. 'I wonder if I could have a word? In private?'

'Certainly.' Marcus encircles her shoulder with a casual arm. 'Shall we go into the corridor?'

'No.' Alix's eyes are on Clara. 'Come up to my office. What I have to say is *very* confidential.' Her ice-cold eyes sweep over me. 'Well... Sarah. Good luck for the reveal. I've a feeling you're going to need it.'

'Why?'

Alix delicately taps the side of her nose, then cups her hand and leans towards me as if about to impart a treasured secret.

'Revelations, Sarah,' she whispers, her breath tickling my ear, 'can cut both ways.'

Marcus is holding the door open. Distant, jagged chords stutter from the other studio. I shiver. The moths immolate themselves against my ribs.

*

The man draws attention to himself in spite of his attempts otherwise. He elbows through the crowd, his arms and legs working frantically, like a drowning beetle. His spare black jacket stands out against the rainbow clothes worn by my prospective judges. While they surge towards the catwalk, seeking the best, most visible positions, he seems intent on fighting his way out of the studio.

Hidden in the dusty, curtained backstage area, I watch, fascinated. Here is someone who evidently wishes to escape this media circus. Someone like me. I long to join him. To burrow down among the rapt faces, to move seamlessly and anonymously in his black wake towards the exit.

The crowd is irritated. A few turn to stare at him, whispering. The shades mark him out as an alien. His thin face is intense under a mop of springy grey hair. He looks neither to the right nor the left, refusing to acknowledge them. He doesn't belong, any more than I do. I find myself creating possible scenarios to explain his presence.

He had a row with his girlfriend, or his wife. He came along reluctantly, to please her, and she said something or did something to piss him off and now he's walking out on her. Or he's a claustrophobic, a sociophobe. Deliberately facing his fear, only to find the reality overwhelming…

He is almost through now, pushing past the stragglers at the back. I silently urge him on, and feel the relief of the open space as he reaches the perimeter of the studio. He is wearing trainers under the formal black trousers. They flash white as he walks, like a sneer. I step forward to get a better view.

'Jo!' It's Clara, grabbing my arm and yanking me back behind the curtain. 'What the hell d'you think you're doing? They mustn't see you until The Reveal.'

'Sorry. Sorry. I wasn't thinking.'

Then Clara grins, a flash of the old, cynical Clara. 'Hey, it's only television. Hardly life and death.'

'Still,' I say, 'it was stupid of me. I was miles away.'

Clara gazes down at the over-excited crowd. 'Look at them. All agog for their five seconds of fame.' She sighs and fans herself with her schedule. 'We'll be ready to go any minute. You know what you have to do?'

I nod. 'I wait until Marcus announces me, then I walk on stage, turn, and go down the ramp on to the catwalk, towards camera…'

'And don't forget to smile!'

'I'll do my best. Grimace, anyway. These shoes are killing me. And they throw me off balance.'

'Never mind,' says Clara. 'In a couple of hours you'll be back at home in your slippers and it'll all be over. At long last.'

Bill inserts himself between us, adjusting my radio microphone. Lisa bustles up. 'Clara, are we ready to go? Gary says the natives are getting restless.'

'Right. I'm coming. Is Marcus ready?'

'He is. Smug bastard.'

Clara grins and turns to me. 'Good luck. You look incredible.'

Incredible indeed. It seems unbelievable that I, Jo Coe, am standing here, practically naked in killer heels and this wispy excuse for a dress, about to be revealed to the mob below, who seethe and whisper and giggle. Each of them longs to be in close-up, in the spotlight. For this they will gasp and clap and affirm to the attentive camera that Sarah Miller is indeed remade and remodelled. Reborn. Wide-eyed and gullible, they will guess her to be ten, fifteen, even twenty years younger than her biological age. *Incredible.*

In the hubbub of the final preparations, I have almost forgotten Alix. The moths in my chest seek sanctuary, dusty wings folding, tiring now. The floor manager, out by the cameras, calls for quiet. The crowd gradually fall silent, their excited heads bobbing like water coming to the boil. Then, at a cue from Clara up in the studio gallery, Marcus's voice rings out, authoritative but with an unaccountable edge of ice.

'Good evening, everyone. You have been most patient. Here, this evening, we mark the end of a long and transformative journey, which I have been privileged…' he pauses to make his point '…to have been part of.'

Hurry up, Marcus, before I change my mind.

'And now, the moment we've all been waiting for. Please welcome our changeling, the reason we're here tonight. Sarah!'

Stepping out into the spotlight, I meet a wall of frenzied sound, a sea of upturned, obedient faces, shrieking, eager, hands smacking together, lips whistling.

I search beyond them for the beetle man. He is gone.

CLARA

It's over.

The lights are dimmed and the cables are coiled. The shiny catwalk has been dismantled and the studio returned to echoing utilitarian emptiness. The audience has done its job and departed. Even the last, straggling groupies who flirted and shimmied around Gary and his team of sparks have dispersed. Up in the distant capsule of the gallery, a fluorescent light flickers as the studio manager checks the room before leaving too.

Jo is sitting on a rostrum across the studio, her backbone curved and her belly sticking out like a child's. The red shoes pose beside her, one fallen on its side as if giving up the struggle to stay erect. In the scarlet dress, she resembles a weary butterfly. Like the one Clara saw once in a butterfly house. She had gazed, fascinated, as it slowly birthed from an ugly, hanging cocoon, then paused, recovering from the effort, its bright wings drying.

Her limbs feel like bricks and her head aches. *I got through.* Hardly with flying colours, but with the material she needs, which is all that matters. She has thanked the studio crew, shaken Gary's hand, praised Bill and been hugged by Lisa. Marcus disappeared abruptly after lavishing overblown compliments on the crew, ignoring Clara and, oddly, Jo.

Only the editing now and it will be finished. Today is March the first. Saint David's Day. Has he forgotten her already? Has he consigned her to the past: an unfortunate incident, handled as best he could? Clara shakes her head to dismiss him and calls across the studio.

'Jo?'

Jo looks up and flaps her hand in an excuse for a wave. She should be in the dressing room or, better still, in a taxi on her way home. Seems they are both too exhausted to move. Clara sighs and picks up her bag. Her mobile is ringing: an unknown number. She turns it off.

The studio door swings open. Marcus. *Hell.* She thought he'd gone. He stands in the doorway, his off-duty grey jacket slung over one shoulder, his pinstriped shirt still immaculate and his briefcase in hand.

'Clara. A word.' His tone is cold and righteous. He clearly expects her to go to him.

'Yes?'

'There's a problem.' He announces it with a kind of triumph.

'Is there?' She cannot think what it might be. The shots are good, the vox pops conclusive. Marcus's skill has been lauded. Several of the women in the audience have asked for his card. He is staring at her. Familiar irritation prickles.

'What problem?'

He indicates Jo with a dismissive jerk of his great head. 'Elsewhere would be preferable.'

Her heart begins to thud. She struggles to keep a calm face. 'We could go to my office, I suppose.'

Marcus shakes his head. He obviously doesn't want to be on her territory for this, whatever it is. She indicates the gallery. He nods.

'Sarah,' she calls. Jo looks up absently, then straightens and frowns as she registers Marcus. 'Go and get changed, why don't you? I'll see you in the dressing room in a while.'

*

In the gallery, she slides automatically into the director's chair. The banks of monitors are blank and empty, like dead, blind eyes. The desk is littered with used coffee cups, water bottles and marked-up scripts. A title page, *THE MAKING OF HER*, lies discarded on the floor. Someone has been playing a game of hangman on it.

Marcus disdains the vision-mixer's swivel chair and pulls over a producer's seat, which he places directly opposite her. He drapes his jacket over the back and lowers his briefcase on to the floor between them.

'Well?' Clara hears the bravado in her own voice, unconvincing and thin.

'What do you know about Sarah Miller?'

A gunshot question, setting her heart thudding. *Thump, thump, thump.* 'What do you mean?'

Marcus hefts the briefcase on to his knees, clicks it open and pulls out a sheet of paper. He hands it to her. She glances at it.

'A filming release form. Where did you get this?'

He ignores the question and taps the paper with one finger, as if the very touch of it is distasteful to him. 'Perhaps you should pay more attention to such… formalities.' He pulls it from her hands and holds it up in front of her. 'Look at the signature.'

There, at the bottom, is a name. It is not Sarah Miller's.

How did Jo, so meticulous in her deception, forget to sign her fictitious name? How did Marcus get hold of it? Who else knows? The familiar precursors of a flush tighten round her head like a noose.

Marcus sharply withdraws the paper as if he expects her to tear it up and replaces it in his case. 'It would seem that this person – this Jo Coe – has taken part in *The Making of Her* under a false name. Deceived the production staff. Deceived me. Deceived *you*.' His eyes bore into her.

Blood is flooding her face. Menopausal guilt. Why, why did Jo have to stumble, right at the final hurdle? And what now? It would be all too easy to lie: to pretend she knows nothing about the deception. She averts her eyes from Marcus's triumphant face and stares through the thick glass of the gallery window down to the studio floor, where Jo's abandoned shoes sit on the rostrum like Exhibit A for the prosecution. Why keep fighting? And what, anyway, is she fighting for? Her career at ProDoCo? Her pride? Maybe there are things better worth her energy. What was it Jo said as they stood looking out at the soft rain?

Maybe you're afraid of letting go.

A profound weariness drags at her limbs. It takes every ounce of strength to turn back to Marcus. To open her mouth. To draw the breath to say the words.

'She's my best friend.'

There. It's out. Without prevarication or excuses.

Marcus shakes his large head slowly. 'Oh dear. How very... irregular. Not professional of you, Clara.'

Sweat trickles between her breasts. She can smell his salt-sour breath. He is still staring at her.

'Whatever possessed you? You had hundreds of other applicants. Alix tells me you dismissed a very suitable woman whom she found.'

Clara rallies. 'Oh, *Alix* told you. I see. And I wonder who passed on the release form?'

Marcus seems unmoved. 'Alix was doing what she thought best. She suspected something wasn't quite... right about Sarah.'

She swivels away from him. 'For the record, I didn't know it was Jo when she applied. I only found out afterwards.'

'With respect,' he says, without an ounce of it, 'you should have dropped her when you discovered who she was. Why did you continue with this charade and commit what amounts to professional suicide?'

Because she said she needed it so badly...

That's the surface reason. But underneath, something less palatable.

Because I'd have lost face in front of Alix and Richard. Clara dips her head. Marcus is still speaking.

'You really leave me no option but to inform Stan Barforth.'

That's it then. She'll be sacked. Her throat is tight. Nausea churns in her gut. How dare he accuse her of acting unprofessionally? *The Making of Her* would never have existed if he and Stan Barforth didn't frequent the same club. But no one would be interested in that.

'Unless...' Marcus tilts his head, assessing her.

'Unless what?'

He steeples his fingers. 'This situation puts me in a very difficult position. It could reflect on my own probity. Naturally,' he adds, 'I would not wish to be party to any kind of deceit…'

'What are you saying, Marcus?'

Marcus leans back. 'Perhaps it might be better for all concerned if you simply resigned. Gave in your notice for… personal reasons. You could finish *The Making of Her* and leave with your head held high. Your character untarnished. Your fine reputation,' his eyes glint, 'intact.'

He needs *The Making of Her* to go ahead. If she admits to a personal interest, ProDoCo will pull the programme and all Marcus's work will be wasted. All that free publicity down the drain. But if she resigns, it leaves the way clear for Alix to take her job and Marcus still gets his precious hour of glory.

'And how,' she asks, 'do you intend to square that with your so-called probity?'

'Uncomfortable as it may be,' he says, 'I'll endeavour to live with it.'

'And if they find out?'

'I will claim ignorance. Whereas you…' he nods down towards the studio floor, at Jo's shoes, '…would only be able to blame it on her.'

Game, set and match. She waits for the familiar fury to build. It doesn't. There's only barren exhaustion. Somewhere, far back behind her eyes, child's tears threaten.

'Think about it.' Marcus closes the briefcase with a final click. Then he stands, his outsize head blocking the exit sign, and departs.

*

In the dressing room, Jo is sitting upright in her seat, her body taut, her face wiped clean and her feet in her familiar flat shoes. A paper cup of cold tea sits on the worktop in front of her. In the mirror, her eyes dart to meet Clara's.

'What?'

Clara slumps into the only armchair. 'Marcus.'

'What's he done?'

'He knows. About you.'

'How?'

She tells her. Jo's face is stricken. Bruised. 'Clara… Oh, God. I must have been tired. Or distracted. But how did he get hold of the form?'

'Guess.'

Jo winces. 'Alix. She kept hinting. And I saw her coming out of your office, weeks ago. When you were out…'

At therapy. Of course. 'She's probably been going through my filing tray regularly, hoping to find something incriminating.'

There's a burst of applause from the studio next door.

'But look,' Jo is clearly casting around for hope, 'surely Stanley Barforth won't sack you for it? You chose me quite innocently.'

'Think he'll believe that? With Alix and Marcus dripping poison in his ears? Anyway, it's probably just the excuse he's been looking for.'

Jo's fingers are twining, untwining. 'You can't let Marcus blackmail you into resigning! It's not fair. It's…'

'It's a stitch-up.' Clara gives a humourless grin. 'Here we are, the pair of us. Stitched up. You literally. Me metaphorically.'

'What will you do?'

Clara walks to the window. Out in the evening street, a line of black limousines wait to carry away the music award winners. Their drivers loiter in groups, muffled in their jackets, smoking, stamping and joking.

'What can I do? If I call Marcus's bluff and carry on with *The Making of Her*, he'll just wait until after it's broadcast and then drop me in it. If I resign, I can walk out with my reputation not entirely wrecked. I can get another job. Although…' she remembers her long-ago conversation with Richard '…I'm probably over the hill.'

Jo stands abruptly, as if she can't bear to be still any longer. 'You can't just give up! You're a fighter, Clara, remember?'

Clara draws two lines with her finger on the misted window. 'Used to be. Frankly, I'm too tired. Maybe it's time to stop. Retire gracefully.' She hates the words, even as she says them. But what's the alternative?

'And hand your job to Alix?'

Stop being devil's advocate, Jo. It won't work. 'Yes. Let her have it. It's only ever been a matter of time.'

Jo is staring at her. 'You're exhausted. Don't make a decision right now. Think about it.'

'That's Marcus's advice.' Clara adds a circle to her drawing.

Jo drains her tea and throws the paper cup in a bin. 'You could go away. For the weekend, I mean. I could come with you. We can talk it through…'

Clara reaches for Jo's hand, briefly. 'Thanks. But I can't face any more discussion.' She turns back to the window and resumes her drawing, adding legs and arms to the stick figure.

Jo says, 'I'm so sorry.'

'Don't be. It would have happened anyway, sooner or later. This was just a good excuse for sooner.'

Dinner jackets and gowns are spilling on to the street, laughing and exclaiming at the cold. Superimposed on them, she sees the reflection of Jo's scarlet dress suspended from a hook on the opposite wall.

'I need to go home,' she says. 'Will you be OK?'

'Of course,' Jo replies over-brightly, though her eyes are gleaming with tears.

'I might actually go away. Get some perspective.'

'Where?'

'God knows. Doesn't really matter, so long as it's a long way from here.'

'You won't do anything…'

'No. I just need to put some space between me and this whole bloody mess.'

Jo moves hesitantly towards her. 'Clara,' she says, 'a hug?'

She feels Jo's arms around her, but she cannot relax or let go. Her spine feels frozen. Jo reaches to smooth her fringe, like a mother. 'Go away then,' she says, 'if it feels right.'

Clara nods. She rubs away the hanged figure on the windowpane, then turns abruptly and walks out.

*

The phone is trilling in the house as she lets herself in. She leaves it to ring.

The first thing she does is to strip off her dank clothes. She twists the shower head to maximum pressure and steps in, the needle-sharp jets reddening her skin. Then she washes, harshly and rapidly, needing to clean out every crevice: to rub and scrub herself raw to rid herself of it all.

Dry, she hurries into the bedroom and begins throwing clothes into a case. The phone rings again. Whoever it is can wait. They can all wait. Now that she has decided, there's an overwhelming need to get out. To disappear. Though she has no idea as yet where to go. Who cares? She'll just jump on the first train and see where it takes her.

She empties her bag on to the bed, deciding what to take. Keys, money, credit cards, paracetamol, tissues.

Dan's box.

And as if the memory of Dan calls up his twin tormentor, she suddenly smells David – fresh cotton and citrus – and feels the warmth of his hands around hers. A deep and visceral yearning gouges a hole in her gut.

The phone display is winking, telling her she has a message. Ignoring it, she picks up the receiver and dials. *I promise, if he answers, that I'll see him. Sort it out.* The phone rings and rings. Eventually she hears the recorded voice of his receptionist. What is she thinking of? It's eleven at night. He'll be tucked up at home now, with Jessica. She's tempted to try him there, but the prospect of Jessica picking up the phone drives her back to the bedroom. She picks up Dan's box.

Big, strong, independent Clara. Running to a man when the going gets tough. She drops the box into her bag, hating herself for it.

She turns automatically to pick up her laptop and put it in her case. She stops. What, after all, does she need it for now? Instead she pulls Jo's journal from its drawer and stuffs that in – for company. She remembers the bag-lady, trundling along with her case of books, offering strangers improving literature. Maybe that'll be her, one day. A batty old woman with a bag full of detritus. Nowhere to go, nothing to do.

Do-be-do-be-do.

PETE

He carefully places the statuette on the cistern, unzips his fly and pees. A stream of relief, smelling strong and umber. His head still rings with the clatter and roar of applause, the confusing cross-talk and the resonating bodies. People had approached him without his say-so. Too close. They had pushed him for words he refused to deliver and clapped their hands on his shoulder, their lips leaving soft wet imprints on his cheeks.

When he had broken away from them and stumbled by mistake into that other studio, panic had hit him all over again as he fought through hot flesh, cheap scent, stale lager breath and sharp elbows, cursing Jongo for blackmailing him into coming, cursing himself for allowing it.

The lavatory flushes. He zips and reaches for the statuette. It's cold and angular in his hand. A lifetime achievement award. An icon for an icon.

What if I just leave it? He imagines the scene: some bloke coming in for a crap and finding it. Taking it home to the wife. *Look what I got, Marlene. Pete Street. Remember him?* He clinks the statuette back on to the cistern and turns to go. Hears the soft sound of flat shoes in the corridor outside. Feels his shoulders tighten. Someone's coming in.

He pulls the cubicle door closed and finds the bolt. It won't budge. He turns, lowers the seat slowly, silently, and sits. He hopes there's nothing shitty on it. His suit. Better to wait it out, though. The thing about being an icon is that people think they have the right to accost you, even in the toilet. To say something – anything – so they can take the encounter home with them. Share it with the lads over a beer. *I met Pete Street. Yeah, really. Getting on a bit. What is he now, fifty?*

Sixty? Sharp suit, though.

The bloke seems in no hurry. What's he doing? Hanging about in front of the mirror, probably. Wanting to use the khasi. Well, tough. Two can play the waiting game.

There's a sigh. Then, ricocheting off the tiles, a scream. High pitched. A woman.

Bloody hell. The air's twanging, echoing the scream back. What if someone's dragged her in here to rape her? He holds his breath, his ears straining towards the sound. No. The woman's alone. And he can sense, as he's been able to all his life, every nuance of her emotion.

Stress. Frustration. Despair. She's venting it because she needs to. Because she knows it's time to let go. He wishes suddenly that he could join her. He could stand out there beside her and together they could howl at the moon, at God, at every fucking pain inflicted. Howl until it's out, gone, clean. But he waits, hearing her fist thumping on the mirror, wincing for her knuckles, until the keening cries wane and stop and there's only jagged breathing. He senses satisfaction. He finds he has been holding his own breath, and slowly, carefully lets it go.

Then – too bloody late to stand and block it – she's there, pushing at the door. It swings sharply open, brushing at his knees.

JO

I rest my elbows on the basin. I feel exhilarated. Liberated. My fingertips buzz with energy as if I have expelled every last trace of Sarah Miller from my soul, along with my own guilty part in Clara's betrayal.

I resented that guilt and the unwelcome return of the old, pathetic Jo shouldering everyone's share of the responsibility. Instinct propelled me down the corridor to the toilet. I didn't know whether I would throw up, cry or smash something. In fact I let rip, from the core of myself. Clara's defeat; Marcus's machinations; Alix's revenge. *Deeper.* Iain's woundings; his affair with Rosalie. *Deeper.* Julia's criticisms; the rejection of my writing. Of myself. *Deeper.* I screamed. I smashed my fist against the mirror. I wailed.

And at last it is done. My throat is sore, my hand is bruised and I am free of it all. Slowly, I raise my head. The face in the mirror is flushed. My eyes are sparkling. I look like an Amazon, a warrior woman. And I need to pee. I push open the door of a cubicle and freeze.

A man – the beetle man – is sitting on the toilet. He looks older, close-to. Deep lines run from his nostril to his jaw. A silver bird dangles from one earlobe. Behind him on the cistern stands a golden statuette in the shape of a guitar. My first, obscure thought is – *Why is he in the Ladies?* My next is – *He heard it all.*

'What the –?' My voice is sharp with mortification. 'Get out!'

He stands, slowly, brushing at the seat of his trousers. He must be drunk, or else he's some kind of pervert, hiding in the Ladies toilets and spying on women. He's still wearing the shades. How affected is that?

'If you want.' His voice is guttural. Dusty. Then: 'Why were you screaming?'

I retreat to the basin. 'I've every right to... to express myself as I see fit.'

He shrugs. 'Yeah, fine. Though doing it in the Gents khasi wouldn't be *my* first choice.'

The Gents? For a moment, I doubt myself. Then I stride to the door, pull it open and point at the female symbol. His head follows my gesture.

'Well?' I wait for his apology. It doesn't come. He simply stands, his face blank. 'Maybe you should look before you come blundering into the Ladies.'

'The Ladies? Fuck.' He runs a hand through the mop of silver curls, disconcerted.

And then I understand.

'I'm sorry,' I say. 'I didn't realise.'

His face stiffens. He stuffs his hands into his trouser pockets and glares at a point somewhere to the right of me.

'What?' His tone is provocative.

'That you are...' I hesitate.

'Blind?' The word is shot at me, as if by a sniper.

I nod, then remember. 'Yes.'

He is silent. His shoulders are hunched as if he is shielding himself. Why doesn't he have a dog, or a white stick?

'I saw you,' I say. 'Earlier. Fighting your way through the crowd in the studio. I wondered what you were doing there.'

'Got lost. Bloody Jongo,' he says, obscurely. His head is down. He is probably half an inch shorter than me.

'Jongo?'

'My manager.'

So he's a musician. Or a singer. 'Should I recognise you?'

'How the fuck do I know?'

Strangely, I am not offended by his tone. I turn to the basin and run water over my wrists.

'You screamed.' He is not to be diverted. The words are quiet, understated. I focus on drying my hands. Does he think I'll tell him?

'I'd had enough.'

'Of?'

'Of feeling bad for other people.'

'You're feeling bad for me.' It's a statement, dry and unwrapped. I consider this.

'No. Why should I? I don't know you.'

He cocks his head like a dog hearing a distant whistle, as if he's straining to hear my thoughts and ascertain their integrity. Eventually, he nods, once. He roots in his jacket pocket, pulls out an old pocket watch, opens the glass and runs his fingers over the hands.

'The car'll be waiting.'

My heart contracts for him. For his pride, for his need to find a formal reason to leave. I reach out and touch his arm. A mistake. He flinches away and turns for the door.

'Goodbye…' The words are thrown over his departing shoulder as he fingers his way through the door and out, robbing me of any opportunity to reply. I stare at the closing door, feeling, for some reason, bereft. Was there something I wanted to say to him? Too late now. I turn to the cubicle to pee and see the statuette on the cistern.

PETE

It takes him some time to gain the road outside. He should've kept Ed with him. The minder from the YUKs was flaky. Unreliable. Too bloody star-struck to stay at his side once the award was presented and the limelight lost.

The encounter with the woman has thrown him, and not just because of its unexpectedness. He walks twice past the ProDoCo entrance before the man on reception asks if he can help. He hears the snap of defensiveness in his own voice as he replies. Without, thank Christ, laying a helpful finger on him, the man accompanies him to his waiting car.

'Here, Mr Street, sir.' He hears the car door opening, fumbles in his jacket pocket for a note and shoves it at the man. Then he tumbles into the blessed, safe interior of the car.

'Home, Mr Street?' Ed's breath is pungent with garlic. Pete sighs. 'Yeah.'

The engine starts. He feels its comforting vibration under his backside. Then the door jerks open again and cold air hits his face, together with a waft of familiarity he can't place. Someone launches themselves into the seat beside him, panting. For a moment he fears a fan, some overenthusiastic groupie. Or a pap. They hang around till all hours in the hope of a good shot.

'Out!' Sweat starts on his skin. Ed cuts the engine and turns to remonstrate with the intruder. 'Now, lady…'

Lady? He sniffs. Yes. It's her. She's shoving something heavy into his hands.

'You left this. I didn't know if…' Her breath is coming in gasps. He is about to tell her to keep it, to take it home with her. Make a good story to tell her old man. Then:

'I thought you might not want it. So I waited a bit, to see if you came back for it. And then I wondered if perhaps you might want it, after all, when you saw it… *oh!*'

To his surprise, he finds himself smiling. 'I *see*,' he replies, pointedly. There's a silence. Then he hears her laugh. He runs his fingertips over the statuette. Finds the shape of the guitar: its long slim neck, the beautiful swelling curves and the tiny dip of the waist between.

'Mr Street?' There's a nudge in Ed's voice.

'It's OK.' He wonders if she'd like a lift, but he can't bring himself to offer it.

'I'm Jo. Jo Coe.' He senses a hand being proffered, but he pretends he doesn't know. He hugs the statuette.

'Pete.' Even to his ears, his voice is gruff and unwelcoming.

'I know. I read it on the award.'

'Joko. You a singer?'

'No.' She sounds surprised, then laughs. 'It's Jo for Josephine. Last name Coe.' There's a pause. 'It's not really mine. The name.'

She's talking in riddles. Maybe he'll ask her. Maybe he won't. The silence between them lengthens. Finally:

'Well…'

'D'you…?'

Their voices cancel one another out. She laughs again. The laugh is like the beginning of a tune. *Uh-uh-uh*, on a rising cadence.

'Want a drink?' He cannot believe he's said it.

'All right.' She sounds calm. Amused.

He takes her to a bar off the Bayswater Road. Nothing fancy. A place he goes, because they're cool with who he is. Threadbare leatherette seats, smell of fags, fug and old beer and something tinny and retro on the jukebox. She has red wine. He has his usual.

'Don't you drink?'

'Not anymore.' He hugs the tall glass and hears the ice clipping the rim. She probably thinks he's an alkie. Who cares? He finds that he does. 'Got done. For drink driving. Long time ago.'

'So you had your sight, then?'

'How I lost it.' *And my life.* He prays she isn't looking at him sympathetically. 'Don't fret,' he finds himself saying. 'It happened.'

'I wasn't,' she replies, and he believes her.

He hasn't sat in a bar and talked with a woman for years. Talked with anyone, come to that. Except Jongo, on the rare occasion Jongo drags him out. And he always regrets that, since Jongo's idea of a night out is some sleazy nightclub with a pounding, crappy sound system and a horde of dancing, high-pitched women he's glad he can't see.

He must make conversation. Ask her about herself. He finds, anyway, that he wants to know.

'What do you do at ProDoCo?' Is she a producer? A make-up artist?

'I don't.' She pauses. He waits. 'Actually, I was taking part in a show.'

'Actress?'

'No.' She seems reluctant to say more.

After a while, she asks him the time. He likes that. The pocket watch tells them it's past midnight. She says:

'Today's a special day.'

'Yeah?'

'My first day of freedom.'

'I'll drink to that.' He raises his glass and feels hers meet it. He wonders if she's just got divorced. He won't ask. She'll tell him what she tells him. People do. Strangers. Because he's blind.

They're ringing last orders and the air is full of leaving. He asks if she wants another drink. She hesitates, then says no. He wants to take her hand but fears she'll think he's asking for assistance rather than intimacy. The limo's waiting outside. They sit decorously together on the back seat, not touching. The scent of her body is stronger now, because he knows it. She gives Ed her address. He repeats it, silently, to himself. Outside her house, they sit for a moment without speaking. He will not ask. Wants to, but will not. Instead he mutters,

'See you.'

Instead of replying, he feels her mouth on his cheek, smelling of lipstick and warm wine. Instinctively he turns to it, searching, and finds thin air. She's gone.

CLARA

The cab smells of sweat and old vomit, which compete with the stench from a pine air-freshener dangling from the mirror. The driver has talk radio chattering out of a speaker located somewhere behind her head: *My girlfriend's seeing someone else and...*

She opens the window. The incoming air isn't much fresher, though infinitely colder. Of course the driver chooses this moment to begin a conversation.

'Off somewhere nice, are you?'

She has no idea. Paddington is the nearest station. She may end up sleeping there, since it's gone eleven. Undeterred by her silence, the driver's telling her about his forthcoming holiday in Tenerife. She allows his voice to lull her and gazes out of the window at the sooty streets, garishly streaked by shivering headlights in icy puddles; at the late-night punters emptying the bars, warm beery breath smoking around them as they head towards the clubs. For an unnerving moment she sees a woman who looks like Jo sitting in a pub window talking to a man in shades. Hallucinations now.

She has never known tiredness like this. It has caught and smothered her. Her head weighs seven tons and thoughts swoop around its heavy cavern, going nowhere. Maybe she'll just sit here in this cab all night. Let him drive her around and talk at her till dawn.

Too late. The taxi is filtering up Cab Alley outside the station and jerking to a halt. She knows better than to ask for help with her bag. She hauls it out and passes a crumpled note through the window.

Paddington is greenish-yellow. The air, the light, the sound are all the same colour. The retail outlets are closed and shuttered, except for a solitary coffee booth and an all-night supermarket where travellers and tramps pick over tired sandwiches and glossy magazines. A pair of matching policemen patrol the forecourt, routing drunks and junkies from their patch. A bedraggled pigeon pecks around the plastic seats. Under the departures board, where the digital clock shows eleven-thirty, Clara hauls her bag off her shoulder and watches it subside heavily on the tiled floor.

The few trains displayed are mostly local. Why did she come? Why didn't she wait until tomorrow? Because she can't stop. Can't wait. Frenetic, exhausted energy is racing round her body and brain. She has to stay on the move. David would probably say it's her way of staying in control. He would probably be right.

She pulls out her mobile, dials Jo's number. Turned off. She'll be home by now, curled up in bed, her ordeal over.

She scans the departures board. The only train going further than Reading is a sleeper to Penzance, departing in fifteen minutes. But Cornwall is Dan's territory. She hesitates.

On the other hand, it is as far south as it is possible to go and the thought of a sleeper is attractive. She can rest while being carried along. A couple pass her, bickering quietly. The woman is wearing a cashmere coat and matching scarf but is complaining about the cold, teetering on too-high heels and using his arm to balance herself. He is wheeling a trolley piled with luggage. Clara hefts her bag to her shoulder and wills her legs to catch up with them.

'Excuse me…' She touches the woman's arm and sees her eyes momentarily register suspicion, her hands tightening on her handbag, then relaxing as she realises that Clara poses no threat. 'Are you catching the sleeper to Penzance?'

The woman nods. 'Though we're actually going to St Ives.'

'St Ives?' Dan. Where he is.

The man says, 'It's on the way. You have to get off at St Erth and change.'

She relaxes. That's all right, then. She can get a ticket to Penzance, go right to the end of the line. She will sit on the train as it glides through St Erth and onwards, leaving Dan and the past in its wake.

In Penzance, she will browse the galleries – there must be galleries – and eat seafood in select bistros. She will contemplate her future alone and in peace.

'Can I get on it without a reservation?'

'It may be fully booked.' The woman wants the warmth of the train.

The man is eyeing his watch. 'Best get a move on, if you want to find out. It's going in ten minutes.'

She heads for the ticket office. There's a single berth, second-class, still available. She buys a ticket to Penzance. All the way.

*

In the womb of the carriage, she pulls the blind down and removes her clothes. Then she gets into the bed, with its heavy tartan blanket and pristine sheets. The responsibility of movement is taken from her. She surrenders to the steady motion, falling into sleep as if into a deep well.

She wakes, as she usually does, in the early hours. It is hot, or more likely she is. Pushing away the blanket, she lies for a while, eyes open. The darkness of the carriage is all-encompassing. The train rocks on, threading its way through southern towns and cities she's never visited. Never wished to visit. She leaves London on rare and reluctant occasions, when filming forces her out.

She is wide awake. It seems somehow inappropriate to switch on the light. She crawls out of bed and fiddles with the blind, at first succeeding only in pulling it further down. Then, with a plastic hiss, it shoots up.

The sea is right beside her. For a moment she stiffens and draws back. But it is a calm sheet of the palest grey, glinting, stretching forever and lit by slivers of stars in a wide, black pinprick sky. The solidity of, presumably, cliffs bulks far away to her right. There is nothing else. No ship, no bird, no person. A wild darkness, keeping its secrets close.

Out over the horizon drifts a bank of cloud. At the edges it is suffused with light. And then the cloud opens to reveal a huge pale silver orb hanging low in the sky, turning the sea to mother-of-pearl.

She pulls the blanket from the bed and wraps it round her, its hairy coarseness scratching her naked skin. Like a man's body against her own. She cannot break away from the window. She feels compelled to stand here, immolated in moonlight, for as long as it takes.

*

As the train begins its steady approach to St Erth station, she is ready. She knew, really, in spite of her equivocations, that she would come here: has known since she tipped Dan's wooden box on to her bed. Together with the bickering couple and a few others, she steps down on to the dark platform. The cold morning air slaps her in the face, smelling of salt and gulls.

*

The little train to St Ives trundles along the branch line, halting at alien-sounding places: Lelant Saltings. Carbis Bay. She gazes out of the window and sees her own reflection in the dark glass – a yellow face, unfamiliar and drained.

A lighthouse winks far away: Godrevy, probably. She remembers Dan describing this very journey to her, his Irish accent becoming stronger in the telling of it. It had been his first trip to St Ives and she'd been too busy, and unwilling, to go with him.

'God, Clara, if you would have only seen it. The light. And the sand was white… well, the palest dove-colour. And the sea. Translucent it was, turquoise green, and an old grey seal there was too, like a moving rock…'

Typical Dan. He always found the poetry in things. His eyes were permanently creased from all his looking. He had been so fired up when he returned. Full of plans. She would bet they didn't come to much. He probably spends his days contentedly sitting on the beach, knocking out the odd table for tourists.

And why not? David's voice. Mild and open-minded.

Why not indeed? Dan never knew the meaning of stress. Relaxation was built into the foundations of his character. Or maybe it was to do with his age. He was, after all, ten years younger than her. He will be just forty now.

She shivers, even though the heater by her feet is gamely pumping air into the carriage. She is fifty. Ten whole, stressful years older than him. It's seven years since she last saw him. She is tempted not to get out when the little train reaches St Ives but to wait, head down, until it sets off back to where it came from and then jump on the first mainline train, Penzance or Paddington. To pretend she never came. What, after all, has she come for? What possible good can come of it?

'Ticket, ma'am?' The conductor is standing over her. She scrabbles in her bag for money. Her fingers bump against Dan's box. She retrieves her wallet and buys a return. When the conductor moves on, she places the box on the table. It sits, full of its secrets, on the quivering Formica surface. It's a poor excuse for this trip. She picks it up, gives it a half-hearted shake and slips her thumbnail, as a lever, into the crack. Nothing budges.

Damn. She drops it back into her bag and sits, biting at the thumbnail. The train is slowing now, drawing into St Ives station. Automatically, she reaches for her laptop case. Then, with a shock… Of what? Disappointment?… she remembers that she has left her laptop at home. And Dan's address is on it.

JO

I chose the new journal because it was red. The colour of blood. Of birth. The colour of the new hair, the dress and those shoes.

Nature abhors a vacuum. I emptied myself, and he came in...

Not literally, I think, blushing. I cross out '*myself*' and substitute '*my life*'.

It is seven-thirty in the morning. I haven't slept. I haven't even been upstairs. When I got home last night, I wrapped myself in the old throw and, with another glass of wine – rich, red and tasting of ripe berries – I lay on the couch and ran through the previous day's events, moment by moment. Saving the best till last.

Of course, I will never meet Pete Street again. It was a fleeting encounter and all the more magic for being so. He didn't get my number or even ask me to call him. He just said *See you*, in that laconic, gravelly way. Which, of course, he never will. That's why I kissed his cheek. He gave me the freedom to do so. He kept a lot of space around himself. And I was drawn into it.

I think of my first sexual encounter with Iain in the Bristol house-box: how he had pushed his hot tongue into my mouth and licked and slurped at my breasts. Devoured me. He had been, as the cliché went, all over me like a rash. I thought I liked it, at the time, perhaps because it proved I was needed. Wanted. If only I had known. Iain was hungry, and I was an available tit-bit.

Pete Street's containment is a seductive contrast.

...a subtle beckoning, a sweet invitation...

His independence – even that spiky, seeming indifference, is a door asking to be unlocked: a boundary asking to be breached.

He smelled of smoke and music...

Stop it, Jo. You are drunk. I stand, feeling the carpet shift beneath my bare feet, and carry the half-empty glass to the kitchen, where, regretfully, I tip it into the sink, watching its red stain invade the white enamel. I've been trying to prolong the illusion. Because that's all it is – an illusion. He comes from a different world. He knows nothing about me. Before he lost his sight, he would have walked past the old, plump Jo without a glance.

Like Cinderella, I kissed him and ran. Unlike Cinderella, I fled because I didn't want him to touch me and find my body beautiful. It would be too painful. The glory of the evening with him had been that he had not seen me: that he had wanted to be with me simply because of who I was. And I would rather never meet him again than know the horror of his wanting me for my body. That body. Not mine.

The phone rings. I almost drop the glass into the sink. For a crazy moment I think it might be him. Then my heart shrivels at the more likely possibility that it is Iain. Another solicitor's letter arrived shortly after our last conversation, instructing me that the house must be sold and the proceeds divided. Perhaps he is ringing to rub it in. No. Too early. Iain is a night-owl, and a sloth in the mornings. I pick up the receiver.

'Jo?'

Clara. I am suddenly wide awake. 'Where are you? Are you all right?'

'Yes, yes…'

The signal is poor. 'Clara, you're breaking up.'

'I know. I'm on a train…' She doesn't say where. 'Jo, can you do me a favour? Can you go to the house and get an address off my laptop?'

For a moment, I am too surprised to reply. Clara, leaving her laptop at home? She's usually surgically attached to it.

'Dan's.' Clara's voice is crackly and unstable. 'It'll be in the address book. Text me with it?'

'You're going to see Dan? Are you in Cornwall? Clara?'

226

The line is dead. Well, well. What a turn-up. No wonder she didn't want me to go with her.

*

Clara's usually immaculate bedroom is in chaos. Discarded clothes are scattered over the bed and a wet towel lies on the bathroom floor. I pick it up and drape it on the radiator to dry. The phone in the hall is winking with a message.

I find the laptop lying abandoned on the bed. Carefully, I open it and switch it on. Last time I used a computer was the night Iain discovered me printing out my stories. It seems so far away, as if it happened to someone else. *It did.* I wonder, as the laptop boots up, whether I will ever write fiction again. *No.* The refutal is instant and automatic. *I was just hanging on Iain's coat-tails. On his reputation.* The thought doesn't convince me but I'm not yet ready, or inclined, to test it.

It takes some time to navigate my way through Clara's files and folders. There are seemingly hundreds of them, most relating to *The Making of Her.* I open one. It's a rough voice-over script for the programme:

Sarah Miller is fifty, fat and frustrated. Abandoned by her husband, she has abandoned herself...

Trite and formulaic. Poor Clara. How she must have hated writing it. Perhaps it would be better if she jumped ship and started afresh elsewhere. Reputation or no reputation, would she ever want to put her name to a programme like this?

I remember my task: to find Clara's contacts file and carefully copy Dan's address. Interesting that Clara still keeps it, when she has always been so certain that she won't contact him...

I am about to switch off the laptop when a thought occurs to me. I find the Internet icon and click on it. When the Google website appears, I type in *Pete Street.*

*

An hour later and I am still sitting on the bed, motionless.

There were hundreds of entries, the most recent detailing his winning the lifetime achievement award last night, the earliest ones recounting his successful solo career. And then there were the ones in between.

I suppose I had heard of him. Vaguely. Pop music has never been my thing. His was just another name they mentioned in passing on the radio. Something terrible or tragic had happened to him, as it so often does in the music business, but I couldn't have said what it was.

The singer was pulled from the wreckage of his car in the early evening and taken to Charing Cross Hospital where his condition is described as critical. He has multiple injuries to his back, legs and head. According to his wife Katia, Street had been drinking heavily. A five-year-old child, thought to be their son, is in intensive care.

I wanted to weep for him. And to shout at him. I wanted to press Delete, though whether to erase the information or our meeting, I did not know. Instead, I continued to read, scrolling down the pain:

Street's wife has announced their separation, only days after he was found unconscious and injured in his car. Their son, Jasper, remains in a critical condition. In a press conference, Mrs Street's lawyer read a statement in which she condemned Street for drinking and driving with a child on board. Street remains sedated. It is thought that he has suffered serious injury to his eyes as well as...

There was endless speculation about the marriage. Street was almost forty and had been with Katia for ten years. I googled Katia and found an image of a small, raven-haired person with a tattoo on her shoulder, her arms round a younger Pete's neck. He looked untouched. Wild. His face, and eyes, were blurred. Recent pictures of Katia showed her with a beefy, over-tanned man and living in Qatar. The child, Jasper, was wheelchair-bound and would never regain the use of his legs. He would be fifteen now. There were no pictures of him.

From this point on there was little information. Just a series of

Greatest Hits albums and the odd article bemoaning the fact that Pete Street no longer wrote or performed. It was reported that he had become a recluse. No partner. Nothing, in fact. The inquiry into the accident confirmed that he had been three times over the limit. The judge at the hearing pronounced:

Mr Street would suffer immeasurably in the future from the loss of his sight, the injury to his son, and the end of his marriage.

He had been given a substantial fine. His manager, Jongo MacBride, had issued a statement saying that Pete was not willing to talk about the accident, which he *deeply regretted.*

This last strikes me as odd. And unlike the Pete I met, however briefly. The information swills queasily around my mind. I have no right to judge him. Yet how could he do it? How could he get into a car, full of drink, with his young son, and drive?

I close the laptop. It hardly matters now. I will not be seeing him again. Traitorous tears are seeping down my face and I wipe them fiercely away.

CLARA

St Ives is almost an island. The map from the Tourist Office shows
a dog-leg peninsula surrounded on three sides by the sea. The water
ambushes her. The town seems stubbornly set on forcing her to face
it: from the uneasy view from her hotel room over the choppy waves
towards the solitary stone chapel on the hill, to the galleries hugging
the alleyways, many closed for the winter, their seascapes hanging
forlorn and unsold on the walls. She can barely imagine the place in
summer as Dan described it: the hot sweet smell of sun lotion; the
shouts of children building dams and castles; crowds of chattering
tourists wandering the cobbled streets in search of souvenirs; the
old seal begging for fish from the boats; cats of all colours sloping
and slinking down to the harbour walls; fishermen unloading their
shining silver catch.

Maybe in summer she would be less obvious; would blend in among
the tourists and the culture-seekers. As it is, she is glaringly visible,
her high city heels unsteady on the cobbles and her black cashmere
coat soaking up the weather rather than keeping it out. The mewling
of the gulls, wheeling and diving over the restless grey surface of the
sea, seems to mock her. More water, in the guise of rain, assaults her
face, needle-sharp and icy. She bought an umbrella from the Post
Office but it was almost torn from her grip when she opened it and
then promptly blew inside out. An old man in a sou'wester winked,
lewdly, as her skirt blew above her knees.

Hell. This place is... is antediluvian. Though postdiluvian – *after
the deluge* – would be more appropriate. She is willing to bet the
shops close at five sharp; those that aren't already shut for the winter.
And half-days on Wednesdays. Everything here seems to operate at

tortoise-speed. Postcards play on the local word *dreckly*, which means the same as the Spanish *mañana*. No wonder Dan chooses to live here. It must suit him perfectly. This visit is reminding her exactly why she could never have a future with him.

She looks for him down each new street and in each stranger's face. Somehow, it's all right to take him by surprise but she doesn't want him doing the same to her.

Her mobile bleeps. Thank God, Jo. The message is short and to the point:

10 Dove Lane

Clara scrolls down the message, hoping for a telephone number. There isn't one.

*

Dove Lane belies its name. She had imagined a row of picturesque Farrow & Ball painted cottages decked with hanging baskets, their gardens dotted with idiosyncratic driftwood sculptures. In fact it is a grim, skulking alley far from the tourist trail, a line of terraced houses splashed with gull droppings, their windows dark and unwelcoming and their stone steps unwashed. Number ten is indistinguishable from its neighbours, except that its net curtains have at least seen soap and water. Surely Dan can't be living here? This is the kind of place people in transition use as a stopgap. He must have moved on by now.

Clara hovers on the steps, unwilling to announce herself, suddenly uncomfortably aware of her London life, of her money, of her career. Of her difference. She is also conscious of a bleak, told-you-so satisfaction – *I knew he'd never amount to anything* – accompanied by a dull pain around her heart at the thought of Dan climbing these stark steps each day and calling this hovel home.

Get on with it, Clara. She is almost sure now that Dan no longer lives here, but maybe whoever does can tell her where he has gone. There's no bell. She thumps on the door, noting the flaking paint.

'Yes?' It has opened a crack. A brown face, unshaven and elderly, peers at her.

'I wonder if... Dan Galloway? Does he live here?'

'Dan? Aye.' The door opens further. The man is no more than five foot tall. Most of his body is covered by a paint-smeared overall. His hands, too, are streaked. He smells of turps and wet cat.

'Is he in?' She hopes not. She cannot bear the thought of walking in on him and having to face his embarrassment. His shame.

'He'll be up the site.'

'The site?' He must be working as a chippie. Or worse, labouring.

The old man begins a meandering description of the route to the site. Clara tries to take it in.

'Will I tell him you came?' His eyes are unsettling, sharp and blue.

'No. Thanks.' In case she changes her mind. 'I'll walk up to the site.'

He nods. By the time she reaches the bottom of the steps, the door has clicked shut.

*

The coastal path is cut into the cliff face and laid bare by the wind. She is the only walker, although 'walking' is an overstatement, given the terrain. Her shoes are already soaked and mud-stained. Her hair, tossed and tangled by the wind and rain, keeps catching in the thorny branches which overhang the path. She is an insignificance here, a tiny dot between the wild air above and the sand below. Immediately beneath her, a cave of black rock gushes water into a foaming pool. To her right, sand dunes stretch to infinity. And to her left lies the vastest, emptiest beach she has ever seen. The tide is out. The wet sand is criss-crossed with ghostly dog-walkers' footprints and the lighthouse she glimpsed this morning is a pale sentinel, besieged by white-headed waves.

This *country* has no truck with her city self. Cynicism and sophistication don't wash here. The wind is tearing away her inhibitions. She wants to stand like a child, arms spread and mouth open in a timeless scream. Only the possibility that the site, and Dan, might be somewhere close by deters her. She imagines telling David about wanting to scream, and how he would smile quietly in response. *Maybe I won't see him again.* She deliberately tests out this thought, as if poking at an aching tooth. And yes, it stabs.

The air smells red-brown, of sodden bracken. Her heels sink in the mud. A bird takes flight from a solitary, stripped branch and coasts over the dizzy space below her, calling to its mate.

Then another sound. The regular thud-thud of a tool hitting wood. She stops and listens. Tries to recall the old man's instructions.

'Where the path goes up, ye'll hear it, like as not. Past the studio, and follow it. Site's at the top.'

There's the studio sign. The path is narrowing now. Here, out of the wind, she can hear birdsong. She pulls off her shoes one at a time, wipes the heels on a clump of grass and runs a hand through her wild hair. Will she embarrass him by turning up like this; cause him trouble with his foreman?

She won't hang around. She'll just let him know she's here, and if he wants to meet later, so be it.

The path grows steeper, the trees thicker and the mud deeper. As she nears the source of the thudding it metamorphoses into a resonant ringing flecked with the scent of sawdust. She steps out into a clearing. A giant structure rears out of the ground: a wooden cathedral, its walls open like ribs and its crossed beams soaring to the sky.

A man is working up there, his legs slung either side of a beam as if he is riding a great wooden horse, spurring it on with each thump of the mallet. A shaven head, nut-brown, a broad back and muscular forearms. Old denims, greyer than blue, scored through and frayed. *Dan.*

At this safe distance he resembles one of David's little sand-tray figures – a toy man going about his business, disconnected by the seven years since he left her home and her life. She feels a fleeting relief that he's doing what he does best; that he has found a job which uses his talent and his passion. Thinking this, it all feels clearer. Why throw a pebble into the pond of his life – and hers – and disturb things? She has come, she has seen him and now she can go, safe in the knowledge that he has survived without her. He is gainfully employed. Whatever lies in the little wooden box belongs to what was, not what is. She can return to her hotel and check out, get on the next train to London and consign Dan to memory.

A bustle in the leaves above her: a fat wood pigeon flaps and crashes among the branches with its mate. She begins to inch her way backward, afraid to turn her eyes from Dan, willing him to continue with his steady work and so remain unaware of her presence and her retreat. Her hands grope behind her, feeling for obstacles. The traitor heels stick in the wet earth. Her heart thuds in time with the man with the mallet, as if he is battering at her ribcage and demanding to be let out. Or in.

'*Shit!*'

The word leaves her lips before she can stop it as the soft skin of her hand encounters a tearing thorn. A drop of blood sits in her palm, rolls and falls. Another. Her head swims. The thudding stops. She presses her stinging hand to her chest and focuses on her feet so that she does not have to look at the blood, or at Dan.

In the silence there's only the soughing of the wind in the tree tops and the contrapuntal sharp cry of a gull. Dan doesn't call to her but she knows he has seen her. Finally she raises her head.

He is immobile, staring down at her. She can't make out his expression. Now he is swinging one leg over the beam to join the other, placing the mallet and chisel carefully on the floor. He steps across the structure towards a ladder and descends, boot by worn boot. Reaching the bottom, he stands looking at her. Some fifteen feet separate them.

'Clara.' He doesn't move towards her.

She scrabbles in her bag for a tissue and bunches it in her palm. She is acutely aware of her appearance – wind-blown, muddy, scratched and flushed. Old. While he looks like the young Dan she once knew.

'You've hurt yourself?' His tone is gentle and apparently detached. The Irish in his voice is suddenly so familiar, so intimate, that unexpected tears start in her eyes. She shakes her head violently.

'I'm fine.'

He leans back against the ladder, considering her. 'And,' he says, as if they are continuing an old, lapsed conversation, 'you came, in the end.' As if he'd always known she would.

'Look,' she says, and hears her voice harsh and unwieldy, 'I was leaving. You'd never have noticed, if it wasn't for that bloody… plant.'

'Wild rose,' he says.

'Whatever.'

There's a pause.

'So,' says Dan. 'What now? Will you be going, or staying?' His voice is relaxed but she can see that he is gripping the ladder. The space between them seems unbridgeable. She avoids his eyes and fixes her own on the edifice above them.

'Impressive.' Even as she says it, she wishes she hadn't. *Patronising*. However, he nods.

'Yes,' he says, simply. It was always his way, she recalls with a small shock. He was a stranger to undertone or irony. Each word was, to him, new-minted and true. She had seen it as a sign of naivety. Of gullibility. Was it?

'Will you look around?' He sounds uncertain.

'What about the others?'

'Others?'

'The other builders. And whoever's in charge.'

He looks at her for a moment, then shrugs. 'As you see, there's only me.'

Her feet take her to him. Closer, he looks older. His eyes seem deeper-set and his wide mouth is tethered to his nose by a series of fine lines. She wonders what he sees in her own face. She can smell him: fresh sweat, wood smoke. She used to know which wood he was working with from the smell on his hands and from the pale curls of shavings clinging to his clothes.

'Oak,' he says as if answering her thought. He gestures at the building. 'Oak framed.' Then he looks down at her hand and reaches for it. 'Give me a look.'

His hands are warm and rough. Unlike David's. She can feel her heart beating against her breast. He gently removes the ball of tissue. She turns her face away.

''Course,' he says. 'You were never fond of the sight of blood.'

She feels her hand being lifted, then the shock of his tongue in her palm. For a moment she feels angry at the invasion. And the intimacy. He releases her hand.

'It's clean now,' he says. 'Stopped bleeding. D'you have any gloves?'

'Yes.' She pulls them from her coat pocket.

He folds the tissue, places it on the wound and watches as she slips the gloves on. 'Shall we go up?'

She nods. Much easier to deal with the reality of his building than with dredged-up emotions from the past.

He doesn't ask why she's here, for which she is grateful. Instead, he shows her over his construction while talking about mortise and tenon joints and roof trusses. He shows her the pegs holding the structure together – *green oak – shrinks as it ages, tightens the bond.* She draws her hand over the live, silky sharpness of the wood, so different from the rigidity of brick and cement. How does he feel, labouring to create this extraordinary home for some wealthy client while he lives in poky Dove Lane with the turpentine-soaked old man? She has a thousand questions to ask him, yet is content for now to be soothed by his voice and awed by the view across the dunes.

'We can see it all,' she says, 'and no one can see us.'

'That's the joy of it,' he replies.

He shows her where the bedrooms will be. She tries, in vain, to imagine walls partitioning the space and defining use.

'When will it be finished?'

'By summer's end. Though Aubrey says that's optimistic.'

'Who's Aubrey?'

'I rent a room from him. He's a painter.'

'And what will you do then? When it's done?'

He raises an eyebrow. 'Move in, of course.'

It's his. She sits down, rather suddenly, on a beam. Dan's face is difficult to read. He lowers himself to sit, cross-legged, in front of her. She smells the warmth of sweat and cloth.

'You're surprised.'

'I... Yes. How did you... I mean...'

'The money? Hard graft. After I left... London...' he does not say *you* '...I took any job I could get and saved all I made. Worked in the Sloop, nights. They gave me my supper. Over the years I got enough together for the materials.'

Why, why did she deny the truth of him? He was never a sponger. Always had a strong work ethic. Had it been more convenient to cut him down, in her memory, to a more manageable size?

'And the land? It must have cost a fortune.'

Dan drops his head. 'My dad. He died a couple of years ago.'

'Sorry.' She never met his father. Meeting parents had been a compromise too far. She looks at his lowered, shaven head and feels an urge to reach out and touch it. He looks up, straight into her eyes.

'You seem... softer... than I remember,' he says. 'But then, memory hardens things.'

She nods, and they sit in silence for a while, each lost in their own private thoughts.

*

That evening, he takes her to the Sloop, a pub lying in the crook of the harbour's arm, its walls covered in paintings. The locals eye her in a cursory way. *She'm from up country.* Not worth bothering with. Clara stares at one of the paintings: vivid swirls of colour lashing at the edges of the canvas as if demanding escape. Its wild spontaneity makes her nervous.

'Aubrey's,' Dan says, behind her.

'What's it meant to *be*?'

'Whatever you see in it.'

'Cop-out.' She wants to provoke him but here her words sound sharp and sarcastic. He grins and shoulders his way ahead of her to the bar.

'Let me,' she says, reaching for her wallet.

'My treat.'

'No, I…'

For the first time there's a trace of irritation in his face. 'Find a seat,' he says, 'if you can.'

Is it her exhaustion that causes her to do as she's told? Once, she would have insisted on paying, or at least going Dutch. Once, she would have won. But there's something harder and more impervious about Dan.

They eat seafood chowder and rough bread, sweet with garlic. The wine, too, is good; heavy with fruit. She swallows the first glass quickly, needing it to take the edge off the awkwardness, and then another. He tells her about his plans for the house.

'A sanctuary, a retreat. Where people can come when they need space. A place for healing.'

The word *healing* grates, reminding her that they are worlds apart. Always have been.

'I'll call it *Vipassana*.'

'Meaning?'

'Clear-seeing. Insight. The nature of reality.'

'For Buddhists?'

'For anyone.' He wipes a chunk of bread in the last drops of his soup.

'Even people like me?'

He looks at her. 'You want a place to escape to?'

She thinks of David and the safety of the yellow room. 'Maybe.'

'Want to tell me?'

So, with the wine's assistance, she tells him about *The Making of Her.*

About Jo, and Alix, and about Marcus's ultimatum. He listens to it all. She does not mention David, or therapy. When she has finished, he leans towards her. She watches his wide mouth as he says:

'And what brought you here?'

She hesitates. 'I don't know.' Then honesty forces her to add: 'Desperation, probably.'

His face closes. 'I see.'

The presence of the little wooden box in her bag whispers to her. Should she take it out now and ask him for the key? She has an image of the lid opening to release a flock of grey birds carrying a bloody heart in their beaks. She focuses on his hands, scored and blistered, which he clasps loosely on the rough tabletop. She remembers those hands, and his mouth, dancing hard and soft on her skin. She is gripped with an intense longing for an extra layer of skin – his, anyone's – to shield her and enfold her.

'Dan?'

He raises his eyes to her.

'Will you stay with me tonight? At the hotel?' Her heart is beating fast, too fast. In the silence that follows, sweat and humiliation drench her body. *Same old Clara, pushing and forcing.* She stands clumsily, rocking the table.

'Where are you going?' He also stands.

'Better go back…'

'I'll walk with you.' He guides her through the drinkers.

Outside, the air is icy. They walk side by side without speaking. She hears the silence of the tide slipping in and smells the sour stain of seaweed in the air.

At the hotel, he leans towards her and touches her mouth with his. His body is heavy, warm and close. Desire catches at her throat and in her groin. She wants to push him against the hotel wall, to force an intimacy, to break down the years: to have him, *make* him. She can feel him hardening against her, his mouth opening to her tongue. *Yes.* Then he takes her by the shoulders and breaks away.

'Tomorrow?' he asks.

'No.' Her body is furious in its desire. *'Now.'*

'Now or never?' he says, watching her, his face shadowed. 'Is that it?'

'That's it.'

He twists away from her and sets off down the hill. The rain spits and smarts on her skin but she stays where she is, waiting for him to turn. To return. She watches his figure recede until he is as small as when she encountered him at the site – diminutive and manageable – the way she's always chosen to see him. Like looking through a telescope, backwards.

*

In the hotel room she throws clothes and toiletries into her suitcase and rings Reception for a taxi. After a long while – *dreckly* – the phone is picked up.

'Can you order me a taxi, please?'

'Yes, madam.' The voice is leisurely. *Get a move on.* 'Where to?'

'The station. D'you know what time the next train to London is?'

There's a pause. 'Sorry, madam. There aren't any more trains tonight.'

Bloody Cornwall. Bloody Dan. *Bloody hell.*

JO

I am on my knees scrubbing the kitchen floor when the doorbell rings. My instinct, after leaving Clara's, was to eradicate all trace of Pete Street from my memory. I had hoped that energetic activity might accomplish this, but the damning articles roll repeatedly through my mind. Why, why, why did I google him? Why couldn't I leave well alone? The doorbell rings again.

Has the estate agent turned up early? He's due at midday, and it's only ten-thirty. Today, the house is to be assessed for value. I am unwashed and sweaty. The red hair has been screwed unceremoniously into a scrunchy and Iain's old jogging bottoms have been pressed, once again, into service. On my way from the kitchen to the hall, I cast around for a means of improving my appearance but cannot find one, apart from wiping away the sweat from under my eyes. Passing the hall mirror, I see that I've transferred a smear of kitchen grime to my face.

Through the glass in the front door I make out a large shadow, shifting impatiently. I open the door with more force than is necessary.

The man on my doorstep doesn't resemble an estate agent. He is broad and florid, grey hair tied back with what looks like a boot lace. His heavy breath is redolent with exertion. Or alcohol.

'May I speak tae the *lady of the house*?' He obviously thinks I'm the cleaner.

'That's me.'

The man's forehead wrinkles and he scans the hall behind me, as if making sure that the real owner isn't lurking behind the umbrella stand. Then he extends a hairy hand.

'Jongo MacBride, at your service. And you must be…?'

'Jo Coe.' I wipe my hand on the jogging pants and take his. His name seems familiar, but his accent distracts me and his physical presence blocks my doorway.

He nods meaningfully at me. 'I have a *message* for you.'

'Oh?' I wonder again if he is drunk.

'Salutations from Mr Street. He requests your company for *a breath of fresh air* at your immediate convenience.'

My mouth drops open in an idiot's gawp. Jongo MacBride. Pete's manager.

'Och, when I say immediate, I dinnae mean instant.' He is clearly attempting tact. 'There's time enough tae clean yoursel' up.'

At the back of my mind Google is regurgitating Pete's shocking past, but it's distant now. Irrelevant. I draw myself up and attempt to look dignified. 'Why didn't Mr Street come in person?'

Jongo MacBride guffaws. Either that or he has caught a large fly in his gullet and is attempting to expel it. 'Och, he's a wee cowrin' beastie when it comes tae *the fair sex*.'

I peer down the road. Yes. Several doors down is the limousine. My heart is jumping. Not with the moths, but with a wicked joy. And some anxiety. I turn to Jongo, who is wiping his forehead on a paisley handkerchief.

'Thank you, Mr MacBride, for taking the trouble to ask, but…'

'You're nivver *turning him down?*' Jongo staggers slightly on my pristine path.

I try to remember that Pete Street is a danger – to his son, to himself, and very probably to me. Yet every cell in my body is chorusing *Yes!*

'Tell him,' I say, 'to ask me himself. Then I'll decide.' And I close the door firmly in Jongo MacBride's face.

For a moment I panic. What if I've scared him away? And then, more prosaically: How can I make myself presentable in five minutes?

I bolt to the bathroom, throw my clothes to the floor and step under the shower. I only have to make sure I'm clean and fresh. I needn't – thank God – concern myself about the shape of my hair or the style of my clothes. This feels like a liberation. I quickly rub my hair dry, glad of its shorn spikes. There are traces of red dye on the towel. I wonder about scent. No. Let him smell me. My skin.

I open my wardrobe. What a conundrum. A blind man: so who am I dressing for? I bundle on jeans and a neutral jersey and check myself in the mirror for neatness. My face, naked under the tousled red hair, looks unprotected and innocent. I reach for the lipstick and its rogue pleasures.

*

Pete Street's face is pale above his black overcoat, like a root pulled from the soil. He stands on my doorstep, his hands pushed deep into his pockets and his head turned from me as if he isn't really here. We wait for a moment in a formal, brittle silence.

I ask, 'Where's Jongo?'

Pete shuffles his trainers. 'Jongo's not my keeper.'

'Then why did you send him?'

'Maybe,' he says, 'I wanted to find out what you looked like.'

My heart seems to be performing acrobatics in my chest. I wait. Then he turns his face to me.

'No,' he says. 'I didn't ask him. What difference would it make?'

'It makes a difference to most men.'

'Me too, once.' He says it briefly, as if it doesn't matter. I realise I've been holding my breath, and let it out.

'Will you come in?'

'No.'

The trainers are tapping now, impatient. He must be cold. There are still traces of frost on the shrubs in my front garden. A blackbird pecks at the frozen ground, flicking earth from its orange beak.

'So are you coming?' He fires the question like a man in a dug-out facing the enemy.

'Where?'

'Wait and see.' He grins sardonically. 'You shouldn't trust me. I'm not trustworthy.' He throws the statement down like a gauntlet.

My heart contracts.

'I'll get my coat.'

He sets off down the path, reaching for the gate at almost the right moment. As he gains the pavement, the limousine draws up to the kerb and Ed the driver gets out to open the door.

I remember my appointment at midday. And the kitchen floor is only half washed. Then I shrug my coat on, glancing at my reflection in the hall mirror. I look all mouth. Sod the agents. I'm going.

*

The limousine is empty save for Pete, Ed and a guitar case, its battered surface a mass of peeling stickers. I wonder what happened to Jongo.

We drive to Kew Gardens. This surprises me. Pete Street doesn't strike me as a man who likes open public spaces. Though I suppose Kew is unlikely to be packed on a cold morning in March. Only the keenest of tourists would come early.

When we reach the gates, Pete grabs the guitar and climbs out of the limousine.

'Chaperone?' I ask, noting the way he holds it between us.

'What?'

'The guitar.'

'Maybe.' He turns to Ed, who winks at me. 'I'll call.'

Kew is frosted like a cake. The grass is pockmarked with bird tracks. The air is cold and still. Canada geese plod and peck among their own frozen excretions. Planes, heading for Heathrow, drone across the sky every two minutes or so. A group of Japanese tourists carrying cameras bend over guidebooks, their high staccato tones a fragment of human music.

Pete sets off rapidly with his head down. How does he know the path? He carries the guitar like a mine-detector and seems disinclined to talk. This is clearly no romantic stroll. I match my stride to his. The air is like glass in my throat.

'I haven't been here for years,' I say. 'Not since I was young.'

'How old are you?' The question is a shock. Somehow, I had taken it for granted that he knew.

'I'm fifty. You?'

'Same.' He supplies the information succinctly, without embellishment. Under normal circumstances I'd find this challenging but now, rather than forcing me to talk, it offers me the freedom to be silent.

We are nearing a great glasshouse. It rears up before us, a translucent mountain. I imagine the doors opening, exhaling moist tropical air like a warm sigh into the silence of the gardens. Pete turns down a path. Now we are in a formal garden with symmetrical beds laid like dominoes, side by side. The garden is cradled by the severe line of a holly hedge. We are the only people in it. Pete slows.

'D'you come here often?' I ask. Well done, Jo. When in doubt, turn to a cliché.

He nods. He is stepping around the edges of the borders with the intentness of a pilgrim treading a labyrinth.

'How do you…' I don't know how to put it. How does he find his way without a dog or a stick?

'Like playing guitar. Practice, then instinct. First I made Jongo come with me. Then I came on my own. Again and again until I knew it.'

'But the people?'

'I'm blind,' he says, 'not insensate.'

'Meaning?' I won't be thrown off by the implied rebuke. A smile twitches at the corner of his mouth and is swiftly despatched.

'Not seeing sharpens things. I sense people by sound and by smell. Like the roses.'

'What roses?'

'In summer,' he says, 'this is a rose garden. Fifty-four varieties. Fifty-four beds. The petals are soft. Each smells of its colour. Like fifty-four women.' He smiles again. 'You can bury yourself in them.'

I imagine him, white-throated, plunging his mouth into petals. The sensuality disturbs me. I ask, 'What does yellow smell of?'

'Tangy. Like a come-on, a flirtation.'

'White?'

'Virginal. Sweet. Misty.'

'And red?'

He hesitates, then: 'Velvet. Hot, with undertones of musk.'

Red, white and yellow scents. His words clothe the bareness of the winter branches. The rose bushes, hundreds of them, stand closed-down and pruned, their brown thorny arms exposed. I remember, and speak aloud, from a long-loved poem:

'Footfalls echo in the memory
Down the passage which we did not take
Towards the door we never opened
Into the rose-garden.'

I dart a look at him. Will he think me pretentious? But he is smiling, a private, internal smile, and then he takes up the refrain:

'But to what purpose
Disturbing the dust on a bowl of rose-leaves
I do not know.'

'What d'you think of Eliot?' It feels as if we are standing on an edge, hesitating between small talk and revelation.

'His words are like fine lyrics. They resonate.'

'You're not how I imagine a rock star,' I say. He cocks his head towards me and the silver bird earring swings. 'What I mean is, you're… precise. Orderly. Aren't rock stars supposed to be wild and chaotic?'

'I've known chaotic.' He is tight-lipped. Then he relents a little. 'But I like edges. Like to know where things begin and end. Anyhow,' he adds, 'I've got to be orderly now. Got to remember where I put stuff.'

How must it be, living without the miracle of sight? Does he have television? Books? What does he see when he closes his eyes? Can he see in his dreams?

'Glad I lost it.' The words are delivered brusquely.

'What?'

'My seeing. Hearing or touching – that'd be the end of me. Whoever's up there understands something about musicians. There are worse things to lose than your sight.'

Like your son, or your wife, perhaps. I long to ask him but sense the fortress of his private hedge, prickly and repelling. Like my own. We are both concealing significant parts of our lives. But I have the advantage: I know about his past. The fact that I have my sight while he has lost his is not a source of guilt. But the fact that I have used my eyes to gain information about him without his permission feels unacceptable. It was all right when he was a stranger, someone I'd met by chance and would never see again but now that he is opening and unfolding into a person, I fear my advantage over him.

He is quickening his stride again and moving on, the overcoat flapping around his thin body. He is the most self-contained person I've ever met.

'Where are we going?'

'Somewhere I can play.' His voice is strained, like that of a man needing a cigarette.

*

The conservation area is Kew's secret. It is remote from the grandeur of the palace and the glasshouses, and an unpretentious path meanders through it. Most tourists, if they ventured this far, would quickly pass through on their way to the river, or to Queen Charlotte's Cottage. Here, there are no manicured lawns and no formal beds. Only a couple of benches, their slats stained with droppings, and two bare trees with bird-feeders hanging from their dark branches.

'Like real country,' I say.

Pete ignores me. He has settled on one of the benches and is removing the guitar from its case. I watch him. Even this feels voyeuristic, for he is curving around the guitar like a lover, his fingers feeling for the strings and his head tilted to its body as if to catch a whisper. Their shared world excludes me and a coldness, unrelated to the weather, creeps into my bones.

He begins to play.

The notes curl into the winter air. I expect them to create smoke, for they are like breath: Pete's breath, soul breath, winding and drifting across the space between us. Slowly, silently, I lower myself on to the bench. He gives no sign that he knows. His attention embraces the wood and gut, coaxing it to cry out in love, in pain. I turn my head away.

Afterwards, in the silence, I watch him dragging himself unwillingly back to the present and wait for him to speak. The air feels paralysed, the branches stark and lifeless. He says nothing, and eventually I ask:

'Was that one of yours?'

His face is white. 'No.'

Why does he need to keep me at arm's length? Self-containment is one thing; rudeness another. I leave him to it.

As if sensing this, he turns again to the guitar. This time I recognise what he plays. Mozart. It reminds me of the rose garden: formal and structured. His fingers are light upon the strings, plucking history from them. This time he turns to me while he plays, as if his playing is merely a backdrop to our conversation.

'When I was a kid,' he says, 'I learned how to sight-read.'

'Did you?'

'No one else in my family could do it. I was the only one.'

'They weren't musical?'

'They were musicians.' His mouth dips into the sardonic smile. 'Hippies. Peace, man.' His fingers glide effortlessly into Fleetwood Mac. I can almost smell the patchouli.

'So they encouraged you?'

'Too out of it most of the time to know I was there. I used to hang round them, asking questions. Only nothing came back.'

I shiver, thrown back to my own childhood, and Julia. Reaching out for love into nothingness, holding myself tight to ward off the inevitable puncturing words. I imagine a young Pete, thirsty as a sponge for information. For affection.

Like me, he was a child of the 60s. He tells me how he was dragged from festival to festival, country to country: an unstructured, anything-goes kind of living. His parents were children themselves with their long hair and floating, dirty cheesecloth. He'd longed for boundaries and he'd found them in music. Music had rules: bars, beat and measure. Regularity. The sight-reading was his rebellion. The language he alone spoke. And the guitar was his secret friend. The body of it, with its dark inner chamber, reminded him that he, too, housed a soul. The taut responsiveness of the strings affirmed the dexterity of his fingers and its voice was an echo of his own. The guitar was direct, obedient: the more so as he grew proficient. When he spoke, it listened. When he asked, it answered, replying instantly to his questioning fingers. The guitar was always there.

'The better I got, the more I tamed it. And the more it became itself.'

'I know…' The memory of taming words, of freeing them, floods me. 'That's how it is for me. With writing…'

In the silence that follows I screw up my face, willing him to continue playing. Instead, he places the guitar across his thighs. I'm aware of movement in the branches above us. A squirrel, flicking its tail, runs along a branch. I bunch my hands together. Pete turns his face towards me.

'So you're a writer,' he says.

'No!' He has drawn back a curtain, flooding me with unwelcome light. Exposing me.

He bends his head to the supine guitar and plays three dissonant chords. 'It's your prerogative, to lie. I don't mind.'

'I'm not lying!' I know I'm overreacting by protesting too much. 'I used to write, yes. Once. Not anymore. Apart from a journal.'

'Why not?'

'Because. Because I discovered I wasn't much good.'

'How did you discover that?' He seems genuinely interested.

'It doesn't matter.'

'I'd have thought,' he says, 'that it mattered a lot.'

The tears take me by surprise, dropping on to my clenched hands. My body hunches, turning in upon itself. After a while I wipe at my eyes and look up at him. His face is turned, unmoving, to the middle distance. I'm grateful that he doesn't try to make me better. After a while he says:

'Want to feed the birds?'

He opens the guitar case and puts the instrument away. Then he stands, feeling in the pocket of his overcoat and withdrawing a packet of peanuts.

'Hold out your hand.' He reaches to me, finding it, and tips me a handful. 'You have to be still. They'll come, in the end.' He retires to the bench.

I stand for a long time, my arm outstretched and my palm upturned. I cannot hear him behind me. Is he still there? *I'm not trustworthy*, he'd said with that sardonic grin. Maybe he has had enough of me and my tears and has crept back to his car. The planes roar overhead, mocking me. The cold seeps into my feet. My arm begins to ache. Of course they won't come. Wild birds don't.

I take a breath to say so when there is a rustle far above me. I don't move but sense the tiny black shadow in the branches. Then another. The tree whispers with birds, little puffballs of blown-out feathers, their quick heads cocking and turning. One flicks down to a branch beside me. I can see its blue feathers and its watchful eye. And – *oh!* – it flies down almost to my hand, but swerves away at the last moment. I try to be as still as the tree, hold my breath, silently asking. And then, in a gasp, it's back: cold feet grazing my palm as it swipes a nut, then flashes away. I am deaf to the roar of the planes: I hear only the beating of wings.

When the nuts are gone I lower my arm and brush my palms together. A brown rat steals out of the undergrowth on to the path and searches for leftovers. I turn. Pete is sitting as I left him, the guitar at his feet.

'You're still here,' I say.

'Why wouldn't I be?' he replies.

CLARA

Another hour and she'll be out of here.

Her bag is packed and ready. Her coat, hanging over a radiator, is presentable apart from a few flecks of mud near the hem. She has made good use of the sleepless night, scrubbing at her shoes in the hotel basin and washing her hair. What was that song from her childhood – about washing a man out of your hair? She has certainly washed the wind and the rain out of her own. It shines and falls around her face in its familiar, angular way. If only Dan had slipped accommodatingly down the plughole with the water. Another phrase sidles in. *Throwing the baby out with the bath water.* She glances at her watch. Another cup of strong black coffee and the taxi will be here.

Sunday. Day of rest. Not, it seems, for the Cornish weather, which gusts and spits against the hotel window. Down on the beaches, grey waves rear, white with froth, humping clumps of seaweed on to the sand. In the harbour, a man, hunched in a wet windcheater, is baling water from a rowing boat which labours queasily on the restless sea.

In Notting Hill, it will be silent now, its residents sleeping in after a heavy week at the office or a night at the theatre. In due course there will be croissants and coffee or leisurely lovemaking; then the Sunday papers and the online chat rooms. London life is lived indoors in winter, in centrally-heated shops and offices and apartments. Weather is a passing nuisance, held off by taxis.

Her mobile is ringing. She sets down her coffee and goes to find it.

'Clara?' Jo's voice envelops her like a warm shawl.

'Jo!'

'How are you? What's happening?'

'The weather's happening.' She moves away from it, to the radiator.

'You?'

'Lots.' There's an underlying seam of, what? – excitement? despair? – in Jo's voice. Clara feels a tremor of apprehension.

'Have you seen Dan?'

'Yes. Yes, I have.'

'And?'

'That's it. I've seen him. End of.' She knows she's being brusque and defensive.

'Clara,…' Jo's voice is distant and bubbly, as if underwater. The signal's breaking up.

The weather is even depriving her of Jo.

'Clara, listen. I met someone.'

'Who? How?' She remembers what she saw, and thought she'd imagined, in the taxi to Paddington: Jo, through the steamed-up window of a bar, talking to a thin man in shades. Is this the 'someone'? Clara suddenly and irrationally blames Sarah Miller, with her new seductive body and her new attractive face. The old Jo, middle-aged, comfortable and shy, would never have done this. Would never have had the opportunity to find herself a new man. How much of Jo will this man want? *Will there be anything left for me?*

'Oh – *oh!*' Jo sounds hyper, like a child after a party. 'Clara, I need to see you. I can't tell you over the phone. Are you coming back tonight?'

There's a knock at the door. Clearly the driver isn't Cornish, since he's early. Suddenly, it all seems too much.

'Just a moment,' she calls to the door. Then, to Jo: 'The taxi's here. I'll call you later. Promise…'

She drops the mobile into her bag and casts around the room for anything left behind, throwing on her coat and forcing her feet into the shoes, which seem to have shrunk after their encounter with the elements. Will the driver carry her suitcase downstairs? Unlikely.

The door is heavy and hard to open. And the corridor's dark. But there's no mistaking the shaven head and the bulk of the shoulders. He is wet and real and carrying a rucksack.

'Now?' Dan says. 'Or never?'

She stares at him. At his mouth. His eyes. The taxi's on its way. Tomorrow, Monday, they'll be expecting her at ProDoCo. The cutting room is booked. Marcus will be anticipating her resignation. A disgraceful, unlikely yet exciting thought intrudes. *I don't have to go back.*

What, after all, would she be returning for? A programme she doesn't believe in. A job she will shortly lose. A friend with, it seems, a new man in her life. A therapist who... she shakes the thought away.

Dan's here. The London things – her job, her therapist, her friend – won't be, soon. Or won't be the way they were. She steps back into the room, allowing Dan entry.

'We can walk,' he says. He, too, looks as if he has hardly slept.

'The taxi. The hotel...' Her thoughts are staccato. Another gust of wind shudders at the window. 'The weather. My shoes...'

'Cancel it. Stay another night. I've a coat for you. And boots.' He dumps the rucksack on the bed and pulls out a heavy waterproof coat, a pair of walking boots and thick socks. Who do they belong to? Her feet are half the size of his.

He sits on the bed while she cancels the taxi and books another night at the hotel. He watches her as she searches through her case for suitable clothes. Everything she has brought is too slick, too smart or too flimsy. She pulls out a couple of cashmere jerseys. She'll layer them. And her Jaeger trousers can tuck into the socks. No point in taking her bag – it'll be ruined in no time. She delves into it, filling the capacious pockets of Dan's coat with tissues, lipstick and purse. At the bottom of the bag her fingers find the wooden box. She turns her back to him and transfers it to the coat pocket. Then she moves to the bathroom to change.

'You'll do,' Dan says when she comes back. He helps her with the boots, deftly lacing them through the metal hooks and pulling tight. Her feet feel secure. Held. He moves close and pulls the hood up over her hair. She can feel his breath warm on her face. She raises her mouth to his but he doesn't kiss her, so she shoves her hands deep into the pockets of the coat, her fingers automatically feeling for the wooden box.

She'll ask him about it today. Soon.

They follow the cliff path and continue walking, past the turning to the site, skirting a golf course where men drive and putt against the wind. He points out the estuary and she gazes at the dark river that splits the land apart before flowing to join the sea. They pass standing stones yellow with lichen and rocks like stubs of ancient teeth that rear from the wet bracken. They walk over sodden fields, their boots leaving sucking footprints in the earth. On the path again, he bends to show her early violets. He doesn't touch her, and they barely speak: something is building between them like a heavy cloud. She is grateful for the narrowness of the path, which means they have to walk single-file. At least the rain has stopped, though the wind fists air at her face each time they emerge from the shelter of the path. She has used wind machines for filming, with their steady, predictable streams of air, but this is an irritable wind that fingers her hair and flicks it into her eyes, pulling it this way and that over her head like a crazed hairdresser.

'Want some lunch?' Dan, walking ahead, turns. She longs for a fire. Mulled wine and hot soup. A sense of ease. Perhaps, warm and close, they can talk. They can say some of the unspoken words that hover between them, too wild and frightening to let loose into this shifting air.

She nods. 'Is there a restaurant near here?'

Dan laughs. 'Yeah. The Ritz. Just over the dunes.' Unusual for him to be sarcastic.

'What, then?' Her words are caught by the wind and tossed away from him.

'What?'

'Where shall we lunch?'

He jerks his head, indicating that she follow him. Perhaps there's a cafe down on the beach. As they descend, her boots catch in bracken, which gradually gives way to wet sand. Dunes stretch as far as she can see. There's no sign of a café, and the only other inhabitants of the beach are the gulls, restless in the air. The tide is out but even so she can hear it beating and grinding and sucking at the sand. She stops.

Dan is way ahead now, striding over the dunes towards the sea. Up, down. Her legs suddenly feel weak and she lowers herself on to a patch of grass, pulling his coat down under her buttocks. The wind immediately ceases. Let him go on. Nothing is going to induce her to go down there, to the sucking sea. Far in the distance, she watches him stop, scanning the dunes, searching for her. Does he think she's left him? She raises her arm and gives a half-hearted wave. Dan walks slowly back.

When he reaches her, he plumps down on the sand, oblivious of the damp. He pulls the rucksack off, unstraps and unzips it. He pulls out a thermos flask – *thank God* – and a couple of grease-soaked paper bags, one of which he hands to her.

The paper is slippery. She peers inside. A pasty. Cold. Or rather, half cold, as if the life's been seeping out of it for some time. She lets it drop to the sand.

'What are you doing?' Dan's biting into his pasty with all the appearance of relish.

'It's cold. And it's carbohydrate.'

'Didn't seem to bother you last night.'

She remembers the hot, garlic-soaked bread and sighs, gesturing at the wind-driven sand. 'Not quite the same ambience.'

'Get over yourself, Clara.' Dan's halfway through his pasty. 'You're not in London now.'

'More's the pity.' She leans over Dan to grab the flask. The tea is hot and strong. It burns her lips. Why does everything here have to be so… extreme? She turns to look at him. 'Don't you ever miss it? London?'

'Some things.' He screws up the empty bag and drops it into the rucksack. 'It wasn't all bad.' A fleck of pastry clings to his lower lip. She wants to wipe it away.

The bird comes out of nowhere, plunging into the sand between them, its wings grazing her face. She sees the headstrong yellow eye, the curved beak stabbing at the abandoned pasty. Wildly, she flails her arms at it and falls back into the wet sand. The gull shrieks and stabs again. She crouches, her heart hammering, protecting her head. Dan is laughing and whooshing at the bird and sending it off, its beak full of pastry.

'Scavenger.' He's still grinning. 'It'll take what it can. You should've eaten it while you had the chance.'

'For fuck's sake!' Clara says. 'I want to go. Now.'

'Not before you've seen the sea.' Dan replaces the flask and kicks sand over the remains of Clara's pasty.

'I don't want to see the sea. I want to go back.'

'Back to London?'

'Yes, back to London! I should never have come…'

'But you did come. And you haven't yet told me why.'

Right.

'To find out,' she says, fingering the angle of the box in her pocket. 'To find out what you didn't tell me.'

He looks surprised. 'Such as?'

She pulls the box out, brandishing it on the palm of her hand. He stares at it for a moment.

'You found it, then.' He makes no attempt to take it from her.

'There was no key.'

'No.'

'What's inside?'

'Does it matter?'

'Come on, Dan.'

'Maybe,' he says, 'the key is what's inside.'

Riddles. Mysteries. *The sound of one hand clapping.* Clara hears her voice sharpen. 'Don't mess with me. Just tell me.'

He hesitates. 'I will. If you'll walk with me. By the sea.' He sets off, his head hunched and his hands in his pockets.

'What about our stuff?' she calls.

'There's no one to take it.'

She trails after him across an expanse of sand that stretches away on either side of her. Even in the distance, the sea is mountainous, sucking up the sand and dumping flotsam in frothy exhalation. Her nightmare. She keeps her eyes fixed on the ground. A vast wet sand tray. No safe edges, no painted base. No David to contain it all. Here a wellington boot, its sole stripped away. There a condom, perished, like some sea urchin. The tide line is ahead of them, a straggle of seaweed, crushed shells and surf-smoothed glass. Dare she cross this line? Dan holds out his hand. She takes it. It's warm and dry. They move towards the sea. Underfoot, the sand is suffused in water. Their boots leave soft footprints, which close up behind them, leaving faint, surrendered tracks. As they near the water, the wind increases. Lean grey gulls are tossed about in the air; their keening cries cut through the hiss and tumble of the waves. She can barely stand. She clings to Dan's lifebelt hand with one of her own, while her other clutches the box. For a moment she is tempted to hurl the box into the air so that it will spiral down and be swallowed by the sea. A wave crashes almost at their feet, sending a mizzle of froth pouring towards her boots. But it stops just short and, like a great empty maw, sighs and sucks the sand from beneath her feet. She pulls at Dan's hand. His lifted face is open to the elements. A stranger's face.

'Let me go!' She has to get away from this.

He holds on.

'Please…' She is shouting against the wind, her plea thrown back into her mouth. 'Let me *go!*'

Dan is staring at her, as if he's seeing her properly. 'What is it, Clara? Why so afraid?'

She's sobbing now, furious with him. With herself. Breaking from his grip, she hurls herself up the beach. The soles of her boots slip on green and brown seaweed as she scrambles, her arms flailing, up to the safety of the dunes. For a moment she is disorientated. Where are their things? Then Dan is behind her, opening his coat to let her in and holding her against the heat of his body. She sobs and shakes.

After a while, he bends his head and rubs his cheek against hers. 'I'll tell you about the box,' he says, 'if you want to know.'

Does she? She's no longer sure.

'But first, will you tell me something?'

His mouth is so close to hers. She longs to find it with her lips, to open him and find a way through without words or explanations. Why does it have to be so complicated?

'Why did you send me away, Clara?'

'You don't want to know.'

'I do,' he says. 'I really do.'

For a long time, she stares over his shoulder at the sea. Then: 'You wanted me to come down here. To leave London. Have children.'

'I did,' he says.

'That night. You wouldn't remember. I… we made love. Without protection.'

How can the silence be so full? The sea, the wind, the gulls. She dares not look at his face.

'I got pregnant.'

'*Fuck*.' In the years they were together, Dan never swore. He is no longer holding her. Cold air eddies between their bodies.

'I knew you'd want it… and… I knew I didn't.'

'So you sent me away.' His voice is stripped, weary. 'You had an abortion.'

'Yes.' She will never, never tell him the rest. The sucking away of their child. The pain – not in her body but in her heart. Her soul. The longing for something that would never be. Someone. She knows it was a girl; they made a girl together. If he knew that she had wanted the baby it would kill him.

They walk back in silence. Already there is an intimation of dusk in the air. The thorn bushes are turning from brown to mauve, while above them a ghostly sliver of moon hangs in the still-light sky. An owl hoots somewhere nearby. She catches the scent of wild garlic.

'Look where you walk.' Dan's voice is clipped. 'There are roots.'

The path is so narrow now that she can barely find a foothold.

Trees arch to each other, forcing her to bow her head. The roots wind from the ground in serpentine loops.

She is cold. So cold she can barely breathe. A combination of shock and lack of food. When she gets to her hotel room, she will crawl into bed fully dressed, pull the covers over her and curl like a child in the dark until it is morning and she can go.

Outside the hotel, she stops. He walks on.

'Dan!' It mustn't end like this. 'Can't we at least say goodbye?'

He turns to look at her. 'We could say goodbye,' he says. His face is dusk-pale. 'Or we could finish what we started.' And he holds out a hand.

Her mind scrabbles to wrench the meaning from the ambiguous words. Is he talking about their relationship? Their quarrel? Their child? Does it matter?

The box in her pocket retains its secret. Perhaps the mystery is what matters, not the answers. *Maybe David was right.* She walks towards Dan and gives him her hand.

*

His room is in the attic, but the smell of turps and oil follows them up the stairs from Aubrey's studio on the floor below. The house is dark, for which she's grateful, and surprisingly warm. Dan holds on to her hand all the way up the stairs, as if she might escape. Her boots leave clumps of mud and sand on the carpet. Whose are they? Some local girl with dreadlocked hair and long skirts? A spiritual type. Someone like him.

Dan pushes the door open. He doesn't switch on the light. There's a large window with a table under it, the silhouette of a chair and, far in the distance, the wink of Godrevy lighthouse. Beside the table, the white curve of a basin. A bed, neatly made. The bulk of an overbearing wardrobe.

'It's all right,' she says, letting go of his hand, 'I won't run away.'

She can't see his expression.

'Take off your boots,' he says, kneeling to remove his own. He pulls off his jacket, hangs it on a hook on the door and holds out his hand for her coat. She shakes her head. 'I'm too cold.'

'I'll get you a drink.' He moves from the table to the basin and switches on the kettle. 'The radiator's hot. You'll soon warm up.' She stands against it, feeling the heat creeping into her buttocks, and spreads her hands over its surface to absorb every bit of warmth.

While the kettle heats, he moves to a corner, bends and strikes a match. A candle flickers on a carved wooden altar: the one which, seven years ago, stood in her own spare room.

The air smells of Dan. Wood and incense. They move in an awkward dance around the furniture to find places to sit. She avoids the bed and perches on the chair. He sits on the rug at her feet. The tea is herbal – ginger and spice; the silence between them is hesitant and anxious.

'Talk to me, Dan,' she says, her body warming with the tea.

There's no clue as to whether he's still angry. He sighs. 'What happened to our child…'

'It wasn't. It wasn't a child.'

But it was. She was.

He ignores her interruption. 'What happened to our child was like everything that happened between you and me.' He is staring at the rug. 'Nothing ever grew between us. Nothing was allowed to.'

'I don't know what you mean. We lived together. We spent time together.'

'We went through the motions. I had a key to your door. We fucked.'

She winces.

'We made love,' she says. 'Didn't we?'

'You can't *make* love.' Dan says quietly. 'Love's either there or it isn't.'

The old irritation rises. 'Maybe love can't be philosophised over, either. Maybe it's just got to be experienced. And if it's not there, it's not. At least with sex you know where you are.'

'In your case,' says Dan, 'on top.' Again, the uncharacteristic sarcasm.

'What are you saying? That I should have been a good little woman? Laid back and thought of Ireland? Come on, Dan. Things have moved along since Victoria.'

Dan leans forward. 'You know what I'm saying. I'm not talking about the mechanics of it. I'm talking about the dynamic between us. Remember?'

'No, I don't. It was all pretty straightforward, as I recall. As you say, we fucked. Simple.'

'It was a fight. Sex was a fight. Always.'

'Was it? In that case, we were right to split up.' She stands and sets her mug on the table.

'Walking out, Clara?'

'What the hell do you want me to do? Stay here? Play wife in The-House-That-Dan-Built? Have babies?' She sees him turn away. 'It can't have escaped your notice that I'm seven years older. *Old*. Past it.'

Her voice echoes harshly around the walls. Dan rubs his fist against his forehead.

'No,' he says at last. 'I don't want you to stay. I just want you to *be*, while you are here. That's all.'

Do-be-do-be-do. The old refrain. The old, impossible criticism that she'd been so busy doing what she wanted that she never let anything – anything worthwhile – just be. Is he right? Did she deny Dan the possibility of love, just as she denied him their child?

'I don't know how,' she says. 'I don't know how to be.'

'Come here…' he takes her reluctant arms and pulls her down beside him, '…while I kiss you.' He reaches for her face, draws her hair back. 'And you don't have to do a thing.'

'But I…'

His mouth is on hers, his lips soft and cold, awakening her. He is searching her out, relentless as the water. *Sex was a fight. Always.* The fight seems to be happening inside her. She wants to push him down on to the mattress. And to push him away. She wants to tear off his shirt, and to tear from the room. Why then is she sitting still, her ears ringing with the silence between them, willing to receive him as he is?

He stands, pulling her with him. She feels the stock of his body against hers. His tongue is in her mouth. A flush – a blood flush – is spreading through her body, like a piece of dried coral that has found water again and is suffused and engorged. She floats in the viscosity of desire, offering no resistance when he pulls off her coat and her jerseys. Everything. His body is harder and leaner than seven years ago. More beautiful. He cups her sex in his open hand, bends to her breasts. Then, much later, he is engulfing her. Filling her with himself. The first thrust is like a wave breaking into her, sucking back, receding, holding: making her wait for the next. For a moment, she pulls back. *Trust me*, his body says – or is it her own? She lets go to him, surrendering to his rhythm, her heart against his, their legs intertwined. Their breath. She is shaking; breaking in his arms.

Afterwards, it is all wet: their skin, her thighs, the sheet. She smells the sea outside the window. Dan is still holding her.

'I've waited seven long years,' he says, 'for this.'

There will be no conception, this time: no child. No second chances. And yet, between them, something new is being born.

'Dan?' she says. 'May I ask you something?'

'Ask away.'

'Can I stay?'

He smiles. A real smile. 'Of course you're to stay. Were you thinking of going back to the hotel?'

'I didn't mean that.'

'What, then?'

'How would you feel if I stayed on for a while? Here, in St Ives?'

The words sit awkwardly between them. His face is shadowed. 'Clara.' The word says it all. He is disappointed in her, expected more of her: and his face is suddenly David's. Why is every man she's attracted to like a father or a teacher?

'I'll go, then.' She slides her legs out of the bed.

'Don't you see,' he says, 'that it wouldn't be right?'

'Why not?'

'You'd be running away. You know that.' He places the palm of his hand against her cheek. 'And neither St Ives or myself should be a last resort.'

'You're not. You wouldn't be.'

'Go back,' he says, and she knows he's right.

'Face the music?'

'Finish what you started.'

'You mean, complete *The Making of Her*?'

'Yeah. *The Making of Her.*' His expression is unreadable.

Later, as he sleeps beside her, she stares at the sliver of moon framed in the window.

You, the first

lost loved one, who never arrived…

Is she beginning, at last, to separate from Dan? Now that she's found him, will she lose him? The candle on the altar is waning, its dying light shivering over the carved wood. Perhaps it is only in the letting go of things, and people, and ideas, that one discovers what one needs. She leans into Dan, breathing in his warm moving breath. Then she gets up and puts on her clothes. She hesitates over the coat. The boots. But she can't walk to the hotel barefoot. She looks at Dan's sleeping form. He would say, Take them. Hunching her shoulders, she plunges her hands into the pockets of his coat.

The box shocks against her fingers. His box. Still there, unopened. Its story and its mystery intact. Why did she try to pry open the heart of him? Why did she ever imagine she had the right to know?

She tiptoes to the altar. No point in kneeling before it. It would know her for the fraud she is. Carefully, she places the little box beside the solitary guttering candle. *My offering*. The nearest she can get to letting it be, letting it go. She bends, blows out the candle and makes for the stairs.

*

She takes the first train back to London. She doesn't sleep, but stares out of the window and weeps.

When that is done, she leaves a message on Jo's mobile.

'Jo? I'm coming back. Looking forward to seeing you. And to hearing all about him...'

Had she considered how Jo might feel when she rushed down here to see Dan? No. She had taken it for granted that Jo would be there on her return, as she always has been; just as she took it for granted that Dan would be here, waiting for her. Has she ever recognised either of them as individuals in their own right? Separate. With their own needs and desires?

The message left, she feels somewhat better. Yet she owes Jo more than this.

What, then?

She hauls her suitcase from the rack and removes Jo's journal. Then she pulls Dan's coat around herself and opens the journal to the first, densely-written page.

PART FOUR

now you lead me to your flame
and you say
you're gonna burn my wounds away
we will tell our truth, and naked, scar to scar,
change the terror into trust
change the water into fire
strip me down, love
tear my lies away like petals
love me, love me not, love
strip me down

Extract from WATER INTO FIRE
Music and lyrics by Pete Street
© Flame Records

PETE

Pete lets himself into the thin, silent house in Islington. His feet scuff at the usual scatter of letters and junk mail and he thinks, as he always does, *ought to get a letter basket.* He leans the guitar against the wall and bends, running his hands over the floor and pushing the letters into a pile. Among them is a large, stiff envelope. He places the bundle on the table by the door for Jongo to sort. Then he retrieves the guitar and climbs the stairs.

In the living room, he takes out his watch and runs his fingers over its hands, an action that brings him a familiar comfort. You can't stop time: you can only witness it ticking by, relentlessly, forever. Four-forty. Early, yet. They'd walked, he and Jo, drunk coffee and walked again, and left Kew when he heard the birds' twilight song, like the swell of applause before the end of a gig.

The song between them had been sweeter than the birdsong and slippery with sensuality. *Stupid. Could have broken my duck. Could* – he deliberately coarsens it – *have scored.* His mouth stretches into a wry grin. Who is he kidding? He didn't even ask her back to his place. Just got Ed to drive to her door. Again, outside, they hesitated. Or rather, he did. No way was he going to make a dick of himself again by plunging at her, guessing where her lips were, and missing. At times like these he curses his blindness; when it forces him to be passive and vulnerable.

He'd caught her scent though, when she leant towards him, and sensed her momentary doubt like a question mark hanging in the air between them. Then her mouth found his and there was nothing more for a few minutes: her soft lips and his yearning. His hands discovered her hair – short, soft and spiked. *Red*, he'd thought, *I reckon it's red.* Digging deeper, his fingertips had found the delicate bones of her skull and he held her head carefully, as he'd held rabbits and mice as a child, mindful of their wild free will. When the long kiss ended, they did not break apart but unwound slowly and reluctantly from one another. Only when they'd pulled apart far enough to sever the connection did he feel the familiar anxiety tightening his throat.

'Come in?' she'd asked, and he thought that she now imagined there was something indissoluble between them. As women do.

As Katia had – Katia, who had spun cobweb threads between them until she had him caught fast. Threads which tugged at his dick until it stood up for her; tugged at his heart so that he sprawled, helpless, at her feet.

So he'd shut her out, this Jo, with his abrupt 'No, thanks.' So what if he'd told her stuff? She'd told him things too. Deliberately, he pulled down the shutters on their shared confidences. Only when he heard the emptiness in the air between them could he breathe again.

And now the evening spreads before him, all the more barren for what might have been.

Evening is usually his best time, when the day joins him in darkness.

Eat. Then play. Or the other way round. That's how he gets through. The guitar beckons him – the only temptation he can succumb to at any time without fear. He sits down and pulls it to his lap.

So she's a blocked writer. Both in the same boat, then. Jo Coe and Pete Street. *Fuck, life's clever.* He liked the way she stood up to him, then faltered, uncertain, like she was only practising being brave.

A series of strangled croaks makes him jump. Bloody entryphone. Another thing he must attend to, or get Jongo to; but before he can press the button, he hears Jongo's key in the lock. He calls down to him to bring the letters up, hears Jongo's breathy and laborious ascent.

'Eh, laddie…' Jongo flings the door wide open as he always does, and Pete winces as it hits the wall. 'I need a word.'

'Stub it.' The same old ritual. Pete smells the dying smoke from

Jongo's cigar, hears the letters slapped on to the table. Then Jongo's heavy tread as he fetches the bottle Pete keeps for him in the kitchen, followed by the clink of glass against glass and, finally, the bitter, enticing scent of whisky. Jongo collapses, wheezing, in his usual chair.

'For Christ's sake, close the window, lad. My baws are *freezing off.*'

'Fresh air's good for you.'

'I'll stick tae alcohol.'

Pete lifts the guitar, feeling for the ridges of the gut under his fingertips. He begins to play, bending his head low over the strings so that their sound blocks out Jongo. Not that he'll speak now. Jongo holds few things sacred, but Pete's playing is one of them. In the pause that follows the end of the piece, Jongo says:

'Eh, *a new one?*'

And Pete wants to hit him. They both know there's been nothing new for a decade. He swallows.

'For fuck's sake, Jongo. That was Purcell.'

But Jongo wouldn't know Purcell's music if it jumped up and bit him. 'How was your date wi' the girlie?'

Don't beat about the bush, Jongo, will you?

'OK.' He feels no need to elaborate.

'Seein' her again?'

'Dunno.' He picks out a few notes. There's a pause as Jongo sniffs appreciatively at his glass then knocks back the contents.

'Now, my lad…'

An intimation of what's coming makes Pete duck his head but Jongo ploughs on regardless. 'A wee bit o' *forward planning* is called for.'

For a moment he thinks Jongo's referring to Jo and almost grins. Jongo quickly disabuses him. 'I've been talking to Flame..'

Now what? Flame Records is his old label.

'And?' He hears the sharpness, born of fear, in his own voice.

'Now, laddie…' Jongo bangs his glass on the table. He must mean business. 'They want you to do some new stuff.'

'Tough.'

He replaces the guitar in its case while Jongo heaves himself to his feet and begins to pace up and down the room, exhaling impatiently. His footsteps come to a halt near the fireplace.

'It's been ten years,' he says.

'Time isn't the issue.'

'No,' says Jongo. 'Mebbe. But the issue needs facing all the same.'

'Why?'

'Because you're *stagnating*, lad. You have a talent. A very particular talent. And the world's *the poorer without it.*'

How dare Jongo imply he's being selfish? That he's deliberately withholding his talent? What the fuck does Jongo know? He takes a deep breath and counts backwards from ten.

'Will you do the mail?'

Jongo snorts. 'Too dark tae read.' A sigh followed by the click of a switch and the sound of paper being shuffled and torn.

'Junk. Gas bill. A wee fan wanting a photo. Junk.'

A definite pause. *What?* The hairs on Pete's arms prickle.

Jongo clears his throat. 'A note from… *she who must not be mentioned.*'

Katia. Bugger. 'And?'

'She says…' Jongo shuffles the paper again. 'Jasper. Taken on his birthday. He places something thin and smooth into Pete's hands. 'Sorry, lad.'

A photograph. He runs his fingertips over a shiny surface that gives him nothing. Why does Katia continue to be so cruel? A photograph of a child – no, not a child, a young man – whom he cannot see and cannot touch. A disembodied voice on a phone line once a month when Katia allows it.

The tawny smell of Jongo's whisky is permeating the room. Getting up his nose. He craves its anaesthesia. Something – anything – to take the edge off the guilt that crouches like a rat in a corner, ready to gnaw at his heart, and the helpless, impotent love which cannot ever be translated into words. Carefully, he returns the photograph to Jongo.

'How does he look?'

Jongo's voice is hearty: 'He looks fine. Nivver better.'

Pete stands, moves to the light switch and clicks it off. Then he returns to his seat and folds his arms around his chest, holding it tightly. Holding it together. Eventually, Jongo says, 'Even more reason to *move on*?'

The pain in his chest tightens into a dagger, which he suddenly wants to stick into Jongo, poor inoffensive sod. He bites his lips, battening down the urge to shout about bulls in china shops, insensitivity, piss-artistry… A lesser man would shut up, right now. Jongo is not that man.

'Just because he's *sufferin'* doesnae mean *you* have to. Do what you do best. Mek him *proud* of you, laddie.'

Too much. Pete leaps to his feet, plunges towards Jongo and stands over him. 'Fuck it, Jongo! You've no bloody idea, have you? No idea…'

He's afraid of himself. Afraid of his body, which wants to lunge and pummel and fist. Instead, he sweeps at the rough whereabouts of Jongo's whisky glass, glad – *glad* – when his hand catches it like a blow and sends it flying across the room to the fireplace, where it shatters on the tiles.

There is a long silence. Then Jongo stands, his whisky breath polluting the air between them, clicks the light back on and shuffles over to the broken glass, falling on his knees to scrabble it together. Pete finds himself worrying for Jongo's hands and moves towards him.

'Ye'll tread in it. Got a dustpan?'

Pete fetches it and hands it down. When the glass is all collected, Jongo carries the pan to the kitchen. There's a crackle of paper, the thud and rattle of the bin, and Jongo returns to the room.

After a long pause, Pete says, 'It's not that.'

'Not what?'

'What you said. I'm not doing it out of stubbornness. Or being selfish.'

He can hear Jongo breathing, taking this in.

'Tell me then, lad. Just tell me.'

The words are buried in his throat, cleaving to it. He hauls them up, one by one. 'There's nothing. In me. Anymore.' *Barren. Scraped out. Finished.*

Tears follow the words; bitter, blinding tears. Except the blinding happened long ago.

'I can't do it. Understand? It's gone.'

The times he'd tried, at the beginning, sitting with the guitar, straining to create something and longing for the comfort that would follow. Then the shock, loaded on the grief, when it didn't happen. He had told himself it'd come right. That he just needed to give himself more time. And yet more time. But nothing came. Nothing ever came again.

The tears are scalding down his cheeks. His chest is convulsing, retching up the pain and the shame.

Jongo says, 'Come here, laddie. Come over here.'

Somehow he crosses the room, crouches before Jongo and is enfolded in the hot bear's cave of his chest.

CLARA

Clara leans on the doorbell.

Be in, Jo. Please.

She is about to give up when footsteps approach and the door is opened.

'Clara...' Jo's face is flushed. 'Come in.'

Clara hefts her bag inside, feeling her tiredness for the first time since arriving back in London. She didn't sleep at all on the train. Nor has she been home. At Paddington, she had jumped into a cab, willing the driver to hurry, so bursting was she with what she needed to tell Jo. For the first time in months, energy and purpose run through her veins. Inspiration even.

Jo opens her arms and they hug. *It's all right. She won't abandon me.* Then, before she can speak, Jo is shushing her and miming, words tumbling in whispers so that Clara can barely catch them, let alone understand them.

'He's here... turned up... I was asleep... can't see... doesn't know about me... don't tell him...' and before Clara can ask her to repeat herself, Jo is pulling her into the living room.

A man – *that* man – is sitting on the couch. She recognises him by the curls and the shades. He rises as they enter. He's wearing an overcoat, as if he hasn't decided whether to stay. His very pale skin contrasts with a black shirt and black leather trousers. He looks out of place in Jo's comfortable room, as if he has been transplanted from an exotic, hothouse life.

'Clara,' Jo is saying, 'this is Pete. And Pete, this is my dearest friend, Clara.'

The man – *who is he?* – holds out his hand. She takes it. His handshake is definite. He says, 'I'll go.'

Jo turns to him. 'No. Stay. Please. I want you to.'

As Jo hurries to the kitchen to make coffee, Clara sits on a single chair, leaving the space on the sofa for Jo. Pete is gazing into space, the narrow planes of his face caught by the morning light. Then she realises who he is.

'You're Pete Street. The musician.'

'Used to be,' he says, and his face becomes impersonal. What does he mean by that? Wasn't there something about him? Some scandal?

'How did you two meet?' she asks.

'In a toilet.' He seems disinclined to expand on this. Clara stifles a snort of laughter. Whatever the story is, he is a very different proposition to Iain. She wonders whether she'll like him and how he will affect her relationship with Jo. Then she remembers her mission.

'Pete,' she says, 'I hope you'll bear with me. I need to speak to Jo, urgently, about something important.'

'Privately?' So he's sensitive.

'Doesn't have to be. But I need to say it.'

'Say what?' Jo enters with a tray and hands out drinks. She sits beside Pete. They complement one another: he all pale and black; she flushed, red-haired and red-lipped.

'Jo. Listen. I can't stay long. I should be in the cutting room...'

'What is it?' Jo sounds anxious. Pete leans in as if to listen for the cause.

'I've read it. Your journal. I finished it on the train.' She stands and begins to pace. 'Jo, it's superb. Extraordinary. Not only beautiful writing, but so moving and... and true.'

Jo is shaking her head. Pete is gazing into his coffee, but his face is very still. What's going on? Clara hesitates, then continues.

'I want to use it. Or parts of it. Will you let me?'

'Use it? For what?'

'Can't tell you just now. Later. But I need you to come with me to ProDoCo.'

'Now?' Jo glances at Pete.

'Please. Will you?'

Pete drains his coffee.

'So,' he says to Jo with the shadow of a smile. 'Seems like you *can* do it, after all.'

'It's just a journal,' mutters Jo. 'Just me writing to myself.'

He stands.

'No,' he says, as Jo gets up too. 'Stay where you are. I can find my way out.' He feels into his overcoat pocket, draws out a card and holds it towards Jo. 'Call me,' he says. 'My address is on there too.'

Jo blushes, leans towards him and kisses him on the mouth.

'I will,' she says, and a subtle vibration seems to pass between them. Then he walks, quite slowly, towards the door, finds the handle and turns it. They listen to his footsteps receding down the hall. When the front door closes, Jo visibly relaxes.

'He's blind, you see,' she says. And bursts into tears.

*

'You haven't told him?'

Clara shifts along the cab seat to allow Jo to climb in beside her. Jo's tears had been brief, like a rain shower. Giving her no time to talk, Clara had grabbed her arm and pulled her, protesting, from the house.

The cab bumps along the Goldhawk Road and through the White City estate. Clara digs her nails into her palms and tries to concentrate on Jo's reply. 'About *The Making of Her*? No.' Jo is gazing out of the window. 'Ironic, isn't it? I get a makeover and meet a blind man. And the awful thing is, I'm grateful that Pete's blind. That he sees *me*, rather than *this*.' She gestures at her body.

'But surely, you and he…' Does Jo understand what she's got herself into? Does she think her relationship with Pete will be a meeting of minds?

'No. Just kissed.'

'So when are you going to tell him?' She's finding it hard to focus, with the journal burning a hole in her bag.

'I don't know.' Jo clasps her hands tightly in her lap. She stares out at the passing traffic. 'I hadn't… anticipated meeting someone. It never came into the equation. I wanted transformation, yes. I got that. I've found a new self, inside. And I like her. I really do. But she comes with this body. And now…'

'Now?'

Jo is silent. Gone into that distant sanctuary of hers.

'Jo, talk to me. Do you regret having this makeover? Was it the wrong choice?'

'It was the worst thing I ever did,' Jo says. 'And the best.' She raises her hand as if to push up a pair of glasses, then frowns and rubs her nose instead. 'The whole process was shocking – not only psychologically but spiritually. It made me see that change is possible. It made me realise I didn't have to live as I had been. It shook up every last atom of me and threw me down in a new pattern.'

Yes. Her journal made that so vividly clear. Clara's fingers stray to her bag and the journal inside. The cab is crawling along Wood Lane, caught in the usual mayhem. Soon, soon. 'And the worst?'

'Now I have to live with it,' Jo says, simply. 'With a body that will never be mine. A cardboard cut-out of a body. Marcus's idea of a body. Sarah Miller's body.'

'Sarah Miller doesn't exist.'

'Exactly.' Jo's eyes are brimming. Clara takes her hand.

'If Pete loves you, really loves you, it's because of who you are. Your heart, your mind, your self. The rest is just skin deep.'

'But skin is part of it, don't you see? Especially for Pete. He understands the world through touch. It's such a vital dimension for him. How can I let him touch *these*…' she gestures at her face, her breasts '…when they're not me?'

Oh, Jo. Must she be so conscientious? Clara attempts to quash her rising impatience.

'It's… complicated,' Jo is saying. 'If I try to explain, will you try to understand?'

'Sure…' The cab is still stationary. Caught in a jam. Exhaust fumes rise into the already-polluted air. The driver is dangling a cigarette out of the window.

'Having the makeover, like I said, was the best and the worst thing. The best is that I've redeemed myself. Found an inner self, a strong self I never knew existed. The worst is that I've betrayed myself. Betrayed my body. My old one, I mean. I'll never feel this body is mine.'

'It's too soon. You've been through a trauma…'

'A self-inflicted one.'

'True, but a trauma nonetheless. Give it time, Jo.'

'I will. I am. But I'm afraid. About Pete.' The words are flooding from her now. 'I'm afraid that if he touches me, I'll feel… like a fraud. I'm scared he'll fall in love with this body – the way men do – and…'

'You don't have to do anything until you're ready.' Is this her, Clara, speaking? She sounds like David. 'So what is it about Pete?'

'Pete,' Jo says slowly, 'is real.'

'Meaning?'

'He doesn't pretend. And he doesn't expect me to. But I'm not being honest with him. I haven't told him about the makeover. And… other things.'

'Give the man some credit. Do you trust him?'

Jo hesitates. 'So far, yes, though he's difficult and complex. If you prod him, he rolls up into a ball and all you get is a mass of prickles.'

'I like him.' Clara realises she means this. Jo's face lightens.

'Do you? I'm glad. But Clara, do you know about his history?'

'Wasn't there an accident? Some kind of break-up?'

'I keep telling myself that it shouldn't matter. But it does.'

'What? His blindness? His past?'

'He almost killed his son.'

'He did what?' Clara tries, and fails, to imagine Pete Street as a child murderer. 'Did he tell you?'

'I googled him on your laptop. That's another thing I haven't told him. Clara, it's so hard…' Jo's face is creased with anxiety. 'How could he do it? He was drunk and driving with his young son in the car.'

Clara tries to align this new dimension of Pete with the man she's just met – a man who gave the impression of integrity and sensibility. 'Perhaps,' she says, 'he's changed. Like you.'

The cab is edging its way past the BBC, past White City. Men and women hurry in and out of the iron gates clutching mobiles and laptop cases. Is there a future in television for her? If she resigns will there be another job to go to? She fingers the journal. She can almost feel the energy crackling from its pages, but Jo is still speaking.

'What happened… the drink-driving, the crash, his son… is important… of course it's important… but it doesn't seem to affect how I feel about him.'

'Maybe,' Clara says, 'you love him.'

Jo is silent.

'And if you do, at some point you're going to want to make love with him.'

Jo flushes again. 'He'll have to wait,' she says. 'Until I know what to do.'

'Don't take too long.' *Like I did with Dan.*

'Cornwall?' Jo's intuition is clearly functioning. 'How was it, seeing Dan?'

How to describe it all to Jo in the space of the few minutes before they reach ProDoCo and with her mind racing ahead to other things? 'We talked. And stuff.'

Jo raises an enquiring eyebrow.

'He told me to go back to London. And he was right.'

'Can you be a bit more specific?'

'Later. Let's just say that I know what I need to do. And be. And that it's thanks in no small part to you. And Dan. And David.'

The cab pulls up outside ProDoCo.

'Last time I was here, I met Pete,' says Jo.

'Last time I was here, I thought the end of the world had come.'

Clara opens the door and hauls the bag with its precious cargo on to her shoulder.

Maybe it has. Or maybe it's only beginning.

*

Four-thirty. It has taken a long time, much longer than she expected. Jo had been nervous at first, her voice high and tense, and Clara had to use all her professional skills to coax her to relax. Every line needed several takes to get exactly right.

But my God, it was worth it.

And now she faces the greatest challenge of her career. Twice the amount of material to edit, in secret, without assistance. She'd never be able to do it if she hadn't managed to sneak time in an empty cutting room while Jo was convalescing. Even so, she has only three weeks to finish *The Making of Her.*

And the other? She fingers the tape marked *Jo's Voice-Over.*

She'll have to work through the nights to get it done. And she wants to. More than anything.

But before she can begin, there's the detail of her resignation to attend to. She turns to her laptop and, fortified with a large black coffee, begins to type.

JO

I turn the key and let myself in, closing my front door on the night. My throat and eyes ache from all the reading and my nerves are jangling after numerous cups of ProDoCo coffee. The house is cold and unwelcoming, as if it senses I will soon be selling it. In the living room, the sofa cushions are still imprinted with the shape of Pete's body.

It's not as if I've actually lied to him.

But isn't keeping quiet about my surgery two-faced? Not to mention my knowing about his accident and its consequences? He has every right to privacy. Don't I, too?

Two-faced. I catch my reflection in Julia's mirror. Have I been?

In the literal sense, yes. There was my old face, with its wrinkles and beaky nose and short-sighted eyes, a face which expressed – blurted out, more like – my whole life, revealing every detail of every year I'd lived. That face no longer exists, except in photographs, and there are few enough of those. Then there is this new face – Sarah Miller's face, with its taut inscrutability: a face without memories or a past.

He brought roses today. Roses the colour of rubies, or blood. I looked for the guitar, but he had come without it. His face had a stripped quality, as if a layer of skin had been torn away in the night. I leaned over the roses to kiss his mouth, ignoring the thorns.

I wondered why he had come. After our parting I hadn't expected to see him again. After the intimacy of our day in Kew, he had refused to enter my house, had turned from me to his blessed limousine and disappeared without a word. I shut the door on him and wept, trying to persuade myself it was for the best.

But this time, when I asked him to come in, he did. I took him by the hand and led him to the living room.

'Again,' he said, when we reached the sofa.

So I accompanied him back to the front door, kissed him again for luck, and we retraced our steps. Watching him counting, feeling his way, I felt an overwhelming gratitude. He wanted to know my house.

'Tell me,' he said, when he was sitting on my sofa, 'about your writing. Why did you stop?'

This floored me. I found myself shaking and prevaricating. 'Why d'you want to know?'

He didn't answer. Silence, taut as my skin, stretched between us.

'My husband...' I watched his face as I said it, and seeing the slight contraction added: 'Ex-husband, almost. He was a writer. We'd... he's written eight plays.'

'We?'

'I helped him with them. Editing... you know.'

'No. But go on.'

'I'd been writing, myself, forever. Couldn't not. But he... well, he found out about my stories and...'

'Stories?'

'Just... yes. Anyhow, he told me they were rubbish, so I stopped.' Pete's head was cocked towards me as if he were trying to gauge what lay beneath my words. Tears threatened again and I covered my mouth with my hands. We sat for a long time in silence, until he said, so quietly I could hardly hear him:

'I have spread my dreams under your feet.

Tread softly because you tread on my dreams.'

He understood. Iain had trodden on my dreams and shattered them.

'Thank you,' I whispered.

Pete Street, for all his sharpness, could walk on eggshells and not break them. Like me, he had a sixth sense for psychic scars. For wounds. And it was at this point that Clara had rung the doorbell.

Would I have told him the rest, if Clara hadn't come? About *The Making of Her*? How would he have reacted?

He's stripping away my defences, layer by layer. I feel all the more alive for it, all the more real.

Can I do the same for him?

I draw the card he gave me from my pocket.

*

The Islington house is four storeys high, the fifth in a conforming row of discreet white-painted terraced townhouses. I know, before I'm close enough to read the number, that the odd one will be Pete's. Painted the colour of bitter chocolate, it stands out, stark and idiosyncratic. Like a single black note on a piano keyboard. The basement windows are barred. Those on the ground floor are shuttered. Every upper window is a charcoal oblong in the dark facade. He must have locked up. Gone away. Then I see a solitary open window and hear the distant notes of a guitar.

So he's here. Sitting in the dark, alone. In this house of his, which could be fortress, sanctuary or prison.

I should have called him first. I finger my mobile. But I needed to come here unannounced to see how I felt about his house, and about myself, before continuing any further. My throat still feels scratchy. Dare I tell him that I know about his past and that I've deliberately held back that knowledge?

I must. There can be no more prevaricating. I pull out his card and key the number into my mobile. I can hear the phone ringing in his room, faintly, one floor up.

'Yeah?' His voice is clipped and sounds harsh. I swallow.

'It's Jo. I'm outside.'

After a moment's silence, he says, 'Come in.'

The front door clicks open.

The hall is unprepossessing and bare, as if no one lives here. Stairs wind down to the basement. To my left, firmly shut, is a door to what is presumably the ground-floor reception room. There's a plain wood table with a stack of mail on it. A letter has fallen from the pile to the floor. I stoop to retrieve it.

'Come up.' His voice sounds peremptory. Is he irritated that I've appeared on his doorstep without warning? *Well, touché.* It's so dark that I can hardly make out the stairs, but the quality of the air changes as I ascend. Down in the hall it had smelt of neglect and regret. Now, my nostrils catch the tang of wood smoke.

He is standing silhouetted in the doorway at the top of the stairs. My teeth are chattering.

'You're cold.' He draws me into the room. 'Sit by the fire.' He disappears into the kitchen. The room is red in the flickering light of the fire – not the fashionable blaring red of the interior design magazines, but a deep, velvety-purplish red. The fire is banked up beneath a vast Victorian marble surround. I sit on a severe, high-backed chair beside it. The guitar lies mute beside his own chair by the open window.

He returns, hands me a glass of red wine and shuts the window. He moves differently here, as if he is part of the room. He doesn't ask why I'm here, but folds himself on to his chair and picks up the guitar. With his self-mocking, sardonic smile he bends to the strings while his fingers pluck out familiar, winding notes. 'Stairway to Heaven'.

'I want to tell you something,' I say, though I would rather sip my wine and allow it to soothe my raw throat. I would rather watch the fire shadows stroke his face as he plays.

He pauses, then slides into a reprise. 'Tell away.'

'I know. About you. And Katia and Jasper.' My voice sounds hoarse and brittle.

His head jerks up. His face is very still and alert. The music between us is gone.

'I had to tell you. It wouldn't have been fair otherwise.'

'Is it fair now?' He is face-down again, over the strings. I don't know how to reply. We sit for some moments without speaking. Then he says:

'Want to have sex?'

The words slice the intimacy of the room. It's as if he's punched

me. How can he be so sensitive one minute and so offensive the next?
I place my glass on the hearth and stand.

'No, I don't.' I draw my coat together. 'I'll go.'

'If you want.' His tone is offhand. He bends to the guitar again.

'For what it's worth,' I say, 'it doesn't make any difference.'

He continues to play, excluding me. But as I reach the door, he
says, 'You believe it, then.'

I turn. He is still playing, but his head is raised towards me as if to
gauge how far I have gone. His earring shivers in the firelight. I see
his throat, shadowed and private, above the black shirt. 'Do you want
to tell me?' I say. 'I'll stay, if you do.'

'Stay the night?' I don't dignify the question with a reply.

'Well?' I ask. Suddenly I feel sure of myself. Of him. Of what's
happening between us.

He stands, placing the guitar on the floor. Then he walks to me
until our faces are so close I can smell his skin. His breath. He lifts a
hand and draws his fingers down my neck to the hollow of my throat.
. Then he sighs. 'Sit down.'

I return to my seat. He moves to the window and stands, his back
to me. 'Ever been caught in a current?' His words are indistinct.

'What?'

He turns. 'Ever been dragged out of your depth?'

'No.'

'When I was kid,' he says, 'we were at a festival in France.
We camped by the river. One night, I went for a midnight swim.'
He sits. 'The water was beautiful. Most beautiful thing I'd ever seen.
Black ringlets, swirling and eddying round my ankles. Beckoning me
in. And cold, so cold.'

I shiver.

'I waded in. When I was up to my waist, the river bed ran out. Just
disappeared from under my feet. I went under. I choked. Tried to
shout for help.' He runs a hand over the guitar strings. 'The current
was like a net. My legs were caught in it. My mouth and eyes and ears
were filled with black water. It pulled me down, and out. I thought I'd

either drown or be taken to sea.' He pauses. 'Anyhow,' he says, 'that's how it was. With her.'

'Her?'

'Katia. My wife.'

I lean nearer the fire, for comfort. 'And Jasper?' The red flames lick and spit at a piece of coal.

'Jasper was the glue that held us together when sex didn't work anymore. I'd try to pull away from her and that made Jasper scared…' his voice breaks '…and when it all got too bad, I drank. To blunt the pain. Stupid shit that I was.'

'Pete,' I say, 'I understand, about the pain. But surely…'

'Understand? I doubt it.' He turns his face from me and briefly removes the shades, rubbing at his eyes as if by doing so he can force them to see. 'Anyway,' he says. 'You know what happened. Don't you?'

'You were drinking. You took Jasper in the car. There was an accident and he was injured.'

'Yeah.' Pete picks up the guitar. 'That's it.'

I look at him. 'I read what the papers said.'

He's singing now, softly, about glitter and gold and certainty. After a couple of lines, he breaks off. 'Ask Jongo.'

'I'm asking you.'

*

They had been drinking.

In Katia's case, provocatively, like a wilful kid let loose in a sweet shop, throwing it down her throat. Anything she could lay her hands on, staring him down as she mixed vodka, gin, wine. Daring him to object. And he drank, too, reluctantly, to escape the roles she forced on him, of parent and minder. Booze never agreed with him. Made him throw up.

Jasper was on the sofa bed in the playroom downstairs, alone with his toys. Needed company, poor little bugger. Katia had been out

all day and he had put Jasper down early after the careful ritual of
swabbing his hands in cream and pulling on the white protective
mittens to help his eczema. The sight of them made him want to cry.
He needed time alone, to think.

She was already half-pissed when she got in. He heard the front
door slam and stepped out on to the landing, jerking his head towards
the playroom door to warn her not to wake their son. She could be so
out of it she'd leave the car slewed half across the street and the door
hanging open. He usually went down to re-park and lock it. But not
tonight. Sod being head prefect. Let her deal with it.

She ignored him, passing him on the landing as if he was just
another step, and headed for the kitchen and the drink. He joined
her there. Poured himself a beer, then another, and another. He
watched her light up a joint, squinting against the miasma of the
setting sun, her black hair haloed in it, the smoke curling up and
around her narrow, knowing child's face.

When they were young together, long ago, he would wind his
fingers in her hair as he came, bewitched by her. Then, over years, he
grew up, while she remained the child-woman of their first meeting.
She taunted him for his sense and precision while she spiralled away
into a feral place he had no wish to enter. Now she stood watching
him watching her. She looked sober but he knew better. Katia didn't
slur or stumble, dramatise or dissolve. Instead, she dried up like
an autumn leaf in the wind, drifting and scraping and carrying a
premonition of ice, her flat Lennon voice sucking the life from the
air between them.

The row came, as it always did, out of nowhere. The beers had
already knocked him off centre and his head was swimming. A coil
of nausea in the pit of his stomach wound upwards. He watched
himself reacting, shouting back at her while she spat stiletto pricks
of venom.

Then the door opened and Jasper was standing there, hair on end,
his face sleep-slackened and moist, his eyes holding a pain and a
doubting which should not be there at five tender years. Pete felt the

soft mitten of Jasper's hand taking his, as if Jasper were the father and Pete the wayward son, and allowed himself to be pulled by his child towards his wife.

'Mummy. Here's Duddah. No fighting.'

Katia focused then. 'Baby,' she said, 'go back to bed.'

Pete picked up the damp bundle that was his son and then, finding his legs unsteady, replaced him on the floor, took his hand and carefully, carefully counted their way down the stairs as they always did, feeling the nausea under his ribs. And Katia followed them, glass in hand, taunting him with an echo of his counting.

'Let me,' he said, when they reached the playroom. He took Jasper in, leaving her in the hall, and sat with his son until Jasper's eyes closed.

She was waiting for him in the hallway, tilting her glass at him so that the contents swilled and swayed. He watched as liquid splattered the wooden floor.

'Yeah,' she said, 'I'm fucked. So are you.' Then she leaned towards him, her breath foul with alcohol and smoke, and spat once, precisely, in his face.

For a moment the shock rendered him speechless. Then he said, as quietly as he could, 'I'm going to leave you.'

'Get out, then,' she said in her flat voice. And she pulled open the front door and waited.

The nausea hit him as it always did, smack between the eyes, his stomach convulsing. He charged upstairs to the kitchen sink, emptying himself into it, spewing out the whole contents of his day. And she followed him, laughing, carrying bottle and glass and pouring herself another drink. Afterwards, as he gripped the sink, his head swimming, heaving, she reached out and ran a cool hand over his forehead.

'Now clear it up,' she said.

This, the last hour of his seeing, was etched with detail like the stitches in a scar. Vomit in the sink. Katia's smoky black hair. The image of the weeping sores on his son's trusting, hopeful hands. All he knew was that he had to get away from her. He knew that if he stayed, he'd kill her, then himself.

He tumbled downstairs, his feet two steps behind him, and barrelled out through the still-open front door of the house and into the car, not registering that the car door was open too. He ground the key into the ignition, jumped on the accelerator and − tyres squealing − drove away from her and her poison and down towards the motorway. Grey buildings slurred past faster than he could think. Dear God, if only he had had time to think. If only he had ignored the car, run into the bloody road instead and been mown down. If only he had looked in the back of the car and checked…

The last thing he heard was *'Dud-dah!'*

He got in the car. While we were upstairs…

And his last, precious vision, before he plunged into terminal night, was Jasper's tear-stained face in the mirror, lunging from the back seat, frantic mittened hands seeking his father's neck but finding, instead, his eyes and covering them for the five vital seconds that sent the car slewing into the central barrier.

*

He sits, head in hands, curled in on himself like a child. I cannot see if he is crying. I want, very much, to go to him. To offer what comfort I can. But I know that he needs to be where he is, back there. He is not ready yet to return.

I sit very still, holding him in my gaze. The fire is dying down, red surrendering to black. After a long time, he stirs.

'Are you there?'

'Yes,' I say. 'I'm here.'

'Now you know,' he says.

He has torn away the official version of Pete Street. He has exposed his heart to me. I feel infinitely humbled.

Is this what our destiny with each other will be? To strip away the layers of protective lies until we get down to the bone? I shiver.

It would be only fair for me to tell him about *The Making of Her*. He has revealed the hardest, deepest, most painful truths to me. Now I must reciprocate.

My face is burning. A wave of shame envelops me. *Fraud*. How, after what he has told me, can I possibly reveal that I allowed my body to be butchered for vanity? His scars are real. Mine are self-inflicted.

He is moving towards me. The fire is almost dead and the room is so dark that I can barely see him, even up close.

'Will you kiss me?' he asks. His skin smells of tears and tiredness. I look at his mouth. Lean to it, and press my lips, once and dry, against his. His response is quick, questioning, his mouth warm, parting my lips, his body right against mine now, his hands safe around my head. Then his fingers slip from my hair, trace a path down my neck, finding a breast…

'*No!*'

He jerks from me as if burnt. I wrap my arms around my breasts. The silence between us is terrible but I cannot break it. He is looking towards me with an expression which I cannot fathom.

'What are you doing?' His voice is harsh.

He thinks I'm like her, Katia: using my body to tease him and draw him out of himself and make him vulnerable, only to deny him.

I reach to him and take his hand. He lets it sit hurt, inert, in mine.

'My love,' I say, watching his face, seeing him straining to find meaning in my voice, 'I can't. Not now.'

He is shaking. His whole body is trembling with tension. This is unbearable.

'Pete,' I say. 'Pete, it's complicated.'

'Yeah?' A ghost of the old, sardonic tone.

'There's something you don't know. About me.'

His face stiffens. 'Tell me, then.'

'I can't. I'm not ready to. I need to see if I can come to terms with it myself first.'

'And when you have?'

'I can't answer that. I'm sorry.'

I watch him. Slowly, he dips his head in a nod. I yearn to offer myself to him and assuage his pain.

If you do, all will be lost. The Voice is speaking. The Voice is sovereign.

He turns from me. 'I'll call you a cab.'

'Thank you,' I say.

I watch him make the call, businesslike now, and cool.

'It'll be here in five.'

'I'll wait outside.'

I cross the room to him, take his face in my hands and kiss him. Then I slowly descend the stairs.

CLARA

...and so, with regret, I am tendering my resignation. I will, of course, finish editing The Making of Her before I leave.

Clara pauses, her finger hovering over the button as the tiny arrow trembles on the Send Mail icon, seeing herself standing on a chair, a noose around her neck. Will she jump? The question is rhetorical. If she doesn't jump, she'll be pushed. Marcus will see to that.

Her sleepless night is catching up with her, and she still has hours of work ahead. Is this an appropriate time to be making the most important decision of her life, a decision which will effectively slam a door on her career? Because in the eyes of Alix and Stanley Barforth, she is old. A three-letter judgement upon her, and upon a whole generation of women.

One click, and she'll consign herself to that anonymous place of has-been.

And afterwards? The unknown. Returning to Cornwall, and Dan, is not an option. The only other safe place is David's yellow room but all she can see there is her forcing her mouth on to David's, and his shocked face, frozen in time. She tries to go back to before, to conjure up the comfort of the sun slanting in on the sand tray, of David sitting cross-legged and bare-footed. What would he say about this decision? Probably what he said about therapy.

'It's up to you. But if you choose to do it, you need to do it wholeheartedly.'

Her heart feels anything but whole. It is scattered, like ashes: some of it in Cornwall, with Dan; some in the yellow room in Camden; some clinging on to her ailing career; and... Cautiously, she places her hands over her heart, feeling the warm beating. Then down to her belly, to where the trembling was, seven years ago. The beating of another, unknown life. The *her* that she and Dan made.

The one who never arrived.

She cannot rekindle that life, or that love. She has carried its corpse ever since, frozen in her guilt and longing. Will the ice ever melt? For a while, in Dan's arms, she thought it had.

She presses a key on the sleeping laptop. Her resignation letter reappears, like Lazarus.

She clicks on Send Mail.

*

'What does it take to be a woman out there in the real world? Bouncing breasts. Beauty. Bedworthiness. Women like me don't count. Under the radar, as far as men are concerned. Even the beer-bellied, balding men. Even the ones with builders' bums…'

Jo's soundtrack is running. Thank God for the journal. Though Jo's sprawling writing isn't easy to read, at least Clara has something to follow. She has highlighted the most telling passages with a marker pen. Now she must listen and cut, listen and cut. Carve out a narrative from the mass of words.

And that's just the sound. When that's finished, there will be the visuals. Then the rough-cut, the fine-cut, the music and effects, the track-laying, the conforming. All to be accomplished in the secret moonlit hours when she should be in her bed. So much for letting go. Here she is, doubling the load, pushing herself harder than ever. And for what? For a swan-song.

From nine in the morning to seven at night, she will tread the familiar hamster wheel, diligently cutting the version of *The Making of Her* she's been commissioned to make. Sarah Miller's unsatisfactory life and body will be paraded before the viewers, who will watch, fascinated, glad that they are not her, yet longing, too, for their own transformation. Marcus will wield his knife to reform that deteriorating flesh into something ripe and edible. And Sarah will return to the world, remade. Beginning, middle and end. A modern fairy tale. The acceptable version.

But at night, when the lights are switched off in the production offices, when Marcus toasts a woman – perhaps Alix – in his club, when the bag-lady finds herself a doorway among the pigeon-droppings, the real work begins. A shame it'll be virtual: digital information held in the computer's memory, pixels on a screen. Back in the old days, the film editor would sit at a Steenbeck machine handling the film, hanging it in seaweed strands for selection, making each cut physically, with a real blade. A real cutting room, rather than a poncy edit suite. Her fingers long for that touching and making. But under those conditions, she could never accomplish what she's doing now.

Her mobile shrills. An unknown number.

'Clara?' A woman's voice.

'Who is this?'

'It's Jessica. David's wife.'

Clara grips the phone, her heart quickening. Jessica's bored tones float into her ear.

'I got your number from Richard and Linnie ages ago. Didn't you get the message I left, on your landline?'

The winking light on the answer machine, before she ran away to Cornwall.

'Clara? Are you there?'

'Yes.' Jessica must be drunk. Why else would she call?

'I've something to tell you. Can we meet?' She doesn't sound drunk.

'I doubt it.' Clara glances at the monitors. 'I'm on a heavy schedule right now. Can it wait?'

'No. I honestly don't think it can.'

Her heart thuds harder. She has to ask. 'Is it David? Is he all right?'

'Yes, yes. On the whole, that is. As much as any of us are.'

Come to the point, Jessica. 'Can't you just tell me now?'

There's a pause. Then: 'I've left him.'

'What?'

'David. I've left him. I told you I would.'

'Yes, but you were…'

'Pissed?' Jessica laughs. 'I was. *In vino veritas.* The truth will out.'

'Why are you telling me this?'

'Please.' Jessica's voice is serious. 'Can we meet?'

'I really am up against it.'

'Tomorrow? For an hour? Say, five-thirty, Kew Bridge?'

'A café would be more civilised.'

'I talk better when I'm on the move.'

Typical. Never mind what anyone else might prefer.

'And I find it easier to converse side by side, rather than face-to-face,' Jessica adds. 'Unlike my husband.'

Clara sighs. 'One hour. No longer.'

'It takes forty-five minutes to walk from Kew to Richmond.'

'In the dark?'

'Dusk. Anyway, I know the path.'

*

Kew Bridge is fading, with coils of mist lying on the river beneath. Jessica is a lone figure leaning on the stone parapet, her auburn hair mutating to mauve in the dwindling light. The setting sun flares a halo of red around a tower block on the far bank. A flock of geese fly over, honking, in a dark arrowhead.

'Clara?' Jessica turns at her approach. She is wearing the orange coat and, with her red hair clashing and tumbling, is the image of an urban fox. 'I'm sober,' she says, as if replying to a question. 'And stone cold. Shall we go?'

They descend the steps to where the river runs, swollen and dark and full of secret currents. Jessica, her breath misting around her, sets off along the towpath. David's wife, who has lain with him, shared his basin and table and bed.

'So. What's this about?'

'Patience,' says Jessica, 'is clearly a virtue which neither you nor

I possess. I suspect we have other things in common, too. Besides, of course, David.'

'You talk as if my relationship with David were personal rather than professional.'

'Isn't it?'

Clara is grateful for the fading light. 'I'm not having an affair with him, if that's what you're implying.'

Jessica laughs, a surprising, guttural sound which she pushes from her throat into the cold air. 'I can't answer for your motives and desires, but my husband is an upright man. A man of integrity. Of course you're not having an affair with him.'

A pale early moon has risen while they've been speaking. It hangs over the river like a silver sphere of honesty.

'I love this river,' Jessica says. 'So dark. So… feminine. Bearing so much along with it. Sometimes, I long to let myself fall into it, like Ophelia.'

The level of the river is rimming the edge of the path and flowing strongly.

'Don't worry,' Jessica says, reading her thoughts again. 'You won't drown, I promise.'

Clara stops. 'How much higher does the water get?'

'Oh, quite high.'

'What if we get caught by it?'

'Don't you trust me?' Jessica laughs again.

'No,' Clara says. 'Why should I?'

'That's fair,' Jessica says. 'But actually, you can.' She sets off again, her shoes tapping on the rough stone path, her hair billowing around her like a cloak. Clara quickens her pace to keep up.

'Is this about David?'

'I told you,' says Jessica. 'I left him.'

'And what has that to do with me?'

Jessica ignores the question. After a while she says, 'We are not a happy combination, David and I. David sticks to the rules. I break them.' She glances speculatively at Clara. 'Are you a rule-breaker,

Clara?'

The cutting room at night, and its secret task. 'Maybe I am.'

'Then you'll understand when I tell you how I met David.'

'Look, Jessica…' She finds herself torn between wanting to know and wanting to cover her ears. What is she afraid of discovering?

'I was married to someone else,' Jessica says, so quietly that Clara can barely catch the words. 'It was going wrong. Badly wrong.' She stops. 'So I went into therapy to try to sort it out.'

Her words hang in the air between them. 'You don't mean…?'

Jessica nods. 'I was his client, yes.'

She remembers David's horrified look as she lurched to kiss him. 'But… didn't it go against his code of practice?'

'Of course! Poor David.' There's a gleam in Jessica's eye. 'Don't worry. We didn't fall on each other in the therapy room. It was all quite proper. I ended therapy. Then I ended my marriage. And, after a decent interval – about a year – David and I got together.' Jessica pauses. 'Then we both lived unhappily ever after.'

A flare of distaste. 'Why are you so cynical?'

'I'm not. I'm just pragmatic.' Jessica begins walking again, hunching her shoulders into her coat. 'I love David, strange as it may sound. But I don't love him the way a wife loves a husband. I know that now. What I felt for him in that direction was need. Which is a very different kettle of fish.'

'Need for what?'

'Who knows?' Jessica pulls her coat collar up around her face. 'I haven't got that far. Father? Brother? Gaoler? Hero? God only knows.' She laughs. 'And He probably does.'

'You mean,' Clara says, 'it was all projection?'

'I see he's got you trained. Fluent in the language of psychobabble. Give something a label and then you can control it.' Jessica laughs again, without humour. 'Which is exactly why it went wrong for us. We each took up a position and neither of us was willing, or able, to back down from it. He was the therapist, the saint. Who married a lush. Mad, bad and dangerous.'

'Isn't that rather simplistic?'

'Perhaps. It suited me to believe it, at the time. His goodness enabled me to be bad, to live at the edge. And I thrive at the edge.' She turns her face to the water. Clara studies her. This Jessica is quicker and sharper than the woman in Linnie's bathroom.

'When did you give up drinking?'

'New Year. Since, in fact, the last time we met. That was my final outing as the villain in the story.'

Clara slows. She needs time and silence to process Jessica's words.

Jessica clearly has other ideas. 'What are your feelings for David?' she asks.

The question comes without warning and catches her off balance. 'I don't understand what you're asking.'

'You like him, don't you?'

Clara hesitates, then nods.

'Well then,' says Jessica, as if this makes it obvious.

'Jessica,' Clara wrestles with an urge to throttle her, 'get on with it.'

'I happen to know,' says Jessica, 'that he likes you.'

Her heart lurches. 'What do you mean?'

Jessica slants a mischievous glance at her. 'Let's get through this bit,' she says, 'and when we come out the other side, I'll tell you.' She looks at the river. 'We should get a move on.'

Water is fingering the path. Even as Clara watches, a sliver of dark liquid seeps across it. Tufts of grass, like dark islands, are marooned in its flow. Not like the sea, which roars and crashes and announces its invasion: this is a silent, insidious encroachment. Like age. Or unwanted understanding.

'We must go back…'

'No point,' says Jessica. 'It'll be too deep now.'

Behind them, the water has closed over the path, carrying rotten leaves and pieces of twig in its current. Her boots are submerged.

'We'll have to take our shoes off.' Jessica's voice is high and childlike. 'What fun!'

She's insane. Clara bends to her boots, surrendering to the inevitable, her feet sinking into the icy water. The water cuts at her like a knife. Rough stones scratch her soles. She paddles cautiously, feeling for the path.

'Can you swim?' Jessica's voice, ahead, is full of laughter.

Dear God. 'The current…'

'Joke.'

'Not funny.'

'Oh, come on, Clara. Live a little.'

This must be how David feels. Has felt. The more Jessica revels in her self-appointed role as daredevil, the more Clara finds herself playing prefect. Stung, she wades on. She can't see her feet but can feel their cold aching. The dark water, oily with God knows what, is halfway up her calves now, swishing and swelling, the weight of it pushing against her legs as she walks. Drops of water from the boots she's carrying are trickling up her coat sleeves. Her teeth are chattering – from cold, or fear, or from the shock of Jessica's revelations.

They wade on in silence. Just as she thinks it will go on forever, she sees her feet reappearing, white and ghostlike, surfacing like two pale fish as the path emerges again above the surface of the water.

'There's a bench ahead.' Jessica's voice is softer, as if she has been calmed by the experience.

'What, so we can sit and admire the scenery?' Now that they are safe, the irritation is returning.

'So we can dry our feet, stupid.'

Clara unwinds her scarf and bends to rub her feet with it, gritting her teeth as numbness gives way to pain. It's difficult to push them into her boots, but the relief of doing so is exquisite.

'Right.' She stands. 'No more beating about the bush. Explain.'

'I've no wish for him to suffer,' says Jessica. 'Because he will, you know. He's used to having me as his ball and chain, used to dragging my bad reputation around with him. I was his project. He deserves to come out of this with something positive. And his blessed sense of duty is likely to put paid to that. Unless he can be distracted.'

'Distracted?'

'By you.'

'Me?'

'All right,' says Jessica. 'Here it is.' She pushes her hands deep into her coat pockets. 'I heard him on the phone to Helen, his supervisor. Talking about you. He said he was struggling with his feelings for you.' She laughs. 'Typical David, eh? Can't just enjoy the feelings. Has to make them into a rod to beat himself with.'

Clara's head is swimming. 'How do I know you're not making this up?'

Jessica smiles. 'You don't. Tricky, isn't it?' She sets off along the path towards Twickenham Bridge. 'So anyway,' she continues, 'I want to kind of... bequeath David to you. See if you can make a better job of it with him than I did.'

As if he doesn't have any say in it. As if she, Clara, doesn't.

'You want to hand him on to me, like a piece of unwanted furniture?'

'Ideally, yes.'

She is crazy. Or, in spite of what she says, drunk.

'I suppose,' Clara says, 'you've met someone else.'

Jessica looks at her. 'Thanks for the vote of confidence.' She pauses. 'But as a matter of fact, I have. In a manner of speaking.'

'Who?'

Jessica smiles. 'Myself.'

'And you accuse *me* of psychobabble...'

Jessica ignores her. 'I've accomplished what some people never do, even with...' her eyes glint '...years of therapy. And I've done it on my own.'

'Please don't tell me that in leaving David you've discovered who you really are?'

Jessica grins. 'No. In leaving him, I've discovered who *he* is. In giving up the booze, I found me.'

Clara looks at her. Jessica does appear clearer, more defined, more sure of herself. 'Do you like this... new you?' she asks.

'Not much. But then I don't like many people. But I do know, now, what I need.'

'Which is?'

'To be fertile. To birth things rather than destroy them.'

'And how,' Clara says, 'does that translate into reality?'

'Who's being cynical now?' says Jessica.

Clara peers at her watch. Only six-thirty. Ahead are the lights of Richmond. She needs to get back to the cutting room.

The stony path has given way to cobbles. The river is corseted now by concrete banks, its surface glazed yellowish-brown by the punctuation of street lights. A gaggle of teenagers lob stones at a floating can. Under Richmond Bridge she and Jessica stand for a moment, looking back the way they came.

'I will have a child,' says Jessica. 'Preferably naturally. But time's marching on. I may have to pay for IVF.' She smiles. 'I can bear it now, you see.'

'Bear a child?'

'Bear life without drink, on the one hand. And bear my own goodness, on the other. Because goodness, as David knows, can be a bit of a burden. I suppose,' she adds, 'he is rather a hero.'

She reaches to Clara and rubs awkwardly at her arm. 'I'm glad we did this,' she says.

Clara finds, surprisingly, that she is too. 'Good luck with... everything,' she says.

'Good luck with David,' says Jessica. 'Whatever you decide.'

And she's gone, melting into the encroaching darkness.

JO

The doorbell.

For a moment my heart leaps, but my head quickly disabuses me of hope. Or fear. Pete is fiercely independent. Proud. I told him to wait, and wait he will. I open the door and a blast of cold air and mizzling rain whips in around the stolid figure on the step.

'Jongo!'

'Eh, it's cold enough tae freeze *a dog's baws off.*' Jongo's protruberant nose is mauve and he's hunched inside a damp-looking tartan overcoat at least a size too small for him.

'Come into the warm.' I step back to allow him to squeeze past me. I gesture him down the hall, following his wheeze into the living room. 'A drink?'

Jongo's rheumy eyes gleam. 'A wee drap o' malt would do me proud.'

'Sorry. I've only got coffee. Or hot chocolate.'

Jongo subsides heavily on to the sofa. 'Educate yerself, my girl,' he says, '*in the pleasures of the spirit.* It's a maudlin world, only improved by a wee dram now and then.'

I wait. He sighs. 'Och, coffee then. Black.'

What brings Jongo to my house? My thoughts tumble as I boil water and get out mugs, spoons and coffee. When I return to the living room, Jongo is standing with his bottom to the fire, steaming slightly. The overcoat gives off an aroma of old spaniel and cigar smoke.

He takes his mug as if accepting a poisoned chalice and proceeds to slurp mournfully at the contents. I take mine to the sofa. The coffee soothes my throat.

'Does Pete know you're here?'

Jongo ignores the question, setting his mug on the mantelpiece with the air of a man who has done his duty. 'D'you have a cold, girlie?' The diminutive is gentle rather than patronising.

'No,' I say. 'I don't think so. I've been doing a lot of talking.' And a fair bit of crying.

Jongo wanders to the French windows, ruminating at the darkening garden, his breath misting the glass. He takes out his paisley handkerchief and mops at it. Then he turns to me. 'What have you done tae him?'

'What do you mean?'

He returns to the fire. 'He was bad enough before. But now he's terrible.'

I tense. 'What happened?'

'He willnae talk to me. He willnae leave the house. He willnae do anything but play that guitar in the dark.'

'I'm sorry.' The words are ineffectual.

'Look, hen…' Jongo peels off the overcoat and lays it carefully on an arm of the sofa. Crimson braces strain over his stomach. 'Pete isn't your *everyday kind.*'

'I know that.'

'He's sensitive. Takes things hard. You have tae treat him with *kid gloves.*' His hand strays towards his trouser pocket and withdraws a sodden-looking cigar, then he appears to think better of it and replaces it.

'Jongo,' I say, 'Pete's a grown man. And I respect him as such. He can deal with it.' I hope I'm right.

'Have you *terminated the relationship?*'

'I'm not sure that we have one,' I say. 'Or rather, I'm not sure whether we can have one.'

Out comes the handkerchief again as he wipes his perspiring forehead. 'Och, I know he's not an easy lad tae get tae know, but…'

'It has nothing to do with Pete.' I look at my hands. 'It's my own stuff.'

'Ye're wed?' Jongo darts a look around the room as if expecting a wronged husband to leap out.

'Yes. No. Not for much longer.'

'Too *soon*?' His tone is earnest.

'I don't know.' He thinks I mean too soon after Iain. If only it were as straightforward as that.

Jongo says, 'Life's short, girlie. Dinnae waste it. Look at Pete.'

'You think he's wasting his life?'

'And his potential. All for a wean who's…' He remembers himself. 'All for nothing. Nothing he can do anything about.'

'I know about Jasper. And the accident.'

'Aye, well then.' Jongo casts me a penetrating look. 'If he's told you that, he trusts you.' It sounds like a reproach.

'Jongo,…' I stand, and my reflection pops up like a jack-in-the-box in the mirror. 'Jongo, please know that I wouldn't hurt him for the world. Which is why I mustn't be with him just now.'

'Ye're talking in riddles.' Jongo's hand is back in his pocket.

'It would be teasing him. And Katia did too much teasing, I think.'

'Eh, Katia was the *personification of problems*. He doesnae need any more o' that. But you're a guid girl, I can tell. And a beautiful one.'

I wince.

'I'm not,' I say, before I can stop myself. 'That's the trouble.'

'Not guid?'

'Not beautiful.'

Jongo's forehead wrinkles. 'Eh, you women. Take a look *in the mirror.*'

'It's not that…' I find myself wanting to confide in Jongo. After all, he's the nearest thing to Pete. 'Can I talk to you, Jongo? If you won't tell Pete?'

'Girlie,' Jongo's gaze is earnest, 'let me tell you something. I think ye're guid for him. I think you can *wake him up.*'

I laugh, in spite of myself. The image of me as a modern-day Prince bending to kiss a recumbent and unconscious Pete Street is ludicrous. And yet… I shake away the thought.

'I've had surgery.' There. It's out.

'I'm sorry tae hear that.'

'No… what I mean is, I've had cosmetic surgery.'

Understanding dawns in Jongo's eyes and his gaze slides down to my chest. 'Boob job?'

'The works. Boobs, facelift, nose reconstruction, tummy-tuck, liposuction…'

Jongo smiles. 'And ye look marvellous, girlie. Marvellous.'

This is just what I feared. Men are hypnotised by exteriors.

'Look, Jongo,' I say, 'I've things to do. I need to get on.' I pick up our mugs in what I hope is a concluding gesture and head for the kitchen. I splash water into the sink, praying that he's taken the hint.

'Eh, hen.' I jump. Jongo is filling the doorway. 'Come back tae the fire.'

I feel tears threatening and lower my head. 'What's the point?'

Jongo's hand is on my arm. 'Come on, girlie.' As if I'm a frightened animal.

I wipe my face on a tea towel and allow him to draw me back into the living room. He settles me on the sofa, covering my knees, inexpertly, with the throw. Then he drags an armchair up beside me and sits.

'Pete,' he says, his breath smelling of tobacco and coffee, 'is stuck. And it's up tae you tae show him how to move on.'

My face is hot. 'How the hell am I supposed to do that? I don't know how to move myself on.'

'I think ye do.' Jongo shifts forward until his eyes are level with my own.

What's he getting at?

If I knew how, I'd do it. Wouldn't I?

Jongo says, 'Pete's given up. He's frozen, back with her an' the boy. The only sign o' life in him is his playing, but he's playing *other people's stuff*, not his own.'

Kew Gardens, and his shutting me out when I asked him if the song he played was his. Aren't the two of us actually in the same boat?

Me, like him, afraid to write. Him shut away behind the beautiful but barred facade of the Islington house. Me caught and held fast by my perfect, lying exterior.

'Claim it,' Jongo says.

'What?'

'Ye have to claim your body.'

'But it's not my body. My body was old and fat and wrinkled. It told the real story. Of my life.' How can I expect him to understand?

'A guid story?'

I sigh. 'No.'

Jongo harrumphs. 'Seems to me, girlie, that ye're making your new body into *more of a problem* than the old one.'

'I feel like I'm cheating Pete…'

'Ye're cheating yoursel'. Of a *full and satisfying life*.'

Jongo heaves himself to his feet and retrieves the tartan coat. I walk with him to the front door and watch as he steps into the rain.

'Don't wait too long, girlie. I dinnae like to think of youse two skulkin' in your houses in the dark.' He withdraws the cigar from his pocket, clamps it between his lips and with a gruff salute, sets off down the path.

*

All very well for him. I open a window to dispel his lingering aroma. Telling me to move on, to claim this body. But how, when my body feels separate from me? Just something to adorn and dress and display; a living, breathing deception. And I'm afraid of Pete falling in love with it.

Why? I poke at the fire, watching the embers shift, redden and die.

Because it would feel as if he'd fallen in love with another woman's body, not mine.

As if he'd been seduced by something false.

I wander to the bookshelf. The lines of books sit hunched, their backs to me. I run my fingers over the familiar spines. Each holds a story. Like mine. And my exchange with Jongo follows me like an echo.

'It told the story of my life.'

'A guid story?'

'No.'

CLARA

Ten to seven.

She presses Play and the penultimate scene of *The Making of Her* unfolds.

She's doing a good job. No one can doubt that. Here's Marcus on stage, introducing Sarah Miller. And here's Sarah, radiant in red, stepping out to the gasps and frenzied applause of the crowd. Slowing the speed works well here. Gary's clever undulating shot of Sarah turning, the lights flaring off her hair and her shoulders, is inter-cut with shots of upturned faces and clapping hands. Doubling up on the applause track creates a triumphant, uplifting climax. Only the vox pops to cut now – the shots of members of the audience guessing Sarah's age – and the final compilation for the end credits. They can wait until tomorrow morning. She ejects the tape.

In the sudden silence, the clock above the desk ticks on. She counts the beats. By seven o'clock, ProDoCo will have emptied for the night except for a few stalwarts like herself, safely embedded in their edit suites. Seven o'clock is changeover time.

Her resignation has been received with calm acceptance by Stanley Barforth.

Of course,

his email murmured,

we are sorry to let you go after your long and successful career at ProDoCo, but we do wish you well for the future…

He probably assumes that she'll retire, like Richard. That she'll take up embroidery, or join the waiting list for an allotment. Put the old girl out to grass.

I'm only fifty. She has been wrapped in the company's ethos for twenty of those years but maybe there's still a future for her outside it. She thinks of Dan, building his new life in the clearing outside St Ives. But Dan is only forty. And a man.

She has not contacted him, nor he her, since she returned to London. She's been too exhausted, lately, to dream, but his gentle presence haunts her days. As does David's. How can she have feelings – powerful feelings – for two men? Each swings into prominence according to her mood, like the miniature weather-house figures of her childhood. Since Jessica's revelations, David's presence has been in the ascendant.

I happen to know he likes you… He said he was struggling with his feelings for you.

He cares for her – which feels like a gift and a threat. He is – was – her therapist. It had felt barely acceptable to harbour secret, erotic feelings about him, and any thoughts that he might return them seem almost… incestuous. And exciting. Jessica has let it be known that the possibility of a future with him is not as remote as she'd imagined, or he'd implied. But Jessica has lived with the reality of David. She knows his underbelly. His humanity. Whereas all she, Clara, knows is the therapeutic facade.

The clock is fingering seven. Energy rises in her veins like mercury. She reaches into her bag, withdraws the other tape and slips it into the machine.

Sounds and images awaken the screen. The story's taking shape. With only Gary's original shots to work with, she's had to be inventive with the visuals, but there are moments, unguarded moments just before she called *action* and just after she called *cut*, when the camera continued to roll, recording fleeting expressions and unspoken thoughts. Here's a fabulous shot of Jo waiting for Clara's tardy *cut*, her almost-naked body exhaling, her face telling its truth in spite of her efforts to maintain a veneer of insouciance. Clara has plundered the shot, slowed it right down and inter-cut it with a close-up of Marcus's pallid fingers poking and prodding Jo's flesh. And she has added Jo's voice, the words from the journal, making nonsense of

Marcus's promulgations.

'He touches me like a piece of meat. I am more than this. I am more than my body…'

Her mobile's ringing. She glances at the display. For a moment, she stares at the name, paralysed. David. Then, almost without her volition, her right index finger is pressing Pause on the computer keyboard, while her left thumb pushes on the miniature receiver on the mobile.

'David…'

'Hello, Clara.' He sounds steady and professional. Formal.

'David, I –'

'Clara, I'm ringing to ask whether you've made a decision about therapy.'

I haven't. How can I?

He's still speaking. 'And it's fine if you've decided to stop…'

It's not fine.

'…but endings are important, and I'd encourage you to have one more session to complete things… Clara? Are you there?'

'Yes,' she manages. 'Sorry. I was thinking.'

'The door's open.' His voice is softer now, and gentle. 'I just wanted you to know that.'

'David, I'm busy right now.' *Coward.* 'Can I call you in a week or so and make an appointment?'

'Yes. Yes, of course.' He pauses. 'Take care of yourself.'

'You too.' She switches the phone off.

Her hands are shaking. She can't focus on the screen. Her concentration's shot. She needs a coffee, strong and black. She heads for the machine in the corridor.

At this rate she'll need counselling. To get over her therapy.

JO

I snap Rilke shut. *A writer for a writer*, Clara said, when she gave it to me.

If I were a writer I would be writing now, regardless of Iain, regardless of rejection, regardless of everything except my need and my longing to do so. Writing a journal doesn't count. It merely serves as a catheter to release some of the pressure and dilute some of the pain. My journal's still in the cutting room, with the passages Clara asked me to read highlighted in yellow, and Clara has disappeared down the all-too-familiar hole of her work. When I ring, she is busy, distracted. Too busy to speak. Too busy to eat, apparently, since she has declined my offers of sandwiches and soup in the cutting room. She has fobbed me off with excuses.

I push my glasses up my nose, my fingers still surprised to find only thin air. It's as if Clara has taken what she needs from me. She has taken my voice and my words for her own purposes, and has refused to explain why.

'Give me a couple of weeks,' is all she said. That time is now up.

This morning the couple who are buying the house came to measure up and plan. I made them coffee, then let them get on with it. They were so full of their future, so focused on each other, that it seemed an intrusion to hang around. Only when the measuring was done did we gather, briefly, in the hall.

'We're going to *love* living here,' said the young woman. Her hair was straightened into pencil points, and she exposed the globe of her pregnant belly like a trophy between her cut-off cardigan and her maternity jeans. The man's hair was greying and his face was lined. He held out his hand.

'I do hope you and your husband will be happy in your new home.'

For a moment, I considered going along with the charade. Then I said, 'Actually, my husband and I have separated.'

The girl's innocent face dropped and she glanced quickly up at the man. 'Sorry,' she said. 'We didn't know.'

We shook hands quickly and they were gone.

Separated. I ponder the word. As if Iain and I were joined at the hip, or at the heart, like Siamese twins, as if sharing vital organs rather than coming together as two whole individuals. Yes. Iain and I were half-people searching for wholeness. That's why in the end it became a power struggle. Life and death. The victor running off with the spoils; the fruits of our endeavours.

I haven't heard from Pete. Why should I? He is stubborn and sensitive in equal measure. As Jongo said, he would sit in the dark forever, if necessary. I could release him from that prison. I could go to him and kiss him and open this body to him and give him comfort.

Claim it. Jongo's words have reverberated through me in the days since his visit. In the nights I've dreamed of Pete, his arms full of blood-red flowers, knocking at my door; and me jiggling a stuck key in a futile lock, opening my mouth to shout at him to wait for me but finding my dry throat empty of sound.

The day is closing. Twilight fills the room like a negative. As I pass the mirror, it reflects only an anonymous, shrouded shape. A person who could be anyone, or anything.

Claim it.

In the bedroom, I dress without switching on the light. I run my hands through my hair. I pick up the lipstick and expose its pointing finger. Is lipstick red in the dark? I wonder at the miracle of colour, seen or unseen, and, by the weak, strained light of the street lamp outside the window, I trace its greasy finger around the shape of my lips. Then I replace the cap with its idiosyncratic, feminine sound – *sshop*. I pull on a coat and scarf, pick up my bag, descend to the hallway and open the door.

*

The first thing I hear is the sound of my own voice.

The cutting room is shadowy, except for the glare of the screens. A pool of white light cast by an Anglepoise lamp illuminates Clara's dark hair and pale face. She frowns at the screen, the arches of her eyebrows mirrored by the dark half-circles under her eyes.

I step into the room. 'Clara?'

Clara jumps and presses a key, freezing the action on the screen. My body – my old body – is caught and held there, preserved like some forensic exhibit in the aspic of technology.

'Jo!' The relief in Clara's voice is evident. 'You've come…'

As if she's been expecting me. Is Clara, too, aware that the fortnight she asked for is up? I've never seen her look so exhausted, or so thin. Yet there's a glitter about her, a suppressed excitement in her eyes.

Clara pulls a chair from a dim corner. 'Sit. I'm going to get another coffee. Want one?'

I shake my head, hypnotised by the image of my body arrested on the screen. Too late to resuscitate it now. I want to take it in my arms, that poor, unloved collection of fat and cellulite and folds, and cradle it and soothe it and care for it. But it's gone. Sucked through a tube and down a drain. Aborted.

I'm roused from my thoughts by voices in the corridor. Clara's, together with the bass tones of a man's. And a woman's – upper-class and laughing. I tense. Please, not Marcus and Alix.

The door opens. Three figures are silhouetted in the light from the corridor. I half stand, clenching my hands. The man, who seems familiar, moves towards me. He is wearing a suit, his stomach straining over his belt.

Clara's voice is tight: 'As it happens, Sarah's here.'

'Sarah.' The man is holding out his hand. I struggle to remember where I've met him. He's staring at my face. 'Goodness. I'd never have recognised you.'

'Sarah,' says Clara, 'you remember Richard? My executive producer, before he threw in the towel. And Linnie.'

The woman, sixty-ish and heavy-boned, smiles, revealing large teeth. Wisps of grey hair escape from a hastily-erected bun. She's wearing a paisley silk dress with a ruffled neckline, and pearls. 'Well, I must say you look wonderful, my dear. Of course,' she adds, 'I've no idea what you looked like before…'

We shake hands. Linnie says, 'We were eating in Hammersmith, and Dickie said, "Why don't we pop in…?"'

'…to remind myself what I'm missing.' Richard has a glint in his eye. 'And, of course, to ask you to join us for supper.'

'Thanks,' says Clara, 'but not tonight.' She bends to the desk and presses a key. My flesh dies away. Richard half raises a hand as if to stop it.

'You're in the thick of it?' His eyes are still fixed on the screen.

'Actually,' says Clara, 'I've just finished.'

'How exciting,' says Linnie. 'Can we see?'

Clara hesitates. 'Sarah hasn't seen it yet.' She glances at me. 'Is that OK with you?'

I nod. What else can I do?

Richard is heading for the door. 'I'll get some more chairs.'

'He's so excited to be back,' Linnie says. 'Though he'd never admit it. The golf club just doesn't have the same allure.'

'How is retirement, really, Linnie?' Clara seems tense. She presses a key on the computer and a tape slides out. She drops it into her bag.

Linnie grimaces. 'Testing. He's like a dog without a bone. I have to keep him occupied, which rather eats into my committee time. Still,' she adds, 'I prefer it to the way he used to be. The way you are.' She taps Clara on the arm. 'You look shattered. When are you going to stop?'

'Soon,' says Clara. 'Very soon.'

The door opens. Richard, pushing two chairs, is followed by a tall, slight figure carrying a plastic cup. My heart drops. Clara looks up. Her expression changes.

'Alix.'

'Found her by the coffee machine,' says Richard, ushering Alix in.

'I thought we could have a group viewing, since Alix was involved early on. You haven't seen it yet, have you, Alix?'

'No.' Alix hovers in the doorway, her face slightly flushed. She casts a glance at Clara. Is she embarrassed after what she's done?

The two women look at one another. An unspoken question hangs in the air. Then Clara nods, more to herself than to Alix. 'Please,' she says, 'come in.'

Alix lets the door swing shut. Richard motions her towards one of the chairs.

'It's OK,' she says. 'I'll stand. I can't stay long.'

Clara picks up another tape, inserts it into the machine and switches off the Anglepoise. My hands move up to my chest to still the beating of the moths' wings. I try to breathe normally. My knees, beneath the desk, are shaking. Alix is standing behind me.

Clara keys in instructions. Is she nervous? Confident? It's impossible to tell.

The opening sequence rolls, ending with a triumphant burst of upbeat chords on the title: *The Making of Her.*

Here are the shots Gary took of Sarah walking down the street, her hair lank and her face bare of make-up as she gazed into sleek shop windows. I remember this. But I didn't know then that Gary had imposed my reflection on those of the mannequins in an ironic image of comparison. I catch Linnie casting me a sideways glance, as if unable to believe that the woman on screen and the one in the room are the same person.

The addition of an impersonal, male voice-over generates a tone of specious sympathy as it describes Sarah Miller, her ageing body and her unhappy life. Then comes the humiliation of the first collection of vox pops, and Sarah's reaction when they are played back. Clara has selected – as she must – the most damning. The sharp vixen faces of the young sniff out Sarah's flaws and failings, and with cruel grins guess her age. Here's Marcus, suave and superior, marking Sarah's body in broad, rough strokes, as if that body doesn't merit anything more precise. And – *my God* – here I am, as I've never seen myself before: an anonymous mass swathed in plastic sheeting, my own, old face unconscious as the knife slices at my eyes, my nose, my nipples, my belly, while Marcus jokes and smiles behind his mask, providing a running commentary as he bulldozes the landscape of my flesh.

I'm so red, inside. Bloody, red meat.

The action rolls relentlessly on. Here's Sarah convalescing, her face and body swollen and black-bruised. She looks like something putrefying and dying, rather than someone being reborn. And here, as if the intervening painful weeks were an irrelevance, is Sarah, rising from the ashes of her life as the final, cosmetic work is completed: the bleaching of the teeth, the cutting of the hair, the make-up, the red dress and the heels.

Here's the crowd in the studio. I strain to glimpse Pete among them, but there's no sign of him. I'm glad. He doesn't belong in this. Sarah Miller walks out on to the catwalk, twisting and turning for the crowd, her new body slomo-ed and haloed and bathed in music, her face a perfect mask above the upturned faces and the clapping hands. Cinderella in her ballgown; a butterfly; a swan. And the final, gushing vox pops, the credits rolling over Sarah as she walks along the High Road followed, now, by men's eyes. I remember Clara's words to me, all those months ago in this very room:

'When I edit, I cut away the dross. Get to the heart of it. Tell the story my way…'

Has Clara got to the heart of this? The answer, unequivocally, is no. Like the mannequins in that shop window, *The Making of Her* is interchangeable with all the others of its kind. The sort of show that Alix would make.

The final credit rolls to the centre of the screen, and stops:

Director and Producer
CLARA WILLIAMS

It looks like an inscription on a gravestone.

For a moment there is silence. Then Richard leans to Clara. 'Excellent,' he says. 'A good job.'

Linnie glances at me with eyes full of sympathy. 'Sarah, dear, what a transformation,' she says. 'You look entirely different.' She doesn't say what she thinks of the programme. Richard turns to me.

'Yes. Well done. Terrific.'

Clara, too, is staring at me, the corners of her mouth lifting, wry. 'What d'you think, Sarah?'

They're all gazing at me, waiting for my praise. I clear my throat. 'It's... flawless.' I catch a puzzled expression on Linnie's face. Richard looks up at the still figure behind him.

'Alix?'

Alix's pale face is a mask. She looks at Clara. Clara stares back. Then, as the silence stretches between them, Alix nods, once. 'It's good. A good programme.'

'Think it'll help the ratings?' Clara's face is expressionless.

'Yes. Probably.' Alix crumples her empty cup and drops it into the bin. 'Better get back.'

At the door, she turns.

'Goodbye, Clara,' she says quietly. 'Good luck.'

As the door slides shut, Richard asks, 'Is Alix leaving?'

'No,' says Clara. 'I am.'

Linnie takes her by the shoulders and plants a smacking kiss on her cheek, leaving a crimson imprint. 'Darling girl, excellent news. I hope this means we'll be seeing much more of you. Unless, of course, you decide to move?' There's a wealth of innuendo in the question.

'You'll be the first to know if I do.' Clara winks unobtrusively at me. 'But actually, moving is the last thing I'm thinking of. I intend to slow down for a while. Maybe even stop.'

I bite down an exclamation. Clara? Slow down?

'Hoorah!' Linnie says. 'And about time, too.'

Richard looks at Clara. 'Is that wise?'

Clara smiles, bends to the machine, ejects the tape and drops it into her bag. 'Who knows?' she says. 'I'll have to wait and see.'

*

Seven-thirty. Richard and Linnie have gone for their meal, Linnie effervescent, Richard somewhat subdued. As their voices recede down the corridor, Clara turns to me.

'Now,' she says, 'tell me what you really think.'

What does she want me to say? I swivel in my chair, seeking inspiration.

'Come on, Jo,' Clara's face is grim and flushed. 'You don't have to pretend. Slick? Predictable? Superficial? Don't hold back.'

I rub my nose. 'It does the job you were commissioned to do, and does it well. All right?'

'Think it would have kept me my job? If I hadn't already resigned?'

'Absolutely.' *But it wouldn't have kept you your self-respect.*

Clara laughs without humour. 'I'm ready for another coffee. You?'

Enough of this charade. I swallow. 'Clara, I came for my journal.' I pull Rilke from my bag. 'And to return this.'

'Of course.' Clara takes it. 'I thought the journal was a gift.'

'So did I,' I say. 'Only I've changed my mind.'

Clara pulls the journal out of her bag and places it on my knees. It's larger and weightier than I remember. I trace my fingertips around its familiar edges. 'So what did you want it for? Why did I have to read from it?'

Clara pushes her hair behind her ears. 'Let me ask you something first,' she says. 'How's it going with the agents?'

'The agents?' My face grows hot.

'Have you heard anything back, yet?'

I long for my old, lank hair to drop forward and hide my face. My fingers continue to rub the journal.

'I see.' Clara wheels her chair forcibly backwards and swivels to the desk. She heaves her bag on to it, rummages inside, retrieves the tape and inserts it into the machine. 'Look at yourself, Jo. Listen to yourself.'

Surely she's not going to force me to watch the whole thing over again?

And Clara presses Play.

PETE

He only notices the cold when the strings disappear under his fingers, though the voice of the guitar changed some time ago: became thinner, higher and complaining, its body leaden and uncooperative. How long have they been sitting here? It hardly matters.

The watch is warm from his shirt pocket. He pulls away the glass, his numb fingers sliding awkwardly over its surface, tracing the hands. Just after seven. He's pushed on deliberately, refusing to give in either to the guitar's lament or to the growling of his stomach. His pants are slipping off his ass. His head's thumping. If Jongo were here, he'd be nagging him to eat. But he's not here. Jongo's laborious attempts to get him to talk resulted in Pete telling him to piss off. For the first hours after his manager's departure, he'd relished the silence. *He'll be back, belly-aching as usual.*

He cocks his head and listens to the empty night as if he can dredge some human sound from it. Nothing. Only the distant swish of traffic on the motorway, the hum of the fridge and the diminutive tick of the watch against his chest. His fingers creep towards the radio, then drop away. Other people's music, other people's words. What's the point?

Light a fire.

Jongo would tell him to switch on the central heating. He says fire-lighting's dangerous for a man who can't see. Sod that. Central heating's like muzak: machine-made and soulless. It dries out the air, his voice and the guitar. He can kindle a fire with his own hands; hear its staccato overture as it spits and crackles, feel its red, real heat beating into the room and, later, its sighing exhalation as the embers shift and settle. Fire has moods. Like a woman.

My love, she'd called him as she left.

He drops to his knees on the hearth. A faint, cold draught issues from the chimney mouth, chilling him further. He runs his hand around the grate. Full of ash. He finds the dustpan and brush and carefully sweeps up the cool grey dust. He carries the pan to the kitchen and empties it into the bin. Then he feels for paper in the recycling box.

He builds the coal around the scrunched envelopes and the sticks of kindling, placing each piece carefully, mindful of his clothes. His fingers are rough with black dust. The cold seems to be seeping into his soul. He stands, hearing his knees crack, and with his clean left hand feels along the wooden surface of the mantelpiece.

Fuck. Jongo lit the fire for him yesterday. What's he done with the matches? He bends to the hearth and runs his hands around its edges. Shuffles on his knees to Jongo's customary chair and searches the table beside it. Only the ashtray, with the splayed remains of a cigar. Either Jongo has thoughtlessly put the matches in his pocket or, more likely, he's taken them with him deliberately.

He could go out to the corner shop. They know him there. And the walk would warm him. He shivers, and not only from the cold. He's got out of the habit of leaving the house; he's sent Jongo, or ordered in, or done without. When did he last go out? When he went to her house. When he asked her about her writing. When that friend of hers came. How long ago? A couple of weeks? More.

Maybe the matches are in the kitchen. He rinses his hands under the tap, then begins a systematic search of the drawers and the worktops. The surfaces are ungiving. Halfway round, on the windowsill, his fingers encounter something hard and solid. *What?* He picks it up. It's guitar-shaped, woman-shaped. The award.

Cold. Like her. Even as he thinks it, he knows he's falsifying her. But she has gone, and left him without a promise. He opened himself to her, made himself vulnerable and she… He lifts the lid of the bin and drops the award in, smelling the ash puffing as it lands.

He continues his search. Microwave, dishwasher, hob, work surface, cupboard. Inside, tins and jars. A bottle, tall and fat; and, sheltering behind a box of cereal, a row of three rectangular packets: his stash of pills. His fingers circle the tall bottle: Jongo's whisky. There was an interview on the radio, some psychologist saying that people who crave spirits are actually craving *spirit*. Does Jongo long for something more, something beyond the harsh reality of the real world? Did Katia?

Does he?

He allows himself to pick up the bottle and shake it. He unscrews the cap and sniffs. The smell burns his nostrils. Fire water. It would do the job. Half of it, anyhow. He shivers again.

Pour it down the sink. Or down his throat. Deliberately, he lifts the bottle to his lips and allows the rim its cold, specious kiss.

She was warm. She kissed him with her whole body; her whole red self.

He lowers the bottle, his mouth yearning for it. For her. If he's going to do it, he might as well make a proper job of it. No half measures. He reaches back into the cupboard and grabs the pills.

To sleep: perchance to dream.

Katia. Emptying pills into the black water. Telling him to drink it, all of it.

In the sink, his fingers find Jongo's discarded glass. He retrieves it, automatically rinsing it under the tap. So cold. He moves to the central heating controls and flicks a switch. The boiler awakens with its dry mechanical hum. He places the whisky bottle carefully on the work surface. Then he lines up the packets of pills beside it – one, two, three. Katia, Jasper, me. He moves back to the radiator and runs his fingers over its surface. Here it comes, the seeping, creeping heat. Water posing as fire. It'll have to do. This is it: his life. The life he settled for. A wave of exhaustion passes through him.

He picks up the whisky bottle and tips. The liquid splashes his fingers.

Then he picks up the first packet and slowly, methodically, pops out the pills.

JO

I am gazing, plump and lank-haired, at the mannequins in a shop window. People heedlessly skirt around me.

'Books are judged by their covers and women like me remain on the shelf… unopened…'

The words. Mine. My voice, too.

I can scarcely breathe. My fingers have found each other and are gripped tight under the cutting room desk. Clara is taut beside me, her eyes fixed on the screen.

Now I'm standing alone on Chiswick High Road. I am singled out, a monument to middle-age, while people with curious faces slow down, drawn by the beckoning camera lens, to assess and judge me. The same vox pops as in the other version, but now Clara has zoomed in on the mouths and the narrowed eyes. She has soft-focused the faces so that they slide into one other. She has made the voices screech and sneer like needles skidding across vinyl.

'Muuuuustbeseeeexty attt leeeeast…'

'Mygran…'

'Oooooold –'

My face. White. Trying not to see them. Trying not to see myself through their censorious eyes.

'How can my skin be so thick, and yet so thin? Why does it stop their eyes but let in their criticisms? What if I could tear this skin away, layer by layer, until there's only the heart of me? Bloody and raw, but real.'

The knife rips across my exposed belly. The flap of skin is raised, smearing and spilling blood over the green surgical gloves. I cannot look, but I have to because it's all true, just as my words are true. It's my experience. My body. Me, Jo. Sarah Miller is no more.

No. She will be back for the transformation scene, the reveal. I find myself stuffing my fingers into my mouth and biting at the perfect plastic nails in an effort to keep them from stabbing the keyboard and stopping the programme right here, while I'm still recognisable. Still myself.

The cutting is finished, but what's this? These shots didn't appear in the first version. Clara has slowed the sewing-together into a ritualistic dance. The needle pierces my flesh, slipping in and reappearing. In, out. It draws the thread in its wake, binding me up, reconciling my flesh, reuniting it with itself. And – *oh!* – the music. Not the shiny, stock music of the first version, but *that* music, soft and slow, hesitant and haunting, each note melded to the needle, to the thread, to the flesh: pulling, holding back, entering, withdrawing. Again and again.

Tenderness. I can think of no other word. Mesmerised, I find my body moving to the tugging notes as my eyes follow the images on the screen. This sequence seems to last forever. I want it to rock with it until… until…

The image is changing now and blending into whiteness. In silence, the camera widens to reveal the bandages slowly, slowly unravelling from my eyes and my face. My body is unwrapped like a precious gift. Not a death after all, but a birth. Not a shroud but a swaddling. Here are the stitches that hold my torn self together. Here are the bruises smearing my face like afterbirth. Here is my swollen body. Full. Full of itself.

'…*my inside on the outside. The pain… the shame I've been carrying all my life…*'

Here is Jo. Gazing at her new face in a mirror, hypnotised.

'…*had to let her go, the old Jo. The worst thing I could have done, and the best…*'

Here comes the music again, stealing inside me, winding and dancing through and around my body, loving me: taking all the disparate, alienated parts of me, binding my heart with my mind with my skin and making sense and sensuality of it all. Of me. Images and music melt together, all red. Blood, mouth, silk, passion, fire…

'It's been the making of me…'

Now there is nothing but the red lips filling the screen, telling their idiosyncratic truth as they move, lusciously – *me, me, me* – lipstick and love, transformation and redemption.

The credits roll silently, red against white. Gary. Bill. Lisa. I half-register Surgeon MARCUS TEMPLETON and Researcher ALIX ST CLAIR. Clara's name and title rise and pass through, disappearing like all the others. Then a final credit rolls and stops, centre-screen:

Written by
JOSEPHINE MILLER

After a long silence, I say, 'I don't understand.'

'What?'

'Why you did this.'

'Don't you?' says Clara.

'For me?'

'Yes.' Clara takes my hand. 'And for me. If this is my swan-song, it's going to be my best.'

It is, it is. Tears are dripping on to our clasped hands. My tears or hers? I am shaking, crying and laughing all at once.

'D'you realise,' I say, 'that you've performed an extreme makeover? On your own programme?'

Clara's eyes widen, then screw shut, her tired face lifting. For a moment, she's the girl at Davina Lucas, when life was all promise and possibility. We laugh, as we did then, unselfconsciously and wholeheartedly.

'So,' I say, as we gradually subside, 'when will it transmit?'

'This?' Clara says. 'Never.'

'What?'

Clara turns to the machine and ejects the tape. 'Like I said, this is for me. I had to take something real away with me. I needed to know I could do it.'

'You won't show it to them?'

'They commissioned me to produce a makeover programme, which I've done. That was the contract.'

'But women – women like you and me – need to see this. Clara, you can't hide it away and pretend it doesn't exist…'

Clara is staring at me. 'Like you've been hiding your writing?'

My eyes are drawn back to the empty black screen. I drop my head, my cheeks burning. 'It's not the same thing at all.'

'No?'

Both of us, consigning our truth to the dark. Both of us choosing invisibility over revelation. I look up.

'I'll do it, if you will. I'll try the agents again.' *Write.*

'And Pete? Will you tell him?'

'Yes. If you'll broadcast this programme.'

Now it's Clara who's hesitating. 'Barforth will never sanction it.'

'He doesn't have to.'

Clara shakes her head. 'He does. Every finished programme has to be approved by him before it's transmitted.'

'You could substitute it. At the last moment.'

Clara bites at the skin around her thumb.

'What's to lose?' I say. 'You're leaving anyway.' I see us again, me and Clara, running out of Davina Lucas and on to the high street, only this time it's me who is dragging Clara. *I dare you!*

Clara's mobile bleeps. 'Oh…' she says. 'I've an appointment with David.' She grabs her bag and her coat.

I stand. 'The music?' I know the answer already.

Clara looks at me. '"Changing the Story". Vintage Pete Street. At least fifteen years ago.'

His music. My whole body is filled with it. The Voice is singing along with it, loud and clear.

He needs you. It's time.

323

CLARA

White narcissi glow in dark Camden gardens. The disk of a full moon hangs low in the sky. As she approaches David's building, Clara's eyes are drawn upwards to anonymous windows. Behind one, he is working. Someone is sitting opposite him: the nervous man, the calm woman or some new, unknown client who is talking, weeping, sifting through private worlds. What secrets are being revealed? What feelings explored? Are their hands playing out stories in her sand tray?

She presses the buzzer. After a moment, the door clicks open and she climbs the stairs, her body humming with anticipation and fear. His receptionist smiles at her.

'Clara. Take a seat. He's almost ready.'

She nods and sits. The humming is rising in pitch. Her legs are shaking, her teeth chattering. She clasps her hands between her knees and breathes deliberately. In and out.

'Are you OK?' The receptionist turns a concerned face towards her.

'Y-yes. Just cold.'

'I'll get you a coffee. You can take it in with you.' The woman busies herself with the kettle.

Clara gazes at the door to his room. There's been no opportunity until now to feel. Caught up in the final, finishing touches to *The Making of Her*, she's been thankful for an excuse to keep going. Now both versions are completed. She's done all she can – for herself and for Jo. She's on the brink of the void she's feared and the emptiness she's avoided.

But first, this.

The coffee steadies her. Something solid to hold. The steam rises and circles; heat reddens her palms. She wants to sit here forever in anticipation of him. No. She wants to get in and get it over with. His door is opening.

'Clara. Come in.' His face is paler than she remembers, and his body less substantial. He stands back to let her pass and she smells him, the familiar whisper of lemon and maleness. The yellow room folds around her. Like flower petals. Like the sun. The candles, filled to their rims and overflowing, waver in the draught from the open door.

Fifty minutes.

She lowers herself into the chair, hugging her coffee. The sand tray is placed to one side of his seat. The sand is white, its surface unbroken, but it's been touched, maybe only a few minutes ago. He has smoothed it ready for her, the next client.

She hears him close the door and move to his seat. When she raises her eyes to his face, he's looking at her, holding her in his gaze, just as he always does. With his balding head and mild expression he resembles a Buddhist monk. Or Dan, meditating on his unanswerable riddles.

'How are you, Clara?'

'You've lost weight.' Her words sound accusing.

'So have you.'

What does he see? A smart, frenetic middle-aged woman, grey with exhaustion? She buries her face in the mug and takes a slug of coffee. It tastes thin and sour. 'I've been working hard.'

He nods. 'So you said.'

Why does it sound like a rebuke? She waits for the anger to rise. It doesn't. The silence stretches between them.

'How would you like to use this session?' His tone is gentle.

'I need to make a decision. Whether to carry on here, with you. Or to stop.' The last thought makes her heart quicken.

She glances at the clock. The second hand clicks on, measuring out their time together. She places the cooling mug on the table, beside the box of tissues, and drops her eyes to his hands. The wedding ring is still there. Has Jessica changed her mind and returned to him? Has it all been an illusion, the product of an overactive imagination, together with some mischief-making by Jessica?

The pain of not-knowing burns through her, together with a familiar compulsion to confront him: *Jessica told me she'd left you. That you have feelings for me. Is it true?* The words whirl and whistle through her body like an angry wind, craving a gap or a crack. She clamps her hands to her lips.

'Clara?'

'I don't know what to do!' Must she lose even this, even him? It's unbearable. She wants to run to the clock and tear off its hands. Stop time.

'About?'

'This! Everything…'

'You don't have to know. And there's no pressure to do anything.' His voice calms her. She lowers her hands.

'I'm sorry,' she says.

'What are you sorry for?'

'For trying to… you know.'

'Kiss me?' His face is still.

'Yes.'

'Clara,' he says, 'if you hadn't… done what you did, nothing would have changed.'

'Exactly.' She remembers her gritty, culpable hands enfolded by his. She longs to return to that place before everything disintegrated between them.

'And you said you wanted change.'

'For the better, I said. Not for the worse.'

He grins, the old lop-sided grin. 'Sometimes it has to get worse before it gets better.'

'Thanks, Sigmund.' She takes another slug of coffee.

'How have you been, these last weeks?' he asks.

Where to begin?

'I went to see Dan, in Cornwall. And I've resigned from ProDoCo.'

'Are the two connected?' She can read nothing in his face. Does he think she ran away to be with Dan? Does he care?

'Yes. And no.' Her heart is beating in time with the ticking of the clock. The last thing she wants is to spend these precious minutes detailing everything that's happened since she last saw him. 'I think,' she adds, because already it seems far away, 'I was searching for something. In Dan.' *And in you.*

'What was that?'

'Something that… I could only find in myself.'

'And have you found it?'

'Yes.' He allows the silence to stretch between them. She can hear the faint flapping and warbling of the pigeons on the sill, invisible behind the drawn curtains. Tears prick at her eyes. *I don't want it to change. I want it to go on like this, forever. I need to believe that this is just another session, which will be followed by another, and another, for as long as I want.*

'I'll do a sand tray.'

He looks at her for a moment, then bends to the tray and slides it into the space between them. She kneels before it and he follows suit, folding himself down on to the rug, cross-legged, bare-footed.

The sand is pale and dry. In St Ives, the beach was wet, cold and gritty. She remembers the shards of shell, the pebbles sucked back and forth by the waves, the wind tearing at her hair. She cups a handful. It's so fine. She can't hold it. It's running like time through her fingers. She needs to stop it. To tame it.

'Some water?'

He moves to the sink and fills a large plastic jug and places it beside the tray.

She lifts the jug, slowly tilting it to allow a drop of water to fall into the sand. Instantly the sand darkens, as if invaded. The shadow spreads a little, then stops. Deliberately, she tilts the jug further. The sand guzzles up the water. The dark stain spreads across the box until the sand lies dull and replete. Still she pours, until the sand is flooded and suffused by water. Bloated. It lies dormant beneath the surface of the water like a drowned woman. The jug is empty.

She pokes her fingers into the wet fudge silt. She paddles her hands in the surface of the water, allowing it to cleanse them. *There. No one else can use it now.* She flicks a gauntlet glance up at him. His face is impassive. She stands, wiping her hands on her skirt, and goes to the cupboard.

The tiny objects regard her. The baby sits curled as she left it, its back to her. There's the television with its flat plastic screen. And beside it, propped up, the figurine of the bride and groom. She picks it up. It sits, rigid, in her palm.

What God has joined together, let no man put asunder.

She runs her finger over the groom. Could he be David? Or Dan? She can't tell. And the bride: Jessica? Herself? The breasts protrude stiffly from the sugary gown, the hourglass waist nips in so sharply that it would never let sand, or time, escape. The lips are a perfect pink pout. A man's idea of a woman. A woman's idea of an ending: a happy-ever-after ending. The icing on the cake.

She turns the figurine upside down. It's hollow. Where the soles of the couple's shoes should be there's nothing but a gaping, moulded hole. And stamped around the edge, *Made in China.*

Nothing is real. Not the sand tray, nor these playthings, nor this charade called therapy. She wants to throw the figurine against the wall. Instead she pushes it to the very back of the shelf and returns to David.

'Now, some clay.'

He does her bidding, unwrapping it, his hands pale against its dark, undefiled surface. 'How much would you like?'

'Just a handful.'

He cuts the clay, leaving the slice lying virgin for her to take. It's slippery and sensual in her hands. She looks at his wide, beautiful mouth. Not smiling. She averts her eyes. Screws them shut. Her longing is a burning, a starving, a dry-mouthed thirst. Her fingers tighten around the clay.

'What's happening?' His voice has eyes.

'I can't…'

'Can't what?'

'Let… let it be. Let it go.'

'Let what go?'

She opens her eyes and stares at the clay and the bars of her fingers surrounding it like a cage. What is she so afraid of letting go of? Her career? No. That's already gone. What, then? She looks into his face, at his mouth, at her fingers that long to touch and stroke.

'This.' Her face is burning. 'You.'

What we made.

He is looking at her as if she is very dear to him. Is she imagining it? Projecting?

'Clara,' he says, 'I'm not going anywhere. You are free.'

Free. Free to stay? Free to walk away? Her fingers are rigid around the clay.

'If I let go of this,' she says, 'I'll have nothing.'

He says, 'Is nothing so very bad?'

'Yes…' Hot tears scald her eyes and run down her cheeks. It's too late. She's too old. Her head drops to her chest.

'Clara, breathe.'

In, out. Air rasps uselessly in her throat. Like a diver with the bends, her chest craves the killing air. She can't stay here, nor can she step out into the void. Her fingers are shaking so much that the clay is going to fall…

'Help me!' The words are forced from somewhere deep inside.

Hands.

Her eyes start open. His hands, cupping hers, just as they did in that last, terrible session. *How dare he?* she thinks, not in anger but in awe. She stares at their joined hands. His are warm, and articulate. Vulnerable, yet supporting her own. Her heart is flailing against her ribs like a bird caught in a cage. Her fingers are numb, her hands heavy, holding the clay fast between them.

You are free.

Slowly she allows her fingers to soften and uncurl until their hands

are a double cup, open like a lotus flower. The clay sits in her palm
like a grey fledgling. Uncertain whether it is ready to fly. Now she
is sobbing. Letting it all go; all of it. Words, incoherent words flood
from her mouth and she does not care, does not stop them, can't even
think of stopping them.

'My heart. My heart…'

Her ribs are parting and her heart – winged, feathery, dripping –
ascends as it did in her long-ago dream. White wings carry her up
into emptiness. Blue space. Endless sky.

*

When she opens her eyes he is there, sitting motionless before her, his
hands still cupped around hers. And the clay is simply clay in their
hands. He, too, is crying. He makes no attempt to stop the tears, or
wipe them.

'I loved you,' she says, and there is no desire for more.

He nods. They sit on, silently, awkwardly, until the clock's tick
intrudes, reminding. Then she withdraws her hands from his, places
the clay carefully beside the sand tray and goes to the sink. Her palms
are smeared and cool with clay. The backs of her hands are still
warm from his. She stands for a moment, reluctant to wash either
away. Then she turns the tap and rinses her hands.

She looks at him. He's sitting as she left him, head bowed, before
the desecrated sand tray. She wants to tell him that it will be all right,
that all will be well, but she cannot.

Sometimes it has to get worse. Before it gets better.

Her heart pumps steadily, warmly, against her ribs.

JO

My heels strike the cold pavement and my breath mists around my face. I am the only real person in the world.

Through half-closed curtains, in dimly-lit rooms, I glimpse stretched-out legs, comatose bodies, eyes focused on the flickering faces of the television screens. A black cat streaks across my path and slips into the shadow under a parked car.

Here is my body, taking me to Pete's house.

I swing my arms, just for the joy of it, and skip along Pete's street. *Pete's Street.* I find myself giggling. I am only halfway up his road but my ears strain to hear the notes of the guitar and my eyes seek the dark shape of his house in the white surrounding terrace.

There it is. I break into a half-run and feel the cold air on my cheeks, my breasts bouncing slightly under my coat.

The house is as shuttered and unforthcoming as it was the last time I came. I stare up at his window. It's closed. That's why I can't hear him playing. I look for the leaping shadows of the fire on the red walls but can see only a darkness. He's there, surely? I feel in my bag for my mobile. My fingers find only my purse, lipstick and keys. I must have left it at home in my haste to get to ProDoCo.

I climb the steps to his front door and press his buzzer. It gives an arrested croak. I press again. Nothing.

Steps behind me. Heavy breathing. I turn, ready to duck and defend myself, and collide with a large, solid shape.

'Eh, girlie, you came. And in the *nick of time.*'

'Jongo!' I breathe the familiar aroma of whisky and cigar.

He is wearing the same tartan coat, plus an ancient fedora hat. He pulls the disreputable handkerchief from his pocket and mops at his forehead.

'Och, hen, did you have to go at such a poke? I could have done m'self *a serious injury* trying tae catch you.'

'Where's Pete? Is he in?'

Jongo spreads out the handkerchief and applies it to his nose, giving a stentorian blow. Glancing up at the window, he says, 'Oh, aye. He'll be in.'

'I tried the bell. It doesn't work.'

Jongo reaches past me and plants a large thumb on the buzzer. There's no sound. He pushes his hand into his pocket and gropes around. Eventually he pulls out a key and proffers it.

'I can't just let myself into his house…' I find myself whispering.

'Eh, you can.' He begins to rummage in his other pocket.

'Jongo, it wouldn't be respectful. He'll be furious.'

'He will. But not *for the duration*.' He draws out the remains of a cigar, together with a battered matchbox. Clamping the cigar between his teeth, he strikes a match and sucks hard on the stump. Then he hands the matchbox to me. 'Take these. Light him a fire. Mek him eat.'

'But…' My protest falls uselessly at my feet as Jongo retreats down the steps.

'Go to it, girlie. And tell him I came.'

I watch the smoke huffing around the brim of his hat as he plods away and melts into the darkness. I turn to the door and press my finger again to the mute bell. Then I knock, my cold knuckles bruising at the wood, but the sound is hollow and even if he is in, he is up the twisting stairs, far away. The key sits in my palm. I see myself, in my dream, jiggling a key in a stiff lock to open a door between us.

I take a deep breath, raise the key to the lock and insert it. It turns smoothly and easily. A tiny push and the door swings open over a pile of letters and junk mail. I gather them and place them on the wooden table. Then I retrieve the key and close the door. The hall smells of despair and disconnection. I reach to touch the radiator. It's hot. I stand for a moment, listening.

'Pete?' My voice sounds reedy and thin.

Only silence. Maybe Jongo's wrong. Maybe Pete's gone away and left the heating on the timer in his absence.

I climb the stairs, treading carefully, though why I fear making a noise, I don't know.

The living room door is open. I switch on the light. The room is empty, a fire laid ready for lighting. Then I see the guitar leaning on the wall beside his seat. So he is here.

The kitchen, too, is empty. In the corner a boiler purrs. I survey the clinical surfaces, devoid of personality. It could be a hotel kitchenette, except for an upturned whiskey bottle on the draining board, a cluster of packets and a glass.

At the far end of the kitchen, a door is half open, and beyond it, a narrow corridor and another curling flight of stairs. Like a tower. I begin to climb. At the top, a closed door, and silence. I raise my hand and knock softly.

Nothing. I push the door open.

A wave of heat. The room is a shadowy hothouse, lit only by moonlight, streetlight.

Pete lies sprawled across the king-sized bed, fully clothed, like an exotic black flower. The duvet is on the floor. Beside him, on the bedside table, lie his shades.

I stand for a moment, transfixed. If he were lying there naked, he could not look more vulnerable, more exposed. He looks so young. So infinitely touchable.

I cross the room quickly and silently, drawn to him by the constant, indefinable thread between us. His face is a white blur in the half-darkness. The silver earring gleams. I lower myself to the floor beside the bed.

Then I see his eyes.

Wide open. Staring at the ceiling. Without a hint of consciousness. *The sink in the kitchen. The whisky bottle. The glass. And the empty packets of pills.*

Suddenly, I am cold. Cold to my bones.

'Pete?' Why am I whispering? Why can't I shout, take hold of him, shake him awake? Shake him alive? My own body is trembling, through and through. What has he done? What have I done?

Then, almost inaudible, a sigh. I bend to his mouth, holding my own breath. Nothing. Then... Yes. A stream of warm air. Another.

In my relief I want to laugh and jump to my feet and dance around the bed like a madwoman. But more, I want to draw close. Closer to his breath. His mouth.

He sighs again. His skin smells of honey. I have to. I have to bridge the gap and take his mouth and fill him with my kiss. I draw closer. Where is my precious moral rectitude now? I am a thief, come in the darkness to steal from him. I touch his lips with my own.

He starts upright and his face crashes into mine. He gives an inarticulate shout. I scramble to my feet, rubbing my nose, and make for the door.

'Jongo?' His voice is sleep-sodden. His hand scrabbles at the bedside table, finds the shades and shoves them on.

'It's me.' My voice sounds harsh and hoarse. 'Pete, it's me.'

Silence. Just our breathing, staccato, in counterpoint.

'What...?'

'It's me. I thought you...'

'What?'

'I thought you'd taken the pills.'

There's a pause, then: 'I did.'

'Pete... you...'

'Only two.' Is that the ghost of the old, cynical smile? If so, it doesn't hang around. 'Had a headache. The rest went down the sink.'

He stands and runs a hand through his curls.

'How did you get in?'

'Jongo gave me his key. The buzzer didn't work. I left my mobile...'

The room smells of warm flesh and disorder. Somehow, this is consoling. He brushes past me and sets off downstairs into the kitchen, where he flicks at a switch. The boiler judders to a halt. Then he moves to the living room, and his chair. With the guitar-barrier on his knee, he faces me.

'Pete,' I say, 'I'm sorry. But I needed to see you.'

'Three weeks,' he says.

I drop my head. 'I know.' I cross the room to him and hold out the matches, shaking the box. It sounds hollow, almost empty. 'Jongo said to give you these.'

'Bugger Jongo.' Pete ignores the matches. I place them on the windowsill and move to the hearth.

'I've missed you.' My words sit between us like stone. I expected no less. I watch his silent profile as he crouches over the guitar, turned in upon himself. Everything about him says *I don't need you. I won't give in.* He won't make a move towards me. Why should he? He's playing now, his fingers feeling their questioning way over the strings, a stark melody without words.

'I had a dream,' I say. 'I was trying to reach you but the door was locked.'

'Yeah?' He continues to play.

'I've been shutting you out, I know.'

'Why?'

'Because... because I...'

Call myself a writer – *and I do, I will* – when I can't seem to put together the simplest of sentences?

'Because I was afraid. That you'd see me differently.'

His mouth curls.

'Yes, see me. You do see me. Not with your eyes...'

He fingers out a chain of notes. 'Then why would I stop?'

'I was wrong.' I want to force him to turn to me, to pull off his impenetrable shades. 'Pete? My love?'

The sound of the strings hovers and dies in the air. He picks up the matchbox and throws it in my direction. It falls near the hearth.

'Love is,' he says, 'as love does.'

I bend to retrieve the box and drop to my knees beside the fireplace. There are only two matches left. I scrape one against the side of the box. The match fizzes briefly, but as I move it to the fire it dies in a sullen trail of smoke. Pete continues to play.

One match. *One chance.* I strike it, my hand shaking. Even my breath might extinguish it. I clamp my lips together. The match flares. Slowly, slowly I move it to the fire and allow the flame to catch at the paper. Once. Twice. The fire creeps along the paper's edge, leaving a jagged black wake. Surely the flame will die before the kindling catches? I'm aware of Pete behind me. He's stopped playing.

The paper is almost burnt through. The coal sits stolidly above it. Between the two, the kindling waits. What can I do but kneel before it and pray?

'Blow on it. Gently.' I hear the tension in his voice. This matters to him, just as much.

I lean towards the fire until my face is down beside it. I purse my lips and exhale, directing a soft stream of air into its heart. A small cloud of ashes puff out and sparks erupt. Have I extinguished it?

No. The flame glows, leaps upwards and reaches out to consume the next ball of paper, licking and curling around the kindling. There's a crackling, a spitting: the kindling catches, flaring at the impervious coals. I can do nothing now but wait, my back aching and the imprint of the carpet burning into my knees.

A flickering. A blue flame cradling the coal.

'Add more coal,' he says, 'a bit at a time.'

I pick up a piece between my thumb and index finger, feeling its sandpaper scrape against my skin. I place it carefully above the flames. Then, unable to watch, I rub my fingers into my palm, and see the coal dust turn my life line blue.

A loud snap pulls my eyes back to the fire. There's a glow now, in the very heart of it. Thin flames flicker yellow as the fire begins to draw. I can feel its breath on my cheeks.

'Yeah,' he says, behind me. I try to cry silently, hunching my shoulders around my body, pressing my fingers to my mouth.

'Jo?'

He's never used my name before. I swallow fiercely.

'Yes?' My voice is croaky.

'Come over here.'

I walk on my knees to him. The guitar lies across his lap like a lover. He makes no attempt to remove it, but reaches out to me across it. I wipe my own wet and blackened hands on my trousers. His hands are warm. I find myself caressing his fingers, feeling my way around them as if I too am blind, finding the calloused tips, the longer nail of his thumb and the soft underbelly of his palm. I watch his face as I do so, feeling tears still rolling down my own. Gently, I withdraw my hands and take the neck of the guitar. For a moment he hangs on to it. Then he allows me to lift it from his lap and lean it against the wall.

'I'm here,' I say.

'To stay?'

'Yes.'

Love is, indeed, as love does. Only this body – my body – can express what I need to say. I stand and kiss his palm.

'Where are you going?' His voice is sharp again.

'I need to pee,' I say. 'I'll be back.'

*

I pull the cord and the fluorescent light floods my reflection in his redundant mirror, casting shadows under my eyes. Rinsing my hands, I study the skin on my face, taut as a string. I inspect my hair, my neck, my nose and my teeth. All, all perfect. Then, slowly, I lift a strand of hair. Find the tiny scar behind my ear.

Turning from the mirror, I pull my jumper over my head, unbutton my blouse and, shivering, pull it off. I unzip my trousers and fold them over the side of the bath. I unhook my bra and dangle it, like a gaudy trophy, from a tap. I step out of my knickers. Pete's silence sneaks in under the door like a held breath.

I stand, naked, at the glass. My body looks greenish in the harsh light. My nipples are standing out, alert. My breasts are full, round and youthful; my stomach soft and smooth. There is the incision, down towards my crotch. Red lines crossed with white. I stand like a child reciting the alphabet, deliberately scanning and listing all the scars that Pete will never see, counting them aloud while the light buzzes above my head.

The soles of my bare feet stick to the fibre of the carpet when I return to the room. Pete is sitting just as I left him, illuminated by the overhead light, his back against the wall. I look down at my body, and then at him. It feels unfair that I have the gift of gazing openly at him. I reach for the light switch and his face, impassive, shifts. He knows I'm here.

The room clicks into democratic darkness. The fire casts its crazy ruby shadows around the room, over my body and over his. I cross the distance between us and kneel before him.

'You've taken off your clothes?' he asks.

How can he tell?

'I can smell your skin.'

He doesn't touch me. I wonder if he despises me for exposing myself to him. It doesn't matter. This has to be done, for both of us. Gently, I lift the shades from his eyes. Then I lean to him, kiss his eyelids, feeling the shiver of his lashes on my lips, the trembling passing like an echo through his body. I kiss his mouth, his fingers, see the fire-shadows leaping over his throat and the red light dancing on the planes of his face as his lips part, opening to me. His hands reach out to find me, feel me. *I am here*, I want to say, over and over. *I am here.*

'Your skin,' he says, with a kind of wonder. 'Your breasts. Your belly.' I almost draw back.

Then his fingers, searching deeper, find the scars. I stop breathing when I feel him pause. I wait while the minute sensitivity of his musician's fingertips traces each line and each division in my flesh, reading them like Braille. *What does he feel? What does he think?* But it doesn't matter. Nothing matters because he knows me, deeper than my skin. Deeper, even, than my blood.

Suddenly, he's crying, wildly and silently, as his mouth finds mine. His fingers play on my skin. He draws me like fire. My sighs leave my open throat and meet his quick hands.

'You,' he says, between kisses.

'Me,' I answer, as my tears fall into his eyes.

CLARA

The cutting room is dark, the screens blank. She stands for a moment before them, saying goodbye. She won't return to the office. Her possessions can be recycled by her successor. The past is a heavy weight and she has no wish to carry it further. She checks her bag. The parcel is inside. Along with the swan-song tape.

*

'Ready to go?' Fergus, the transmissions engineer, takes the tape from her.

'Ready,' she replies.

'I'll bin the old one, right?'

'Thanks.'

'Bloody Barforth,' he grins. 'Never knows when to leave well alone, eh?'

'Well,' she says, 'it was just a last-minute alteration.'

'Hear you're leaving,' he says. 'Pity.'

'Not really,' she says. 'It's time for a change.'

*

The ProDoCo foyer is empty.

'Night, love.' Darren glances up from The Sun.

'Night, Darren.'

The doors hiss open and close behind her.

EPILOGUE

David Wood opens the door to let out his last client of the evening. His receptionist, half-shrugged into her coat, looks up.

'Oh, David. Clara Williams dropped by. Left you this.' She's holding out a flat, oblong package. He takes it.

'I'll be off, then?' She's hurrying to get home to her husband and her family.

''Night.'

He carries the parcel into his room and closes the door. He sits for some time without opening it. Then he slips his finger under the tape.

The book is well thumbed; its leaves curling. Poetry by Rainer Maria Rilke. The word *Works* is half-obscured by what appears to be a splash of bird-dropping. He turns to the title page. No inscription. No message. But there's a bookmark. He opens it at that page, where words are highlighted in yellow marker pen:

You, the first
lost loved one, who never arrived...

He reads the poem slowly. Nothing to hurry for, or towards. There was only ever a bird, singing through both of them. Yesterday. Separate. In the evening.

*

Clara sits by the early-evening river. She's warm from her walk, but not uncomfortably so. The hot flushes are abating. Pigeons bob and peck around her ankles as she scatters crumbs from her sandwich. A young moon hovers like the ghost of a promise, reflected dimly in the dark water.

The reverberations from *The Making of Her* continue to lap at her. According to Lisa, Stanley Barforth's apoplexy was short-lived, lasting only until the tributes from viewers began pouring in. Now, ProDoCo forwards the messages and emails in batches, apparently with his blessing.

She feels inside her bag for a tissue to wipe her hands. Her fingers brush against the letter which came this morning, out of the blue.

Seems she's wanted, after all.

There's a beating in the air. Two great silhouettes, white necks outstretched in perfect synchronicity, descend in a long wake, skimming the surface of the water.

She breathes in, and fancies she can smell spring.

*

Pete sits by the window in his tall, thin Islington house. The guitar's calling to him, distracting him from Jongo, who's ensconced in his usual chair, sipping whisky and giving forth. Pete shifts his attention from Jongo's voice to the settling, crackling fire.

He's been impatient and antsy since that programme. *The Making of Her*. Since he heard his music intertwined with Jo's voice. Something stirred then, something which whispers and turns inside him now, longing for a way out. He can't concentrate. Not on Jongo, not on the fire. What was it she said? *Tearing back my skin, all the layers, stripping me down…*

He stands, picks up the guitar and makes for the stairs.

'Where are you off tae, laddie?'

'Just… downstairs. For a bit.'

Jongo says nothing. As he descends the stairs, Pete hears the scrape of a match and the smoky suck of Jongo's cigar. Fuck it. Let him get on with it.

His heart beats a noisy percussion as he stops outside the door to Jasper's room. He finds his hand on the doorknob. He can hear the steady click of fingers tapping at a keyboard, then a pause before it begins again. Relishing the sound, he quietly says:

'Jo?'

– and the tapping stops.

'Yes, my love?' Her sweet voice.

Tempted as he is to go in, he refrains. She doesn't want him there. Nor should she. Jasper's old playroom is her place now. In it, she's giving birth to her words. But it's not just that. The insistent murmuring in his own belly pulls him away. His fingers tighten around the neck of the guitar.

The steps to the basement are steep – steeper than he remembers. He feels his way down the banister. The guitar knocks against the wall and he jumps. The air smells of disuse.

The key is in the lock, just as he left it ten years ago. His hands are shaking, sweating. But the melody and the words are filling his body and straining at his fingers.

strip me down, love
tear my will away like petals
love me, love me not, love
strip me down

He turns the key and opens the studio door.